I0747712

Fools, Angels

and the

DEVIL

FOOLS, ANGELS

and the

DEVIL

A Prelude to the Series
THE SONGS OF WAR

ROBERT FAULK

Fools, Angels and the Devil
Copyright © 2023 by Lady's Slipper Books Inc.

All rights reserved. No part of this publication may be reproduced, distributed, or transmitted in any form or by any means, including photocopying, recording, or other electronic or mechanical methods, without the prior written permission of the author, except in the case of brief quotations embodied in critical reviews and certain other non-commercial uses permitted by copyright law.

Galleon Publishing, Moncton, Canada
www.galleonbooks.ca

ISBN
    Print book: 978-1-7780781-8-7
    ebook: 978-1-7780781-9-4

GALLEON

TABLE OF CONTENTS

Preface VII

Chapter One 1
The Calling

Chapter Two .17
Money isn't Everything, but it's Close.

Chapter Three 41
Some People are Worth It.

Chapter Four 57
All Beginnings are Difficult

Chapter Five 73
Where Fools and Angels Meet

Chapter Six .83
There are no Shortcuts to a Place Worth Going

Chapter Seven 95
Hear no Evil; See no Evil.

Chapter Eight 117
One-Way Loyalty is a Dead-End Street.

Chapter Nine 135
Brünnhilde

Chapter Ten 145
She Loves me, she Loves me not....

Chapter Eleven 157
Irreconcilable Differences

Chapter Twelve 169
A Fork in the Road

Chapter Thirteen 177
   Roads that Bend

Chapter Fourteen 189
   Everything Works Out in the End

Chapter Fifteen 197
   Everything Worthwhile is Difficult

Chapter Sixteen 203
   The Devil Tightens his Grip

Chapter Seventeen 219
   Some Rules are Intended to be Broken

Chapter Eighteen 231
   When the Devil Schemes, Nature Trembles

Chapter Nineteen 241
   Creating Something Beautiful

Chapter Twenty 249
   It's Worth Doing Because it's Hard

Chapter Twenty-One 259
   The Worst Thing That Can Happen

Chapter Twenty-two 273
   All is Not Yet Lost

Keep your Friends Close—your Enemies Closer . 285

Message from the author 287

Your Next Book 288

A Song of Sorrow 289

About the Author 290

PREFACE

ARCHDUKE FRANZ FERDINAND CARL LUDWIG JOSEPH MARIA was the presumptive heir to the Austria-Hungarian throne. He was also indirectly responsible for starting the First World War when his chauffeur took a wrong turn on the way home from visiting a hospital in Sarajevo, Serbia. Gavrilo Princip wouldn't have shot the Archduke and his wife if their driver hadn't gotten on the wrong street.

The Austrians immediately blamed the Serbs and demanded they hand over control of their country to Austria. Serbia, as expected, refused, and Austria declared war on them.

Russia, allied to Serbia, declared war on Austria, and Germany, allied to Austria, declared war on Russia. Russia mobilized a vast army and France joined them to declare war on Germany. England decided to support their friends in France, and the generals on both sides rejoiced.

Germany pleaded with France to stay out of the fight, pointing out Germany would be squeezed between them and Russia, fighting a war on two fronts. They would have no choice but to attack.

Holland and Belgium are inconveniently located between Germany and France, leaving Germany no choice but to cross them to get at France, lighting the fuse on *The War to End All Wars*.

The war changed Russia forever, birthing communism in its most popular form. The Russian Revolution became a bloody civil war, culminating in the brutal murders of the Tsar and his family and a power struggle within the country that lasted for decades.

Four years later, in 1918, total mortalities from the war were in an order of magnitude neither side could accept. The Allies counted six million dead soldiers, Germany and its allies about four million, and both sides had lost about ten million civilians. The world economy had ground to a halt—millions starved.

The German people marched in the streets, called national strikes—Mothers who had lost sons screamed at politicians, and Kaiser Wilhelm wanted out. Negotiations were one-sided because, with the people against them and refusing to fight for the *Vaterland*, the Kaiser and the German generals had no options left. With defeat staring at them, Germany signed an open-ended Armistice, ending the fighting on November 11, 1918. The treaty containing the stipulations would come later in a document called the Treaty of Versailles.

The infamous treaty, signed on 28 June 1919 at the Palace of Versailles, seven months and a few days after the last shot was fired in World War I, codified the peace terms between Germany and the victorious Allies. The treaty put one hundred percent of the responsibility for starting the war on the German people, imposing harsh penalties on the nation. The Allies forced Germany to abandon territory populated with Germans and to pay massive and unrealistic reparations. They also insisted on the complete demilitarization of the country, leaving it destitute and defenceless.

Germany had ceased fighting in November of 1918 without defined provisions, conditional upon the Allies' promise that negotiations would be based on U.S. President Wilson's "peace without victory," as outlined in his famous *Fourteen Points* speech to the U.S. Congress on 8 January 1918. To undermine the German cause, the Allies had dropped leaflets on Germany and communicated diplomatically that their intention was to negotiate a fair peace, and the German people had believed them.

On this basis, The German government stood its army down, docked its navy, and grounded its air force, leaving Germany defenceless and with no negotiating position other than Wilson's verbal assurances.

Consequently, when Germany entered the palace to sign the treaty, they found that the Allies had broken their promise; the final terms of the Treaty of Versailles had nothing to do with Wilson's *Fourteen Points*. The European generals who had started the war had dictated the terms of ending it, laying the foundation for the next one. The treaty humiliated Germany and the German people while failing to resolve the underlying issues that had led to war in the first place. Economic distress and seething resentment caused by the treaty within Germany fuelled the rise of Adolf Hitler, the National Socialist Party, and all the misery that followed.

CHAPTER ONE

The Calling

June, 1933

If I cannot fly, let me sing.
Stephen Sondheim

HEINZ METZGER BENT DOWN to look under the Mercedes, his reward for years of work, and said to his son, Peter, "What are you doing to the car? I drove it yesterday, and it worked fine." He straightened up and got to the point, "Elizabeth said you wanted to talk to me."

Heinz had bought this, his first car, a well-used but well-maintained 1925 Mercedes touring car from his boss, for a price he couldn't refuse, as much for the pleasure of working on it as to drive it. Fortunately, as things would turn out, he had passed the mechanical gene on to his son, Peter, and working on it was candy to both of them.

Peter's father was in charge of the M.A.N. Augsburg machine shop that built prototypes designed by the research department of the M.A.N. Corporation. A manufacturer of heavy machinery, trucks, and engines, M.A.N., an acronym for the cities Mannheim, Augsburg and Nürnberg, where their facilities were located, had survived the post-war economic disaster and the depression mainly through the efforts of men like Heinz and the engineer he worked for, a *Maschinenbauingenieur* and head of the R&D department.

The research department had designed a line of marine engines for the *Kriegsmarine*, the German navy, using the Bosch high-pressure fuel injection system—at the time, the best in the world—and was modifying the prototype in preparation for manufacture. In June of 1933, M.A.N. had a backlog of engine orders for submarines, ships, and heavy *Lastwagen*, trucks built in the M.A.N. factory in Nürnberg for the German *Verteidigungsministerium*, the Department of Defence.

Now that the engine was ready for manufacture, the research department was beginning work on a Krupp contract for the under-carriage of a new *Panzer*.

Peter answered his father without rolling his creeper out from under the car. "I'm oiling the linkage on the brakes—they're getting a little stiff. Why don't you pump them a few times while I lubricate them?"

Heinz, usually a patient man, knew Peter was testing him but decided to humour him.

"Okay, I'll pump them, but the brakes are fine."

Heinz climbed into the leather driver's seat, still immaculate but softened by age. Before he pushed the pedal, he made sure the cloth Peter had laid there to protect the leather was under him. Heinz smiled when the pedal moved, but it took so much effort that he realized his son was right; corrosion was accruing somewhere in the mechanical brake system.

He seldom drove the car and recently hadn't had time to work on it, so the problem had sneaked up on him, and Peter had found it. Heinz was proud of his son… the best natural mechanic he had ever seen, and his dream for Peter was that he would become a mechanical engineer.

"Okay, wait a minute while I crawl under the front." Peter grinned at his father, then disappeared under the front of the car. "Okay, pump it now."

Heinz pumped the brake, and each stroke became easier. "Yes, you are right; it's getting better."

It took close to an hour before Peter was satisfied. He did what he could with an oil can and a grease gun and said, "I'm going to take the drums off the wheels later to get the rest. We can talk while I put the tools away."

Heinz followed his son to the small workshop he had con-structed in the backyard before he had built the house. It was filled with hand tools and metal-working machinery, the best Heinz could afford. As soon as they could turn a screwdriver, Heinz had taught Peter and his brothers how to use every tool and machine in the shop—something akin to teaching fish how to swim. Peter's brothers, Rolf and Dieter, born a year apart and five years before

Peter, had never had an interest outside of mechanics and had chosen careers as machinists in the M.A.N. research and development division where Heinz worked.

Unlike his brothers, Peter was not like his father in any way, with the solitary exception that he obsessively loved fixing mechanical problems. At the end of his fifth school year, Peter qualified for *Gymnasium,* the only path to university. He studied French and Spanish because he had to, excelled in mathematics and logic because he loved the subjects, and Heinz dreamed of someday working alongside his engineer son. But Peter had a second love, which Heinz hoped would disappear if he ignored it.

When he was eight, Peter sang in a boy's choir and music, particularly singing, soon became his first love. He was heartbroken when, at thirteen, his voice changed, forcing him to leave the choir. However, two years later was singing again, this time in the Lutheran church's senior choir. The Schweitzer family was registered as *Evangelisch*—Protestant—and attended the church. When it became apparent that Peter had an exceptional voice, the church organist, who knew nothing about singing, gave him singing lessons. Every month he sang a solo, bringing tears to his sensitive father's eyes and loving smiles to his mother's face. Heinz and Elizabeth became Peter's biggest fans, but Peter's father still considered singing nothing more than a diversion.

Peter put a set of box-end wrenches in the toolbox and didn't turn around to face his father. Heinz patiently waited, knowing his son had something on his mind. The last time was to talk about working with him in the M.A.N. shop, so Heinz was shocked when, out of the blue, Peter said, "Dad, I want to talk about a singing career instead of engineering."

Heinz's first reaction was to yell at his son, but having already gotten two sons through puberty, he had learned to be as subtle as a man of limited vocabulary who couldn't spell diplomacy can be. He said, forcing himself to be calm, "But weren't you accepted at Heidelberg University to study engineering?"

Peter said, "Yes, I was accepted in the first round, but I don't want to be an engineer; I want to sing.

Heinz clenched and unclenched his fists; he recognized the symptoms of panic and said, "We should talk about this with your mother."

"I've already talked to her, and she said I should discuss it with you."

"I'm sorry, Peter, but I need Elizabeth. You and I can't talk about this without your mother." Heinz left the shop, half-running into the house, and Peter followed, knowing this was not good. He had thought his father would be happy about his choice of a music career, considering Heinz's reaction when he sang in church.

Elizabeth was waiting for him in the kitchen, and when Heinz said, "Elizabeth, I…" she interrupted.

"Sit down in your chair, Heinz, and please don't say anything until I'm done."

Peter arrived, and Elizabeth guided him to the chair opposite his father.

"I want to…." Peter started, and Elizabeth said, "The same goes for you as for your father. Be quiet and listen."

Peter looked at his father and shrugged. Heinz looked at Elizabeth and said, "Okay, we're ready."

Elizabeth was born to Jewish parents, Moshe and Hannah Metzger, and had married outside her faith and below her intellectual level. Her parents had resisted at first, then insisted on a Jewish wedding. Eventually, when time had healed the wound, they accepted Heinz into the family, not as a Jew but as some equivalent.

However, Elizabeth was stricken from the Jewish roles because she married a traditional German with a Protestant name. Consequently, she was registered with the German Einwohneramt as Evangelisch, meaning nothing except she had to pay an eight percent church tax to the Protestant church instead of ten percent to the Catholic church. But it also meant her children would grow up in the Lutheran church, something Elizabeth's parents found difficult to digest.

Elizabeth had only known classical music as a child, and Heinz bought her a radio and gramophone so she could listen to Bayerische Rundfunk's frequent classical music concerts. She had also collected many classical music recordings, and she and Peter spent hours listening to the gramophone, mesmerized by the music they both loved.

When Peter's voice changed, halting his singing in the boys choir, he lost the will to do anything. He became depressed, his schoolwork suffered, and he stopped talking to his teachers and parents. Elizabeth tried everything she could think of to snap him out of it. She found recordings of everything she thought he might like, but the only ones he wanted to hear were of Italian operas. He spent hours sitting in front of the speaker, quietly imitating the singers using his dreadful transitioning voice.

Heinz created workshop projects he could build with Peter, but as soon as he could sneak away, Peter headed for the gramophone.

And then Elizabeth found a recording of Beniamino Gigli singing "Spirto Gentil" from Donizetti's "La Favorita," and Peter wore out the record in a month. Elizabeth bought recordings of other singers, sopranos and tenors, singing lieder and opera. Still, Peter listened to the worn-out recording of Gigli's Spirto Gentil every day, sitting beside the phonograph and nudging the needle when it stuck in a track. Finally, Elizabeth bought a new recording but restricted Peter's listening to it to once every night.

Desperate, Elizabeth took him to the church organist and asked her to teach him to sing, and Peter insisted on singing Spirto Gentil a capella at his audition. The organist listened with tears in her eyes and, when he finished, said, "It would be an honour to teach you, Peter, but you must do much more than develop that instrument. I will teach you to be a musician, but I can't teach you to sing… that must wait until your voice is ready, and then I will find you a singing teacher."

Frau Schmidt was out of her element teaching vocal technique, but it was Peter's good fortune that she knew it. However, she was a violin virtuoso and understood musical expression with strings, and Peter lapped it up like cream.

Three years later, when Peter told Frau Schmidt he would study engineering, she panicked and called a friend who played in the Munich Opera orchestra. Her friend called the *Direktor* of the *Hochschule für Musik* in Munich, someone every professional musician within two hundred kilometres knew. A few days later, Frau Schmidt called

Elizabeth, and a week after that, they took Peter to the Odeon concert hall to sing for the director.

Peter was terrified as he walked onto the stage, the first one he had seen. Frau Schmidt, equally frazzled, dropped her music on the floor when she sat down at the piano. She retrieved it and began playing Schubert's *Die Forelle*. Not having performed in years, she stumbled over the notes, but Peter sang the Lied with feeling and tempo, dragging her behind him.

Sitting in the centre of the orchestra section, the school director asked loudly, "Do you have something higher, perhaps an opera aria?"

Frau Schmidt shuffled her music and said, "I have another Schubert lied, but I can't play it very well... and I think...." She fumbled through the sheets.... "No, I seem to have forgotten it...."

"Never mind," said the director. "I will find a pianist and call you later to discuss what we can do."

Peter said, "I can sing an aria for you without the piano."

The director smiled and asked, "Which arias do you know?"

"I can sing all the arias that Beniamino Gigli and Enrico Caruso have recorded."

The director, still smiling, said, "Why don't you sing the one you like the best?"

"Alright," said Peter, "I will sing *Spirto Gentil*, Fernando's aria from La Favorita by Gaetano Donizetti." He had introduced the aria precisely as Frau Schmidt had taught him.

The director put up his hand. "Perhaps something simpler. That is one of the most difficult arias in the lyric tenor repertoire."

"I can sing it better than any of the others," said Peter.

"Na gut." said the director, smiling and waving his hand, *"Wie du willst!"*

Peter looked at Frau Schmidt. "A 'd' please." She smiled as she plunked the note.

Peter lost himself in the first phrase, singing with Fernando's broken heart. He sang without effort, and the top notes flowed with the same ease as Gigli sang them. When he finished, he was smiling, and tears streamed down his cheeks. The director said, "Frau Schmidt, would you play the 'd' once more?" She played it, and the director said, "As I thought, Peter went sharp."

Peter said, *"Es tut mir leid,"* and hung his head.

A few days later, when Peter and his distraught father came in from the shop, Elizabeth said to Peter, "I have a letter for you from the director of the *Musik Hochschule* in Munich—she held it out in her hand—why don't you read it?" Peter took the letter and read it twice before giving it back. She passed it to Heinz. He read it aloud.

"Peter can study at the school at no cost, but he must audition for *Herr Professor Garcia,* and they say he is the most distinguished teacher in Germany. If he is accepted, the school will pay his living expenses."

Elizabeth put her hand on her husband's. "Yes, and these people know about singing. You have heard Peter sing... you can hear the beauty, can't you?"

Heinz slumped his shoulders and looked at his hands. "Yes, sometimes he makes me cry."

"He must study music; he must sing. He cannot be an engineer because his soul is that of a singer."

Heinz looked at Peter, sighed, and said, "I will do whatever you want me to do. If you both think this is what Peter should do, then it's alright with me." He turned and headed for the shop.

Peter worked at M.A.N. with his father until September, then took the train to Munich for the first day of classes and the audition with Professor Garcia on Monday, the eleventh of September, 1933. The train left Augsburg at 07:32; it took forty-five minutes to reach the Munich *Hauptbahnhof* and another twenty minutes to walk to *Odeonplatz.* His audition was at ten, and he found Professor Garcia's studio at nine. Singing sounds came through the door as he sat down on a bench beside a well-dressed, beautiful girl who appeared to be about his age. He pointed to the space on the bench next to her and asked, "May I?"

She nodded, and as he sat down, he said, "I have an audition with Professor Garcia at ten... do you know whether it's okay to sit here until then?"

She answered, "I will also audition with Professor Garcia. I was told to wait on the bench until my lesson time, then knock and go in. My audition is at nine-thirty."

The sounds from the studio came from a soprano, a powerful voice vocalizing into the stratosphere.

"I think I heard a 'd' above high 'c,'" said Peter, amazed. "I didn't know anyone could sing above a 'c.'"

The girl said, "Of course, lots of sopranos can—as a matter of fact, she just sang an 'f,'" then explained, "I was born with perfect pitch."

The singer bounced around on notes that caused nightmares for most sopranos while Peter, trying to be inconspicuous, looked closely at the beautiful girl sitting a few centimetres from him. Finally, he gave up his pretence, looked straight into her face and said, "You are the most beautiful girl I've ever seen."

"Merci beaucoup," said the girl, then switched to German because it had become obvious her mediocre German was better than Peter's bad French. "Please forgive me that I don't speak good German, but if I am accepted in Professor Garcia's studio, I will take language lessons, *oui?"*

Peter forced himself to look away and fiddled with his hands, regretting that he hadn't worked harder at French. He thought for a minute, turned to her, held out his hand and said, *"Je m'appelle Peter Schweitzer."*

She gently laid her hand in his, smiled a smile that broke his heart and said, *"Je m'appelle Juliette Durand; je vis à Bruxelles."*

"Je suis ténor," said Peter, as though that were the only thing he could think of to say. *"Je suppose que tu es une soprano."*

Juliette looked at Peter as though she had just put a slice of lemon in her mouth and said, "I am a lyric coloratura soprano, and I can sing as high as the one in the studio, although not as loud." She looked at Professor Garcia's door. "I never sing that loud... My teacher said that I should protect the beauty in my voice, *n'est-ce pas?"*

Peter said, "My teacher plays the violin and the organ, but she doesn't know much about singing. She taught me how to read musical notes, and I taught myself to sing Spirto Gentil from La Favorita by Gaetano Donizetti. When I sang it for *Schuldirektor Siegmund von Hausegger,* he accepted me in the Hochschule, even though my voice isn't trained yet. I will sing it for Herr Professor Garcia." Peter said quickly, "I suppose that's why we're here....because our voices aren't trained, aren't we? I mean... " Peter stopped talking, and Juliette turned away.

But he hadn't taken the hint and started again.

"I could sing it for you sometime."

"What?"

"Spirto Gentil...Gigli...from La Favorita...that's an opera. I will sing it for you someday. I can sing it just like Gigli."

"That would be nice, if you must."

He went on, undeterred by her cold attitude.

"I went to the National Socialist rally in Nürnberg and heard both Adolph Hitler and Ernst Röhm speak. The rally was called *Reichsparte-itag des Sieges,* the 'Rally of Victory' to celebrate the National Socialist victory against the old Weimar Republic."

"Congratulations, but I have no interest in Adolph Hitler's political nonsense."

"Nonsense? My father works for M.A.N., and Hitler saved his job when he rescued the German people from the terrible economic problems caused by the Versailles Treaty and the world banks."

Juliette looked at her watch, and Peter went on, driven by nerves. "Next year, when Professor Garcia has taught me how to sing my audition arias, I'm going to get a job singing in an opera house; my teacher said I should wait until my voice matures. She said my voice doesn't need much work on the technical aspect, but I will have to work hard on learning how to sing the tenor *rep...reper...uh....* " *Repertoire* wouldn't come out right, and, aware that he didn't belong there, Peter felt something like shock when he realized from her expression that she was thinking the same thing, and worst of all, she felt sorry for him.

Juliette looked at the clock on the wall opposite the bench and said, "It's *repertoire.* I have to go to my lesson now," as she stood up. She waited a few seconds while the second hand swept to the twelve, knocked, and opened the door to a blast of sound.

The singing stopped mid-phrase, and almost immediately, a tall, broad-shouldered Nordic blond woman who would tip the scales at fifty kilograms more than Juliette swept out of the room without looking at her. She passed Peter without a sideways glance—Peter watched Juliette shrug, enter, and close the door.

Juliette's singing, a shadow of the volume and resonance of the previous singer's, barely carried through the door and didn't last more than a minute before the teacher's loud voice interrupted. Peter couldn't understand the muffled words, but a few minutes later, Juliette sang a few scales, accompanied by what Peter generously interpreted as encouragement from Professor Garcia. Peter couldn't understand the words the professor and Juliette exchanged, spoken in at least two romantic Latin-based languages, but he recognized a lot of energy in them.

The more Juliette sang, the more the professor's encouragement sounded like threats. He shouted something about his *petite fille*, banged four notes on the piano, and Juliette screamed the arpeggio. He punished the same notes again, then again, and Juliette's screams sounded more resonant with every attempt. Finally, the teacher said enthusiastically, *"Si—Eso es todo…Eso es Bueno!* Then, *Ja! Du hast es! Wunderbar! So sollst du singen!"* The rest of the half-hour passed with periods of shouting in several languages, male and female screaming and yelling in the universal language of anger and frustration, and finally, the quiet voice of the Professor punctuated by Juliette's sobs.

A man Peter guessed would be almost thirty had been pacing the hall during Juliette's lesson. Twice he had walked up to the thick door, and once, during a particularly violent screaming match, had put his hand on the lever that opened it. The screaming stopped, the man pulled his hand back and stood still, staring at the door as the professor banged three notes on the piano; Juliette screamed the pitches as though she and her teacher were going to kill one another.

The anxious man let go of the handle, shook his head, and resumed pacing.

The clock opposite the bench clicked on precisely ten o'clock when Juliette burst out of the studio, crying, ignoring the anxious pacer, who tried to keep up with her as she passed Peter. His gaze followed them down the hall.

"Well, Do you want to audition or not?" Professor Garcia shouted from inside the room. Peter hurried through the open door, and the Professor, who sat behind a long grand piano, said, "If you don't know enough to close a door every time you pass through it, you can go somewhere else to learn to sing!"

Peter gently closed the door but didn't hear the latch click.

"*Mierda!* Close the damned door as though you mean it! Are you a child?"

Peter put a little more effort into it, but the latch didn't quite make it. He looked at Professor Garcia, who was looking at the ceiling. He dropped his eyes to meet Peter's, and Peter slammed the door so hard the glass rattled.

"That's better…now, stand over there." Professor Garcia pointed, waited a few seconds, then stood up from behind the piano, took Peter's shoulders in both hands and steered him to the middle of the room. He returned to the piano.

"What do you want to sing?"

Peter stammered, *"Spirto Gentil.* It was written by…" Professor Garcia cut him off.

"Do you have the piano score with you?"

"No, Herr Professor, I don't have any music… I learned it from a recording by Beniamino Gigli." He stressed Gigli's name.

"*Maldita mierda!* God help me—not another arrogant, stupid tenor!" He began playing the last few bars before the tenor entrance on the recording, talking as he played, so Peter would have had to interrupt him to come in on time.

"At least you copied the best tenor in the world… I suppose it could be worse—you could have chosen Caruso, but he hasn't recorded this aria, has he?" He stopped playing. "I can tell you why Caruso doesn't sing it… He can't sing it—it's too difficult—but you think you can… Amazing, isn't it? Perhaps you should sing a different aria… I can play anything you can sing."

Peter shook his head and said, "No, I can sing this one."

Professor Garcia started playing again, his frustration showing in his treatment of the piano. When he reached the bar where Peter should be

11

singing, Peter didn't recognize it. Garcia stopped, began at the beginning again, and said, "You had better come in this time—if I remember correctly, this is the tenor aria you said you could sing." Peter had never heard a piano play the Aria's accompaniment and almost missed his entrance again but recovered in time to sing half the first phrase before the piano stopped. Peter continued, assuming the professor had forgotten the notes and would let him sing without accompaniment, but Professor Garcia raised his hand and shouted, "Stop!" And Peter stopped singing in the middle of a word.

"Where have you sung this aria?" The professor asked the question as though he expected the answer to be a concert hall in Vienna.

"In our living room."

"Never in another room?" asked Professor Garcia, laughing sarcastically. "What about the bathroom? Perhaps you sing it when you are in the bathtub?"

Peter suddenly remembered. "Yes, sir, I always sing in the tub."

"And I have been told that you sing in the Lutheran church in Augsburg. And your former teacher plays the violin quite well."

"Yes, sir, I used to sing in the boys choir, and now I sing in the adult choir. I also sing a solo once a month."

"'Sang' in the adult choir…you are done singing in choirs for a while. And what was your last solo?"

"'Then shall the righteous….' It's from *The Elijah* by…."

"I know perfectly well who wrote Elijah, and I know he was a Jew. If you sing any of his music here, you will be expelled. What else?"

"I sang *Thou Shalt Break Them* from *The Messiah* by…."

"Georg Friedrich Händel. Sing it now."

"I don't have the music."

"Do you know it or not?"

"Yes, sir, but if you are going to play it…."

"If we are going to work together, you must stop insulting me."

Professor Garcia began the aria, stopped, said, "Wrong key…" then started again, but noticeably higher.

Peter sang the first word, sensed the tuning was higher than he had ever sung the piece but kept going as Professor Garcia banged the piano so hard that Peter worried he might break it. When he sang the first 'high A,' Professor Garcia slammed the cover down on the keyboard and shouted, "Don't you dare sing that in falsetto!" and Peter stared at the tall, broad-shouldered Spaniard and asked, "What's *falsetto?*" thinking it must be a Spanish word.

"Sing the note." He banged it on the piano. "Just that note."

Peter sang the note. Professor Garcia looked at the key, banged it again and said, "Sing it louder."

Peter tried, but louder wasn't there.

"Caw like a crow." Professor Garcia made a perfect impression of a cawing crow.

Peter tried to emulate the professor's crow three times and thought he was close when the professor said, "Your crow is sick. Try this." He squeaked like a mouse.

Peter tried to imitate the mouse, and Professor Garcia yelled, "Relax, squeak, relax...." Peter repeated it a dozen times until the tension in his throat subsided, and his squeak had become even a little musical.

"Sing this." Garcia played a note, slid down a fifth and played another. When Peter hesitated, he said, "If you don't trust me, get another teacher... if you do trust me, do what I tell you without hesitating. Now you've got to squeak again."

Peter laughed, then squeaked. Professor Garcia squeaked four times, and each time Peter imitated him.

"Now this." He slid down a full octave. Peter imitated the *glissando,* and Garcia raised the pitch, repeating the sound. Peter copied him, and Professor Garcia raised the pitch a third time, then a fourth, until the top note was somewhere in the ether. Peter followed Professor Garcia and found himself somewhere he had never been, where his head became light, and he began to laugh.

"Why are you laughing?"

"That can't be right. It's too easy, too high, and too much fun."

Professor Garcia said, "Are you afraid? I assure you, it is safe, and it's right." He banged a note on the piano and played a descending arpeggio. "Throw the note out like a crow, or a mouse, and I will tell you when to go down. Do not think; if you do, you will not succeed."

When Peter hesitated, the professor relaxed his shoulders and put his hands in his lap.

"Singing is not an intellectual occupation; after shitting, pissing, and one other item, it is the most primitive thing you can do. There is nothing to singing but raw emotion, and you must clear your mind of logic… if you can find logic in singing, you can explain the existence of God." He repeated the arpeggio. "Sing, Peter, like a lion roars, as a crow calls its mate or protects its babies."

Peter nailed the note, and Professor Garcia said, "Louder!" Peter surprised himself when he increased the volume without breaking his voice. "Softer. Don't think—just do it!" Garcia indicated 'soft' with his hand by patting an imaginary dog. Peter brought the sound back until the professor said, "Now, down the scale," and played the notes of the scale. Peter followed him down but ran out of breath before the last note.

Peter laughed… he felt like dancing as he asked, "What was the note?"

The professor chuckled. "It doesn't matter. It was high enough… for now."

"That's not falsetto. But the high notes I was singing before were falsetto… *nicht wahr?*"

"You are right, Peter, that is not falsetto, and yes, you were singing in falsetto before. The sound you are making now is the one a tenor makes when he wants the women opposite him on stage to fall in love with him, and that sound is why you must learn to sing."

"What now?" Peter asked, "How long before I can sing an opera?"

"Sit down, Peter." Professor Garcia pointed to the only chair in the room, and Peter sat on it while the professor leaned against the piano.

"How many people do you think can find a seat in the Munich Staatsoper *Zuschauerraum?*" Professor Garcia swept his arm as though looking out from the stage into the audience. He didn't expect or wait for an answer. "I will tell you… about two thousand. There are five balconies, and the stage is bigger than your father's house. When you stand in the middle of that stage, you will sing to the most important person in the theatre. She is sitting in the back row of the fifth balcony, paid half her monthly pension for her seat, and the woman is hard of hearing. That woman must fall in love with every note in your beautiful voice." He nodded when Peter opened his mouth. "And the most difficult part is this. If you sing with the resonance you need so the lady can hear you, you cannot hear the orchestra!"

Peter thought for a moment and asked, "How many people would hear me if I sang like I do now?"

"Perhaps those halfway back in the orchestra seating, and maybe someone seated in the front row of the first balcony... if they have excellent hearing. But perhaps not so many as that because the orchestra, if it's not a good one, will likely drown you out."

"How do I make my voice bigger?"

"Bigger, resonant, accurate, flexible, durable... I cannot tell you how... there is no single or simple explanation, as there is no explanation for a Stradivarius violin. You must trust me to build your instrument and let me teach you how to play it."

Professor Garcia looked at Peter in a way that told him not to interrupt.

"You are fortunate to have the raw material I need, and if you do precisely what I say, you will have exceptional high notes and beautiful, resonant low notes. Unfortunately, you are intelligent for a tenor, which can sometimes be a hindrance." He appeared to consider whether to say more but then went on.

"These are all rare qualities in any singer but truly a miracle in a tenor. And that is why you must believe in me as you were taught to believe in God, without question or modification, because sometimes what I say and do might seem... shall we say... ridiculous?" He walked to the door and put his hand on the lever. "I want you to come at nine o'clock tomorrow and wait with Mademoiselle Durand, whose lesson is at nine-thirty. Do not tell her about your session with me because everything you do and hear in this room stays here. This was not a lesson but an examination of your potential so I could decide whether to take you as my student."

Peter said, "I can't be here at nine. The train...."

"That's alright, temporarily, but you must find a *Wohnung* close to the school—not more than a ten-minute walk."

"But, I can't afford...."

"Don't worry, I shall arrange a *stipend* for you. It will be enough for your living expenses, and I will have an address for your accommodations tomorrow. You will find them adequate but not luxurious."

"But...."

Professor Garcia opened the door, and a young man with a leather case in his hand passed Peter.

"Out... your time is up. You are now my student, and you must obey my rules, or I guarantee you shall regret it."

Professor Garcia smiled. Peter firmly closed the door and danced down the hall until he met students coming up the wide stairs.

Chapter Two

Money isn't Everything, but it's Close

About ten years earlier

Once you've tried it, you will realize that being wealthy is much better than poverty. People who don't believe that have never been wealthy.

JULIETTE HAD NO IDEA HER PARENTS WERE FILTHY RICH until she was halfway through an expensive private school. She accepted as normal that a man with a gun followed her everywhere, and a chauffeur waited in a Rolls Royce at her beck and call. A butler opened the door for her and closed it behind her… a maid cleaned the house—another served tea when Juliette got home from school… all perfectly normal if one is civilized and insanely wealthy.

Art and music were the basic staples of life in the house of one of Europe's most respected art and jewelry dealers. Juliette didn't know that not everyone lived as she did and wouldn't have cared if she had known.

Whenever her parents took her to the Monnaie Theater, Juliette sat in the third row of the orchestra section, the most expensive seats in the house. She had attended her first symphony concert, Gustav Mahler's First Symphony, with her mother when she was three. When the conductor paused at the end of the third movement, a funeral march through the forest, Juliette whispered to her mother, *"Mama, ils ont joué 'Frère Jacques,'"* the first sound the little girl had made since the cuckoo call in the first movement, and her mother said, "Yes, the theme of that movement was based on *'Frère Jacques.'* Now, no more talking."

Veronique had already told Juliette she would take her to the symphony when the king invited Jacques and Veronique to sit in the Royal Box with him and his family. But Veronique wanted Juliette's music education to include this symphony, and Brussels might not offer another opportunity. Furthermore, she wasn't sure Juliette wouldn't disturb the people in the Royal Box, so mother and daughter sat in the family's *abonnement* seats.

Veronique played Mozart and Bach on the piano while Juliette was still in the womb, and after her daughter was born, Juliette slept in a basket under the piano. When her little girl graduated to a crib in her own bedroom, Veronique sang her to sleep with Schubert, Brahms, and Schumann lieder, sprinkled with French *Chanson,* from *Renaissance* to modern.

Juliette played the piano as soon as she could reach the keys while sitting on her mother's lap or crouching on the bench. Veronique taught her to play children's songs with one finger, then two fingers, and then with both hands. When Juliette discovered the phonograph, Veronique had to restrict her daughter's listening time.

Juliette's first voice teacher was recommended to her mother by the music director at the Monnaie Theatre. Mademoiselle Monique Desjardins had sung lead roles in several operas, and Veronique also knew her from solos she had sung with the local Bach choir.

Before she told Juliette who would teach her, Veronique took her daughter to one of her prospective teacher's concerts. When her mother introduced Juliette to Mademoiselle Desjardins after the concert, the little girl had heard enough that she could barely contain her excitement.

However, when the next day the chauffeur parked the Rolls Royce in front of a narrow townhouse in a low-income neighbourhood, Veronique had to coax Juliette out of the car with the promise of a strawberry croissant for lunch.

When Juliette hesitated in front of the door, her mother asked, "Do you want to learn to sing like Mademoiselle Desjardins?"

Juliette nodded.

Veronique dropped the knocker on its plate, and a few seconds later, the door swung open. Monique Desjardins smiled, shook Juliette's mother's hand, and said, *"Madame Durand. Entrez, s'il vous plaît."*

Juliette cautiously followed her mother and curtsied when Veronique introduced her to her teacher. The woman, who had only reluctantly agreed to teach a six-year-old child, leaned over, put her face level with Juliette's and said, "Would you like to sing for me?"

Juliette shook her head.

Mademoiselle Desjardins said, "Then I will sing for you, *n'est-ce pas?"* and took her hand. Juliette resisted; Mademoiselle smiled, looked at Veronique, and the little girl relented.

They passed through a comfortable parlour to a small studio that appeared to have been added to the back of the house as an afterthought. Veronique sat on the only chair in the room, an uncomfortable plain hardwood chair designed for eating brief meals at a table or, more likely, to discourage parents from listening to their child's lesson. The teacher put Juliette in the crook of the baby grand piano and began singing a children's song as she played a simple accompaniment. Juliette looked at her mother; Veronique made a sour face and waved until the teacher stopped.

Perhaps you could sing something more mature; I suggest the lullaby from Humperdink's Hansel and Gretel, if you know it."

"*Mais oui,* I have sung Gretel many times. But, for a child… it is a legitimate opera—difficult to sing—certainly not a children's song."

Veronique smiled a smile that said everything without a need for words. Mademoiselle's shrug said, "Okay, you are paying," as she turned to the keyboard and began playing. At the correct place in the music, she began singing, "*Abends will ich schlafen gehen…* "and Juliette began singing Hänsel's harmony line in a clear voice, and in German. Halfway through the first verse, when Juliette stumbled on a word, Veronique halted them with her hand and asked, "Can you please sing Hänsel? Juliette knows the soprano role better than the mezzo."

"*Mais oui,* " said the excited teacher, and Veronique said, "Please, from the beginning."

Halfway through the verse, Veronique stopped them and asked Juliette, "I would like you to talk to Mademoiselle Desjardins—perhaps Mademoiselle has time for milk and a pastry…."

To avoid surprises, Veronique and Mademoiselle Desjardins had arranged everything beforehand, and Juliette's new teacher smiled knowingly and nodded.

Veronique stood up. "When shall I tell our chauffeur to pick up my daughter?"

"Before six," said Mademoiselle Desjardins, "but after five. Juliette and I have much to talk about."

"Bien!" said Veronique, nodded to her daughter and said as she left the room. "I will see myself out. The chauffeur will be outside the door at six."

And so began Juliette's love affair with Mademoiselle Desjardins. Veronique paid Mademoiselle Desjardins enough to give up half her studio, and Juliette spent all her spare time there. Juliette sang in amateur vocal competitions, winning most of them, but her crown achievement was singing Gretel in a school production at the Monnaie Theatre.

Nine years later, when Juliette was almost sixteen, oratorio and concert engagements began pouring in, and her singing career began. A few months before her seventeenth birthday, her father called her into his office.

"I have a friend in the *Münchner Staatsoper* who knows the *Münchner Musik Hochschule Direktor,* Siegmund von Hausegger, and you have an audition with Professor... It's here somewhere... Ah, here it is... Professor Miguel Jesus Garcia on Monday, the eleventh of September. Veronique has spoken with your teacher, and Mademoiselle Desjardins agrees that Professor Garcia is an excellent teacher. She has also agreed to work with you every day until you audition." He grinned at his daughter. "Marcel will accompany you to Munich. Be nice to him."

"Do I have anything to say about this?"

"Of course... what would you like to say?"

Jacques knew he was in trouble with his only child. He had made arrangements without talking to her, but his friend had needed an answer on the spot, and Jacques couldn't think of a reason why it shouldn't be "yes, and thank you." He watched the storm clouds gather on Juliette's face and braced himself for the inevitable blowback. The only thing that could make it worse would be for Veronique to walk through the door.

Unfortunately, Jacques' worst fear was listening on the other side of the door, and she opened it.

Her first words were, "I did not speak with mademoiselle about losing her star pupil… " Veronique crossed the room to stand in front of him and added… "Because *you* neglected to tell me." She put her hands on her hips, always a bad sign, and said, "I did, however, follow your instructions and arranged a lesson for every day next week." She pointed her index finger at her husband's long nose. "I am afraid you have put me in a very awkward position with Juliette's teacher, who is incidentally also my friend."

Seeing her father's discomfort, Juliette jumped in on the attack. "Daddy, you can cancel the audition—I don't want another teacher. Monique said that I can begin auditioning with agents in October, and she believes I will have a contract before Christmas."

Jacques ground his perfect teeth. The water was getting deeper and colder.

"Mademoiselle Desjardins doesn't know whether you are ready. You must sing for a teacher who teaches the best voices in the world, like Professor Garcia."

"Daddy, I can sing all the lyric soprano repertoire. I have ten arias that I can sing perfectly, and I will get a job when I audition."

"But you don't have any experience at that level… and don't tell me mademoiselle does. She is a good singer, but she is *not* a diva."

Veronique flanked him. "Jacques, you are wrong about this. I have heard Juliette sing those arias, and our daughter can sing them as well as anyone I've heard, even on recordings!"

Jacques hung his head; he was in too deep. He looked at his daughter and braced himself, knowing he was about to insult her, and knowing from bitter experience she wouldn't take it well.

"*Ma cherie,* the school director says you need at least four years in the opera school and at least two years with a teacher like Professor Garcia. I can't be the one to tell you whether you are ready; only the school director and the professor are qualified to make that judgment."

"Okay, Daddy, you've said what you think—now call the *Hoch-schule* and cancel the audition." Sparks flew from Juliette's eyes as she turned on her heel and charged past her mother, slamming the door behind her.

Jacques stared at the door and said, "I can't get anything right with that girl. Those nuns have ruined her!"

"You should have talked to her first. You are the person she wants most to please, and you just told her that she can't sing well enough to get a job. Singing is in that child's soul! How could you be so cruel and... and... stupid?"

She slammed the door behind her.

Jacques was feeling sorry for himself and his wife's words were still ringing in his ears when the telephone rang. He answered, "Durand here," hoping for good news.

A familiar voice said, "Jacques, I think you should cancel your daughter's trip to Munich. Röhm's S.A. bastards are organizing into gangs and hunting down communists and Jews! Women aren't safe on the street, especially beautiful young ones like Juliette."

"What about the police... don't your people control them now?"

"We have a certain amount of control, but I cannot guarantee your daughter's safety, even with the *Polizei*. Röhm is Hitler's closest friend, and the Führer is allowing him to throw his weight around. Everyone but me is afraid of that fat prick!"

"I might not send her in any case—she and her mother think her voice doesn't need any more work, and I will have to let you know what they decide. But Juliette is neither communist nor Jew, and I'm sure we can find a way to protect her from Röhm's thugs."

"I will await your call, and if she comes, you have my assurance we will quietly watch over her from afar. However, I cannot openly help you or give any guarantees."

Jacques said quickly before his friend could hang up, "Our mutual contact in Switzerland received your package, and it is now safe. Perhaps you could find a way to do more for my daughter."

The voice smiled over the phone.

"It is a pleasure doing business with you, Jacques, and I will do my best regarding your daughter. Perhaps, for now, it would be better if she had someone from your side looking after her directly, preferably someone who can use a substantial and deadly weapon, although I cannot officially condone...."

"...I will send a man with her who fits that description...for now."

Jacques hung up the phone.

Juliette came downstairs after spending half an hour crying, then another half-hour thinking. She confronted her mother at the piano in the living room.

The weather was warm, the doors to the long verandah were open, and birds sang their goodbyes to summer.

"Mama, I don't know what to do. Papa could be right, and your opinion could be clouded by your desire to protect me."

"So, do you think your father wants to get rid of you?" Veronique stopped in the middle of a beautiful line in a Chopin Ballad. "You are right about me wanting you to stay home... Munich is the most dangerous city in Europe, and you are too young, headstrong and self-absorbed to be sensible."

Juliette refused to be deflected by the veiled insult and asked, "Do you know anything about this Professor?"

"Not a lot, but what I know tells me he is as hard as Krupp steel. Jacques' friend in Munich did some research through the school director, and Professor Garcia has a reputation for screaming at his students. But despite that, he teaches world-famous singers who sit on a boat for two weeks crossing the Atlantic Ocean to spend a week working with him."

"I have a lesson today; I will ask Monique if she knows anything about this man."

"Oh, dear, that might not be a good idea... she will be upset if she thinks you might leave and, well, Monique has great plans for you, and I hate to disappoint her."

Juliette looked into the gardens in the backyard. A single maple tree out of a dozen nearly identical trees was beginning to turn red. Every year it changed colour weeks before the others, always to red, while the others, when they finally turned, were yellow. Juliette decided if she were a tree, she would want to be the red one.

"But what if Daddy is right? What if my voice is too small for the opera stage, and this man could make it bigger? I can hear that Mademoiselle Desjardins' voice is really not big enough for opera... perhaps...."

Juliette went to the piano, reached around her mother and pressed 'middle C. She sang it, then pushed it as loud as she could, lifting her diaphragm as Monique had taught her. The note became only slightly louder, still not as loud as the single key on the piano.

"Mama, why don't you come to my lesson today? We can have tea with Monique."

Veronique spread her hands, then sighed, *"Trés bien;* I will go with you."

Juliette's lesson began with the usual arpeggios and scales, then Mademoiselle Desjardins opened her *La Bohème* score to the fold at the end of the first tenor aria. She played the closing bars, singing the tenor's request for the soprano to tell him her name. Juliette began, *Mi chiamano Mimi...* and stopped.

"Do you think the audience will hear me sing that if I were singing in a large house... say... Munich?" Monique put her hands on her lap, and Juliette went on. "I'm singing in the bottom fifth of my voice, a sixty-piece orchestra is playing, and Munich has a vast *Zuschauerraum*, one of the largest in Europe. Will anyone hear me tell Rudolpho that my name is *Mimi?* Do you honestly think my voice is big enough for an opera stage like Munich?"

Monique leaned ahead and fiddled with the page, pressing it flat.

"Juliette, you have the most beautiful voice I've ever heard, but beautiful voices are rarely big voices. You are barely one-metre fifty-five, and you weigh how much?...fifty, fifty-five kilograms? Big voices don't come in tiny packages like that."

"But I want to sing Mimi and Violette and Desdemona...."

"You can sing those roles on the concert stage, but not in the *Münchner Staatsoper*. I've taught you a dozen arias, and you sing them beautifully enough to get you into a small theatre. And then there is your oratorio and concert career...."

Juliette decided to wait before she dropped the bomb. Tea would soften the blow.

"My mother and I would like some tea. You made it from dried black currents the last time we had tea together, and I would love to have it again. Can we talk about where you think I can go with the voice I have while we sip our tea?"

Monique stood up, closed the score and said, "I think that would be a good idea. There are several options, and we should discuss them."

The gas burner on high heated a kettle of water in less than three minutes, and it took all of that to prepare the teapot with the dried currents and find three croissants and plates.

Juliette poured the tea, then sat opposite Monique—Veronique sat between them at the end of the table.

Monique sipped her tea, put the cup down and asked Juliette, "Now, tell me what you are thinking. Where is this doubt about your voice coming from?"

Veronique said, "It didn't come from me."

Juliette touched her mother's hand. "I want to sing opera. I don't mind singing concerts and oratorios, but my heart is with playing a role on the stage. I love acting as much as singing, maybe more. But both together... that's what I was born to do!"

"I can attest to that!" said Veronique.

"Alright," said Monique, "where do I come in?"

Juliette's tea was getting cold, but she didn't take a sip before she asked, "Have you ever heard of the singing teacher... I think his name is Miguel Jesus Garcia? He teaches at the Munich *Gesangs Hochschule.*"

"Heard of him? He's probably the most famous voice teacher who ever lived! He gives master classes all over the world—and famous singers come to him from America when they have voice problems! Why, I've heard he gave Rosa Ponselle a lesson when he held a master class in New York, and now she won't let anyone else touch her voice!"

"Who's Rosa Ponselle?

"I have neglected your musical education, haven't I? Rosa Ponselle is an American soprano, the best there has ever been, and likely the best there will ever be. She sings your roles at the Metropolitan Opera and is about your size but muscular. As far as I know, she has never had a singing teacher other than Garcia."

"So, how does she sing in a big house like that? How can her voice be bigger than mine?"

Monique shrugged her shoulders. "If I knew that...."

Veronique asked, "Is it possible to teach that?"

Monique said, "Yes, I think so because all big voices started with a baby's cry, and babies are pretty much equally annoying."

Veronique smiled meaningfully. "What about a teacher like Garcia? Does he know how to do that?"

"Let me put it this way. This tiny house is all I have in this world, and I would give it to Professor Garcia if he would teach me for only a year!"

"What about Juliette? What if she studied with him—do you think he could make her voice big enough for opera?"

Monique looked from Veronique to Juliette, then back. "What are you really asking? Of course, he can make her voice bigger *and* more resonant, and he wouldn't sacrifice any beauty. I can't do that, and I don't know anyone else who can. But his class is always booked years in advance, so it's a moot point, isn't it?"

"Juliette has an opportunity to audition for Professor Garcia next Monday. Would you be offended?"

Mademoiselle Desjardins jumped to her feet, spilling her tea as she did.

"Offended? That's the most wonderful news I've heard in my music career! I have been awake nights trying to think how I can give Juliette what I know she needs. Everyone who hears her says she has world-class talent, and you certainly have the money to develop it, but I am at the limit of my expertise. I've done no harm to the beauty of her instrument, and Juliette is musically a much better singer than when she came here. But more is there, and I don't know how to get it. However, I guarantee Professor Garcia will get it, if she can pass the audition."

Juliette's eyes brimmed with tears as she reached across the table and put her hand on Monique's.

"I don't know how to thank you."

"Your father will take care of that!" said Veronique.

Marcel Guignard, bodyguard, chauffeur, and who knew what else, sat opposite Juliette in a first-class compartment on the train from Aachen to Munich. He read because he had nothing else to do, and Juliette wanted his attention, so she snatched the book he was reading and slammed it shut.

"I want to talk."

He reached for the book. "That book is only for adults!"

Juliette looked at the front cover, plain white with a woman's stylized head. The title was *Le Dieuxième Sexe* in large black letters, and the author was Simone de Beauvoir.

"The second sex? Are you trying to learn something about women?" She had removed her shoes and now used her big toe to lift the right leg of his pants. "You only need to ask." She giggled.

"Now, that is what I don't understand. I am eight years older than you; my job is protecting you from leaches like me, yet you tease me with your toe." He laughed. "Luckily for you, I like working for your father."

"How is it lucky?" She waved her hand and said, "Don't answer that."

Juliette pulled her foot back and spread her long skirt evenly over her lap.

"I saw you sitting at the back when I sang my last concert. Now, I want you to tell me what you think of my voice, and I am ordering you to be honest. If I don't believe you, I will tell Daddy to fire you!"

Marcel wriggled uncomfortably on his plush seat. "I wasn't really listening; I was waiting for you. I didn't want to waste gas driving back to the house and then back to the Monnaie Theatre."

"That's not an answer… you're fired!"

"Juliette, I know nothing about singing and less about sopranos. You have a beautiful voice; that's all I know."

"But I don't want just a beautiful voice… I want an exciting voice." She put her toe under his pant leg again. "Does my voice turn on your motor?"

"No, no… I mean… Hell, Juliette, give me my book." He tried to grab it, but she held it against her breasts, telling him with her eyes to come and get it.

"Do my high notes thrill you? Tell me the truth, or I'll tell Daddy you molested me!"

"Ha! I molested you... do you even know what that means?"

"I don't need to read about it to know what that means... now tell me the truth! Dammit, I want the truth—stop running around a pole!"

"Alright, Mademoiselle Durand, I will tell you what I think." He looked out the window for a minute, then looked at Juliette with an expression that reminded her of her father, specifically when she needed to hear an unpleasant truth.

"I love your voice and your singing when you sing at home. Your voice is *intime,* and I find a concert hall takes it away and leaves only a little girl's voice."

Juliette pulled her feet back, leaned against the window and watched the forest and farms pass the train. "Precisely!"

She thought about her voice and her dreams. She didn't want a pretty or beautiful voice; she wanted an exciting sound that would stiffen the hairs on people's necks. She needed to thrill her audience, make them laugh and cry... she couldn't do that with a pretty or even a beautiful voice if they had to strain to hear it. She needed a big, resonant, exciting voice that would bring people to their feet, shouting, *'Bravo,'* again and again while she bowed, left the stage, returned, and left the stage again and again until she became too tired to give them more.

Yes, that was the voice she wanted, and she would get it, or she wouldn't sing!

"Thank you, Marcel. You should be honest with me all the time."

"Don't count on that," said Marcel as she handed him his sexy book. "I've learned that honesty gets me in trouble with women."

They checked into the *Bayerische Hof,* and Juliette slept well, despite her apprehension. She woke early, while the sun still struggled to peek over the horizon. The tea with Monique had settled Juliette on the right path, and she was convinced Professor Garcia was the next step on that road. God had given her a beautiful voice and taken care of the roadblocks, and she told herself God wouldn't have guided her to this point if Professor Garcia weren't going to jump at the chance to teach her.

As she pulled a comb through her long black hair, admiring her reflection, she imagined herself on the stage with a handsome tenor, singing *La Traviata,* or perhaps *La Bohème* duets with the tenor, to a swooning audience.

Juliette began singing Mimi's aria to herself, imagining the same handsome tenor listening intently to her beautiful voice. Halfway through the aria, Mimi asked the innuendo-laden question, *"Lei m'intende?"* coquettishly suggesting, "Do you *really* know what I'm saying?" and the handsome tenor answered with an evocative, *"Sì."*

A knock on the door, using the secret cadence Marcel had insisted Juliette learn, brought a "Come in… it's not locked" out of Juliette and a *"Ma petite fille,* what did I tell you about locking the door?" look from Marcel as he entered and threw himself in one of only two comfortable chairs in the room.

"It's time for breakfast…do what you do, and from now on, lock your door! There are some bad cats in Munich these days."

Juliette laughed at Marcel as she returned from the makeup table in her dressing room and picked up her purse from the desk beside him. She said, mocking him with her tone as he struggled to get out of the soft chair, "Marcel, don't be such a mouse. There are armed guards in the hall, the stairwells, the lobby, and outside on the sidewalk. How much safer can we be?"

"Juliette, if Röhm thought there were communists or Jews in the hotel, he would find a way to get to them."

"But I'm just a little Catholic Belgian girl; what would Röhm want with me?"

"Röhm, nothing… but the thugs that work for him… they would think of something unpleasant to do with you." Marcel opened the door.

"Juliette, you are a naïve almost-seventeen-year-old girl, and Röhm's *Sturmabteilung* is a collection of gangs—dangerous thugs and hoodlums. They rape women and murder people, ostensibly communists, Jews and homosexuals. Wealth offers no protection; in fact, Röhm's squads look for wealthy people to rob, then justify the robbery by saying their victim is a Jew, or worse, a *Bolshevik!* But Röhm is playing with fire by attacking the people who got Hitler where he is."

Juliette dismissed Marcel with a wave of her hand. "It's all politics, and I'm not interested. Right now, I need a cup of coffee and a croissant."

After a short walk through the old city to Odeonplatz, they arrived at the school an hour early. Marcel, who Juliette knew wasn't sure where Professor Garcia's studio was, asked the first person he saw entering the building that stood at the address they had been given.

The young woman was about Juliette's age, five centimetres taller and overweight. Juliette guessed she was a soprano.

The young woman confirmed Juliette's suspicion when her warm speaking voice said, "Go up the main stairway to the first floor, turn left, then sit on the bench until your lesson time. His majesty's name is on the studio door." Her impeccable German was coloured with a beautiful French accent.

Juliette asked in French, "Are you in Professor Garcia's class?"

The girl laughed and quickly picked up on the inference. "God, no, he hates sopranos!" She paused, snapped her fingers and said, *"Oh, merde,* are you auditioning for him today?"

Trying to sound confident, Juliette said, "Yes, I have an appointment with Professor Garcia at nine-thirty." The girl smiled sympathetically; Juliette ignored the implication and asked, "Do you know where I can warm up my voice?"

"Come with me. You're beautiful—that won't hurt, but you'll still need all the help you can get."

She led Juliette to the bench, pointed at a clock opposite a door with Garcia's name on it and said, "That's *God's* studio. Sit on the bench when your voice is ready, and go in when your time comes. Don't wait; just barge in!"

She took Juliette across the hall into a large room with a grand piano. Juliette put her music on the piano bench and turned around. The girl had closed the door and was waiting to say something.

"This is only one of ten identical practice rooms." She swept her hand around the spacious room, stopping at the piano. "If a room has a number but no name, you can use it if it's not occupied. You can't reserve one, but most of them are empty at this time of day; that's why I'm here… by the way, my name is Michelle Landry, and I'm from Lyon."

"Juliette Durand, from Brussels." Juliette shook the girl's large hand and asked, What's he like? I've heard he's the best teacher in the world!"

Michelle laughed from her belly, a sure sign of a singer's voice.

"He thinks so, and I guess he might be, but I can't stand him! I auditioned for Garcia a year ago—the worst experience of my life! I was relieved when he sent me to Frau Kirschbaum."

A soprano voice pierced the closed door to the room, and they stopped to listen. Juliette had never heard a sound that powerful, especially considering it came through two doors and a hallway! She asked Michelle, "My God, is that one of Professor Garcia's students?"

"She's not a student; she sings in the Metropolitan Opera and comes here for a week before the opera season for a 'tune-up' with him. She's Norwegian."

"What's her name?"

"I don't pay much attention to Met singers, and I've forgotten, but she's famous in the United States, and I think in England too. She never sits on the bench and never speaks to us mortals." Michelle opened the door to leave, and with only the studio door between Juliette and the source, the sound coming from Professor Garcia's studio shocked her. How could a human voice make such a sound?

"I'll be down the hall if you want a shoulder to cry on."

Juliette laughed, but the expression on Michelle's face killed any mirth she felt. Michelle left the room, closing the door behind her.

The piano was a two-metre Steinway grand, and as Juliette sat on the bench to try it out, she tempered her expectations for a practice studio piano. But the sound was exquisite, and even to her perfect ear, the tuning was as accurate as a piano can be tuned, and the 'voicing' was excellent to her educated ear. The quality of the piano hinted at the quality of the school, heightening Juliette's desire to get into Professor Garcia's class.

Juliette sang a few scales, then began Mimi's aria. The sound improved with every note until, when she reached the aria's climax, she knew from experience her voice was as good as it could be. She resisted the temptation to sing Violette's 'Sempre libra," a much more difficult aria, closed the cover and went to the bench in the hallway. Marcel had seated himself discreetly on a hard chair two doors down the hall.

The barely credible singing sounds penetrating the professor's door thrilled Juliette but also awakened a gremlin of doubt. Instinctively she knew she would never come close to having a voice like that, no matter who taught her—that sound was a gift from God—but she also knew in her heart that her voice contained the same thrill. That sound was buried in her imagination, and she needed Professor Garcia to uncover it. She would do whatever was required to get him to help her.

A young man about her age pointed to the seat beside her and said in native German, "May I?" She smiled and nodded.

He immediately notified Juliette that he would audition for Professor Garcia at ten, and she told him how everything worked while thinking, *"he's a tenor for sure."*

The voice in Professor Garcia's studio vocalized to the 'F' above 'high C' so easily Juliette's heart sank. Huge voices were not supposed to be able to do that.

"I think I heard a 'D' above high 'C,'" said the tenor, obviously as amazed with the sound as Juliette was.

Juliette wanted to scream but settled for correcting him. "She sang an 'F,'" then added, "I have perfect pitch." She wanted to say, "And you are proof that tenors have no pitch," but restrained herself.

Juliette had sung with many tenors, all of them stupid, tone-deaf, and lecherous. In her considerable experience, their priorities lay first and almost entirely with their beautiful voice. Above everything else in their self-absorbed lives, all tenors were obsessed with their holy grail, the indomitable 'high C.' Sopranos came a distant second, but only if they were pretty and worshipped tenors. Everything else was trivial, except perhaps Italian food and alcohol.

As the voice behind the door ran up and down arpeggios and scales, making sounds Juliette had considered reserved for animals and birds, Juliette's mood descended into despair. She groaned to herself as the voice practiced Mozart's "Queen of the Night" aria in a key her perfect pitch told her was a half-tone higher than the original.

"You are the most beautiful girl I've ever seen."

The tenor stared at her, pleading for something, but Juliette didn't dare guess what, so she said, *"Merci beaucoup."* She realized she had replied in French and said in German, "Please forgive me that I don't speak good German. I learned it in school and my father speaks it, and when I am accepted in Professor Garcia's studio, I will take language classes."

He looked away, fiddled with his hands, held out his right hand and said, *"Je m'appelle Peter Schweitzer,"* with an ugly German accent.

Juliette didn't react at first. A tenor who spoke a second language? She had never met one who could speak any language well. Perhaps she was wrong about him... maybe he was a baritone.

She gently laid her hand in his, smiled the smile she used on children and said, *"Je m'appelle Juliette Durand; je vis à Bruxelles."*

"Je suis ténor," said the young man, ruining Juliette's baritone thesis, and then to prove he was indeed a tenor, said, *"Je suppose que tu es une soprano,"* with the ugliest accent she had ever heard.

Juliette looked at Peter with a mixture of disgust and sympathy, reminding herself of why she hated tenors. She decided to amuse herself by playing his game for a few minutes.

"I am a lyric coloratura soprano," she said in German, "and I can sing as high as the one in the studio, although not as loud." She looked at Professor Garcia's door. "I never sing that loud. My teacher said that I should protect the beauty in my voice, *n'est-ce pas?"*

The tenor, whose name she now knew was Peter, raised Juliette's hackles by ignoring her comment. He said, "My teacher plays the violin. She doesn't know much about singing, but she taught me how to read musical notes, and I taught myself to sing *Spirto Gentil* from *La Favorita* by Gaetano Donizetti. My mother bought the recording of Beniamino Gigli singing it—he sings it better than anyone—I sing it just like he does."

Oh, great, she thought; *he learned to sing from a recording. If that pompous ass passes an audition for Professor Garcia's class and I don't, I will quit singing!*

The tenor went on, "When I sang it for *Schuldirektor* Siegmund von Hausegger, he immediately accepted me in the *Hochschule.* I will sing it for my audition with Herr Professor Garcia."

Juliette turned away, trying not to laugh.

"I could sing it for you sometime."

Juliette, not believing her ears, blurted, "What?"

As she tried to decide whether this tenor was an egotistical idiot or naïve, he went on, explaining, "Spirto Gentil... Gigli... La Favorita... I will sing it for you. I can sing it just like Gigli."

"That would be nice." She tried to put an expression on her face that would discourage him, but he surprised her by turning to politics.

"I went to the National Socialist rally in Nürnberg and heard both Adolph Hitler and Ernst Röhm speak. The rally was called *Reichsparteitag des Sieges;* it was to celebrate the National Socialist victory over the old Weimar Republic."

Juliette decided to cut him off.

"Congratulations, but I am not interested in that nonsense." Juliette was reminded of a quote attributed to King Henry II: "Will no one rid me of this troublesome Priest?" which prompted four of his knights to put Thomas Becket to the sword. Juliette thought, *Where is a loyal knight when a damsel needs him?*

"Nonsense? My father works for M.A.N., and Hitler saved his job when the party rescued the German people from the terrible economic problems caused by the Versailles Treaty and the world banks!"

Juliette looked at her watch… under two minutes to go. She looked at the clock on the wall facing her, and it agreed. She hoped Peter would keep his mouth shut when he saw her looking at the clock, but he didn't take the hint, once again proving he was a tenor.

"Next year, when Professor Garcia has taught me how to sing my audition arias, I'm going to get a job singing in an opera house; my teacher said I should wait until my voice matures. She said my voice didn't need much work on the technical aspect, but I will have to work hard on learning how to sing the tenor reper...rep...uh..."

Juliette looked at her watch again, said, "It's *repertoire,*" and then, "I have to go to my lesson now," as she stood up. She was surprised that a tenor would use a sophisticated word like 'aspect,' but actually found herself feeling sorry for him when he struggled with *repertoire*.

She stopped at the studio door, held her knuckles a few centimetres from it and waited until the second hand on the wall clock swept past the twelve. She knocked and opened the door. A tall, broad-shouldered blond Nordic woman who would tip the scales at over a hundred kilograms stopped mid-phrase and looked at the clock in the studio. The professor stood up from the piano and went around it to shake her hand. The woman picked up her leather music case, and Juliette was left with the impression the woman would have run over her if she hadn't stepped out of the way. Juliette firmly closed the door behind her.

Juliette tried to hide her nervousness as she met Professor Garcia halfway across the room and shook his outstretched hand.

"Ah, Mademoiselle Durand. I am afraid your audition may be for nothing; my studio is already full."

Juliette resisted the need to throw her music at the smug Spaniard. She said, "I have come from Brussels to sing for you, and I have thirty minutes before the tenor I was sitting beside will audition for your 'already full' studio. During that time, I will sing *Mimi* for you."

"Mademoiselle, since I have been informed you have been singing since you were six, you will know there are different rules for tenors—an unfortunate fact of opera life." He smiled. "But it is also a fact that I save a spot or two for exceptional voices, even sopranos. Sing what you have brought, and we will see what you are made of."

Juliette gave him her piano score of La Bohème; the Professor sat on the piano bench, opened the score to Mimi's first act aria, pressed the pages flat and looked at Juliette. She nodded, and he sang the last line of the tenor aria that led into hers.

Juliette began with all the sound she could get out of her vocal cords without injuring them and was humiliated when Professor Garcia banged on the piano and said, "I can't hear you," as he hammered the keys.

Juliette controlled the urge to tell him to take his feet off the keys, but after the third phrase, she stopped and said, "How can you decide whether I can sing if you can't hear me? Perhaps you *would* hear me if you accompanied me instead of trying to destroy the piano!"

"Mademoiselle, have you ever heard a baby cry?"

Juliette thought for a few seconds, trying to find a connection between a baby crying and his ruthless treatment of Mister Steinway's piano.

She said, "Of course. I've heard many babies cry." She was tempted to add a sarcastic comment but needed his approval more than she wanted satisfaction.

"A baby typically weighs between three kilograms, and we'll take fifteen kilograms as the maximum for my purposes. Now, I think a determined and upset baby could be heard over my attempts to damage this fine piano. In fact, no one would care about my terrible playing if that baby were beside the piano as you are. They would focus on the baby—do you agree?"

Juliette thought for a moment and decided he had a point. She reluctantly said, "I agree."

"Am I close when I estimate your weight at fifty-five kilograms?"

Juliette wasn't uncomfortable talking about her weight—she was proud of her trim, solid figure. Still, she sensed that Professor Garcia was about to upset everything she had assumed about singing and her voice. She said, "Fifty-four kilos when I left Brussels."

"Close enough. Our baby is still in her mother's arms at ten kilograms. Would you agree that you weigh more than five times as much as this baby?"

She reacted without thinking of the implication. "Professor Garcia, I am sixteen, almost seventeen years old, and you treat me like a child! Your comparison between my voice and a baby's screams is insulting and inappropriate. The baby is attempting to annoy its mother, and I am making music with my voice. I am creating something beautiful; I am not trying to annoy everyone until I get whatever it is that I want!"

"All right, Mademoiselle, I understand. Now, humour me and let's hear what you can do if you want to truly annoy someone. Let's say you've caught your husband in bed with another woman—and let's say she's your best friend."

Professor Garcia sat at the piano and played the last tenor line. When Juliette didn't come in, he asked, "Do you have a problem with the idea of screaming mademoiselle?"

"The pitch is too low. If I were angry, I would scream higher."

"All right, let's go to *'Cosi gentila, il profumo d'un fiore…'* But let's not worry about the smelly flowers—remember, you just caught your husband in bed with your best friend!"

"But…"

"Do it! This is not a concert, and this studio is not a democratic institution!"

The Professor hammered the phrase before *cosi* and Juliette came in with all the power she could find without risking damage to her vocal cords. He stopped playing on her second note and clapped his hands.

"Bravo, Mademoiselle, you have an exquisitely beautiful voice, but your mother, seated in the first row, is the only one who can hear you. I drowned you out with a single piano, and you can trust my word that the orchestra score is marked *forte* in that spot. Don't you think sixty instruments playing the volume requested by the composer will cover your sweet voice?" He banged the piano. "I just fucked your sister… scream at me or get out of here!"

He played a few bars before her entrance, and she hardened her abdomen as Mademoiselle Desjardins had taught her, put every scrap of strength she had into supporting the sound, and on the second note, Professor Garcia screamed, *"Cri… Cri strident!"* She tried so hard that she felt faint.

He stopped playing and shouted, "I guess your future husband has nothing to worry about, does he?"

Juliette felt tears of frustration filling her eyes.

She screamed at him, "But I will hurt my voice!"

"Exactly that!" said the Professor. "Now do that on these notes!" He played an arpeggio leading to the 'A' in the aria.

Juliette supported with everything she had and sang the arpeggio.

"Sacre bleu! Scream at me!" He banged the notes, and Juliette began to cry.

"*Mierde!* How long are you going to cry? You've wasted half the lesson already… if you want to waste the rest of it whimpering, then leave!" He banged the piano on the arpeggio, yelling, "*Cri, mademoiselle, cri strident! Cri! Cri!* My five-year-old daughter can scream louder than that!"

Juliette forgot her training, dropped her support and screamed the notes. The sound bounced off the hard plaster and hurt her ears. He banged the notes again, and she screamed on the pitches, tears running down her face. As he yelled, "*Oui, mademoiselle, oui!*" she screamed the notes louder, but the sound was not what she expected; it was becoming less a scream and more round. He stopped banging the piano, and she stopped screaming.

"That is enough, mademoiselle… you don't want to injure your voice, do you?"

The professor came around the piano and stood behind her.

"Do not be afraid, mademoiselle—I am touching you with my wife's permission." His hand slid around her to press on her abdomen from behind. He said, "Sing a note…any note."

Juliette picked a random note in the middle of her range and sang it as loudly as she could.

"*Mon Dieu,* mademoiselle, you have the stomach muscles of a boxer. I am certain that if I hit your stomach, I would surely break my hand! I know nothing about boxing, but I cannot believe you want to be a *boxeur!*" He added pressure and said, "Humour me… scream for me again."

Juliette screamed the arpeggio, and Professor Garcia yelled, "Relax, let me do the work!" as he pressed her stomach. The sound became louder, and the hard edge began to disappear.

"*Si—Eso es todo…Eso es Bueno!*" He released her and went back to the piano. "You have it! *Ja! Du hast es wunderbar! So sollst du singen!*" He went to the piano bench as quickly as he could, played the arpeggio and shouted, "Breathe! Move your abdomen!" as he banged the arpeggio.

She screamed and tried to move her frozen stomach muscles, but the harder she tried, the more rigid they became. Garcia ran around the piano, yelled, "Scream, Juliette! *Cri strident!*" and pushed her stomach. It moved, reluctantly at first, then smoother as she relaxed and let his hand do some of the work.

He said, in an almost kind voice, *"Bueno! Para! Para! Para!* and Juliette stopped.

"Come to the piano bench. I want you to show me how strong your stomach muscles really are."

He pulled the bench back from the piano, sat on the edge and leaned back with his toes under the keyboard. He put his hands behind his head and lowered his upper body until his torso bent backward over the bench, making a smooth buzzing sound as he lowered, then raised himself.

He stood aside, pointed at the bench and said, "Try it."

Juliette could feel her stomach muscles trying to move, but when she was halfway down had to give up.

"I didn't hear any noise. I want those *Zees!*"

He stood alongside her and said, "Trust me… I will support you… you can let yourself down on my hands."

Juliette began her *Zees* and leaned back. Professor Garcia put his hands under her shoulders and at first supported her so the *Zees* were smooth, but gradually, as she passed the point where she knew she couldn't pull herself up, he took almost all the support away. She panicked, stopped her *Zees,* and rolled off the bench onto the floor.

"Coward!" He said and pointed to the bench. "*Feige*—get up on that bench!"

"You lied to me!"

"I don't think it's the first time someone has lied to you, but this time it was for your own good."

"You told me I could trust you, and then you let me fall!"

"Your parents and your priest lie to you… I do not. And I did not let you fall. The problem is you—you don't trust me."

"I won't do that exercise! If you can't teach me without that, I don't want to study with you."

"Well, if you don't do precisely what I tell you, I won't teach you. So, get out; your audition is over."

"But I want to sing!" Juliette was suddenly filled with dread. "I need a teacher who can make my voice bigger." Tears flowed as if a dam in her eyes had burst.

"Let me see. You want me to teach you how to sing like a grownup, but you don't want to do what I tell you… is that about right?"

Juliette sobbed, "Yes, I want you to teach me, but I don't want to lean back on the piano bench."

Juliette cried uncontrollably as he pushed her toward the door. He said, "Leave your music here and come back tomorrow morning at the same time. I must audition three more sopranos today, and one of them might have more potential than you. I will consider taking you as a student, but only if you learn to trust me."

He opened the door, and Juliette involuntarily sobbed as she ran past the bewildered tenor, who looked at her with disbelief and apprehension. Marcel followed her down the stairs and out the door to the sidewalk.

He walked beside her for a few minutes, and when she didn't explain her tears, he said, "Do you want me to call your father and see if we can hurt that bastard?"

Juliette stopped, faced Marcel, wiped her tears with a handkerchief she carried in her sleeve and said, "Don't you dare tell Daddy! I hope you reserved the room for another night… I've got another lesson tomorrow morning at nine-thirty."

Obviously frustrated, Marcel spread his hands and asked, "Are all singers crazy?"

Juliette said, "Probably, and I think sopranos are the worst," and walked toward the Bayerische Hof.

CHAPTER THREE

Some People are Worth It

Rejection and failure are voices telling you to keep digging until you reach acceptance and success

As THEY ROUNDED THE CORNER A BLOCK FROM THE HOTEL, Marcel put his arm in front of Juliette to block her way. Wondering why he had stopped her, she looked where Marcel was watching two brown-shirted *Sturmabteilung* officers drag a man out of a shop with a front window full of women's hats.

The man escaped, ran onto the street and stopped a car that almost hit him, but the brown-shirts caught him before the driver could get out. A second vehicle and several pedestrians stopped to watch the soldiers beat the man with their clubs. They knocked him down, then kicked him with their heavy boots. Covering his head, the man curled up like a fetus, then moved his arms down to protect his ribs when the beating concentrated on his torso.

Marcel said, "Stay here; I'm going to stop this," leaving Juliette on the sidewalk. She watched him approach the ruffians, smiling like he knew what he was doing. Juliette heard him say, "What's going on here? What did this man do?" The soldiers stopped beating the man and turned to face the intruder.

One of the *Brownshirts* grinned, exposing a mouth full of brown teeth as he said, "He's a Jew; he sold a hat to a German, and now we will teach him a lesson. Stay out of it, or you will get the same." He turned to kick the man again.

A woman who had run from the millinery wrapped her arms around the SA officer, who ignored the impediment as he tried to kick the man on the ground. She pulled him back, screaming, "Leave my husband alone. We will give you money!"

Before Marcel could stop him, the man suddenly turned and hit the woman in the face with his club. Blood poured instantly from her cheek, her body went limp, and, without a whimper, she fell hard onto the cobblestones and lay there like a discarded rag doll. The Brownshirt pointed at her and laughed, showing his nicotine-stained teeth. "Look at that! I only hit her once!"

Marcel hit the officer with the tobacco-stained teeth on the back of his head, grabbed the hand with the club and spun him around, shifting the man's attention from the shop owner and his wife. The Jew, bleeding and in great pain, tried to crawl to his motionless wife.

Marcel hit the Brownshirt in the throat, felling him, and, as the second officer tried to draw his pistol, a man wearing an SS uniform appeared on the sidewalk and fired a shot from his Luger, aimed high enough it wouldn't hit anyone, but low enough to hear the bullet whiz past. No one moved.

"Dass reicht aus!" shouted the SS officer, waving his gun at the Brownshirt with the half-drawn pistol. "I would be delighted if you would give me a reason to shoot you. You and your comrade are under arrest."

"You cannot arrest a member of the SA," said the tobacco chewer. The SS officer smiled as a second black-uniformed officer appeared, stepped into the street and handcuffed both SA soldiers. Marcel backed away as two policemen ran around the corner with pistols drawn.

The first SS officer said to Marcel with a wave, "Leave us. Take your young lady and go to the hotel. Someone will call."

Marcel took Juliette's hand and led her down the street. She tried to get an explanation of what had happened, but Marcel said, "Wait until we are in our hotel rooms. I need to think."

It was almost noon when Marcel dropped Juliette off in her room and said, "I have to telephone your father."

An hour later, Juliette heard him use the secret knock and unlocked the door. As he headed for a comfortable chair, he said, "Those SS officers have been following us since yesterday when we got off the train. Your father made an arrangement to have them assigned to protect us."

"I didn't see any SS officers until today... Assigned? By whom?"

Marcel smiled. "Your father has a friend in Munich who has more than a passing amount of influence in the *Schutzstaffel*. He is very high in the Munich SS, and at the moment, there is no love lost between the SS and Röhm's gang of hoodlums."

"But who were those awful men in brown uniforms, and why did they beat the man who sold a hat to a German lady?"

Marcel said, pointing at the bed, "Sit down. You need a lesson in politics."

Juliette sat on the bed, and Marcel dragged his soft chair over to sit facing her.

"You do know that Paul Von Hindenburg, the German President, appointed Hitler chancellor in January?"

Juliette shook her head. "No, I thought he was still the leader of the NSDAP, the National Socialists."

"He still is the National Socialist Party leader."

Juliette was confused; Marcel saw it and said, "Let me explain."

He stood up, walked across the room and returned to lean on the back of the chair.

"A couple of years ago, Hindenburg found a loophole in the German constitution that allowed him to effectively neuter the *Reichstag*. Then, using technical parliamentary rules, he made the President of Germany a dictator in every way but name. But then Hitler came along and put Hindenburg in a political corner, forcing the aging president, who was under the illusion he could control the upstart leader of the National Socialist Party, to name him Chancellor. And he did precisely that on January thirtieth this year. A few months later, Hitler double-crossed Hindenburg by placing the Chancellor above the President." Marcel sat down and began talking with his hands.

"His power consolidated, Hitler turned to his *Sturmabteilung* hoodlums under Ernst Röhm. They had been his hired bullies for the past five years, ostensibly protecting National Socialist Party members at rallies, and Hitler turned this gang of thugs loose on everyone who opposed him.

On February twenty-seventh, someone conveniently, at least for Hitler, set fire to the *Reichstag*, and Hitler used it as an excuse to declare what amounted to martial law. A month later, using questionable political maneuvring, Hitler forced the *Reichstag* to pass what he called *"Das Ermächtigungsgesetz*. The act enabled the Chancellor to do anything he wanted, despite objections from any other branch of government. And in July, six months after Hindenburg made him Chancellor, Hitler banned all parties but the National Socialists.

"Are you telling me that in six months, Hitler took over Germany? He has absolute power to do anything, even beat up that poor man because he sold a hat?"

"I am telling you that in Germany now, Hitler has equal status with God. As for the man who sold the hat, Hitler ordered a boycott of all Jewish stores sometime in April, and since then, Jewish stores are not allowed to sell to non-Jews. The law is seldom enforced, but that was the excuse those thugs used to beat him." Marcel stopped as Juliette lowered her head, waited, then continued when she looked at him.

"Hitler banned trade unions in May, and in June, when the workers objected, the SA beat twenty-three people to death in Berlin for no reason other than they opposed Hitler and the National Socialist movement. Since then, all over Germany, the SA has ransacked Jewish businesses and beaten their owners. A month ago, Hitler offered to allow Jews to go to Palestine if they gave most of their possessions to the National Socialist Party, using the logic that they had gotten their education and earned their money at the expense of the German people."

"So, what has this to do with me? I don't vote in Germany, and I am not a Jew. I don't even know a Jew, so why should I worry?"

"Those SA thugs are not fussy about who they beat up, and there are reliable stories of them raping women."

Juliette spread her hands. "You are here to protect me, and the hotel has guards all over the place, so what's the problem?'

"Your father needs me in Brussels, and if you study here, you will need someplace to live. There won't be guards, and the SS can't protect you."

"Okay, I need you to say what you mean… are you saying I must give up on studying in Munich?"

"No, I have no idea what you should do, but your father and mother are worried that Germany could fly apart at any moment. They want you to study in Belgium or France, and I'm supposed to talk you into getting on a train to Brussels tomorrow morning."

Juliette stood, and Marcel got up to face her.

"I am going to finish my audition tomorrow morning. If Professor Garcia takes me, I will study with him, and please remind my father when you call him that he is the one who insisted on my coming here."

"I heard Garcia yelling at you, and I saw how upset you were when you came out of his studio. Why would you want to study with someone who does that to you?"

"I cried because I knew he was right… I sing like a little girl and will never sing diva roles on a big stage unless I have a bigger instrument. It is hard to give up what I've always done, and I suspect he yelled at me to find out whether I would choose the pretty voice or the singing career. I know he will push me so hard I'll cry, and I might not get to the opera stage, but he is my best hope. I don't care how often he yells at me, and I don't care how ridiculous his exercises are—I will do whatever it takes to build a voice that will carry over an orchestra!"

"But it is dangerous in Munich—singing can't be worth the risk. You are not safe alone on the streets, even in broad daylight. Surely there is a teacher in Belgium who can teach you to sing opera."

"Marcel, there are many teachers who could teach me to sing opera, but only a few teachers in the world who can build an operatic voice. Rosa Ponselle is the most famous soprano singing today, but her voice wasn't taught; she was born with it! And it doesn't hurt that she is ten centimetres taller than I am and built like a *camion.*"

Marcel looked at the ceiling. "I'm not allowed to pick you up and carry you to the train, so I guess I will have to tell your father that you are staying here at least until your audition is over."

Juliette said, "Tell him to hire someone who lives in Munich to look after me. I am going to study with Professor Garcia, and I am going to sing in Germany."

Marcel called Jacques and gave him the bad news, expecting a tirade, but Jacques said, "That's what I expected; her mother would have done the same. I like her idea of hiring someone in Munich to protect her, and I will look into it, but I will still have a problem with Veronique. She will accuse me of being soft on Juliette, then spend the night on her knees pleading with the Virgin to make Professor Garcia send her daughter home."

Relieved that he didn't have to force Juliette into something she refused to do, Marcel said, "I don't think you should expect Garcia to send her away. She took a lot of abuse in her lesson today, and she cried and gave as good as she got when it came to screaming, but he told her to come back tomorrow morning. After all that screaming, yelling and crying, she still thinks he is the best teacher in the world, so I think you should call your friend and tell him to find a guard for her."

"Alright, Marcel, I trust your judgment. You must stay in Munich with her until either she comes home or needs to find a place to live. If she stays, we will send whatever she needs, and I want you to find a suitable place for her. You can't leave until you introduce her to whoever will look after her security."

Marcel hesitated. He wanted to ask Jacques how he expected him to talk her into letting him do that, but decided there was no point until she decided to fight him. He said, "Juliette might not like me picking out her apartment, and I doubt she will agree to the guard, but I will try."

Jacques said, "If you have a problem, tell her to call me."

When Marcel told Juliette about the call, she ate her evening meal in almost total silence. Marcel read the *Völkischer Beobachter*, neatly folded so the article he wanted to read was the only one showing.

Juliette asked, "Is that the Munich newspaper?"

"No, but it used to be before Goebbels took over. Now it spreads its filth over all of Germany."

"Then why do you read it?"

Marcel put the folded rectangle on the table.

"Juliette, if you stay here, you need to keep up with German politics, and this piece of trash is where you should start. It is one tirade after another against communists, Jews, and democratic socialists, but that is where Germany is right now. This newspaper is essential to maintaining and strengthening support for Hitler against his enemies as Goebbels constantly changes the focus to match the Party's objectives."

He put his finger on the article. "This rubbish says the Jews can leave anytime they want. It says Palestine is open to them but doesn't mention that they must leave their possessions behind for the National Socialist Party. The article suggests America and Asia as destinations but doesn't tell the reader that it requires a lot of money, which the government won't let the Jews take with them—or unique talent, like a master's degree in physics."

"But what does it all mean? What can the Jews do if the Brownshirts beat them, like that man and woman you saved?"

"They can do nothing. Every Jew should get out of Germany, even if they have to go to hell and give up everything to do it! In only six months, Hitler has set up what can only be a plan to eradicate them from German soil. He allows the Sturmabteilung to run wild against them and makes it clear there is no limit to what he will do to get rid of them."

"I'm glad I'm not a Jew."

"Yes, you are fortunate, but you are a target even if you only have a Jewish friend, so be careful who you hang around with, and, especially, who you talk to. There is no guarantee that the SA won't attack you just because you are a foreigner—the Sturmabteilung is going beyond beating Jews, and no one is safe, Jew or Gentile. If you are in the wrong place at the wrong time...."

Juliette decided that a croissant and espresso breakfast would probably not help her voice and opted instead for a boiled egg, Semmel buns layered with butter and jam, and sliced cheese. She washed the unappetizing mixture down with apple juice and black coffee while Marcel read *Der Stürmer*. She tried to read the back of the paper, and Marcel put it down.

"Do you want to read something worse than the *Beobachter? Der Stürmer* is Hitler's favourite paper... he reads it cover-to-cover every week."

Juliette was disgusted. "Why don't you just tell me about it."

Marcel put the paper aside. "I've read about all I can take for now anyway. But I recommend you read it every week so you know what is happening in Germany. The article I was reading goes further than even Hitler openly wants to go. Julius Streicher, the owner of the paper and the head of the National Socialist Party in Franconia—Nürnberg is in the centre of Franconia—has been openly advocating the expulsion of all three-hundred-thousand Jews living in Germany. In the article, Streicher makes a thinly veiled threat of physical extermination if Jews don't leave Germany of their own volition, leaving all their possessions behind in exchange for their lives!"

"I don't want to read such nonsense. I don't want to be seen reading it, and I don't want anyone to think I approve of anything that rag prints!"

"But if you want to know what Hitler is planning… I need to follow what is happening in Germany, and if *Der Stürmer* prints a suggestion, Hitler almost literally carries it out. This is why I am disturbed by that article. I ask myself, 'Is this where Hitler will eventually go?'"

Juliette shook her head. "No one would dare try that! Jews own many banks and newspapers, don't they?"

Marcel shook his head. "The National Socialists are taking over the papers. Until March this year, Munich had a liberal socialist morning paper, the *Münchner Post*, but it and dozens of others are no more—replaced by National Socialist publications like this trash." He nodded to the folded paper.

Juliette stood up and said, "I want to get to *Odeonplatz* early, and I don't want to talk about Jews and National Socialism. But Marcel, there is something I don't understand."

"Just ask."

"Why would a French-Canadian chauffeur speak fluent German and need to be interested in German politics? And why does this chauffeur carry a pistol in his pocket? Don't lie… You put it in your pocket when those SS men showed up. And, I know Daddy has a lot of money, but he could never buy the SS…."

"I am a chauffeur because I like driving expensive cars, and I came to Belgium because I wanted to see Europe, and, of course, your father pays me very well. My mother was born in Alsace and left when Germany annexed the area in 1871. She speaks German and French equally well, as do I. What was the other question?... Oh, yes, the gun. Your father insists I carry a pistol when I'm with you, and I assure you I know how to use it." He patted his pocket.

"He knows the political situation here because he is an art dealer, and Munich is a very active market. He uses me as his agent because I speak German fluently, and he expects me to know what is happening here. Several SS officers own valuable paintings and priceless jewellery stored in your father's Swiss vaults, and it is in their interest to see that nothing happens to your father's daughter."

"And you drive daddy's Rolls because you like to drive nice cars? Marcel, you may drive Daddy's car, but you are not his chauffeur!" Juliette smiled.

Marcel pulled out his pocket watch.

"It's time to go."

The practice room Juliette had used the previous day was unoccupied, and when she arrived, she could hear Michelle through the adjacent door, working on her scales.

After an hour of lying awake in the middle of the night, Juliette had concluded that she had to change her attitude if she wanted to learn anything from Professor Garcia. He had been hard on her, but she had pushed back on what he tried to teach her. He was right—she couldn't learn from him if she continued to fight, and there would be no point in him wasting his time on her.

Juliette went directly to the piano bench and pulled it away from the piano until she could sit on the edge with her toes under the keyboard. With her hands behind her head, Juliette leaned backward to the point of no return and couldn't lift herself upright. She rolled sideways, stood up and thought for a minute. Positioning herself for another try, Juliette put her hands on the bench instead of behind her head, theoretically lightening the load her abdomen would need to raise. When she reached horizontal, she stopped, held the position for a few seconds, then returned to sit upright. Adding 'Zees,' Juliette managed three more situps before her muscles demanded a timeout. She sat for a moment, thinking that perhaps Professor Garcia would say she was cheating and insist she put her hands behind her head. But she was willing to bet he wouldn't.

She stood, put her hand on her stomach and pushed, relaxing muscles until air flowed freely out of her mouth. She hit a B-flat on the piano and tried to nail it with a scream but scared herself when the sound split into pieces. She tried it a tone lower; it worked, but Juliette was sure it wasn't right.

She decided to leave the high notes until her lesson—it wouldn't do to go into the studio without a voice!

Juliette sang scales and a few arpeggios until she felt confident her voice was there, then went to the bench. Peter Schweitzer sat there, smiling as she approached. It was still ten minutes before she could knock on the studio door, so she couldn't avoid talking to him.

"*Guten Morgen,* Peter; why are you here so early? You know you can use that practice room to warm your voice, *n'est-ce pas?*"

"I never warm up my voice… my teacher said I should let her do it."

"*Mais oui… Je comprends,*" said Juliette, "But if I went into my teacher's studio unprepared, she wouldn't let me sing."

"I wouldn't know how to do it. I heard you singing scales through the door, and I tried to sing with you, but I can't sing that fast."

Juliette smiled. "*Exacta!* That's why I sing scales. Most music is written as variations of scales, and when we sing with an orchestra, the conductor decides how fast to play the piece based on the singer's ability. The faster she can sing, the better her chances to keep her job."

Peter hadn't thought about singing scales and didn't think he would like it. He asked, "Do tenors have to sing scales?"

"Every singer sings scales! Professor Garcia will teach you to sing them, but scales will be the least of your troubles. *Non?*" Juliette laughed like a raucous barmaid, and Peter decided to change the subject.

"Are you going to be Professor Garcia's student? He told me I could study with him, but I can't live in Augsburg because the train takes too long. He said I must live in Munich, but my parents said they can't afford that."

"Of course, you will have to live near the school. You must find the money if you want to study here." She wanted to say something positive, so she looked at the clock and said, "Why don't you sing your aria for me... the one you learned from the Gigli recording." She pointed at the clock. "We have five minutes."

Peter shook his head. "No, I've decided to stop singing for anyone until Professor Garcia tells me I'm ready."

"Good idea," said Juliette. "I have also discovered that I will start from nothing. I've thought about it, and it makes sense... I must build my musical instrument before I can play it, *non?*"

Peter nodded. *"Jawohl, moi aussi!"*

Juliette opened the anthology of soprano arias she had brought with her. Mademoiselle Desjardins had picked out half the arias as audition pieces, but after only half an hour of abuse at the hands of Professor Garcia, Juliette knew she couldn't sing any of them well enough to get a job in the smallest opera house in Germany.

The second hand swept past the six and began the climb to precisely nine-thirty. Juliette's hands sweated; her knees shook, and her tongue and mouth felt dry as she knocked on the door. She was pushing down the door handle when the door opened and swung toward her. She stepped aside, and the baritone she had heard through the door smiled at her. He said, *"Hola! Buenas Dias, signorita,"* then marched down the hall before she could figure out which language she should use.

Garcia's cheerful voice said, "You came back! I doubted that you would but hoped that you might."

Juliette noticed that Garcia's generous beard bent outward, and his eyes twinkled when he smiled. Her apprehension eased a little as he walked toward her and stretched out his hand. She took it and impulsively said, "My voice is warmed up, and I would like to show you my 'Zee' situps."

"You practiced that? My dear, I don't expect you to do situps on the piano bench until you are ready... on the floor will do for now, and if you can't lift yourself, your hands can be on your stomach, or you can push yourself up if you need to. Your abdomen muscles and bottom ribs should be flexible and free to control your diaphragm; that's the point of those exercises. Your muscles are working against one another; they can't move, so neither can your diaphragm." He chuckled. "Supporting a singing sound requires little more effort than breathing while running or walking briskly, but we'll deal with that later. However, I *am* pleased you tried."

Juliette went around Garcia, and he turned to watch her adjust the piano bench. She put her feet under the keyboard and hands on her stomach, then smoothly buzzed her way to horizontal and back to vertical. Her voice fluttered slightly but was noticeably better than when she'd done it thirty minutes ago.

"I am impressed, my dear, but we will work on that later. First, I want to discuss my plan, and you may not want to do it. Please sit on the chair."

Juliette's heart jumped. What he had said had made it clear that he would teach her, and she didn't care about the conditions. She had to control a sudden urge to jump up and scream.

"I want to conduct an experiment, and I got the idea for it when I heard Peter's voice immediately after yours yesterday. As you will learn, if you don't already know, when it comes to working with singers, most teachers, conductors, and stage directors think of themselves as psychiatrists. Believing the key to a singer's success is manipulating their mind, they talk the singer into thinking they can sing when the sound they produce is garbage. For those who don't know anything about singing, a singer's problems are always psychological; they believe the singing voice can be controlled using emotions."

Professor Garcia grabbed the back of Juliette's chair, and she turned so she could look into his eyes.

"I do not belong to this group…they have more mental problems than their students. I believe the singing voice is as physical as walking, running, jumping and bending over…the only difference being the muscle group. The production of a singing sound that will carry to the back row in a large theatre is physical—it is not a mental exercise. However, when the muscles know how to make the sounds, emotional expression becomes not only possible, but the range of that expression is unlimited. And that brings me to my experiment."

He crossed the room to the door, and Juliette's excitement waned as quickly as it had grown. Her teacher had always used mental exercises and emotions as a basis for the sound quality; she had even applauded when Juliette's emotions triggered tears.

The professor opened the door and motioned to Peter. He said, "Come into the studio—this concerns both of you."

Peter looked around to be certain Professor Garcia was beckoning to him.

"Yes, Peter, I'm waving at you. Come into the studio."

Peter walked in, stared at Juliette, and the professor closed the door.

"Sit down on the piano bench; this will take a few minutes."

Professor Garcia began pacing and talking.

"Listening to both of you yesterday, I heard remarkable similarities in your potential and hindrances to achieving it. I also heard two voices with incredible blending potential." He stopped pacing and looked first at Juliette, then at Peter.

"I propose you take your lessons together; that means you listen to one another as well as to me. I might even ask you to help me with what I am trying to do, and if we don't accomplish anything else, we might get a pair of good teachers out of this experiment."

He stopped pacing, looked from one to the other and said, "Well, what do you think?"

Juliette and Peter looked at one another, Peter with a broad grin and Juliette utterly perplexed. She turned to Professor Garcia and asked, "If I say no, will you still take me as your student?"

"I don't want any misunderstandings, so I will make this as clear as I can. I am taking both of you because teaching teachers as well as developing voices has fascinated me for a long time. I also like teaching my students how to blend their voices with others, a rare quality in an opera singer. What I want to do with you is a natural progression for me."

"I didn't hear an answer to my question," said Juliette.

"It's hard to be direct because I don't know what I would do if you refused. I would need a few days to decide, but I would consider it a gesture of good faith on your part if you would trust me, as you did with the buzzing on the piano bench." He pointed at the bench.

Juliette was cornered. She looked at Peter, trying to decide whether studying with Professor Garcia was worth putting up with this arrogant, musically ignorant National Socialist tenor. Refusing to work with Peter on Garcia's terms would tell the professor Juliette didn't believe his concept had merit, so why would he teach her? There was really only one choice if she wanted to sing opera.

Peter's expression looked pitifully like a dog about to be whipped, but that wasn't why Juliette turned back to Garcia and said, "The more I think about your idea, the more I like it. But will we get the same number of lessons?"

"You will have an hour of shared technique lessons with me every day, Monday to Friday, for as long as you need them. Three times a week, as part of the opera school, you will each have a one-hour session with a *répétiteur* who will teach you your music. Also, as part of the school, you will have two one-hour German and two Italian lessons weekly, and Peter will study French and Italian diction while Juliette..." He pointed at her... "You will work on your German. Both of you must study music theory and history as well as basic composition, and if you fail..." He looked pointedly at Peter... "You will be kicked out, and if that happens, you and Juliette will no longer be allowed to study with me."

Juliette opened her mouth, but the professor read her mind.

"If you both do your part, I believe I can prepare you for auditions two years from now. In three years, you could be on a stage."

"We don't sing in public until then?" exclaimed Juliette. "I have singing engagements in Brussels for next summer!" She hated to think of not performing for two years.

"Oh yes, I insist that you sing in public. Every Tuesday and Thursday evening, we have an *Übungsabend,* an informal concert in front of your peers, followed by *Kuchen und Kaffee* at the *Mensa* cafeteria. You will probably have to reserve a spot, but they also respond well to spontaneous performances."

He leaned on the piano as he looked at Peter. "I don't mind if you sing with your friends or an occasional solo in church, but tell me before you agree to anything more. And no choir singing for at least a year." He looked at Juliette. "I understand that you must fulfill certain contracts, and I will prepare you for them."

Peter said, "I still need a place to live, and I can't afford to rent."

Juliette nodded, relieved to know she could still sing. "I am in the same situation as Peter, except for the lack of money, but Marcel will find a suitable small *Wohnung* for me in a few days. I'm not fussy; I can be comfortable in three or four rooms—a hundred twenty square metres will do, but I need an acceptable kitchen, a bathroom with a large tub, and lots of heat and hot water. In the meantime, I will stay at the Bayerischer Hof."

Professor Garcia laughed. "I have good news for Peter, but perhaps not so good for you. A benefactor made a *Sängerhaus,* a former private residence with ten bedrooms available for the *Hochschule,* complete with a cook, housekeeper and a piano. It's in the *Altstadt,* close to *Odeonplatz,* and I took the liberty of reserving a room for each of you—you only need your suitcase."

"Do I have a private bathroom?" Juliette considered whether she should tell Professor Garcia what she thought of a room without a bathroom.

"No, but there are two bathrooms that everyone can use, one on each of two floors, the upper floor for males and the second floor for females, and both have bathtubs and lots of hot water."

Juliette shook her head. "Thank you, but I would rather have my own apartment, and I will need maid service if I am going to spend the required time on my music. I suppose it might be interesting to share a home with other singers, but there are probably many more deserving singers than I and my father can afford...."

The professor interrupted, shaking his head. "No, it's not a choice. The room is part of the package when you study with me."

She made one last try as she said, "I must ask my father whether I can live with other students. He insists I have someone to protect me."

Peter said, a bit too eagerly for Juliette, "I will protect you!"

Juliette's smile was close enough to an outright laugh that the effect was the same. She decided to take the sting out of it by asking Peter, "Do you carry a gun?"

"Well… no, of course not! But I could buy one!"

She smiled. "It's not that easy. Have you ever fired a gun?"

Peter looked at his feet.

"Do you know how to fight?"

Peter wagged his head once, just enough that Juliette caught it.

"Well then, I guess Daddy will have to find someone else."

Peter looked up, and Juliette didn't enjoy the beaten look on his face as much as she thought she would.

Chapter Four

All Beginnings are Difficult

God, grant me the serenity to accept the things I cannot change....
Reinholt Niebuhr

MARCEL HAD INSTRUCTED JULIETTE to wait in the *Mensa* for him to return from apartment hunting, and Michelle appeared before Juliette finished her first piece of *Kuchen*.

"Where's Peter?" Michelle put her cup of coffee and a piece of *Apfel Strudel* on the table and sat opposite Juliette.

"Oh, he's gone home to get his suitcase."

"I heard you two were moving into the *Sängerhaus*. Somehow, I find it hard to believe you would agree to that. What's going on?"

Juliette thought about what to say, and ultimately decided the truth wouldn't do.

"Oh... I decided I wanted to be around other singers, you know, the university experience. "

Michelle smiled. "Uh-huh... and the moon is made of cheese."

"No, seriously, I'm all right with it. Just because my father is rich doesn't mean I'm spoiled. It's true...I'm not used to sharing a bathroom, but I'll get over it."

Michelle chuckled. Juliette drank a slug of coffee and went on.

"I can make do as long as I have my own room."

Michelle shook her head. "Bad news, Juliette. All the rooms in the *Sängerhaus* are for two students. You will be sharing a room with another soprano... a Mezzo."

Juliette dropped the piece of *Kuchen* her open mouth was expecting.

"But, I can't live with another person... I need privacy!"

"That's what I told Professor Garcia."

"He spoke to you about me?"

"He and I are still on speaking terms, and since I've been here a couple of years, he thinks I can help you get used to associating with the rabble. You're probably the reason I got a room in the *Sängerhaus!*"

Juliette tried not to consider the implications of Michelle's comment. She said, "So, we can see one another occasionally." She used her wet fingertip to pick up the last crumbs of the *Kuchen* she had dropped.

Michelle played with her coffee cup as she said, "We will see one another a lot more than that! I got the room because I agreed to have you as my roommate."

Juliette was surprised when she felt relieved. She had never had a sibling or a close girlfriend and was attracted to Michelle. She liked the idea of a close friend.

"I didn't mean to sound spoiled, but I've never had to share anything, and Papa has always given me everything I wanted. I'm looking forward to sharing a room with you."

Michelle laughed. "To tell the truth, I was excited when Professor Garcia asked me. The room is free, and I could never afford the rent in Munich, so if I hadn't gotten it I would have had to go home. I should thank you."

Marcel somehow got a cup of coffee from the counter without Juliette noticing, and she was surprised when he sat beside her.

He looked at Michelle, asked, "Who is this?" and stood up. Michelle half-stood and shook hands with him across the table.

"Michelle Landry... I'm Juliette's new roommate."

"Uh... roommate? You're going to share the *Wohnung* I found?"

Juliette interrupted as Michelle opened her mouth to answer Marcel's question. "You found an apartment in four hours? What's it like?"

"Your father's Munich friend had already found an empty apartment a block from the school. It has four rooms; a big kitchen with a beautiful table, a living room with a bay window, and a huge bathroom with a bathtub you can swim in. You can each have a private bedroom, but I'm afraid you must share the bathroom."

Juliette felt a surge of joy that went over a cliff when she remembered what Professor Garcia had said.

Suddenly depressed, Juliette said, "Oh, God, that sounds incredible, but Garcia said I have to live in the *Sängerhaus.*"

Marcel laughed and said, "Don't tell me you're going to do it!"

The more Juliette thought about it, the deeper she sank. "He didn't give me any choice."

Marcel chuckled as he said, "Your father would never be able to get you to do that!" His chuckle became a laugh. "I can't wait to see his face when I tell him you are sharing a room with another woman!"

Marcel calmed down when he saw the disdain on Juliette's face and changed his tone as he asked her, "What is it about this professor that gives him that kind of power over you? You are the most stubborn person I know—it's useless for anyone to argue with you!"

"Professor Garcia has something I want more than anything, and I can't get it anywhere else. I only know that I must learn to sing; I don't know why or how, but I know this man is the key."

Marcel shrugged his shoulders. "I'll cancel the *Wohnung* and tell your father what you are doing when I go to Brussels this afternoon to get your things. He probably won't believe me, so maybe you should call him from the hotel."

The *Sängerhaus* disappointed Juliette—ten rooms with two students in each, but only two bathrooms—how could she live with that? Marcel carried two suitcases into the room and, noticing clothes and a book on one of the narrow beds, laid Juliette's bags on the other.

Juliette dumped an armload of coats and boots on the floor and said, "This won't work! I can't live with another woman, even if it is Michelle; I need my own room and a private bathroom!"

Marcel picked up her suitcases. "Okay, we've still got an hour before the train leaves. The taxi is waiting outside, and we can pick up my suitcase at the hotel."

"No... wait... Marcel, what should I do?"

"That's the wrong question. The only relevant question is this: Do you want to sing?"

"You know the answer."

"I thought I did, but now I don't think I do. Aren't you willing to give up *anything* to sing…?"

"But I've always had a private bath and toilet. And I can't sleep with someone else in the room—what if she snores?"

"What you said is a description of who you are now, nothing else. You will change, or you will live with your parents for the rest of your life. No one else will be able to afford you!" He put down the suitcases and squeezed the knobs on the back of a hardwood chair beside Juliette's bed.

"I grew up in a shack on a dirt road with an outhouse in the trees behind the house. I bathed in front of the kitchen sink using cold water and lye soap… if you've never used lye soap, you don't know how painful cleaning your body can be! If you want sympathy because you have a friend sleeping in the same room and a warm bath six meters down the hall, then Juliette, you've come to the wrong place!"

"You think I'm a spoiled brat, don't you?"

"No, I think you are a pampered rich woman, and I try to stay as far away from those people as I can! So far, your mother is the only exception I've met, but I suspect she grew up without much money."

Juliette was holding back tears when the door opened, and Michelle Landry stood in front of her. The tears began to spill over as she laughed and threw her arms around Michelle.

"I'm so glad you're my roommate!"

Michelle put her arms around Juliette and said, "Oh, you poor thing. This must be a terrible adjustment for you." She let her go and stood back. "It won't be so bad… I don't snore, and I can work around your little quirks—I had five brothers and four sisters—it might even be fun. I'm a Mezzo-soprano, and you're a lyric… We can sing ourselves to sleep every night with the *Jardin* duet from *Lakmé.*"

Marcel had his hand on the door lever as he said to Juliette, "I will leave now. You are safe here, and you will get an education in how other people survive and even enjoy life together."

He opened the door, then turned around. "Don't go anywhere alone or without a male escort."

Juliette threw her arms around Marcel and kissed his cheek. "I will be fine, Marcel. Maybe I can even learn not to be one of those pampered women. I do want you to like me."

Marcel peeled her arms from his neck and said, "No, that's not what I meant...."

"Go, Marcel, or you'll miss your train." Juliette pushed him out.

The following afternoon, Juliette and Michelle were sitting on their beds facing one another when someone knocked. Michelle raised her voice and said, "If you are men, come in; we're naked!"

The handle rattled, then became quiet. A voice said, "Michelle?"

Juliette said, "There are two of us... I'm Juliette."

"Uh... can we come in? The door is locked."

Michelle said, "We? How many?"

"I'm with Peter Schweitzer. He's new here, and he says he knows Juliette."

Juliette said, "In that case, you can come in."

She unlocked the door, and a tall, heavy, dark-skinned man with slicked-back black hair and an Italian nose came in, followed by Peter.

Michelle said, "This large animal is Agostino Carracci... he's from the mountains in northern Italy, from a village called Mezzolombarda. He can't ever go home because no one can find it on the map."

"*Si, si, è Vero...* I must stay with Michelle for the rest of my life!" Michelle put out her hand—Agostino kissed it, then pulled her against him and kissed her mouth. "*Si, Sono un Uomo condannato;* I am condemned to die in Michelle's arms."

He let her go and put his arm over Peter's shoulders. "I am rude. I haven't introduced my roommate... I would prefer Michelle, but Germans and their rules... Anyway, Peter Schweitzer is my second choice. He's a tenor, but I forgive him because he can't help it."

Michelle said, "This is Peter's singing partner, Juliette Durand. She is a lyric soprano, and everyone knows how they feel about handsome tenors... Peter hasn't got a chance!" Michelle took Agostino's hand, and Peter stared at Juliette with a broad smile.

"Agostino is a baritone, and I am a mezzo-soprano, so we have two pairs, which makes a natural quartet, *n'est-ce pas?*"

Michelle led them to a small table in front of the window with four chairs surrounding it, and they all sat down. She asked, "White wine, anyone? I have one bottle of sweet chardonnay… sorry boys."

Juliette saw the smug look on Peter's face and couldn't resist wiping it off.

"Peter is out of luck if he thinks this soprano is looking for a lover…I already have one."

Peter's smile disappeared, replaced with a lost puppy look.

Michelle noted Peter's broken heart and said, "Lovers are like clothes…it's a good idea to change them as often as you can." She gave each person a teacup and saucer.

Michelle poured the wine into the teacups, saying, "Kind of like the first act in Bohème, isn't it? This is all the wine I've got, so sip it slowly."

The loaves and fishes story came to mind when they extended seven-tenths of a litre of wine into a four-hour conversation. They talked over one another, interrupted whenever an idea or opinion popped into their head, then apologized. They laughed at one another's stories and bad jokes and, in a few hours, became lifelong friends.

Darkness fell, Michelle found dry bread and cheese, and they washed it down with small sips of wine.

Juliette said, "Professor Garcia promised me a cook and a housekeeper. Where are they?"

Michelle said, "Not on weekends, and during the week, we only get one meal a day… *Abendessen* at six… We're on our own the rest of the day."

Juliette looked at the ceiling, whispered "Liar" to herself, then asked, "And the maid?"

Michelle laughed. "Maid? What maid?"

"The one… oh, never mind. But if we don't have a maid, who makes the beds and washes the floors and windows?"

Michelle smiled. "The cook leaves a list on the bulletin board at the front entrance. We rotate the window-washing, floor-washing in the hallways and sweeping the sidewalk. Everything in the room is up to whoever lives in it. I sweep the floors and make my bed every day, but Agostino lives in a room a pig would break out of."

"If you show me how, I will do my share," said Juliette.

Michelle tried not to laugh, but that made it worse. "You don't know how to sweep a floor or make a bed?"

Agostino said, "Don't look at me… I pay someone to do my share."

Juliette was suddenly elated. "Then that's what I'll do!"

Peter said, "No, I will take your turn. My parents taught me how to do those things when I was so young I can't remember."

"Okay, just tell me how much, and I will pay you," said Juliette.

Peter wilted, and Michelle shook her head.

Agostino and Peter left at ten, and Michelle told Juliette, "If you want the bath, you can have it… I bathed a couple of days ago."

"You don't bathe every day?" Juliette didn't hide her shock.

Michelle smiled and looked away as though preparing to explain God to a child, then turned back to face Juliette.

"Juliette, hot water is expensive… as a matter of fact, water is expensive. It would be best to not flush when you pee, use only a small glass of water to brush your teeth once a day and take no more than two baths a week. And don't put more than ten centimetres of water in the tub." She paused, then added, "Those are the house rules."

Juliette tried to reconcile rules she had never had to obey. At first, she thought of saying something critical but, in the end, decided she had to start adapting now, or her new-found friends would disappear, and her singing career might be over before it started. She said, "I had a bath at the hotel last night, so I'm okay."

Michelle reached out and touched Juliette's hand. "It will be alright once you learn the routine."

Juliette had also brushed her teeth at the hotel when she got up, but she kept that to herself.

"I want to brush my teeth… do I have a glass here?"

Michelle went to a cupboard, pulled out a glass, and said as she handed it to Juliette, "I brush my teeth twice a day too, but don't tell anyone."

Juliette had been outed and didn't try to hide the blush on her cheeks.

The bathroom was clean, and Juliette left it that way. She looked in the toilette for a minute, started for the door, then went back to flush it. When she returned to the room, Michelle smiled and said, "I flush every time too."

The following morning the quartet walked the five minutes to the *Conservatoire* together. Agostino and Michelle each grabbed a practice room, and Juliette took Peter into another. She said, "Stand there," indicating a spot where she could see him and then sat at the piano.

"If we are going to work together, I don't want to waste everyone's time waiting for your voice to warm up. Do this…." Juliette yawned. Peter laughed. Juliette waited. Peter yawned.

"Now, yawn with a sound—like this—" Juliette groaned as she yawned. Peter followed.

They groaned for a few minutes, then Juliette said, "Now, a relaxed glissando up and down an octave, starting on this note." She banged the middle 'c' and slid her voice up and down a full octave. Peter imitated her. She asked, "How did you find pitches in your church choir?"

"I sing notes that fit, and the organist taught me to follow the notes on the page as they go up and down." He added, "I know the notes and all about sharps and flats. My teacher also taught me key signatures, but I don't know anything about chords."

Juliette put her hands on her lap, thought about singing with a tenor who couldn't name the chords, and decided it didn't matter. She shook her head, looked at Peter and said, "You will take music theory in the *Hochschule,* but I will also help you."

Juliette ran her fingers up and down the keyboard, trying to lead Peter astray, but he sang every note accurately and did every glissando in the centre of the pitch. She played a few major scales slowly, and Peter found the pitches, then played minor scales with the same result.

When Juliette thought she had Peter's voice ready for the lesson, she could hear the sound and natural musicality that had gotten him into Professor Garcia's class.

Ten minutes later, Juliette knocked on Professor Garcia's door, stepped aside to let the dramatic soprano who had been torturing her ears pass, and got a slight smile for her trouble.

Professor Garcia stood up at the piano and said to Juliette as he went around it to shake her hand, "You are prompt... a good start considering you are French."

"Belgian," she said as the professor turned to Peter and squeezed his hand. "And we're only late for Spaniards; they never show up on time."

Professor Garcia chuckled, sat down on the piano bench and ran his fingers up and down the keyboard, playing the smoothest and fastest three octaves of minor scales Juliette had ever heard.

He lifted his hands, flexed his fingers, and said, "I think it is imperative to warm up any instrument before you play it, and Juliette, I want you to continue to warm up Peter's voice until he can do it himself. I heard enough through your door to know you can play the piano, so you can introduce him to scales if you like—and perhaps you should do a few arpeggios in his middle range. This morning, I will teach both of you a few exercises that might seem unusual to your musical ears, but from now on, turn off your brain... and don't ask questions unless I tell you to."

For the next week, Juliette and Peter squeaked, screamed, yawned and pulled their larynges until Juliette feared she would swallow hers. Professor Garcia didn't tell them what note they were singing, but Juliette's sense of perfect pitch made that redundant anyway. The answer was strange enough that she didn't tell Peter, who didn't seem to care whether a note was low or high or somewhere between. He opened his mouth, and the sound came out, or it didn't. His voice sounded ugly for the first week, then found beauty in a different part of the vocal cord. She sensed the same thing happening to her, and excitement became part of the lesson.

Michelle and Agostino studied with Frau Professor Kirschbaum, an oratorio and concert singer respected in all of Germany for her interpretation of Bach and other Baroque composers. They had a year under their belt, and Juliette found their sound quality was already beautiful.

As she sat on the bench listening to Michelle's Mezzo-soprano through Frau Kirschbaum's door, Juliette thought she heard a dramatic soprano and decided to ask Professor Garcia why she was wrong. And at the same time, she wanted to ask why he took fifteen minutes twice in the morning and every afternoon to smoke a cigarette on the singer's bench. Despite contrary rumours, smoke did affect her voice.

When she asked her questions, he used the need to knock the ashes off the end of his cigarette to buy time. Two small tables, one on each end of the long oak seat, held two tin ashtrays.

First, he decided to break a hard and fast rule and tell Juliette what he thought of another teacher's student.

"Everyone imagines the sound of their voice as they hear it in their head, and most are disappointed when they hear it on a recording. Even the most famous and self-centred diva is initially disappointed when they hear a recording of their voice. The singer is in love with the sound they hear resonating in their head and will resist any attempt to change it, especially differences in resonance and power."

"But why can't Michelle's voice be simultaneously beautiful and dramatic?"

"Of course, it can be both. But does Michelle actually *like* the dramatic sound when it resonates in her head? You have heard my Norwegian dramatic soprano through the door... what do you think of her voice?"

Juliette didn't know how she should answer. She was in awe of the power and resonance but wasn't impressed by the beauty. Professor Garcia took her off the hook.

"I see you are not sure how you should answer. I can tell you that teaching that voice is not pleasant, and I could not accept two students with voices like hers. My studio reflects sound back to the listener, and that much power assaulting my ears for half an hour is all I can take. Her voice is brutal at close range, but in a large theatre... it is truly a thrilling and beautiful experience. She has been booked in major opera houses for the next three years and earns more in a year than I will earn in my lifetime."

Juliette wasn't convinced. "I don't understand why beauty has to suffer."

Professor Garcia pulled on his cigarette, drawing smoke as deep as he could, satisfying an urge that demanded it. He tapped the ash into the ashtray and looked at the clock. He had three minutes.

"Beauty doesn't need to suffer when the sound grows... but it must sometimes be sacrificed to emotions—it depends on what is being expressed. That woman has an exciting but beautiful voice when singing in a large theatre. But in a small room, it's brutal!"

Juliette hadn't sung anything but arpeggios and scales since her first lesson, and while she knew she hadn't lost any of her range, she could hear a hardness in her voice that disturbed her.

"I hear an edge coming into my voice and perhaps also in Peter's, and it seems ugly."

"That is temporary. Your sound will be more beautiful than the pretty sound you had, particularly in the middle range, and you will thrill your audience with vocal gymnastics and high notes that will penetrate a large orchestra. But you can't look for beauty to convey anger or extreme joy. Look at Violette's *Sempre Libra* aria, and listen to Rosa Ponselle sing it. 'Sempre Libra' is a song of joy, regret and frustration. If you sing it beautifully, your audience will go to sleep. If you sing exciting high notes, you will break hearts...If you give only beauty, your audience will be bored. This aria sets Violette's character for the rest of the opera, and Violette must be a strong woman to survive what Verdi has in store for her!"

"But what about Michelle? Is she a mezzo or a dramatic soprano?"

"I have listened to Michelle several times, and she is a mezzo-soprano. Her voice could be trained to sing the dramatic repertoire, but she would not be happy. Her personality and attitude are not dramatic; she is sweet and lovely, and Michelle can't pretend to be otherwise. If a truly dramatic sound escaped her lips, she would immediately stop and refuse to do it again. She has an excellent teacher and a brilliant career ahead of her."

"When will I sing in public?"

"Whenever you want, but I recommend waiting until your voice is settled—perhaps in three or four months."

Juliette knew she was going to cry. She said, "I need to sing, or I will die."

"Okay, how about an *Übungsabend*. You can sing in front of your friends. Bring something to the lesson tomorrow."

Peter found Wolf's *Harmonielehrer* impossible to understand and wound up most nights in Juliette's room, writing simple four-part harmonies for uncomplicated melodies until he began understanding rudimentary composition and chord theory. Once he saw the patterns, his engineering mind grasped the mathematical principles of harmony and the 'circle of fifths,' and he blazed through the book. But music theory was still something he thought should exclusively belong to composers and conductors.

The quartet gathered around the piano in the *Wohnzimmer* every few days after the evening meal. *Abendessen* was always on the table when the cook went home at six pm, and the boarders were left to clean up. The fun started when the last dish was washed.

Madrigals are songs from the Renaissance period—from the beginning of the 15th to the end of the 16th centuries and extending until they overlapped the time when Baroque became the rage. They are intricate, usually unaccompanied, sometimes naughty poems set to musical lines. They are fun to sing, delightful applications in blend and musical expression as the multiple lines rotate in importance, and, if sung well, are balm for the voice. There is no hard rule for the number of individual parts, but generally, there are two or more, often up to six or even eight. All singers like to talk, but talking is terrible for the singing voice, so in 1933 when opera singers got together, they sang madrigals. And with twenty singers in ten rooms and a living room with a piano, there weren't many evenings in the *Sängerhaus* when at least four singers weren't available to sing.

Two months into the fall semester, Professor Garcia still forbade Juliette and Peter to sing in public, but madrigals were allowed. A five-metre row on the bookshelf in the *Sângerhaus* living room was devoted to dozens of books filled with that intricate music. Almost every evening, the singers gathered in an approximate circle, facing their fellow hopefuls, singing from books of Latin, Italian, German, and English madrigals. Juliette sat cross-legged with Peter on her left, and Michelle sat on the other side of Peter, with Agostino between a soprano and bass none of them had ever met. Juliette chose a lewd song from a book of Italian madrigals and gave everyone their first note.

Peter had never heard a madrigal before singing his first a month before but found himself holding his own with the experienced musicians. He learned the technique of sight-reading madrigals, and the nuances, such as bringing his voice to the front when the tenor line dictated it. Juliette sang first soprano, the top voice and usually the melody, while Peter and Michelle waded around in the middle, singing the 'filler' notes of the chord. Agostino and the new bass plodded along at the bottom.

A month before, Michelle and Agostino had to hold back so they wouldn't cover Juliette and Peter, but now they found themselves balancing their voices at a level as loud as they could comfortably sing.

The new bass and soprano had arrived at the school late, enrolling in the opera school as transfers from the *Berlin Musikhochschule.* Two students who dropped out for unknown reasons made room for the new arrivals.

The bass, Wolfgang Ziegler, was short, overweight to a debilitating degree, and blatted like a sheep, consistently under the pitch. He would never succeed in the music world—there were too many tall, well-built basses and baritones who could sing on pitch.

The soprano, Gutrud Bergmann, had the opposite problem. She was two metres tall, built like a Charolais bull, and had the voice of a bird. It was obvious to everyone that they were not there to study opera.

As the evening progressed, Juliette caught them staring at her too often to be natural. They could not read their musical line, and during the break, they stayed in the living room rather than drink tea in the kitchen with the quartet, speaking in indecipherable low tones. At the end of the session, they said goodnight and left. The quartet sprawled on the soft living room chairs and sofa and talked and sang until half an hour before midnight. When they finally decided to go to their rooms, Juliette told them her plan.

"I was thinking we should take a night to celebrate. We've been working hard, and I think it's time to go out."

Peter said, "Your father would insist we stay out of the beer halls and keep together."

Juliette said, "Yes, I agree, no *Bierstuben*. I was thinking about a nice dinner, two bottles of excellent house wine, then the cinema. The *Deutsches Theater* is showing *Der Blaue Engel,* a film Marlene Dietrich made a couple of years ago. I saw it in Brussels and would like to see it again; it has great music, so we can call it research. Remember Dietrich's song, 'Falling in Love Again?' That's the theme song of the film."

Michelle shook her head sadly. "I can't afford the dinner or the ticket, so I'm out."

Juliette took her hand. "Michelle, you misunderstand… Papa transfers money to my account every month, and it's far more than I need. He has, *in absentia,* offered to buy the tickets and pay for dinner for all of us if you keep the SA hoodlums from beating me up!"

"I can't accept," said Michelle. "My Papa won't let me take charity."

Agostino put up his hand and said, "I'll take it!" Peter did the same.

Juliette shook her head. She said, "This is not charity… it is a friend sharing what she is blessed with. But if you insist on looking at it insensitively, I suppose it's a spoiled rich girl paying for protection and attention. But, okay…if Michelle doesn't go, the whole thing is off."

"I have nothing to wear." Michelle's tone told Juliette not to hurt her pride by offering anything more.

"Michelle, my father makes me dress like a pauper, as you have probably noticed, so the 'Brownshirts' will think I'm a worker. Your clothes are better than mine, I assure you. Michelle, they will let us in the restaurant and the theatre as long as we can pay."

Agostino said to Michelle, "I want to go, but I can't afford it if Juliette's Papa isn't paying. I think Peter is in the same position, and you are spoiling this for us. Why don't you try thinking like an Italian; take whatever you can get, say, *Grazie,* and if you were *really* Italian, you wouldn't even have to mean it!"

On Saturday, the twenty-fifth of November, the quartet ate a very expensive dinner in the Bayerischehof, then walked down Sonnenstrasse, turning onto Schwanthalerstrasse. It took fifteen minutes to reach the

Deutsches Theater, and the seats Juiette had reserved in the middle of the first row of the first balcony were the best in the house.

The film captivated everyone, and when it was over they sang "Falling in Love Again" as they turned toward home. Almost immediately, a grey Mercedes stopped beside them. They stopped walking—four brown-shirted SA soldiers got out of the car, two with pistols drawn, and surrounded them.

"Papier bitte!" A soldier who appeared to be an officer put out his open hand to Agostino. Everyone dug out their identification papers… Agostino, Juliette and Michelle gave the officer their passports, and Peter gave him his *Ausweis*.

"I don't see your religion marked on your passport," said the officer as he flipped through the document Juliette had given him… *"Bist du eine Judin?"*

He returned everyone else's papers but kept Juliette's passport, thumbing through it and finally saying forcefully, "You are a pig Jew, and you were in the theatre. A sign on the door clearly says 'KEINE JUDEN'… you couldn't have missed it! You are under arrest and must come with us!"

Peter said, "She is not a Jew! She is Catholic!"

Juliette tried to grab her passport, and the officer hit her so hard with his big fist that she fell to her hands and knees, spitting blood.

She tried to understand what was happening, but the blow jumbled sounds and pictures in a tangle of gibberish. Lights and faces spun in a whirlpool of black and white images as Juliette fell sideways when she tried to get up.

The officer kicked her twice before Peter grabbed his brown uniform and tried to pull him back. One of the soldiers hit Peter between his shoulder blades with his rifle, knocking him on top of Juliette. The two soldiers holding Luger pistols stepped in front of Agostino and Michelle, and Michelle started to cry.

Peter put his arms around Juliette and hung on as the officer kicked him, trying to force him away from her, shouting, *'Saujudin'* every time he struck them.

When Peter couldn't hold on any longer, he fell sideways, shouting, "She's not a Jew!" while trying to catch the heavy boot in his hand.

Finally, the soldier with the rifle pulled his officer back.

"She's a worker… don't kill her, or there will be hell to pay!"

The officer straightened his uniform and said to the rifleman, "You and Rolf must take her to the police station. Tell them we arrested the Jew because she was in the Deutsches Theater." He watched Peter trying to get to his feet, smiled and said, "I advise you not to protect Jews. I am letting you go, but I would find another girlfriend if I were you—you won't see this one again." He looked at Michelle and Agostino, pointed down the street and screamed, "Get out of here! All of you!" He waved to the remaining soldier, who still clutched his pistol, and said, "Put the pistol away and come with me; there will be others!" He headed for a crowd walking away from the theatre.

Juliette struggled to her feet, helped by the rifleman on one arm and Rolf, a soldier who looked too young to shave, on the other. She staggered, but the world resumed its upright position after a few steps. Her ribs and face hurt, but she could walk on her own.

Agostino helped Peter to his feet, and Peter said, "Follow Juliette and stay with her if you can. I must make a phone call and will meet you at the police station as soon as I can."

Fortunately, Marcel had insisted Juliette give Peter her parents' number. He found a call box, dialled, then held his breath.

Chapter Five

Where Fools and Angels Meet

...Nay, fly to Altars; there they'll talk you dead;
For Fools rush in where Angels fear to tread
Alexander Pope from *An essay on criticism* (1709)

THE ANNOYING RING OF THE TELEPHONE BESIDE THEIR BED wakened Jacques and Veronique Durand. Accustomed to such sleep interruptions and instantly awake, Jacques lifted the receiver on the second ring, knowing that such calls never meant good news.

"Monsieur Durand, it's Peter Schweitzer. Your daughter's been arrested by the *Sturmabteilung.*"

"Who arrested her, and why?" Jacques asked with a pleasant French accent that nevertheless expressed an intense sense of urgency.

"Four of us went to the *Kino,* and SA Brownshirts stopped us when we came out. They accused Juliette of being a Jew and said Jews weren't allowed in the theatre. There is a sign that says, *Keine Juden.*" Jacques heard Peter sob before he said, "They beat and kicked her... I tried to stop them, but I couldn't. *Es tut mir so Leid. Ich....*

Jacques cut him off. "There's no time for that. Where did the soldiers take her?"

"They're walking to Polizei headquarters."

Jacques took a few seconds to clear his mind, then said, "Peter, you must do precisely what I tell you. First: Do not try to rescue Juliette. Second: I want you to follow her at a safe distance and call me again if anything happens, good or bad! Do you understand?"

Peter said, "Yes, Sir, I understand," and Jacques Durand hung up the phone. He dialled a Munich number he knew by heart, and a sleepy Bayern accent answered on the third ring. The familiar voice confirmed that Jacques had dialled correctly.

Jacques said, "Jacques Durand here... my daughter is in your police station. If I do not receive a call from Juliette in one hour telling me she is safe at home, I will be forced to call our mutual friends!"

The soldiers half-carried, half-dragged Juliette toward the police head-quarters for all of Munich, a formidable group of buildings surrounding a courtyard and a ten-minute walk from where they had arrested her. Juliette knew Peter would call her father, and he would need all the time she could get for him. She had to prolong the journey as much as possible.

Halfway to the station, when the young soldiers stopped for a smoke, Juliette turned her back, put two fingers down her throat and threw up most of the expensive dinner and two glasses of wine she had consumed and not yet finished digesting. The young Brownshirts quickly moved to a safe distance as she sprayed her ammunition on the sidewalk and a significant patch of cobblestones in the street.

Michelle and Agostino were following Juliette on the other side of the street, and Michelle ran to her.

"Are you all right, Juliette?" Michelle spoke to her in French.

Michelle held her up. The young soldiers stayed a safe distance away, wanting nothing to do with their charge until she finished making her mess. Juliette knew they would shoot her if she tried to run.

Juliette whispered, "I'm okay, but we must go as slowly as possible." She put her head down and retched as though she were dying. The soldiers leaned against a building a safe distance away, smoking and laughing while keeping one eye on their prisoner.

Peter caught up before the soldiers finished their cigarettes and rushed to Juliette's side. She put her arms around his neck and whispered in his ear, "Get out of here. Don't worry; I will call Papa when I get to the station."

Peter whispered, "I already called your father. He told me to follow you."

"Enough!" said one of the soldiers as he hurried to pull them apart.

Juliette said, "I will be alright, Peter. Go home."

Juliette doubled over, put her fingers down her throat and managed to throw up again, spraying smelly liquid over the soldier's brown uniform and boots before he could jump aside. He joined his partner, and they lit another cigarette.

An iron gate protected the entrance to the Munich Police headquarters, but it was open when the SA soldiers pushed Juliette through it. They led her up eight stone steps and through a heavy wooden door. Agostino and Michelle followed a few metres behind them as the sound of the soldiers' hard boots reverberated off the plastered walls.

They approached a counter behind which sat the only uniformed person in sight. The woman, who would be the perfect casting for Wagner's *Brünnhilde,* was reading a book. She waited until a few seconds after they reached her before she marked her place and looked up. She gave them a second to speak, and when they didn't, she asked impatiently, *"Na...und...* What do the children want now?"

The young rifle-carrying soldier blushed and said, "We have arrested a Jew who was unlawfully in the Deutsches Theater." He indicated Juliette and waited.

Brünnhilde waited for a question, and when the soldier didn't ask one, she said, *"Na... und?* What do you want from me? You are soldiers, not police; as far as I know, you have no right to arrest a civilian."

She opened her book and began reading.

Rolf whispered in the rifleman's ear, "Papers—we need papers."

The soldier carrying the rifle turned back to Brünnhilde and said, "Uh... We need papers so we can prove we brought her here."

Brünnhilde said, "She doesn't look Jewish to me." She examined Juliette's face from a distance, then said, "Step over here so I can see you."

Juliette liked the direction this woman was taking, so she pushed the soldier aside and stepped up to the counter. Brünnhilde carefully examined Juliette's face and said, "She is French—this woman is definitely not a Jew!"

"But we have her identification, and it doesn't say she is Catholic as she claims."

"Let me see it." The rifleman passed Juliette's passport over the counter. As Brünnhilde opened it, she asked, "Where does it say she is Jewish?"

The rifleman reddened. "Uh… I didn't look… uh…. "

"*Bube,* this is a Belgian Passport; they ignore religion in their documents. And this young lady's name is Juliette Durand, hardly a Jewish name. Now, tell me why you think she is Jewish."

"Uh… I don't know… uh…." And then he made a decision.

"We have an informer."

The woman put a piece of paper on the counter and said, *"Na, gut.* Write down your informer's name, and include the address. We will need to interrogate this person." She laid a pencil on the paper. *"Bitte, schreiben sie jetzt!"*

The soldier looked at his partner, who shook his head, then said, "Uh… I don't know if I'm allowed to tell you that. I *can* say this person lives in the same building as this Jew; he knows her, has examined her actions closely and is convinced she is Jewish. He has told us that she disagrees with the National Socialist cause and has also said serious things about the Führer, as a Jew would."

Brünhilde said, lifting the passport, "Well, perhaps your 'informer' doesn't exist, or perhaps he wouldn't know a Jew from an angel."

She looked at Juliette… "Are you a Jew?"

Juliette shook her head and said, "No, I am not a Jew."

"And there you have it, *Junge.* In addition, I have reliable information that Mademoiselle Durand lives in Brussels. Her father is a prominent art dealer, and Juliette was christened in the Brussels Cathedral. But if you insist, the SS can be here in a few minutes if you want to discuss it with them. However, I don't recommend waking them at this time of night."

The soldier with the rifle said, "Uh….no. Our orders were only to bring her to the *Polizei Präsidium;* what you do with her is your business."

Brünhilde's smile contained a dismissal. The soldiers stretched their arms in front of them, said, "Heil Hitler!" and marched out of the police station, leaving Juliette and her friends standing in front of the smiling Brünhilde's desk.

Juliette said, "What do I do now? Those soldiers beat me up, and they should pay for that!" She showed the woman her bloody lip; it had stopped bleeding but was swollen. She had other bruises but wasn't going to show them to this woman unless it was absolutely necessary.

The woman said, "At the moment, I am in charge, so I can release you. I received a call just before you arrived, and, for a worker, you have powerful friends." She leaned over to Juliette and whispered, "I wouldn't press this any further—Hitler will take care of those SA sewer rats when the time is right! Go home and call your father."

Juliette didn't like the woman but smiled pleasantly, took her advice, and left with her friends.

The quartet walked to the *Sängerhaus* without saying anything, locked the door and searched for Wolfgang and Gertrud. When they couldn't find them, they went straight to the living room.

Juliette called her father to confirm she was alright and then hugged Peter. "Thank you for calling Papa. That could have been much worse if that woman hadn't been on our side!"

Michelle said, "That soldier said they have an informer in the *Sängerhaus*, and we all know who it is."

Peter said, "Yes, but what do we do about it? They probably have spies everywhere."

Juliette said, "If they return, we can face them together." She looked forward to the confrontation. "And when I tell them what I think of their despicable actions, they won't want to sing madrigals!"

Michelle said, "I think we should ignore them." Agostino nodded.

Juliette asked Peter, "What do you think of your friend Adolph now?"

Peter hadn't expected Juliette's attack, and it took him a few seconds to realize that she had referred to his support of Adolph Hitler.

"The *Sturmabteilung* soldiers that attacked you are under Ernst Röhm, not Hitler. Röhm supported Hitler when the National Socialist movement started but broke away from what he thinks is Hitler's weakness. Röhm now calls for a 'New Revolution' against communists and democratic socialists."

Juliette said, "So… you think Hitler is okay with the Jews, and you think it's okay if the SA goes after communists and socialists, as long as they don't beat up the Jews?"

"No, that's not what I meant to say."

"Okay, that's what you said… tell me what you meant to say."

"Röhm hates Communists and socialists even more than Jews. As you saw tonight, he orders the rabble he has enlisted in the SA to hassle the Jews, but communists are his real targets. Röhm's hoodlums are supposed to concentrate on Hitler's political opposition. Adolph Hitler won't put up with the SA's persecution of Jews much longer because they are the backbone of the German economy."

Juliette laughed sarcastically. "Do you actually believe Goebbels' rubbish? Do you think there is a limit to Hitler's madness? Do you think it doesn't matter if he persecutes communists and socialists?—that they don't have rights?"

Peter's mouth fell open, and Juliette stopped laughing.

"Surely you are not that stupid and naïve! You must realize that when he is done with the communists, he will go after the Jews precisely *because* they own so much. And, of course, Hitler will seize the assets of the 'backbone' of the German economy!"

"No, that's not right! Hitler is just keeping the party together; the party's extremist wing wants to kick every Jew out of the country! Hitler has already answered them with a decree that Jews may leave if they want to, but he is trying to keep them here by charging a departure tax based on their net worth—after all, they got rich on the backs of the German people. Hitler doesn't want to hurt the Jews; he wants them to stay here and invest in their businesses."

Peter wanted to bring up his Jewish grandparents, both of whom worked in a Munich high school, his grandfather as a teacher and his grandmother as an administrator, but decided to say nothing.

Michelle and Agostino sat on the sofa, but Juliette and Peter remained on their feet, facing one another like two dogs, both claiming a bone.

Juliette put her hands on her hips and raised her voice. "Haven't you been paying attention to what's happened to your country? Hitler was appointed chancellor by that old fool Hindenburg on Monday, January thirtieth… do you know what he did on Wednesday?"

Peter shook his head, thinking perhaps he shouldn't have let this get out of control.

"He suspended the *Reichstag*—I understand that to be your democratically elected government—am I correct?"

Peter nodded.

"Now, tell me, Peter, what do you think he did on Friday?"

Peter was in trouble, and he knew it. He said, "I don't know," hoping that answer was safe.

Juliette waved her arms around. "What troubles me is that I, a Belgian girl, have to tell you that on Friday, the second day of February, nineteen thirty-three, you lost your country, and worse, you don't know it!"

Juliette said, "Marcel made me buy *Der Stürmer* to learn what is going on. He said, 'If something appears in that paper, Hitler will eventually do it.' That *Zeitung* is full of anti-Jew and anti-communist drivel. It's sickeningly violent, racist, and filled with hate for anything or anyone not Aryan."

"I haven't read it." Peter wanted to go to bed.

"Let me summarize where your pal has led his country since he became chancellor. He became chancellor eleven months ago and almost immediately made the President subservient to him. And then, before the end of February: freedom of assembly… gone; freedom of the press… gone; then Göring made the SA an auxiliary police force with the power to shoot people. And then there was the suspicious fire in the *Reichstag* that Hitler used as an excuse to issue a decree giving the National Socialists the legal right to eliminate all opposition by whatever means they see fit, including murder—the euphemistic term they use is execution. And then, in March, the National Socialists, your beloved NSDAP, won 44 percent of the vote in the *Reichstag*, allied themselves with the far-right nationalists, then eliminated them and all other parties. In late March, Hitler created courts to judge anyone who opposed him, built Dachau and Oranienburg concentration camps to hold them, and the *Reichstag* that he now controlled voted to give him unfettered and limitless power!"

Peter tried not to raise his voice but had lost control. He screamed, "Don't say any more. There is no evidence of any of that!"

"Evidence? Those are facts; those things happened! You saw the evidence tonight! I was arrested for being a Jew, which I am not… but what if I had been?"

"I'm going to bed." Peter turned to leave, but Juliette grabbed his arm and said, "I'm not done yet!"

"You have no right to judge Hitler any more than I have to judge the Belgian king. You just want to believe that Hitler is a bad leader because you and all of Europe are jealous of Germany. While all of Europe is suffering, the German workers are becoming wealthy. The German people are the most productive in the world, and the world can't stand that!"

Juliette let Peter go. She had lost control, and she regretted it. She wanted to back up but didn't know how, so she followed Peter, saying, "In April Hitler stripped the states' powers, threw all communists, social democrats and Jews out of the civil service, and decreed that Germans could no longer buy anything from a Jew… hence the man I saw being beaten." Peter opened the door and kept going without answering.

"In May, Hitler banned all existing trade unions, putting all workers under one umbrella controlled by the elite industrialists in the National Socialist Party."

Peter stopped and faced Juliette, but she kept going.

"In June, Hitler outlawed all parties except the NSDAP, the National Socialist Party, and membership to any other political organization is now punishable by death! He has killed even the dream of democracy!"

Peter opened the door to his and Agostino's room. Juliette kept going.

"Hitler's government passed a law to sterilize anyone who has a hereditary disease or is mentally disturbed. This law can now be used to sterilize or even kill anyone who speaks against the government. Hitler has already laid the groundwork for that by claiming that anyone who opposes him must, by definition, be mentally ill!"

Peter spread his arms in frustration. "Please, Juliette, we must sing together or be thrown out of the school. Can't you believe what you want and leave me alone? Why do you care what I think or believe about Hitler?"

Juliette knew the answer but wasn't going to say it. She looked around the room—clothes lay everywhere, the beds were unmade, and the floor was filthy.

She breathed deeply and changed her tone as she said, "You two are worse pigs than I am. Why don't Michelle and I clean this room for you and Agostino... but you must promise to keep it that way."

Peter looked at Juliette's sweet face and said, "Do you promise not to criticize my politics?"

Juliette didn't have to think; she said, "Not unless you change them."

She turned and said as she walked through the door, "On second thought, you can clean your own room; I promise not to come back."

Chapter Six

There are no Shortcuts to a Place Worth Going

In a way, being an opera singer is like being a very romantic sixteen-year-old who falls in love with great passion and conviction every month
Renee Fleming

PETER WAITED FOR THEIR LESSON with his back against the wall rather than sitting on the bench beside Juliette. Neither had said a word to the other since Saturday, and on Sunday he had stayed in bed until noon, pretending to sleep, letting his mind go places that were not healthy to visit.

He asked himself whether he could be wrong about Hitler. His mind returned to his father's job, the revived economy, and the Western Allies' cancellation or postponement of German reparation payments—all to the credit of Hitler's policies. Germany thrived; it was building roads and railways, ships and aircraft. Cars came off the assembly lines at a record pace; unemployment had dropped from forty percent before Hitler to under twelve percent and improving every month. Real wages had risen, and the German people's pride was back. People sang in the *Gaststätten* and played chess in the parks.

Peter had to admit there were casualties, and they were regrettable, but politics was a tradeoff; freedom and prosperity had to be earned and paid for by someone. No one, not even Juliette, could deny that substantially fewer people suffered under the new regime than the old one!

Peter hadn't discussed his distress with anyone, least of all with Juliette. He had gone for a long Sunday afternoon walk and eaten in an *Imbiss*—two fat *Bratwurst mit Sauerkraut* from a vendor's cart in *Maximillianplatz*. While sitting on a bench eating his Wurst, Peter decided to accept Heidelberg University's offer to take him into their engineering program. He could still register for the winter semester, and the more he thought about it, the more exciting the prospect of designing machines became.

Under Hitler, there was a whole new world of opportunity for engineers and technicians. Peter was sure he would like to work for a company like M.A.N. in the product development department, perhaps with his father.

For the first time, Peter saw Juliette as an intellectual force he couldn't challenge as an equal. His strength lay in engineering logic, not music—and certainly not in politics. Juliette relied on human factors and emotions, things an engineer's soul must put in the category of rumour and speculation. His world was based on a single simple philosophy: does it work?

The clock reached nine-thirty, and Juliette had her hand on the lever when Professor Garcia's studio door opened, and he waved Juliette and Peter in.

"Come in, come in—I've got a date for your *Übungsabend* debut." Professor Garcia talked as he led them into the studio. "Actually, I think this could work out quite well."

Peter closed the door and stood to one side.

Professor Garcia turned to him. "I'm sorry, Peter... I'm ignoring you... I apologize." He took Peter's hand and shook it, then put his left hand over Peter's and shook it slowly as he said, "I want you to know that I am thrilled with your progress, Peter." Garcia's bright eyes confirmed what he was saying.

Peter pulled his hand back. He looked out the window at leafless trees and gentle snowflakes drifting through them. Why had the professor picked this particular morning to say that? Peter decided to say what was on his mind before it got harder to do.

"I must apologize—to you and also to Juliette because I am quitting the music program as of now. I have been accepted into engineering at Heidelberg, probably for the winter semester but certainly for the fall session. Meanwhile, I will work at M.A.N. with my father."

Juliette felt her face burning. Peter had been sullen since Saturday night, and she knew why... she had torn his heart apart with her words.

She had intended to present him with the facts, to force him to see the light and reverse course, but had obviously done the opposite.

Since Saturday, Juliette had admitted to herself that she cared for Peter, but his support of Hitler was more than her affection for him could accept. She had lashed out at the thing that stood between them, and she regretted it. When the prospect of never seeing him again was suddenly a reality, Juliette wanted to take it all back, undo what she had done, but the words wouldn't come.

Juliette hesitated, undecided, but finally said, "I understand, Peter, and I suppose this has something to do with Saturday night. I shouldn't have attacked you like that, but I won't take anything back because it is the truth. Hitler is the most dangerous man in the world, and your silence is a vote for his twisted principles. I will work with you, but not if you discuss Hitler or his policies. If you are set on studying engineering, and I must return to Brussels, so be it."

Professor Garcia walked to the window and watched the snow fall past it for a few minutes before he turned around and spoke quietly.

"My country is the most politically confusing in the world. Since we wrote a constitution in 1812, we have had a dozen coups and revolutions. That constitution was trashed, then rewritten and trashed again as a succession of coups changed the governing power. Spain is divided between Galatians, Catalonians, and Spanish Nationalists, all armed and dangerous. Our government includes socialists, communists, anarchists, advocates for democracy, anti-religious, pro-religious, nationalists, monarchists, nationalist-monarchists, and a long list of minor factions, each aligned with a fervent just cause. The consequence of this political mayhem is that nothing gets done." Juliette stirred...he stopped her with his hand.

"Currently, our king is in exile, and a Republican socialist has dictatorial powers, but his hold on it is tenuous at best because the Nationalists have the army behind them. We expect another revolution or coup soon because that is how Spanish politics are done." He looked at Juliette, then Peter.

"Now, why don't we sing and let someone else sort out the politics?"
Juliette shook her head. "No, I..."

"You cannot know what Hitler will do with his power. If you did, you would be the first who could predict the future." Professor Garcia turned to Peter.

"You are not right to support Hitler, but it is your choice. Fortunately, you are not a Jew, but if you were a Jewish shop owner in Munich, I assume you would feel differently about the man who is trying to bankrupt you."

Peter said, "I think.... "

"No, Peter, you don't think. You are making a colossal mistake if you take the easy road and quit now, for you will lose the most precious thing you have...yourself. You *are* a singer, and your engineering mind is sometimes an asset, but there are times when you should just accept that art is based on instinct and emotion, unsupported by numbers or cold facts. You have the heart, soul and voice of an opera singer, and you have come to the right place at the right time, something few people accomplish."

Professor Garcia's voice broke as he addressed both Juliette and Peter. "You don't know it now, but you two belong together like a key in a lock. Your voices tell me that, and you will hear it when you sing the third act of La Bohéme on December fourteenth. I love teaching both of you, not one without the other, and your audience will love you too. But first, I need two years to make your voices shine." He looked at Peter. "I need your commitment today. Are you a singer or an engineer?"

Peter looked at Juliette, confused. The thought of giving up on singing had broken his heart, but so had Juliette's rejection, and he couldn't bear being close to her.

Juliette smiled. The look on Peter's face was pathetic. She saw his love for her despite a broken heart. Could she live with his political beliefs? She said, "I promise not to do that again. I care for you and don't want you to leave, but if you say a word about Hitler...."

Peter felt a glow inside, and tears threatened to give him away. He swallowed, cleared his throat and said, "I want to stay, but I thought you hated me."

Juliette impulsively put her arms around Peter, then pulled back.

"If you… I could…" Juliette stepped away from Peter, frustrated with her feelings for him.

She said, "*Mon Dieu,* Peter, I love to sing with you, even if you are a tenor!"

Professor Garcia rushed to the piano, picked an opera score off the cover and handed it to Juliette.

"I have two piano scores of the opera. You must read from one score until you buy a new Peters edition. Michelle and Agostino will also need scores, but I can work that out."

Juliette knew the opera and said, "Can't we sing it as a duet?"

"No, no, for the *Übungsabend,* you must have a Musetta and a Marcello, and you already have a mezzo and a baritone who will sing with you. We shall begin where Marcello meets Mimi. I reserved enough time to do the entire quartet."

Juliette shrugged her shoulders. "We can ask them."

"I have already spoken with Frau Kirschbaum. She said they would be glad to do it."

Juliette put the score on the music stand and opened it to act three.

Garcia said, "Beginning at number eight, the Allegro. Marcel says, "Mimi?"

"Okay," said Juliette, "I've got it."

Professor Garcia played the first note and sang, "Mimi?"

Juliette read her line and hadn't finished the phrase when Professor Garcia said, "I'm sitting in the back row. I can't hear you!"

"But there is no orchestra until the second bar."

"And are you planning to sing like a little girl and then suddenly become a woman on the second bar?

Juliette looked out the window and sang the phrase to an imaginary person across the street.

"Very good. This person has paid a lot for the seat and wants to hear every word you sing, so sing to them, not to me—I'm the orchestra under your feet." Professor Garcia asked Peter, "Tell me, did you hear that in the back row?"

Peter said to Juliette. "Yes, I could feel the sound vibrating!"

Garcia played chords for emphasis as he said, "All right. No more little girl sounds; don't mess with your face... relax, enjoy the sound." He smiled. "Can you do it again?"

Juliette had to try three times, and each time the sound improved. When the lesson was over, she felt she would never lose it again.

The foundation Professor Garcia had laid in the first three months of technique lessons had changed everything about Juliette and Peter's voices when they sang their *Übungsabend* debut. They walked out on the small stage filled with trepidation and excitement, confident they could sing it well, but that tiny rascal doubt still sat on their shoulder, whispering in their ear.

When the pressure was on, would their cords retire into a no-man's-land between their new-found technique and the one they had known and trusted for years? Peter had quickly grasped the new resonance principles—he was older, and his voice's beautiful natural tenor resonance made it easy for him. The multiple 'B flat' notes now sat in a perfect spot—Puccini had written those phrases for a voice like his.

Juliette had found her opera stage resonance, but her 'little girl voice' still sneaked in. She found herself relying on Peter's voice to carry hers through the long unison passages and was afraid he would let her down.

The beginning of the quartet was a dialogue between Juliette and Agostino, who turned out to be a honey-coloured baritone with a naturally big and resonant voice. Agostino's sound was solid and beautiful, but Juliette felt her sound penetrate through it with an intensity that excited her. Even Michelle's rich mezzo was no match for Juliette's focused overtones. In the dress rehearsal, Juliette had shocked herself with the reverberation of her voice off the studio's plastered walls, cutting through everyone with little effort.

Peter found his resonance could easily match and blend with every member of the quartet, and he became so relaxed his emotions almost wrecked him when he said *Addio* to Juliette. They finished their last pledge of love close to tears.

The student audience, the most critical a performer can face, was silent when the last musical sound died. Juliette and Peter held one another and waited for what seemed an eternity, and then the audience exploded with clapping, foot-stomping and yells of 'Brava.' The quartet left the stage, returned, bowed individually, and then with the pianist. It took ten minutes to get off the stage, and they were euphoric, still high on adrenalin when they left the building to walk home.

Juliette, walking arm-in-arm with Michelle, talked about singing and home while Peter walked alongside Agostino. Agostino gestured with his hands as he told Peter about singing Marcello in an amateur opera production. He described a dress rehearsal that had gone perfectly but a premiére that had been an unmitigated disaster, and Peter bent over laughing as Agostino recounted the missed entries and creative lines substituted for forgotten ones.

Most of the *Sturmabteilung* leadership had been uprooted and replaced by Röhm between his becoming Defence Minister in 1930 and when Hitler grabbed dictatorial power in January and February 1933. Ernst Röhm embraced the ruffians of German society as members and leaders, expanding the role of the *Braunhemden* from gangs of bullies who intimidated political opposition to a three-million-man military force to be reckoned with.

Röhm's competition, the *Reichswehr,* was limited by the Versailles Treaty to a hundred thousand men while self-appointed rulers of society, the SA 'brownshirts,' hunted communists, Social Democrats, immigrants, Romani, Jews and homosexuals. Their efforts to reform these individuals' attitudes concentrated mainly on beating them until they learned to stay out of sight.

Dietrich, Manfred and Uwe, all eighteen years old and members of the SA since a week after Hitler came to power, were out on their Thursday night prowl after filling their bellies with beer at the Löwenbräukeller. Armed with clubs, they stalked anyone on their list of targets, especially Jews. The Music Conservatory, a straight shot down Briennerstrasse from their hangout, was the best source of communists, homosexuals and women in the city, and they began by splitting up and lurking in places where light from the streets didn't reach.

Thursdays were concert days, and when the music ended, the marauders could count on a flow of young girls and homosexuals streaming down the sidewalks. Most nights, they watched while drinking beer and smoking cigarettes, talking about rape and murder as though they were experienced in those subjects. Sometimes, there were stragglers, women alone or in pairs—elite women dressed in provocatively short skirts that barely covered their knees. Sometimes there were *Schwule,* artistic gay men who couldn't or wouldn't fight back.

The boys got their high from imagining beating and raping women, and sometimes they actually caught a homosexual man and beat him senseless. Tonight they struck a bonanza… two women wrapped around one another and nothing but two *Schwule* men walking behind to protect them.

Dietrich was the unit's strategist and decided, after checking for SS and police, to follow what he now considered his prey.

He watched the group cross the street to enter the Hofgarten, a perfect spot to intercept them. Dietrich's plan was the usual… Force the students into the trees surrounding the garden and have their way with the women on the grass.

He crossed the street behind the quartet with Manfred and Uwe on his heels. They caught up to the women halfway along the park's edge that led to the Galeriestrasse exit.

When Juliette heard running footsteps she turned around, but was too late to avoid Dietrich. He put his arm around her neck and threw her on the ground like a sack of potatoes. Michelle screamed and reached for Juliette's attacker, ignoring Uwe, who hit her hard between the shoulder blades. Seeing that his friends had the women under control, Manfred passed them and met Peter head-on.

Peter's older brothers had taught him how to fight, and although he hated them for it, Rolf and Dieter had left him no choice but to learn the practical skill of defending himself against a determined opponent. As that training kicked in, Peter instinctively stepped sideways, tripped Manfred as he passed, then kicked him in the ribs when he hit the ground.

Agostino glanced at Peter and took two steps toward Dietrich as a shiny object slipped from his sleeve into his big hand. Waiting for Manfred to get up, Peter was elated when he saw Agostino's hand slash across Dietrich's back, leaving a streak of red on the soldier's brown shirt as he screamed and fell sideways away from Juliette.

Peter and Manfred, mesmerized by Agostino's quickness, watched him as he spun to face Uwe, who was trying to figure out what had happened to Dietrich. The flash in Agostino's hand struck again, this time on Uwe's hip. Uwe staggered, pulled out his club and faced a smiling Agostino, blood pouring down his leg, pain and surprise on his face.

Manfred, struggling to regain his feet, left Peter an opening where a well-aimed kick would do the most damage to an eighteen-year-old boy, and the toe of Peter's leather shoe left the young SA soldier crying in the fetal position.

Peter turned to Juliette, now on her feet. Satisfied she was alright, he hit Dietrich, who was struggling to his feet, with all his weight behind the punch. As the boy fell, Peter gave him the same treatment Manfred had gotten.

Michelle immediately pounced on Uwe, hammering the back of his head with her handbag. He turned around, she grabbed the surprised boy's club and hit him in the face, breaking his nose. He fell, and Agostino, fascinated by her fury as she used the club to beat its helpless owner, took it from her before she killed him.

Agostino said to Manfred, still writhing on the ground, "Lie down beside your friend, or I will put this into your heart." He showed the boy his skinny knife.

"Where did the knife come from?" asked Peter as Manfred crawled over and lay beside a barely conscious Dietrich. Peter grabbed Uwe's collar and dragged him over to his friends.

Agostino opened his hand so Peter could see the magnificent handle attached to a shiny eight-inch blade.

"It's a stiletto, an assassin's knife, designed to kill people like these who attack you on the street."

Peter looked more closely at the graceful weapon. The blade was a simple, clean piece of bright steel with no sharp edges like a traditional knife but a needle-sharp end. The slash it made on Dietrich's back looked serious; it bled as though Agostino had cut something important, but Dietrich's blood flowed evenly, not pulsing like it would if the dagger had cut an artery.

"Where did it come from? I've never seen you carrying it."

Agostino slid the knife point-first up his left sleeve, then stretched out his arms to show it was invisible. "I carry it when I anticipate the possibility of something like this." He looked at Manfred, bent like a pretzel, still holding onto his genitals and moaning. "You don't do so bad yourself."

Juliette had taken Dietrich's club from his belt, and when he moved, she whacked him on the back, being careful to hit the wound. He yelped, and Juliette laughed.

She looked at Agostino's stilleto. "I could carry one of those in my purse, couldn't I?"

Agostino laughed. "I would have to teach you to use it, and the first rule is never to pull a knife if the other guy has a gun. Maybe you should get your father to buy you a pistol for your birthday… I recommend a little six-millimetre Beretta."

Juliette smiled. "My father would never trust me with a gun!"

Michelle kicked Manfred half-heartedly, said, "Stay there until we're gone," took Juliette's hand and smiled like a cat. "Shall we go home and celebrate?"

"What are we celebrating?" asked Peter, "La Bohéme or Agostino?"

Agostino kissed Juliette's hand. "We will celebrate your successful opera debut, of course!"

Peter walked beside Agostino, who couldn't stop smiling. He decided to ask why. "What are you so happy about?"

Agostino said, "Victory is sweet. And you didn't do so badly yourself, although you had the smallest and dumbest of the three." He chuckled.

Peter said, "Will you tell me where you learned to fight like that, or are you Italy's secret weapon?"

"To begin with, I am not as young as you. When I was your age, I had no money for university, so I enlisted in the Mountain Infantry, what the Italian military calls their *Alpini*. I was in the Fifth Regiment,

Third Battalion and spent two years running around the Dolomite mountains in a handsome felt hat with an eagle feather stuck in it."

"And you learned to fight with a knife in the mountains?"

Agostino shook his head. "The stilleto is an Italian invention from the Middle Ages… used by knights to penetrate chain-mail armour. The sharp point will go through thin metal and find chinks where the armour is riveted together. My battalion had the opportunity to learn how to fight with a stilleto in the Sicilian school of knife fighting, and I've always carried one since. I had one when those SA bastards arrested Juliette, but they had guns, and a stilleto is no match for one of those. However, later I could have taken out both of the soldiers who took Juliette to the police station. I didn't do it because I hoped for help from the police."

"This can't go on; Hitler will take care of the *Sturmabteilung.*"

Agostino laughed cynically. "Are you thinking that Hitler will stab his best friend in the back? If he does, then who do you imagine will take care of Hitler?"

CHAPTER SEVEN

Hear no Evil; See no Evil

It is tempting to accept evil in the face of its existence because the worst evils appear banal, and silence grants one anonymity. But acceptance and silence do not eliminate responsibility

WHEN JULIETTE ARRIVED home for Christmas, she had only a few days to learn Bach's joyful Christmas Cantata, BWV 110, *Unser Mund sei voll Lachens*. Madamoiselle Desjardins had convinced the bishop to have the Bach Chamber Choir and Orchestra perform the exuberant piece in the cathedral, highlighting the morning service the day before Christmas.

The soprano part is only a short duet with the tenor, but Juliette approached it with high spirits. She had sung with the local chamber choir before she went to Munich and with the tenor half a dozen times in various oratorios and concerts. She went to rehearsal on Saturday expecting to sing full-out to be heard.

Juliette sang the first choir number with the soprano section and immediately got a stern look from the conductor despite pulling back to a fraction of her power. She pulled back further; he smiled and nodded. As the twenty-five-member chamber choir and twenty-piece Baroque orchestra bounced along at close to full volume, Juliette found the perfect blend using a relaxed sound that wasn't close to her full voice. The notes flowed as though Bach had written the piece for her.

Almost any empty Cathedral's reverberation time is nearly eight seconds, and the sound has to be carefully controlled to hear nuances of music or to understand dialogue, and learning to adjust volume and resonance is an essential consideration for priests, conductors and soloists. Juliette had never experienced a need to adapt, even in the most resonant of those cold stone churches. Her full voice had always been ideally suited for those rebounding sound waves, and blending her resonance into the acoustics of the building was a new experience for her. She was surprised and excited by the satisfaction she felt.

When the orchestra began the lilting opening to the duet, Juliette assumed she would need everything to match the tenor and the sound of the orchestra behind her. The first word was *Liebe...* and Juliette's 'e' rang against the stone walls so loudly that the conductor indicated that she should pull back. The tenor immediately gave Juliette a sour look and came in with a weak sound, not the voice she remembered.

The conductor put both hands up in a 'stop' sign and turned to Juliette.

"Mademoiselle Durand, regrettably, there is no solo part in this cantata for you, and I am sure the audience would appreciate hearing the orchestra and tenor. *S'il vous plaît;* save your wonderful *forté* for Monsieur Verdi."

"Je regret," said Juliette, working hard to conceal her excitement.

The conductor tapped his baton and began again, and Juliette sang her line, thinking, "I can sing Bach, and it's easy... *Mon Dieu!* I can sing Bach!"

When the duet ended, the bass sang his aria, *Wach auf!* God instructed his flock to love one another joyfully, and although the bass's voice was beautiful, Juliette missed the excitement she heard from singers in Professor Garcia's studio.

When the choir sang again, Juliette joined them, singing a chorale filled with full-bore joyfulness, inserting herself effortlessly and seamlessly into the soprano line.

Waiting for the performance on Sunday morning, Juliette felt none of the nervous tension she had always experienced when singing Bach. She sat alongside the anxious tenor in front of the orchestra, confident she was in complete control for the first time in her performing life.

Twenty-five minutes of pure joy flew by, and when the cantata was over, the audience clapped in the church, interrupting the service and ignoring the thousand-year-old rule of silent etiquette. When the shocked conductor recovered, he had the soloists bow together, then the orchestra, and finally, the choir. The audience clapped harder, and the bishop and priest joined them until the conductor signalled Juliette to bow alone. When she did, the church erupted, and tears of joy burst from her dark eyes.

Peter arrived at the *Sängerhaus* on the first day of January to find students filling plates with peeled potatoes, bean and potato salad and fried schnitzel from the table in the dining room. Agostino and Michelle waved to him from the end of the line, and Peter picked a plate from a pile on the buffet and joined them.

The high plastered ceilings and bare walls reflected excited voices, their chatter a dense cloud of seemingly random words picked from a half-dozen languages. Michelle and Agostino let two students into the line ahead of them so they could talk to Peter.

"Juliette is in the living room," said Michelle, "and we'll sit with her when we have our food." She winked. "The first thing Juliette asked when she arrived was whether you were here yet—she has something to tell you."

Peter felt a surge of excitement. Perhaps she would agree not to bring up Adolph Hitler again if he didn't.

Peter wanted to tell Juliette about singing in his parents' church, how easy it had been, how the sound had rung from the walls and vaulted ceiling. He had sung, "Then shall the righteous…" from Mendelssohn's *Elijah*, a piece he had sung in the same church a few weeks before going to the Hochschule to study with Professor Garcia. But Peter feared she would ruin his mood by bringing up something her father had told her about Hitler. He was intimidated just thinking about the man Juliette idolized.

A brand-new *Volksempfänger* radio, a product of Goebbels' propaganda department donated to the *Sängerhaus* by the benefactor who owned the house, sat on a low table in the living room. It was tuned to *Deutschlandsender,* the national station where all of Hitler's speeches were broadcast and the station on which he would give his New Year's address. Someone shouted, *"Ruhe! Der Führer spricht,"* turned up the radio's volume so everyone could hear, and the talking stopped when the announcer introduced

Adolph Hitler. After a pause, the Führer gave a short speech.

"And so the goal of our fight for the German nation in an external sense as well is none other than that of restoring to our 'Volk' honour and equality of rights and of making a sincere contribution to avoiding future bloodshed, which we former soldiers of the World War can envision only as a new catastrophe of the nations in a Europe which has gone mad.

"Thus we leave behind us the Year of the German Revolution and enter into the Year of the German Restoration as National Socialists with the mutual pledge to be a sworn community, filled by the single ardent desire to be allowed to serve our German 'Volk' for the benefit of its peace and good fortune."

There was a short silence; the announcer said, *"Heil Hitler,"* and regular programming resumed, as did the students' conversation. Someone switched the intrusive radio off.

Agostino told Peter, "Juliette talks of nothing but her voice—I think she has fallen in love with her teacher."

Peter ignored the insinuation, nodded, and stepped ahead as the line moved. "I think I know what she's going to tell me. Yesterday, I sang the same piece I had sung six months ago in the same church. I was nervous when I started, as I always am, but I was excited at the end of the first phrase. It felt wonderful, and I don't think I will ever again be afraid to sing anything!"

"I envy both of you," said Michelle, suddenly sad. "In fact, I'm jealous."

Michelle reached the food first and stopped talking to load her plate. Agostino pretended he wanted to get to the schnitzel before she did, then graciously kissed her and stepped aside.

He laughed. "You don't need to be jealous… You've got me!"

At six-thirty, it was dark outside the window except for overlapping light pools spreading across the paving stones below the streetlights. A bright moon cautiously peeking over the roofs on the other side of *Schönfeldstrasse* illuminated the *Sängerhaus,* and Peter pulled the chair Juliette had saved for him sideways so he could see it. The move coincidentally put him close enough to touch her.

FOOLS, ANGELS and the DEVIL

Juliette and Peter's chairs faced the street, and Michelle and Agostino sat behind them, where they could watch the moon rise over their shoulders.

The foursome exchanged Christmas-at-home stories, including a reiteration of Juliette and Peter's singing experience.

Michelle said, perhaps joking, but perhaps not, "You two make me sick! Have you no pity for us mortals?"

Knowing Michelle still felt jilted by Professor Garcia, Juliette said, "You and Agostino have beautiful voices and perfect techniques—why would you let anyone mess with that? Peter and I started from nothing, and we have a long way to go before we can sing as well as either of you."

Agostino said, "Whatever Garcia is doing for you is working. Even bad tenors are envied by every singer who isn't one, but Peter has a world-class voice. As for you," he pointed at Juliette, "you have the face and voice of an angel, and when we sang the 'Bohéme' quartet, I wanted to stop singing and listen to you! You only have to worry about becoming one of those condescending divas everyone loves to hate!"

Michelle said, "Don't forget her petite figure. Juliette will make any tenor look good, even a short, fat, arrogant one. When I stand beside most tenors, I look and feel ridiculous. Even if he sings like a frog and I sing like a goddess, the audience ignores me and showers love on the tenor."

Juliette said, "Michelle—they look ridiculous standing beside *you*."

"It doesn't matter how you look at it; I would get more singing jobs if I looked like you or had Peter's voice. But I guess life isn't a competition between equals, is it?"

Juliette was trying to think of a way to encourage Michelle when shouts from the street carried into the room. A flash lit the darkness, and a gunshot reverberated from buildings built tight against the sidewalk. A woman under the window screamed, a man cried out, and male voices shouted, *"Halt, oder Ich schiesse!"*

Agostino jumped to the switch, turned off the lights and shouted, "Everyone on the floor, and be quiet!"

Michelle, Juliette and Peter lay on the floor under the windows, against the wall and below the window ledges.

There were more shouts and screams, flashes, rifle shots, and then laughter mingled with cries of excitement. Juliette raised herself, peeked over the sill and, in the circles of light under the streetlights, saw three bodies lying in the street. Two men sat, obviously injured, on the curb under an adjacent streetlight. SA Brownshirts approached the wounded men and clubbed them with rifle butts until they lay still. A covered *Lastwagen* drove down the street, stopped, and SA soldiers loaded bodies into the back.

The students gathered close to the windows, and a female voice said, "Why doesn't someone stop them? Where is the *Polizei?*"

Agostino said, "I'm afraid the police can't help you against the *Sturmabteilung* rabble."

A few women cried; others prayed for the souls of the people being dumped like sacks of potatoes into the back of the *Lastwagen*. A second truck pulled up, the soldiers threw the remaining bodies onto the load bed and jumped into the back, and it followed the first one, accelerating to catch up. Both vehicles turned left at the end of the street.

The only light in the living and dining rooms was the light left over from the streetlights six metres below, and the only sound was the whimpering and whispering of shocked students. Agostino turned on the lights, and immediately a frightened girl screamed, so he turned them off as he said, "They're gone now. We need the lights to eat."

A frightened male voice said, "We should stay down with the lights off until we're sure they won't come into the building."

Agostino replied, "They aren't after us... they're after communists, socialists, Jews..." he looked around... "and also homosexuals but, of course, there aren't any of those here."

Juliette said, "I suggest that anyone who is still afraid should go to their room while we finish our dinner."

Five people left the room, and when the last one had closed the door, Agostino turned the switch, and light flooded the room.

He returned to his chair behind Juliette and said, "It is a beautiful moon, Isn't it?"

FOOLS, ANGELS and the DEVIL

Tears streaming down her cheeks, Juliette looked at the cold bright ball approaching the corner of the window where it would soon disappear, and said, "I used to love to watch the moon rise from my bedroom window...."

The music school moved the *Übungsabend* concerts to mid-afternoon so every student could be home before darkness fell on southern Germany. And still, several times a week, someone was harassed by brownshirts on suspicion of some imagined offence.

The city's residents complained, and even the *Münchner Beobachter,* the weekly propaganda newspaper run by the National Socialists, hinted in editorials that Munich's residents had their "noses full" of the SA's "reign of terror," openly criticizing the prolific debauchery and violence in the *Sturmabteilung.*

And then *Der Stürmer,* the weekly National Socialist newspaper that Hitler read from front to back, took up the cry. Even Hermann Göring and Heinrich Himmler jumped on the wagon, discrediting their archenemy, Ernst Röhm.

Until then, Hitler had ignored Röhm's homosexuality and reliable rumours of wild parties. He had appointed him defence minister in his new government, giving him command over three million armed men. But Röhm went over the line when his brownshirts beat German citizens indiscriminately, shot those who ran, and tortured innocent people in cellars. Röhm made no secret of his intent to have a "Second Revolution," and he had the men and arms to successfully do it. He lived in a fantasy world destined to come crashing down when it became a threat Hitler could no longer find an excuse to ignore.

"I think you both should read this." Agostino dropped a newspaper on the piano bench next to Juliette. It was the *Frankfurtervolksblatt;* the date on it was Saturday, 27 January 1934.

The day was Sunday, and Peter and Juliette quietly worked on a love duet from Don Pasquali, *Tornami a dir que m'ami,* "Tell me again that you love me—" pure sexual foreplay.

101

They stopped singing and looked at the paper, folded so only the editorial page was visible. Peter read the headline: "Writer Hanns Johst Interviews Adolph Hitler."

In the interest of their singing careers, Peter and Juliette had sworn off politics, and Peter dismissed Agostino by stating, "We are working on our music... take it away."

But Juliette picked up the paper, scanned the interview, and began reading the article.

Desperate, knowing this would not lead anywhere good, Peter pleaded with Juliette.

"Please don't read that. We need to work on our music."

Whenever they heard of another beating or killing by the SA, Juliette blamed Hitler for the brutality on Munich's streets and dismissed Peter's explanation that Röhm had gone rogue. He learned not to respond when she switched on a rant and to change the subject at the first opportunity. Peter was delighted when Professor Garcia gave them the duet and a week to memorize it. Juliette even seemed happy to learn the love duet with him. What their relationship didn't need was a political discussion centred on Hitler!

But Juliette didn't stop reading as she got up from the piano and found her way to the soft chair she had staked out in the window facing the street.

Peter went to the chair beside hers and waited, his worry increasing as Juliette read. He took it as a bad sign when she reread sections, following the lines with her finger, and his worst fears were confirmed when she finished reading, looked at him with what he knew to be a sure sign of a storm on her face, and passed him the paper. He tried to avoid taking it, but she insisted, saying, "Read it and tell me Hitler isn't going to try to control every detail of German life! That man is pathologically arrogant!"

Peter read and reread every Hitler response to Johst's questions, searching for what Juliette had gleaned from Hitler's words but couldn't find it. When he finished, he looked out the window, avoiding her while trying to figure out how to escape a fight. She waited until he gave up and let his helpless gaze find her blazing eyes.

He said, "I don't see where you get that from this interview," and Juliette was waiting for him.

"Read the last phrase! If you have half a brain, that should be enough!

Peter read aloud, *"For everything which does not feverishly press for work and affirm its faith in work is condemned to extinction in the sphere of National Socialism."*

She looked at him, every fibre in attack mode. "Well, don't you see it?"

"What?" Peter saw nothing more than an affirmation of Hitler's belief in the power of work and the working man and his denunciation of anyone who didn't do their share.

Juliette stood up, looked out the window at a bird trying to get a drop of water hanging on the edge of a roof tile, and vowed to hold her temper. The sun gained strength as the days lengthened, and during the warm time of day, the water on roofs melted and dripped from the edge to land on the sidewalk. She turned around to face Peter, determined to teach him how to recognize Hitler's manipulative art.

"That phrase puts the entire interview into the light. Those words condemn everyone who disagrees with Hitler's vision to obliteration. The 'work' he refers to are the plainly-stated goals of the National Socialist Party—a euphemism for Hitler's goals. There is no code for extinction—Hitler says it directly!'"

She was dismayed to see Peter's blank stare and said, "Listen to him—Hitler uses that word a lot. Think about the meaning!"

Peter reread the phrase, trying to see work as a political goal, but failed to see anything negative. He kept his head down until it would have been evident to a child he couldn't face Juliette, then looked at her and said, reluctantly, "I don't know how you get that out of what I'm reading."

Juliette took the paper from Peter, found the place she was looking for and read, *"In a certain sense, I had to 'naturalize' the term worker and subject it once again to the control of the German language and the sovereign rights and obligations of the German Volk."* She passed the paper back with her finger on the quote, saying, "Hitler has always used the term *Volk* as a term that describes the German Aryan people, excluding communists, socialists, immigrants, Jews, Romani, the mentally weak, the handicapped, and, of course, homosexuals. He also excludes the people he thinks of as the 'Bourgeoisie.' In other words, you, if you become an opera singer, and me because my father is rich, will have no place in Hitler's society and will be made 'extinct.' Precisely what do you think that word means?"

Peter read the passage twice, then said, "I read that Hitler has expanded 'worker' to mean all Germans...."

Juliette interrupted, "No, not all; he means Aryans. He excludes Jews or communists... and certainly everyone who disagrees with him—hence the words 'German language,' 'sovereign rights,' and 'obligations.'"

"You aren't German, and you are telling me what Hitler is saying? Six months of German lessons doesn't make you an expert!"

"The quality of my German has nothing to do with this! I learn languages easily, but I've been working on music since before I could talk; music is my first language. I could speak Dutch, Walloon, French and some German before I went to school, and knowing more than one language helps a person interpret what is being said in any language."

Juliette sensed her control slipping and wanted to stop what she knew might destroy the relationship she had built with Peter. She had tried unsuccessfully to deny her feelings for Peter, but she could never accept him if she had to ignore his approval of Hitler's transgressions. She made it her mission to convince Peter that Germany's Chancellor was the Devil incarnate!

"Peter, Hitler has made deception into an art form. He twists and manipulates what he says, hiding his real intentions behind a wall of ambiguous words, and to get to the truth, you must untangle whatever comes out of his mouth. When Adolph Hitler uses words like 'extinction,' 'eliminate,' and 'condemn' when referring to communists and Jews, he is systematically diminishing their value in German society. Eventually, the Aryan majority will become accustomed to Hitler's hateful rhetoric against his targets and won't complain when he actually eliminates them!"

Frustrated by Peter's puzzled look, Juliette said, "Peter, you should pay attention when Hitler says God ordained him to lead Germany! You should listen carefully—he believes what he says!"

Peter remained seated, trying to find a way to end this, but Juliette wasn't ready to stop.

"Hitler has, in one year, destroyed democracy in Germany, eliminating all political parties except the NSDAP—the National Socialist Party. He has given himself the right to deal with any person who crosses him in any way he wishes. Judges, courts, and the police have all been castrated; they have no power except through Hitler. There is no protection against those brutes who roam the streets, beating and killing people without repercussions. You are relatively safe if you are a white German worker who hates Jews, communists and homosexuals, but everyone else is in grave danger! We had proof of that a few weeks ago!"

Peter stood up, looked at Juliette with an expression that she interpreted as resignation and said, "I've had enough, Juliette... we've got to sing that duet at our lesson tomorrow, and I'm not ready. Do you want to help me work on it or not?"

"No, not tonight. Professor Garcia won't expect us to have it memorized, and I can sight-read it."

Juliette felt sick. She wanted to hold Peter but, simultaneously, felt a burning need to beat some sense into him. The conflict in her heart made staying in the same room with him impossible. She said, "I'm going to skip the madrigals tonight," and ran up the stairs to her room, where she burst into tears.

Peter was on his feet before dawn, quietly dressed himself so he wouldn't wake Agostino, and went to the living room to work on his music. The Don Pasquali duet was a simple melody for both voices, but Peter was not a good sight-reader—he was dreadful. Peter knew when a note was wrong but needed time to pound the right one into his head, and stumbling around, looking for notes in front of Professor Garcia, was not something he could envisage without breaking into a sweat.

Peter sat on the piano bench, put his music on the stand and began softly plunking his line while singing softly; he didn't want to wake anyone. He couldn't play his line of notes anywhere close to the speed marked on the score, so he left out about half of them, hoping the ones in his head were correct. Immersed in the effort, he didn't hear Juliette approach him from behind.

"You're up early," said a voice close to his ear, and his 'fight or flight' reflex kicked in. His arm swept the music from the stand, scattering the pages.

Juliette laughed, put her arms around his neck and kissed his cheek. "Oh, Peter, I'm sorry. Last night I couldn't sleep, so I got up early and came downstairs to sit in my chair and watch the sunrise. I thought you knew I was there and chose to ignore me."

"I didn't see you," said Peter, "and if I had, the last thing I would do is ignore you."

She sat on the bench beside him. "Move over… I'll play, and we'll sing the duet together."

They worked on their music until other students came, then made coffee and sat at the table to wait for the designated shopper to return from the bakery with fresh *Semmel*. Yesterday's rolls wouldn't do.

Agostino sat beside Peter and Juliette, and Michelle sat opposite them. Agostino fiddled with his coffee cup as he said, "I want to apologize for giving you two that interview. I had no idea you would make it into such a big deal!"

"It's not your fault, Agostino," said Juliette. "Peter and I can't agree on who Hitler is, and it has become too important to both of us."

Michelle leaned toward Juliette, glanced at four other students sitting at the table, and said, "You shouldn't talk about it here. Can't you leave your political ideas outside? You must both calm down; otherwise, you could get in trouble!"

The shopper returned with two paper bags full of rolls and put them in the middle of the table. Juliette took one, bit a piece off and mixed it with a drink of coffee. She chewed as she looked past Michelle.

Agostino whispered, "She agrees with you, but she's afraid. I also agree with you, but I'm not afraid, so if ever you need help, I will come."

Juliette smiled. "I promise not to make trouble. I will sing with Peter, but I won't discuss politics with him."

Agostino said, "I don't believe that, but I know better than to contradict you." He chuckled and passed the jam to Juliette.

Juliette and Peter were early for their lesson and spent the extra time working on their breath support. The main breathing exercise Professor Garcia had taught them was simple and voiceless and could be fun. It began with a rhythmic "re-pe-te-ke, re-pe-te-ke," then transitioned to "sh-sh-sh-sh, ss-ss-ss-ss, ch-ch-ch-ch, and finally, at half the speed, expelling as much breath as possible, "woosh—woosh—woosh—woosh." The point was to move the diaphragm muscles as far as possible while letting the breath flow freely, unimpeded and relaxed.

They walked back and forth, wooshing, sshing, and re-pe-te-ke-ing until their muscles cried, "no more!"

When they stopped, they looked at one another, and Juliette hoped she didn't have the same stupid look on her face he did. Peter's face was a mask of desire, and she feared hers was the same.

They practiced the duet while walking around the room, trying to avoid looking at one another as they occasionally crossed paths. The short duet required very few corrections, and they both had it memorized when they opened the studio door at ten o'clock.

"All warmed up, I presume?" Professor Garcia shook hands with them and indicated the music stand in the crook of the piano. "Do we need that?"

"No, Maestro, we don't," said Juliette, and Peter nodded.

"Then stand in the middle of the room." The professor indicated the centre of the room, laughed and said, "I suppose you would have that figured out by now, wouldn't you?"

Garcia sat down on the bench, shuffled his music, and played the introduction but stopped at the exact second they opened their mouths.

"What are you going to do, suck an egg?"

Juliette looked at Peter, and he looked at her as confused as she felt, and she said, "We are going to sing the duet from the third act of Don Pasquale, aren't we?"

Peter nodded vigorously.

"I'm not very interested in whatever you were going to sing—I was hoping you had worked on the love duet I gave you."

Juliette and Peter exchanged glances; she said, "That's the one we worked on!"

"I don't think so," said the professor. "Ernesto and Norina are in love… she's a widow, and he is a very horny guy. They wouldn't stand a metre apart and look at a piano."

Juliette could feel her face burning, but felt better when she looked at Peter. His face resembled a 'sailor-take-warning' sunrise.

The professor waved his hand, indicating they should turn. "Come on, face one another."

Juliette and Peter turned but looked at Professor Garcia or the floor.

"Closer. Touch one another; look in one another's eyes; breathe the same air!"

They met him halfway—standing as close as they could without touching. Juliette didn't trust herself to go further.

Professor Garcia *harrumphfed*, then played the introduction again, letting them sing half the first phrase before he stopped them with a flourish of his left hand.

"You will enroll in the opera school this fall, but I would appreciate it if you would start practicing your acting skills here. This is not very complicated…you are in love…you are competing for words to describe how much you love each other!" He crashed the keys on the piano. "What's the point in teaching you to make beautiful sounds if you can't act like you are in love? Name me one opera that isn't about love!"

He stood up, leaned over the piano and glared at them. "I don't care what is or is not going on between you. Even if you were married to someone else, you would have to cheat on your spouse when you sing this duet!"

He sat down, looked at the music, then at them, smiling sweetly. He said, "I want love, contact, sex… nothing else!" and began playing.

Juliette moved as close as she dared, looked at Peter, and started singing. The professor kept playing, shouting, "Closer!… Closer!" until Peter and Juliette's mouths were so close they could feel each other's breathing. The sound blended into a delicious resonance, caressing their ears and making Juliette giddy.

At first, Peter and Juliette avoided looking into one another's eyes, but then, as they sang, his gaze locked on hers. Her voice thrilled him, and he had to fight to keep the tears in his eyes from running down his cheeks. Phrases flowed and spread like oil on a pond—and when Peter forgot his entry in the middle of the duet, the shock woke him as though someone had turned on a bright light. He stopped singing, and Juliette stopped a bar later but held her eyes on his. He wanted desperately to kiss her, and he knew she felt the same, but Professor Garcia broke the spell before they could move.

"Now, that's what I call acting!" He stood up, turned and looked out the window. His eyes glistened when he turned back to look at Juliette and Peter. "You two have just proven what I have thought to be true since I sang my first note. The human voice comes from the soul through a window that can be intentionally opened. For one beautiful moment, you were in love, and I heard that love in the sound of your voices!"

The following day, Hitler spoke to the Reichstag, and his speech was broadcast into German homes through the miracle of radio. Peter planted himself in front of the government-supplied radio with five other students, including Agostino. Juliette got up from her chair beside the window and left as soon as the tubes warmed up and the radio began to hiss. Agostino tuned it, and the announcer introduced Adolph Hitler, the Chancellor of Germany.

The usual pause preceded Hitler's first words, staged, as usual, for his grand entrance.

"Today, in retrospect, we call 1933 the Year of the National Socialist Revolution, and one day an objective assessment of its incidents and events will judge it right to put this name down in the history of our Volk. What will be regarded as decisive is not the moderate form in which this revolutionary change took place externally but the inner greatness of the transformation this year has brought to the German Volk in every sector and in all facets of its life."

Peter and everyone listening except Agostino nodded their heads and stared at the source of Adolph Hitler's voice.

Hitler went on, marking his accomplishments as the product of the work of others—those who supported him and the National Socialist State. Agostino groaned when Hitler hailed the successful union of all the Protestant churches under his control by crediting to the churches themselves the 'spontaneous decision' he had forced them to make.

"…we all harbour the expectation that the merger of the Protestant Land Churches and Beliefs to form a German Protestant Reich Church might truly satisfy the yearning of those who believe that, in the muddled dividedness of Protestant life, they must fear a weakening in the power of the Protestant faith. This year the National Socialist State has clearly demonstrated its high regard for the strength of the Christian faiths, and hence it expects the same high regard on the part of the confessions for the strength of the National Socialist State!"

Agostino mumbled something about Hitler's eloquence covering his dastardly deeds.

Hitler waded for a few minutes through a stream of self-congratulations. Having eliminated his competition, Hitler then summed it up: *"It was one of the happiest hours of my life when it became clear that the entire German Volk was granting its approval to a policy which exclusively represented its interests.*

Agostino mumbled, for Peter's ears, "He got forty-four percent of the vote; I guess the other fifty-six percent don't count as *'Volk.'*"

Hitler trashed the former monarchy, then took on the economy, congratulating his National Socialists Party for each success, point by point.

"Through a judicial application of subsidies and cutting taxes on capital… We have already made our first general assault on unemployment. In a quarter of the time I asked for before the March elections, useful work has been found for a third of the unemployed. We attacked this problem from all directions, and this is what ensured our success."

Agostino whispered in Peter's ear again. "The man can talk; I'll give him that!"

Peter said, his voice full of respect and wonder, "He is the best speaker I have ever heard!"

Hitler's sycophantic monologue then congratulated the people for having the good taste and wisdom to elect him and the National Socialists to lead their country.

"Curiously, he doesn't mention that he has increased his chances by eliminating all the other parties." Agostino kept his voice low, but his baritone voice's natural resonance carried across the room.

Hitler spoke of future plans. *"Some of the measures which were introduced will not be fully appreciated until the future. This applies particularly to our promotion of the motorization of the German transport system together with the construction of the national freeway system, the Reichs-Autobahnen."*

Hitler paused for applause, and a buzz of approval went through the musicians glued to the radio.

The Führer then attacked the emigrating Jewish community as *"Degenerated Emigrants"* who *"quitted"* the scene for *"purely criminal reasons."*

He took on the communists. *"...A number of Communist ideologists believe it necessary to turn back the tide of history and, in doing so, make use of a sub-humanity (Untermenschentum) which mistakes the concept of political freedom for the idea of allowing criminal instincts free rein...."*

Agostino said, "He is setting up the Jews and communists for something they won't like!"

Peter joined the others in 'shushing' Agostino.

The speech turned to foreign affairs, blaming *"Emigrants"* for turning foreign governments against the National Socialists. Hitler attacked the Austrian government for its *"persecution"* of National Socialism by not allowing their flags or symbols in Austria.

He denied that Germany intended to attack Austria, saying, *"I must emphatically reject the Austrian Government's further allegation that the Reich would even plan, much less carry through, any such type of attack against the Austrian State."*

Hitler paused for the applause. Agostino looked at Peter, who was staring at the radio, and shook his head.

"Peter, we should go. You need to get away from this!"

Peter turned to Agostino. "I think this man is saving Germany from itself. Everyone has said he wants to take over Austria, and you just heard him say he would never do that! He is being ridiculed by people who emigrated from Germany, people who hate Germany."

Agostino said, "Those emigrants are Jews—and Communists who fled for their lives or were kicked out of Germany. They are telling their stories to the foreign press."

"I don't care what you say; I am only interested in the facts. The German people want National Socialism. They want Hitler to give them the same rights and freedoms as other nations have, and I believe he will do that for us!"

When the applause stopped, Hitler began discussing relations with France by saying the only contention point between the two nations was the 'Saarland,' and he proposed a plebiscite to solve it.

Agostino went to the window and looked into the quiet street. Nothing moved; no mechanical or biological presence made a sound. He remained there until the end of the broadcast, then sat in Juliette's chair.

The only girl listening to Hitler went to the kitchen, and three male students gathered around a small table in the living room to play a game of skat. Peter went to his chair and sat beside Agostino.

"I didn't know you hated Hitler—how can you hate him when he has done so much for Germany? Nothing in that speech isn't true; Adolph Hitler has done everything he promised he would do."

Agostino continued to look out the window. "I guess I'm looking at him from a foreigner's point of view. I come from a part of Italy that is about equally Italian and German-speaking. We spoke German at home... well, mixed with some Italian words that one shouldn't say in German. So, I understand the German language, and I am a student of politics."

"Then you will know that Hitler wants only equality among nations for Germany. Why should our army be restricted to a hundred thousand men while our neighbours build modern armies? Why should German citizens not have the same rights to unrestricted travel and freedom from harassment when they display National Socialist emblems in other countries? People who hate Hitler emigrate to other countries, and immediately the foreign press interviews them. Of course, those people hate National Socialism—that's why they emigrated—and they lie about those who remain here; they say we persecute Jews and Communists—in fact, anyone who opposes Hitler. But that isn't the responsibility of National Socialism; that's the *Sturmabteilung* and Ernst Röhm!"

"Peter, Hitler took Germany out of the League of Nations because he didn't want to play by international rules. He passed decrees against the Jews, effectively telling them to get out or risk him writing some dastardly decree removing the right to leave Germany from them forever. Since August last year, Hitler has only allowed Jews to leave if they donated a large percentage of their assets to the National Socialist Party. Despite that condition, many Jews have left, and more continue to leave if they can find a country willing to accept them as immigrants."

Peter said, raising his voice, "But if they remain, they can still run their businesses or work. Germany needs the Jews to stay; the tax when they leave is barely enough to pay for the economic damage to Germany. If I were a Jew, I wouldn't worry about Hitler's plans!"

Agostino shook his head. "Peter, where have you been for the past year? Last April, Hitler implemented a decree that non-Jewish German citizens were forbidden to buy from a Jewish merchant, effectively putting many Jewish shops out of business. Less than half of one percent of Germany is allowed to buy from a Jew. A strange thing about this decree is that it forbids a non-Jew from buying from a Jew, but the Jew is punished for the offence, not the non-Jew who broke the law!"

"You are twisting Hitler's words, just like Juliette does!"

Agostino slowly wagged his head and looked at the floor. "Peter, you should thank God you are not a Jew. Since he became chancellor, Hitler has taken almost all rights away from them, declaring them non-citizens. A Jew cannot work in the civil service or join the *Reichswehr*. The police laugh while their shops are vandalized. If they own a shop or factory, they do business with a gentile at the risk of Röhm's bullies beating them to death or dragging them off to *Dachau*." He spread his arms in frustration. "Peter, we saw Hitler's minions shoot unarmed people in the street without trial or the right to defend themselves! Freedom in Germany is conditional. Everyone who isn't Hitler's notion of German is less than human—he called them *Untermenschen* in the speech you just listened to. That is no one's notion of real freedom, not even for those who have it."

Agostino glanced at the card players, who seemed more interested in his discussion with Peter than their cards. He said, "I'm going upstairs," and left Peter looking out the window.

A heavy fist hammered four closely spaced blows on the *Sängerhaus* door. Daylight was a threat but not yet a reality, and the insistent, violent pounding could only mean an emergency.

Juliette, the designated shopper that morning, had brushed her teeth and dressed for her walk to the bakery, so she ran down two flights of stairs and opened the door just as the fist smashed against the door for the third sequence of blows. A fat, familiar-looking *Sturmabteilung* officer with brown teeth pushed her aside, and three SA soldiers crowded into the Foyer.

"We are looking for Agostino Carracci. You must direct me to his room!"

Despite her fear, Juliette said, "This is a private residence, and I must ask you to leave immediately!" She stood before the big man—David standing before Goliath without the slingshot.

"Search the house!" said the big man, swiping Juliette aside with a massive hand.

The Brownshirt soldiers carried rifles—the fat man had a Luger on his belt. He drew it, started up the stairs, then turned and shouted, *"Hans, komm mit!"* A young man with a rifle joined him, and the fat man said, *"Dummkopf, mach das Gewehr fertig!"*

Peter woke with the first blow on the front door; Agostino was already on his feet, and seconds later was in his pants with the braces flipped over his shoulders. He quickly strapped his little dagger's sheath on his forearm before putting on his shirt, and, as the former *Alpine* soldier slipped the stiletto up his sleeve, he returned Peter's stare, saying, "Just in case," and Peter nodded.

Peter was pulling on his pants when the bedroom door shook under the assault of a large fist.

"Wir suchen Agostino Carracci!" The angry shout didn't sound like the shouter intended anything good for Agostino.

Agostino let him hit the door again, checked his left sleeve and opened it. He said, "That would be me," and smiled as though he were the one with all the aces.

The fat man with the yellow teeth said, "I'm arresting you for treason against Germany."

Agostino grinned pleasantly and said, "You are mistaken… Treason can only be done by a German citizen. I am an Italian citizen."

The big man laughed and swung his fist at Agostino's head, but when his fist got there, Agostino's head was thirty centimetres to the right.

"Shoot him!" said the fat man. "He is resisting arrest."

The boy lifted his rifle, and Agostino's arm straightened like a snake snatching a mouse. The *Alpine* soldier's right hand pulled the gun into the room, and his left pushed the young man onto the floor, landing him on his butt. He flipped the gun, worked the bolt with an expertise born of a thousand hours of practice, and the shell flew out of the chamber. With a flip of his wrist, the magazine landed on the bed.

Peter's jaw was wide open when Agostino passed the empty rifle to the dumbfounded SA officer, patted his shoulder, and said, "I surrender. We will let a judge decide whether or not I committed treason."

He stepped around the soldiers and smiled at a group of half a dozen students dressed in their nightshirts. He said, "Excuse me," passed them, and the soldiers followed him down the stairs.

Juliette met Agostino's entourage at the bottom, stepped aside to let them pass, then stopped Peter, who trailed them dressed only in his pants.

"What's going on?" The shock on Peter's face told Juliette that he probably wouldn't know any more than she did.

"They are arresting Agostino for treason."

"Treason? But… he's Italian!"

Agostino waved to Peter and Juliette from the step.

"Don't worry about me. Tell Michelle I will see her when the war is over."

Juliette started to ask, "What war?" but decided to keep her mouth shut.

Two Police officers visited the *Sängerhaus* two days after Agostino's disappearance. They questioned everyone who had been in the living room the night before the SA soldiers had taken him away, and those who had been there when Agostino had willingly gone with them.

The following Saturday, the *Münchner Beobachter* reported on the back page that four SA officers had been attacked and murdered by what was suspected to be a gang of ten or more Communist thugs. Their vehicle and bodies were found in the *Höhenkirchener Forst*. The police established the cause of death in the case of two of the four SA members to be stab wounds and gunshot wounds for the others. The report assumed the men had been lured into an ambush.

And then, on Sunday, the day after the newspaper reported the SA officers' deaths, Michelle said goodbye to Juliette and Peter while Juliette tried in vain to control her tears. As she cried and hugged her friend, Juliette admired the strength with which Michelle took her lover's disappearance—she even seemed cheerful as she boarded a train heading for Vienna.

As Michelle waved from the train window, Juliette said to Peter, "She needs to go home to grieve; her family is very important to her." She waved, then wiped her tears with a lace handkerchief.

Peter smiled, not in the least sad. "Michelle's home is in the opposite direction. And I wouldn't write Agostino off just yet."

CHAPTER EIGHT

One-Way Loyalty is a Dead-End Street

An enemy can never betray you...a betrayal, by definition, involves a friend

PETER AND JULIETTE HAD THEIR OWN ROOMS for the rest of the semester, and immediately Juliette declared hers off-limits to Peter and made it clear she would refuse any invitations to come to his. However, they still met in the living room to work on music and sometimes to sit in the bay window and talk. Juliette would not allow the conversation to turn to politics, and when Peter asked her to go to the *Hofbräuhaus* to hear Hitler speak, she refused to answer.

On Sunday, the twenty-fifth of February and the day after Peter heard Hitler's speech, they were sitting in the window watching snow whirl and twirl down the street when Peter made the colossal mistake of trying to share his excitement.

"I was in the *Festsaal* at the *Hofbräuhaus* last night. I had never seen it before and..."

"I have no desire to see or hear you describe anyplace your insane ego-centric devil has ever been, least of all where he started."

Peter watched waves of synchronized snowflakes work their way down the street, lie on the paving stones for a moment, then spin away in a miniature whirlwind. He wanted to share his excitement with Juliette, to tell her Hitler had rejected violence, instead declaring his intention to reaffirm his dedication to the people's will. He would call for a referendum to get their approval for what he had done and intended to do in the future. Not once had Hitler said "I...," only "we...." He had said "Volk," meaning 'all the people,' at least a dozen times in ten minutes.

"If you had heard him..."

"No! I don't want to hear anything he has to say!" She threw the blanket off her legs and stood up. Peter touched her arm and said, "I'm sorry… please stay."

Plainly avoiding looking at him, Juliette curled up in her chair and wrapped the blanket around her. Neither spoke for several long minutes.

Juliette looked around the room; there was no one there but them. She looked out the window and asked, "Do you really think they took Agostino to the forest to kill him?"

"Yes, probably… There are rumours that Röhm's butchers kill people in that particular spot."

"And you don't think Röhm is doing Hitler's bidding when he commits murder? You don't hold Hitler responsible for those people who were shot under our window? You think Hitler didn't sanction Agostino's death by allowing the SA to run through the city's streets like rabid dogs?"

Peter knew better than to answer. He stared at the snow but didn't see it.

Juliette forged on. "You know that someone in this house heard Agostino maligning Hitler and reported him, don't you? And you know that's why they killed him!"

Peter shook his head. "I've told you… They didn't kill him, or at least one of those soldiers would still be alive."

Juliette looked into Peter's eyes when he turned to face her. "So, where is he? And how did he kill four armed soldiers?"

"I told you I watched him put the stiletto in his sleeve, and two of those men died of stiletto wounds. I watched him disarm one of those soldiers so quickly I couldn't believe it. And you saw what he did when those SA caught us in the gardens." Peter waited, but Juliette didn't say anything. She seemed lost in thought. Finally, she said, looking for a ray of hope, "But how could he do it? He's an opera singer, not a killer!"

"The Italian army taught Agostino how to kill with a knife…and not just any knife…a stiletto. No regular army teaches their everyday soldiers to fight with anything but a rifle and a bayonet."

Juliette smiled. "So, Agostino is not an opera singer." She wanted to hug Peter but settled for saying, "Peter, you are on Agostino's side—you hope he killed Hitler's minions." She turned her head to watch the swirling snow. "You make me feel there is still hope for both Agostino and you."

Juliette tried but could not get past Peter's loyalty to Hitler, and the magic they had found with the *Don Pasquale* duet was gone when they performed it at an *Übungsabend* to thunderous applause. Professor Garcia rarely attended his students' concerts but made an exception when he sat in the last row. Juliette correctly interpreted his immediate exit when the clapping and cheering began as disgust with what he saw and dreaded facing him at their lesson the following day.

Peter and Juliette entered the studio at ten, passing one of the Professor's international students on his way out. As usual, Professor Garcia shook their hands and then sat at the piano. He said, "If you expect a comment on yesterday's performance, I will only tell you that what I heard was not a love duet—it was a vocal exercise—well done, but not opera, and it certainly had nothing to do with love. Somehow, you lost everything you had achieved in the studio." As he spoke, he ran his fingers up and down the keyboard with his foot on the soft pedal.

"No matter what is going on between you, it illustrates your immaturity as performers—and that's something we must work on."

He paused, looking from one to the other. They both knew he had more to say. He put his hands on the edge of the piano and leaned toward them. "I took the liberty of ordering some music for you at the library. You can pick it up after the lesson."

He paused again, began massaging the keys and said, "I don't want you to sing for a few weeks, not even madrigals with your friends. I must work on individual muscles, which will not be pleasant for either of you." He put his hands on his lap and looked from Juliette to Peter.

"The search for power and resonance is slow and painful, but the search for emotion doubles the pain and is nearly impossible to sustain over time. You must both learn to fake it—what we call acting—no matter what else is happening in your life."

Juliette and Peter suffered through a gamut of vocal gymnastics and scales for an hour, leaving the studio with their voices shredded. As he led them to the door, Professor Garcia said, "It will take a few days to recover from that workout, so stay away until Monday. Do not talk more than necessary." He put one hand on each of their shoulders. "We are entering the hard work phase, but only for a few weeks—then we will see what you can do with roses in Tirol. You might even learn to sing a love duet without actually loving one another."

When they arrived, the library had copies of Carl Zeller's *Vogelhändler* reserved for them.

Juliette said, "I know this operetta—it's fluff. What can we learn by singing this trash?"

"You know it?" asked Peter. "I've never heard of the opera or the composer."

Juliette laughed with a touch of sarcasm. "*Operetta,* and I'm not surprised you've never heard it. I've heard it but never sung it, and I don't want to sing it now. Professor Garcia will have to find something else."

Three days later, Juliette dropped her copy of the 'Rose' duet on the piano and said, "Professor, I came here to learn to sing opera, not popular music. I don't want to sing this."

Professor Garcia grinned like a Cheshire cat and said, "It doesn't matter what you think or want; I have a good reason for giving you that music. You are a coloratura soprano and will eventually sing this style of music, or you won't have a job in a German opera house. Neither of you is ready for Grand Opera, and this is not complicated or challenging vocally, but it does require you to act in a role that you seem reluctant to play. Modify the choir part for soloists, and in a week, I expect the piece to be memorized."

"But…"

"I agreed that you could be my student under the condition that you sing what I tell you to sing. You and Peter made a glorious mess of the *Don Pasquale* duet, and we must correct your attitude before you sing the opera repertoire you say you want to perform. It is much easier to work around bad habits than to cure them, but if you take a bite from the sour apple instead of avoiding it, the cure is for life."

He softened his voice. "Juliette, I promise you will sing operetta in a *Repertoire* theatre with partners who disgust you, and you will have a short career if you don't learn to act and sing the role the audience came to see and hear. The small theatres where you will begin cannot afford to stage only expensive Grand Opera. They need operettas to fill the theatre and pay the bills. If you look at them carefully, those money-makers are written for the house sopranos, tenors, and basses they have in the ensemble. In a pinch, even a good choir singer can replace the principles."

Juliette looked at the score. She thought about the voices required to sing *Vogelhändler* and realized Garcia was right.

"I hadn't thought about that, I guess."

"Everything is about money, isn't it? Verdi, Wagner and Zeller wrote for money, not some grand holy plan ordained by God. You will sing Zeller, Lehar and Strauss because it's your job, and you will learn to see and hear their genius."

It was two months, well into May and beautiful spring weather when the duet was ready for an *Übungsabend*. Juliette had made peace with Peter's obsession with Hitler, and Peter accepted that as long as he supported the Führer, Juliette would not get closer than friend and colleague.

Juliette bought a small bouquet of red roses and wore a *Dirndl*. Peter borrowed *Lederhosen* from his father's youth, and, to the audience's delight, they nuzzled and cuddled their way through the scene. Juliette forgot about Hitler, Röhm and the National Socialists, and their voices floated through the scene as they looked into one another's eyes. Professor Garcia sat in the back row and stayed to clap with the audience, then joined the students who gathered around and jealously waited while he congratulated them.

At night, the streets of Munich became ever more unbearably violent. Every Saturday, the *Münchner Beobachter* reported beatings and murders, mostly of Communists and Democratic Socialists, but occasionally Jews, all committed by the *Sturmabteilung*.

Despite the approaching darkness, Juliette and Peter decided to go to the *Spatenhaus* restaurant to celebrate, Juliette still in her *Dirndl* and Peter in his *Lederhosen*. The expensive restaurant was across from the opera house, and Juliette's father was buying *in absentia*.

They walked down *Residenzstrasse*, holding hands for the first time since they had begun their musical journey in the *Hochschule*. It happened naturally, instinctively, while they were talking and walking, without asking whether they should or could. Twice on the nine-minute journey, they self-consciously let go, but a minute later, their hands found one another. After the second time, Juliette pulled Peter's hand to her mouth and kissed it, and Peter sealed the deal by doing the same.

Residenzstrasse was lined on both sides with shops under three storeys of apartments. The mostly Jewish shop owners lived upstairs and rented at least one floor to carefully chosen tenants, and Juliette and Peter passed several shops with anti-Jewish insults painted on the shop windows. Juliette and Peter said nothing when they passed the first shop with *SauJude* painted on its windows, but Peter stopped and stared at the second one. He said, "This is Röhm's doing," went to the window and tried to wipe the words off with his sleeve.

He said, disgusted, "It's painted... the owner will have to buy new windows."

Further down the street, their way was blocked by cars and people watching something. As they approached, the sounds of shouting became clear—someone was begging to be forgiven, and as they reached the scene, four SA soldiers hit and kicked an old man while a woman tried to stop them. The beating continued even when the old man stopped protecting himself. A dozen people gathered around the scene stood in silence, their heads lowered.

The woman threw herself over the old man, sacrificing her body. The crowd looked away, murmuring sympathy for the couple, but afraid to do more.

Peter shouted, "Stop, you'll kill them!" and started toward a Brownshirt who was hitting the woman. A soldier standing beside the one doing the beating laughed, then shouted as he pointed his rifle at Peter, *"Bist du ein Saujude? Willst du 'was davon?"* Juliette shouted, "Stop beating them! Leave them alone!" A few voices in the growing crowd said, "That's enough... stop beating those people!"

A voice shouted, "They're Jews… beat them until they go to Palestine!" Another pushed him, saying, *"Halt's Maul!"* The first voice retaliated, but another threatened him, then another, until he shut up.

The only one with a pistol on his belt, the soldier who seemed to be in charge looked at the crowd, judging where the power lay. He finally said, "We'll take them with us; put them in the *Lastwagen."*

The crowd waited until the Jews were in the back of the lorry and it had driven away before they dispersed, most speaking openly about SA brutality, but a few were cursing filthy Jews and Communists.

Juliette and Peter walked the final two minutes in silence. Just before they reached the restaurant, Juliette stopped Peter, took his hand and said, "You don't hate Jews."

"Of course not—Jews aren't different from us."

Juliette pushed Peter's hair back. "And you are brave. You were the only one willing to fight for those people. If you hadn't, those brutes might have killed them!"

Dinner was the best meal Peter had ever eaten. Afterward, on the walk home, he forgot the restaurant and the food when Juliette pulled his head down so she could kiss him… not the pecks she had given him until now, but a passionate embrace with pressure, arms around his neck, lips pressed, their breath combined, and the street spinning. She finally let him go, breathless, her eyes shining.

The school term ended on Friday, the twenty-ninth of June, and the students went home, except for Juliette and Peter, who decided to spend the weekend together before parting for the summer. Juliette called her parents to say she wouldn't be home until Monday.

When darkness fell on Saturday, Juliette and Peter were at the piano working on music. Professor Garcia had given each a piece of opera to learn over the summer, and Juliette spent the afternoon helping Peter with his aria from *Der Freischütz* by Carl Maria von Weber. The deceptively melodic but challenging music was filled with mood-swinging, sometimes dark, black-magic themes.

A year of work had improved Peter's musical skills, and he sang Max's first wretched pleas for an explanation of his bad luck without a mistake. Peter vented Max's despair, then switched mood to recall the days when, as a hunter, he had stalked through the forests, confident that he would come home with meat for Agatha's table.

Peter was halfway through the lilting melody when shots echoed in the street. Juliette screamed, whacked the piano keys, and the telephone rang.

As the telephone clanged its urgent call to answer it, Peter said, "Those were rifle shots!" and ran to the light switch. He twisted it, instantly thrusting the room into semi-darkness. Scattered light from the street vaguely defined shadows that marked the furniture's location.

Juliette ran toward the telephone—another shot—Peter caught her, pushed her down to her knees.

"Stay down!" He forced her to bend over. "Don't get up until I tell you!"

Peter crouched low, ran to the telephone, lifted the receiver and said, *"Sängerhaus; hier spricht Peter Schweitzer."*

"Peter… Gott sei dank! Hier ist Marcel. Wie geht's in München?"

"Not so well—someone is shooting in the street. Juliette and I are the only ones in the house. Everyone else has gone home."

"Yes, I know…Juliette called her parents and told them you were staying. That's why I'm calling."

Peter felt a load come off his shoulders. "What should we do?"

"An SS car will pick you and Juliette up in a few minutes when the shooting stops. He will honk twice long, a pause, then one short. Don't turn on the lights or go outside into the street until you hear the horn!"

"Where will it take us?"

"To the *Hauptbahnhof,* where you will put Juliette on the train to Frankfurt, and I will meet her at the *Treffpunkt* in the station. You must go home to Augsburg and stay there!"

"What's happening?"

"Your friend Hitler has had enough of Röhm and the *Sturmabteilung.* The SS is purging the SA and their boss, and you and Juliette must get out of there; Munich will be messy for a few days."

There was a moment of silence, and then Marcel said, "Don't go outside until the car signals you! Two long honks, a pause, then one short."

The receiver clicked; the line went dead.

Peter walked to Juliette, hunched over. She was on her knees, shaking, and he took her hand.

"That was Marcel. An SS car will pick us up when it's safe and drive us to the *Hauptbahnhof.* I will put you on a train to Frankfurt, and Marcel will meet you at the *Treffpunkt* there."

Juliette said, "Okay, but you should come with me to Belgium. Germany isn't safe."

Juliette thought Peter was smiling but couldn't see his face clearly enough to be sure. He said, "There is nothing I would like more, but my father needs me to work in the M.A.N. shop with him, and I need the money."

Staying below the sill, Peter led Juliette to the window, thinking he would watch for the car. He raised his head until he could see uniformed men running on the street. As he watched, a rifle shot brought a man in a brown uniform down; another shot rang out, but no one fell. The wounded soldier crawled to the sidewalk while a dozen men dressed in black and carrying rifles ran past him. He propped himself against a wall in a sitting position and drew a pistol out of his belt. He sat motionless and, a few seconds later, let a black-uniformed SS soldier with a rifle pass him, then shot him in the back. A second SS soldier shot the wounded SA soldier with a machine pistol. A dozen *Sturmabteilung* soldiers appeared, chasing the black uniforms down the street. A *Lastwagen* stopped, and ten Brownshirts with rifles poured out the back and ran to the doors of nearby houses.

Peter asked Juliette, "Is the door locked and bolted?" She shrugged, and Peter thought it must be locked but couldn't remember whether he had slid the heavy bolt into its socket. Bent over, he scurried across the room, stood up in the hallway and moved quickly to the stairs. Running down them as swiftly and quietly as he could, Peter found the door locked but not bolted. He slid the bolt into its place and was on the third step when someone banged on the door with what Peter guessed was a rifle butt.

The man shouted, "Everyone out of the house, or I will break down the door and kill whoever is inside!"

Peter went to stand inside the door and waited while the soldier smashed his gun against five centimetres of the strongest wood that grows. The gun's butt was no match for black oak, and after a few minutes of hammering, the soldier left to search for easier prey.

As the shooting and shouting faded, Peter went upstairs to the kitchen and chose the longest knife he could find for himself and a smaller one for Juliette. As he laid hers on the low table in front of her, he looked into her frightened eyes and said, "Don't worry, they can't get through that door, and there are bars on the downstairs windows."

Peter sat at the bay window where he could see the front door, and Juliette sat on the sofa, shivering.

Tepid daylight lit the room when a horn woke Peter. Everything ached from sleeping in Juliette's chair. Peter looked down and was excited to see two gray Mercedes cars parked next to the curb.

Juliette propped herself to a sitting position on the sofa, swung her legs around and stood up.

Peter wasn't sure he had heard the correct signal, but Juliette said, "That's the signal. Grab your suitcase!"

A black-uniformed man standing beside the front Mercedes waved to Peter, and the horn repeated the signal.

Three SS-uniformed soldiers exited the second gray Mercedes, all holding *Schnellfeuer* machine pistols.

Juliette looked at the cars, then at Peter. "Are you certain they will take us to the *Bahnhof* and not to jail?"

"Yes, Marcel said they will drop us at the train station."

Juliette said, "I'll get dressed."

Peter laughed. "Dressed? You are dressed!"

Juliette said as she stopped at the bottom of the stairs, "Don't be silly. Take those suitcases to the car; the others are in my room. I'll be ready in five minutes!"

Peter carried the suitcases down the stairs, opened the door, and the SS officer standing on the sidewalk beside the front car rushed to take them from him and put them in the trunk.

"Juliette will be here in a few minutes." Peter looked at the open door and turned to the officer.

"Is it over now? Is the shooting over?"

The officer shook his head. "No, it has only begun. Hitler is taking over the *Sturmabteilung,* and Röhm's days as Minister of Defence are numbered. The SS is taking over the cities from his thugs. Last night, the SA went mad, roaming the streets all over Germany looking for Communists, Socialists and Jews. The German people are tired of them. Hitler has to do something, and last night was the trigger. Everyone wants discipline and *Ordnung,* not bullies beating people on the streets!"

Peter said, "That was what we saw last night, and I thought Hitler would stop them, but the SA seemed to be winning."

"Their winning is over… we have them on the run, but it is still dangerous to be on the street."

Juliette came out of the *Sängerhaus* carrying a handbag and gloves, wearing an expensive hat, and dressed in a classy dress, a la Marlene Dietrich. Peter had never seen the outfit before—following her father's instructions, Juliette had worn peasants' clothes, and Peter had forgotten how jaw-droppingly beautiful she was.

She pointed at the door. "There are two more suitcases and a trunk in my room."

Peter and two of the SS soldiers fetched the luggage, and it filled both cars' trunks.

The SS soldiers got into the second car, and the officer who had talked to Peter indicated he and Juliette should sit in the back seat of the lead Mercedes, then slid into the front passenger seat. Juliette didn't miss the irony that SS soldiers made her feel safe for the first time since Marcel had left her in Munich.

The SS cars waited outside the station until Peter and the officer watched Juliette board the train for Frankfurt, where she would meet Marcel and change trains for the Brussels leg. They then drove Peter to Augsburg, leaving him at his parents' house. The trip took twice as long as usual due to slow-moving military convoys.

The officer watched Peter climb the stone steps and try to open the locked Schweitzer door, something his parents typically did only at night. Peter dropped the knocker twice on the brass plate, and a moment later, his mother opened the door and threw her arms around him before he could step into the house.

"We've been trying to find out what's happening. We were so worried when we couldn't reach you!"

She let him go, he stepped over the threshold, and Peter's father went outside, waved at the SS cars and shouted, *"Danke Schön"* as they drove away. He followed his son into the house, and Elizabeth locked the door behind them.

Elizabeth said, "The radio warns everyone to stay inside with their doors locked until the police say it's safe. We are supposed to stay away from the windows because SA soldiers are running through the streets, beating and killing innocent people!"

Peter's father said, "We won't need to lock the door when Hitler's SS is finished putting Röhm's gang of murderers in its place!"

His mother said, "Thank God for Adolph Hitler… can you imagine Germany if someone like that animal Ernst Röhm were chancellor? You wouldn't have a job… I wouldn't dare go to the market… How would we live?"

Marcel and Juliette sat facing one another in the first-class compartment he had booked from Frankfurt to Brussels. Juliette had only gotten a "Not now" from him as he met her at the *Treffpunk*, then checked her baggage to Brussels. As the train left the Frankfurt station, he turned away from the window and said, "It's not safe to talk in public about what's happening in Germany right now, but it's safe to ask your questions here."

Juliette's anxiety had increased as she sat in a crowded compartment on the train from Munich to Frankfurt. She had avoided talking to anyone, and Marcel would now bear the brunt of her apprehension.

"What's going on, Marcel? Last night we heard shots and watched people shooting and running in the streets. It was hard to know who was the hunter and who was running for their life!"

"Adolph Hitler has ordered the SS to take over the streets in every city in Germany." Marcel quickly added, "I know that because your father told me, and his sources are reliable."

"But why?" asked Juliette. "Isn't Röhm Hitler's best friend?"

"A man like Hitler has no real friends, only useful people who stay close because they want to bask in his power and popularity. Later, they stay because they are afraid to leave. That's why Röhm was at Hitler's side in 1923 when the putsch failed and was arrested along with Hitler. He received a fifteen-month sentence, which was suspended. Hitler got five years and served nine months in a comfortable cell."

"That doesn't seem like much for treason."

"Hitler was already popular in southern Germany, and a more lengthy prison term might have made more trouble than it was worth."

"So, how does society stop a man like Hitler?"

"Society can't stop him now; he has the power of the people behind him. During his nine months in prison, Hitler wrote the first volume of *Mein Kampf,* a crude autobiographical diatribe that twists and spins small truths into erroneous assumptions about the inferiority of other races. His ramblings say he would eliminate Slavs, Jews, communists, Romani, and all other non-Aryan races from a superior German society. Everyone assumes that he means he would kick them out of the country, but perhaps he is signalling more than that."

Juliette shivered, although it was warm in the compartment, and interrupted Marcel.

"I can't believe he means he will do what you are insinuating, but nevertheless, he frightens me."

After a short pause, Marcel went on, "Hitler also advocates the levelling of a pure Aryan German society—that everyone, workers and elite, would be equal. A racially pure working man reads Hitler's book as a manifesto promising to raise him to the elite level."

"But, what about Röhm? Doesn't he have the same view of race superiority?"

"Yes, and no. Röhm is also a social leveller, but in another context. He believes German society can achieve economic equality by taking money from the rich and giving to the poor, crushing monopolies, heavily taxing corporations and giving the money to the workers. He supports strong unions and says he will prosecute strike-breakers."

"Sounds alright to me!" said Juliette.

"It didn't work in Russia. The Bolsheviks removed all incentives from the workplace, and the economy collapsed."

"The Russian people revolted against a czar and got a dictatorship under another corrupt leader—far from equality. The Russian economy collapsed for many reasons, none of which have anything to do with incentivizing workers. A level society can be achieved without destroying the economy, but a dictator can't do it. In a level society, the people choose a leader from among themselves, and they have a guaranteed opportunity to replace that leader at regular intervals. Give the people a chance, and they will build the kind of society they want."

Marcel laughed. "What have I done? I see you've taken my advice to pay attention to politics, and now... so much wisdom from a sixteen-year-old!"

Juliette was pleased Marcel had chosen to compliment her and decided to return to the topic of Hitler.

"I'm seventeen. You forgot my birthday." Juliette chuckled. "So...tell me what has happened that Hitler decided to go after his best friend?"

"Seventeen...I guess that explains it. I apologize for missing your birthday." Marcel grinned, and something dangerous stirred in Juliette.

"Best friend might be a stretch, but certainly Röhm was and still is, enamoured by Hitler."

A question jumped into Juliette's mind, but Marcel put his hand up in a stop sign.

"After Hitler's release from prison, Röhm joined him to continue the National Socialist revolution. However, he was dismayed when his hero seemed determined to take the movement forward without breaking the law. Hitler drew his power from the people, using propaganda based on the German capitulation that ended the Great War and, later, on the disastrous Versailles Treaty. Hitler believed that breaking the law would turn the people against him, deflecting their attention from where he wanted it."

Juliette jumped in, "But why do you make him sound reasonable?"

"If you listen to his speeches, he is reasonable." Marcel waved off Juliette's frustration and went on.

"Finally, in 1926, Hitler broke with his friend when Röhm insisted they use the violent rabble in the SA Brownshirts to take over the country. Hitler would not sanction Röhm's armed rebellion, so, in 1928, rather than fight his friend, Röhm went to Bolivia to work as an advisor to their armed forces."

Juliette said, "Hitler didn't want to break the law? That doesn't sound right!"

"You've been reading propaganda… Adolph Hitler has never broken a German law since the putsch, at least none that can be proven. He has always avoided giving a direct order, leaving that to others. He doesn't write anything down and regrets having written his books. Already, his words are damning him."

"Okay, if Röhm went to Bolivia, what's he doing here?"

"Four years ago, after he had the SA under his control, Hitler called Röhm to lead them again, this time as Chief of Staff, believing he could control his friend. But just in case he couldn't, Hitler kept his position as *Oberster SA Führer*, the supreme commander of the *Sturmabteilung*, making him Röhm's direct boss."

Marcel, who had been looking out the window as he spoke, turned to Juliette.

"Hitler's precautions, in retrospect, seem prophetic. Although still loyal and subordinate to him, Röhm surreptitiously took the *Sturmabteilung* in another direction, and it was during this time that Röhm's 'Second Revolution' idea reared its head with the motto, 'Down with capitalism, up with Socialism… take from the rich and give to the poor!' Röhm's SA attacked anyone who opposed the new revolution—strike-breakers, capitalist corporations, communists, Social Democrats, and a new target—Jews. But unfortunately for him, Röhm persecuted the financial backers of Hitler's vision of National Socialism."

Juliette thought she had learned who Hitler was in school and everything she had read and heard since, but this was new. Marcel was silent while she looked out the window at newly planted fields rushing past, thinking about what it meant. She said, "I've never read *Mein Kampf.* I suppose Hitler's National Socialist revolution was based on the book?"

Marcel shook his head. "No, National Socialism doesn't look like the book at all. Present-day Hitler doesn't advocate a sudden or violent revolution; he believes the ideal racially pure society, as he sees it, should be built from the ground up, beginning with the youth. In fact, Hitler said recently that *Mein Kampf* is "...meaningless fantasies from behind bars." He said that now that he is chancellor, he regrets writing it."

Juliette tried to reconcile the Hitler she had framed in her mind with the man Marcel described, but the result was confusion.

"You are telling me I should understand how Peter feels about Hitler."

"Juliette, I am not telling you anything. If you look at Hitler's actions, you will see a man who thinks he is a god. His followers believe God appointed Hitler to save Germany, and, from their point of view, they have the results to prove it. Hitler has delivered for them, and this business with Röhm will only get the *Führer* more rabid followers. He will gain power when he destroys his friend."

A week later, Veronique and Juliette were sitting on the long verandah of the house at 6 Saturn Drive in Brussels when Jacques reported that Röhm was dead, shot under a direct order from Hitler. He said the SA body count included five *Sturmabteilung* generals, a colonel, and dozens of officers who paid the ultimate price for crossing Hitler.

"The man who now demands to be called *Der Führer* took the opportunity to clean up all the deadwood opposing him, and my sources put it at well over a thousand casualties. My information is that Röhm was planning a coup against Hitler. The papers confirm that he was homosexual and was hosting an orgy when Hitler personally arrested him, but I would take that with a generous dose of salt."

Juliette said, "The devil let the SA leadership dig their graves, then pushed them into it." She raised her glass, "A toast to the most devious, narcissistic weasel who has ever lived!" She shrugged her shoulders. "So, he has taken over the *Sturmabteilung;* what now?"

"We think he will put the SA under Himmler's control and expand the *Geheime Staatspolizei,* the *Gestapo,* outside Prussia, where Hermann Göring initially set it up. In April, despite Göring's protests, Hitler put the Gestapo under Himmler's control. This politically controlled and motivated secret police force is now the agency Himmler will use to monitor the German people. They will collect information from secret sources cultivated from within the ranks of the people and will use it as they see fit. It has the potential, along with the Ministry of Propaganda under Goebbels, to be the most powerful force in Germany. As commander of the Gestapo and with his friend Heydrich controlling the SS, Heinrich Himmler is now the most powerful man in the country."

Veronique sipped her tea, then said, "Except Hitler, of course."

Jacques said, "Perhaps. Hitler, like most politicians, thinks he is in control. Still, in every practical sense, Joseph Goebbels, as head of the *Propagandaministerium,* Heinrich Himmler, as head of the gestapo, and Reinhard Heydrich as leader of the *SS* under Himmler, have the real power. Hitler is a lion-tamer. He must feed and care for them because a hungry lion is a dangerous and unpredictable animal."

Juliette suddenly thought of Peter and her criticism of his admiration of Hitler. Peter's father owed his job to the *Führer*, and the family felt indebted to the man who had saved Germany's economy from a complete and permanent collapse.

Juliette caught herself justifying Hitler's usurping of power. He had become a dictator in one short year, and he had done it legally. Eighteen months later, Hitler had turned the economy around; workers were united with him because they had jobs and could feed their families. Juliette didn't doubt the streets were safe—she and Peter could walk to the theatre without worrying about the SA arresting or beating them. Hitler had removed her last arguments against him by executing those responsible for the chaos, even his close friend, Ernst Röhm.

CHAPTER NINE

Brünnhilde

Using power without subtlety is nothing but brute force; applying power with it is an art form

JULIETTE CURLED UP IN HER CHAIR, positioned as usual to watch the front door of the *Sängerhaus*. Marcel had delivered her to Munich on the earliest train possible, intending to return to Brussels without staying overnight. Waiting for Peter, Juliette had been watching students return to the residence for hours, and the streetlights were on when Peter approached, put his suitcase down and dug his key out of his pocket. As he fumbled with the lock, she fought the urge to run downstairs and fling her arms around his neck. She was sure he intentionally hadn't looked up to see her in the window because he wasn't sure how she would react to him now.

She sipped her tea, a brew that the label, *Nerventee*, insinuated would quiet her nerves. It tasted like boiled hay; no one would drink it except for the effect it was advertised to give. She was quite confident it wasn't working as she waited for Peter to come to the living room. Peter hesitated at the first-floor entrance to the community rooms, then climbed the two flights of stairs to his room as Juliette's excitement crashed and burned.

Fifty metres before he reached the *Sängerhaus,* Peter saw light in the bay window and deliberately avoided looking up, afraid Juliette would be there, curled up like a cat in her favourite chair. Peter was terrified she hated him and was trying to think of a way to reject him. Forbidding his head to look up, Peter attempted to open the door with one hand and dropped his keys. He put his suitcase on the step, tried again with both hands, and, when he succeeded, leaned over to pick up his bag.

The wind blew the door shut; Peter caught it before the latch clicked, swung it open, and entered the foyer. He looked across the entrance and up the stairs, trying to decide what to do, postponed the decision until he reached the first landing, then took the steps one at a time, counting them as he went.

Peter hesitated at the landing, which led to the kitchen, dining and living rooms, lost his nerve and went up the stairs. When he reached his room, the door was open and a short, sturdy man, probably still a teenager, jumped up from the chair he had been sitting on. Peter presumed the unopened suitcase in the middle of the space between the beds belonged to the interloper.

"I'm Felix von Finckenstein." He stretched out his arm as he approached Peter, forcing him to put his suitcase on the floor. "Please call me Felix." He had used the familiar 'Du' pronoun. Peter lifted his hand, and Felix grabbed it as though he were drowning.

"I assume since you are here that we are roommates?" asked Peter, also using the familiar pronoun.

"Jawohl," said Felix, in a tone that usually includes a salute. "I have left the choice of beds to you."

"Thank you, Felix; I've been sleeping on the bed next to the wall."

Felix grabbed his expensive leather suitcase, adorned with a brass plate displaying an impressive coat of arms, flung it on the bed next to the drafty window, and undid the straps with a dexterity born of familiarity and routine. He said, "The rest of my luggage is at the *Hauptbahnhof*... I will take a taxi to get it tomorrow."

Peter laid his well-travelled canvas suitcase on his bed, turned to Felix and said, "I hope we can get acquainted later. Right now, I want to meet a friend downstairs."

"I haven't eaten yet... perhaps you can show me where they keep the food."

Peter smiled. "They feed us once a day; otherwise, there is bread and cheese and sometimes Wurst in the kitchen *Schrank*, but you must clean up when you are done. Most students eat out in the evenings."

Peter decided to leave his unpacking until after he talked to Juliette, hoping Felix would go somewhere else to eat. But, alas, Felix followed him down the stairs and headed straight for the kitchen cupboards.

Juliette forced herself to remain curled in her chair until Peter crossed the room, then stood up and smoothed her skirt as he took the last steps. She smothered a laugh when he tripped on the carpet, and although he caught himself in time, the look on his face betrayed the damage to his ego.

Juliette met him with open arms. She said, "I'm so glad to see you, Peter," with all the sincerity she could muster. She squeezed him as tightly as she could, turned her face up and found his lips.

Bracing his feet so he wouldn't fall, drunk with relief and a rising passion, Peter kissed Juliette as tenderly as he could, but when he began to pull away, she put her hand behind his head and pressed herself hard against him.

They lingered, turning the kiss into much more, ignoring the other students in the room who began hurling lewd comments at them.

When they came up for air, Juliette guided an unsteady Peter to his chair—she had dragged it next to hers, and both faced the window. She had usurped the small table from under the telephone and covered it with two plates, each with two pieces of *Butterbrot* and four slices of cheese. Two bottles of *Pils* filled the space between them. Peter sat down, put one of the plates on his knee and slapped a piece of cheese on a slice of thickly buttered *Vollkornbrot* while Juliette popped the tops on the beers.

"Why didn't you write?" asked Juliette while she prepared her black bread and cheese. I wrote to you, but you didn't answer."

Peter stopped chewing and swallowed a piece of bread whole. He choked for a few seconds, tried to talk before he should, choked again to clear his windpipe, then found his voice. "I didn't think you would want me to."

"Why wouldn't I want you to? I thought we had gotten past that before we went home."

"Uh… I thought… uh… Hitler… uh…" Peter searched for the words he wanted, but Juliette interrupted before he found any.

"I've decided we shouldn't talk about that man ever again. If you want to talk about Hitler, go outside and howl at the moon—and don't come back until you're over it!"

Peter drank a swallow of beer, then asked the only question he could think of.

"Uh… how was your summer?"

Juliette smiled. "My summer was fine—no, better than fine. I sang a Bach Cantata, his two-hundred and eleventh, for the Bach Kammer Orchestra in Brussels. It's called the 'Coffee Cantata,' and it was a lot of fun."

Peter bit into the bread, then pushed cheese in his mouth behind it before he chewed. Relieved to have a topic that wouldn't get him in trouble, he asked, spitting crumbs, "How do you write religious music about coffee?"

Juliette laughed. "I don't, and neither did Bach. It's secular music."

"So, that means it isn't religious?"

"Aren't you studying music history?"

Peter said, "Of course, but they didn't teach me that."

Juliette relaxed, sensing how hard Peter was trying.

"Well, most composers wrote both kinds of music. When he was sixteen, Puccini wrote a religious cantata for tenor and choir that would suit your voice perfectly. And then he wrote his first opera."

"I would like to learn to sing Bach," said Peter determined to score points, but Juliette laughed, and he couldn't figure out whether that was good or bad.

"Bach is the last composer you will learn how to sing. It takes a profound technique for a tenor, entirely different from opera."

"Will Professor Garcia teach me to sing Bach?"

"No, I doubt it. But if you're good, I'll teach you someday."

Peter felt his face burning and turned away. He wanted to ask Juliette what he had to be good at but decided that would be a bridge too far.

When the food and beer were gone, Juliette got up from her chair, smiled seductively, took both plates and the empty beer bottles and said,

"I would ask you to my room so we could talk privately, but I have a new roommate who will show up at any time. I see you've got one too." She cocked her head toward Felix, who was surreptitiously watching them.

Peter said, disparagingly, "He's a 'Von.' His name is Felix von Finckenstein. I think his suitcase cost more than my father's car."

"Ah, a nobleman. He won't like your friend, Hitler."

She stood on her toes and pecked Peter on the cheek. "I'm going to wash these dishes and go to bed. We have a technique lesson at nine Tuesday morning and repertoire at three Tuesday afternoon. Let's work on your 'Max' aria tomorrow."

Peter followed Juliette to the kitchen, where he made a token effort to help her by wiping off the counter with a dirty dish towel. She took it from him, washed it in the sink, hung it up, and then pushed him up the stairs with Felix on her heels.

Juliette opened her door, said *"Gute Nacht"* to Peter and giggled as she closed it and turned around.

"My, you are a cheerful young lady, and that can only mean one thing!" said a voice from the bed farthest from the door.

Juliette stared at an incarnation of *Brünnhilde,* the Valkyrie princess from Wagner's 'Ring Cycle' operas. Brünnhilde sweeps onstage to the most exciting music in opera, the *Ride of the Valkyries*—music that would excite a stone—the legend in front of Juliette walked across the floor to stop between her and the bed she had marked with her pyjamas.

The woman was at least a hundred and twenty kilograms of muscle and bone and towered twenty-five centimetres above Juliette. Thick blond hair spilling over her shoulders reached halfway down her back, framing a sharply defined Nordic face. Juliette's jaw dropped, words froze before they reached her vocal cords, and Brünnhilde took over with the speaking voice every woman wished she had.

"My name is Hildegard Dietzel, and I'm from Bremen when I'm not in Hamburg."

The voice bounced off the walls, the fifth note of an octave below any woman's voice Juliette had ever heard. Juliette stretched out her hand, and it disappeared in Hildegard's powerful yet gentle grip.

Juliette said, "My name is Juliette Durand. I'm from Brussels."

"I can see by the expression on your face that you hadn't expected a roommate, at least not one like me. And so that we get it all out, I was also told I would have a room to myself."

Juliette got her hand back and said, "Yes, I was told the same thing last year, but everything worked out just fine, and I'm sure we will work it out."

"I'm not so sure. I fart like an overfed cow and snore like a train going uphill. Honestly, I don't do feminine well."

Juliette couldn't hold the spontaneous laugh that leapt to her throat. It took a long ten seconds to get it stopped, and then Hildegard started. For thirty seconds, her laugh buried Juliette's.

Juliette said, "Don't you think I could get used to it?"

"What, the stink or the noise?" Hildegard chuckled louder than Juliette could yell.

Juliette immediately liked the woman and smiled reassuringly at her. Hildegard stroked Juliette's hair as she would a child's.

"Poor dear. How old are you? Eighteen, nineteen? Certainly not more than twenty! I am twenty-five going on thirty-something, and I've been around a few blocks. Some idiot told me I'll be here for two years, but no one can live with me for that long! We will have to fix this as soon as possible."

"Who are you studying with?"

"A Professor Garcia… I've never sung anything for him, but I have a lesson on Tuesday at nine."

"Strange, so do I."

Hildegard was right about the snoring, but it turned out to be intermittent. When the roar awakened Juliette, she emptied her bladder so she could sleep later in the morning. When she returned, she went to Hildegard's bed, put her hand on the massive forehead and said, "Shhhh," as softly as she could. Hildegard mumbled something, rolled over and breathed softly.

Juliette woke again at daylight and looked at the clock on the night table beside her head; the little hand was on the six, and she didn't bother to check on the big one. She couldn't remember seeing the short one pointed straight down except when it was time for *Abendessen*.

"I see you're awake," said a voice, and then Juliette remembered.

"I think so. Isn't it still night?"

"No, the sun is up. Most people call it morning."

Hilde sat in front of the dressing table, looking in the mirror as she combed her long hair. *"Achzehn, Neunzehn, Zwanzig."* She laid the brush on the table. "Sometimes I wonder if long hair is worth the work; it isn't as though men look at it."

Juliette shook her head to clear the cobwebs, swung her legs over the side of the bed, stretched her arms and yawned.

Hilde said, "You aren't a morning person, and I can't sleep if the sun is up. This isn't going to work, is it?"

Juliette decided to lie. "I've had enough sleep. I sometimes get up late, but like to get going early most mornings."

Hildegard said, "Oh, so you lie—and let me guess—you have a horrible temper!"

"Oh, I can be quite nasty; just ask my boyfriend."

"Peter? I've heard he's a sweetheart. All the other sopranos wish you would die!"

Juliette asked, "How long have you been here?"

"My father and I came a week ago to scout things out. He doesn't like the idea of his little girl so close to Hitler's lair."

"So, you don't like Hitler?"

Hildegard harrumphed. "Don't tell me a nice Belgian girl like you would fall for that little pissant's bullshit!"

Juliette laughed at the descriptions but was happy to hear where Hilde stood. It helped that she would state her position without knowing where Juliette's allegiances lay.

"No, I won't tell you that because I hate Hitler, the National Socialists, and everything they represent! But tell me, if your father is concerned, why doesn't he hire someone to protect you?"

Hilde went to her night table, lifted a lace handkerchief and revealed a small pistol.

"That's a six-millimetre Beretta, a girl's best friend. Even when you don't think I have it with me, I do." The tiny pistol disappeared in her big hand.

"Do you think you need that now that the SA has been tamed?"

Hilde laughed from her belly. "I hate that little fucker, and now that Hindenberg is dead and he's made himself *Der Führer,* he can kill anyone he wants out of his way. Also, reading the fine print, he has pardoned himself retrospectively for murdering a thousand people on the 'Night of the Long Knives.'" She snorted. "The little twit thinks he's made himself God of the German people!"

Juliette smiled. "You should talk to Peter. I know he went to the National Socialist Party rally this past weekend with his father, but he doesn't dare mention it to me."

"And you still speak to him?" Hildegard held Juliette's gaze for long seconds, put her finger on Juliette's nose and said, "You love him, don't you?"

Tears sprang to Juliette's eyes; she lowered her head and nodded.

"Well, don't fight with him—that little National Socialist prick has your Peter for now, but the day will come when... Never mind, but trust me, that day will come!"

Juliette decided she felt safe with this woman.

Juliette was dressed at seven when Hilde said, "Time for breakfast. They will give us all the eggs, Wurst and bread we want, and enough coffee and juice to drown us."

"When did that happen? We only got one meal a day last year."

"Apparently, National Socialism is good for something. They throw money at German culture as long as no Jews are involved." Hilde laughed with a generous dose of sarcasm.

"A Jewish businessman donated this house to the Hochschule before he took his family to America. He also left money behind on condition it is used to maintain the house as a student residence. Someone found out the money was going somewhere it shouldn't and has put it right. The money left by the Jew means we don't have to clean anything but our room, we get fed three times a day, and there is clean linen for the bed every week."

"How did you find out all of this?"

"My father owns a few buildings and a pier in Bremen that the *Wehrmacht* needs. If he asks a question, he usually gets an answer."

Juliet said, "Mine is an art dealer. He has a lot of money and some influence around here."

Hilde smiled. "Perhaps our fathers should talk—art and politics would be common interests."

The cook had spread food on a table with room for ten people, half of the students in residence. Fortunately, only six showed up that early for breakfast.

Hildegard's table manners were exemplary. She handled cutlery as though she had trained for years and ate as delicately as a bird, accomplishing a lot in a remarkably short time but doing it in a way that gave the illusion she hadn't eaten much at all.

Juliette wasn't fooled. While she ate one egg, a piece of bread with two slices of cheese and Wurst, drank a small glass of juice and sipped a cup of coffee, Hilde devoured three times that amount of food, drank two glasses of juice, and was on her third cup of coffee when Juliette wiped her mouth with a linen napkin and said, "That's all I can eat."

Hilde put down her coffee cup and said, "I could certainly eat more, but I must watch my weight." She smiled at Juliette. "Don't I wish I looked like you!"

Everyone showed up for the evening meal, traditionally bread, cheese, Wurst, a salad or fruit, and a beer. But tonight, as a welcoming gesture and perhaps as a start on compensation for stealing the money the Rosenstein family had 'donated' to the school, the students had a choice between quail and venison. All ten rooms were full, lessons began the following morning, and twenty excited young students gathered in the dining and living rooms, all competing to be heard.

Singers' voices are trained to be resonant and generate a lot of noise, and Juliette found the din intolerable. An hour before the evening meal at six, a half dozen students in the *Wohnzimmer* gathered around the piano and tried to plunk Roberta Niesen's rendition of Otto Harbach and Jerome Kern's American hit, "Smoke gets in your eyes" on the piano.

Juliette and Peter had grabbed their favourite seats in the bay window and were listening with Felix and Hildegard. Finally, Hilde said, *"Ach, diese Amateuren, sie machen mich Verrückt,"* and went to the piano. She said, *"Bitte...,"* pulled the plunking pianist off the bench and sat down. Everyone backed up when Hilde spread her arms and brought them together so that her fingers locked and her joints cracked. She blazed a minor scale three octaves up and down the piano with both hands, said, *"Na, Gut!* Is everyone ready?" and the singers looked at one another.

Hilde played the introduction to the most popular song in Germany and began to sing in English:

"They asked me how I knew my true love was..." then stopped when no one else was singing.

"If you don't know the words, just hum. I will sing them through once, and then I will teach you."

Juliette watched Hildegard with tears blurring her vision as the majestic woman's incredible voice made everything in the room vibrate. The singers began to hum an accompaniment in four parts, and their combined voices were barely enough to matter but sufficient to turn the simple melody into a masterpiece.

The cooks in the kitchen hummed, the waitresses stopped what they were doing and stood in the doorway to listen, and no one who wasn't humming made a sound.

CHAPTER TEN

She Loves me, she Loves me not…

To be someone's hero, you must first love them more than you love yourself

THE FOLLOWING MORNING, Hilde again dragged Juliette to breakfast at seven, and Peter wasn't downstairs at eight when Hilde insisted she had to warm up her voice at the school at least an hour before her lesson. Juliette knocked on Peter's door and told a sleepy voice that she would see him at the studio.

Half-running, never quite catching up, Juliette felt like a child trailing behind her mother until Hilde noticed her struggling to keep up and slowed her pace.

"Juliette, you must learn to tell me when I'm going too fast. When I am walking, my mind is usually somewhere else."

Juliette looked up at her friend and asked, "Where is your mind now?"

"I was just wondering why you don't complain about my snoring or other, shall we say, unladylike manners."

"You woke me twice last night… once when I wanted to pee, and the second time I touched your forehead; you immediately rolled over and stopped, so it's not a problem."

"You're the first person who hasn't complained."

They walked in silence until they reached the studios, and Hilde led the way to the one she had been using since she arrived.

No other singers were there, so Juliette took the practice room next to Hilde's so she could hear what she knew would be a remarkable voice.

Juliette listened to her warming her voice for a few minutes before she plunked a middle 'C' to sing her first exercise. She jumped the fifth, then returned to the original note through the third.

Juliette listened to Hilde sing a scale, and the dramatic soprano's incredible sound resonated better in Juliette's room than her own voice did. She sang an arpeggio, using every bit of concentration she had and all the power she dared, but still lost badly to the powerful sound coming through the wall.

Juliette sang ten minutes of scales and technique exercises, then waited for Hilde to take a break. When she stopped five minutes later, Juliette put her score of Antonin Dvořák's *Rusalka,* a Czech opera she had never heard of, on the piano and opened it to the *Song to the Moon* in the first act. Professor Garcia had given it to Juliette before the summer break and told her to memorize it, which she had done. Her hands hovered over the keyboard, ready to play the introduction, when Hilde began playing the same piece. Juliette put her hands on her lap and listened.

Hilde sang the aria perfectly on pitch and musically correct, but without something that, as Juliette listened, she finally put her finger on. The aria required a smooth beauty Juliette felt was missing—Rusalka's plea to the moon wasn't a demand. She decided Hilde's power was misplaced in the piece and wondered why Professor Garcia would give it to a dramatic soprano. Juliette closed her score without singing the aria and went to wait on the bench. Peter and Felix were there, laughing at something.

"If either of you wants to warm your voice, the room I was in is free."

Peter said, "No, I don't need to do any exercises... we've been talking since we left the *Sängerhaus.*"

Juliette said, "Peter, that's the opposite of warming your voice."

Felix laughed. "I never warm my voice... that's all hooey!"

Juliette thought perhaps that was why he didn't get in with Professor Garcia but kept her thoughts to herself.

A minute later, Frau Kirschbaum, on her way to her studio, stopped in front of Felix and said, "Is your voice warmed up?"

Felix looked at Juliette and Peter, turned to his teacher and said, "I was waiting for a practice room."

"I'm done with mine," said Juliette sweetly but with a touch of 'I told you so.'

At that moment, Hilde came out of her practice room; Peter jumped up and said, "I'll take that one."

When Hilde sat down, she and Juliette were alone on the bench and had five minutes to talk.

Juliette said, "Garcia gave us the same aria—I wonder why?"

"The moon aria? He gave you the moon aria?"

"Well… yes, why not?"

"Because it's so low; it lies perfectly for my voice."

Juliette shrugged. "I've been singing it all summer, and it seems to work."

Hilde sat for a few minutes without saying anything, then asked Juliette, "Why do *you* think he would do that?"

At that moment, Peter and Felix came out of their practice rooms, and the second hand on the clock swept past thirty seconds from nine o'clock. Juliette decided to consider the question rhetorical and stood up.

"It's time to go," she said, and Peter followed her to the door. Hilde waited until the second hand had reached the twelve,S and Juliette had opened the door before she caught up to them.

"Welcome to the new school year!" said Professor Garcia. "I assume you are all acquainted." He turned to Juliette. "How do you and Hilde get along?"

Juliette connected the dots. "Fabulous! I want to thank you for putting her in my room."

Professor Garcia looked at the piano keys but didn't entirely hide a guilty grin. He turned to Peter.

"Peter, I had nothing to do with Felix. He's with Frau Kirschbaum."

He rubbed his hands together and said, "Why don't we see what we've got here? The three of you won't be taking lessons together all the time, but I think it would be healthy if you worked together when I can see a mutual benefit." He took Hilde's hand and guided her to the crook in the piano.

"I want you to face Juliette and Peter, who will sit on those chairs." He pointed to two hardwood chairs and looked at Peter. "Put them against the wall so Hilde can sing to you."

147

While Professor Garcia sat on the piano bench and opened the cover, Peter put his new leather music case on the floor, took a chair in each hand and placed them where the professor had indicated. He sat down beside Juliette.

Garcia looked at Hilde and said, "I heard you warming up, so let's do a few technique exercises just to open the pipes."

He played what Juliette's perfect pitch told her was the top 'c' and played an arpeggio going down an octave.

Hildegard folded her hands in front of her, took a deep breath, nailed the 'c' with a sound that would break a window in the next block, then carried the devastating sound down an octave.

"Wow, I'm glad to hear that you can do that! If the air raid siren breaks down, the city can just put you at an open window!" The professor took the edge off what could have been an insult by chuckling and adding, "That's as much sound as I've ever heard come out of a human throat."

Shocked by the shrillness of the sound, Juliette couldn't believe that would work, even for Brünnhilde.

Professor Garcia looked at Juliette for a moment, then said, "Juliette, please tell me what you are thinking."

Juliette looked at her hands, and when no one broke the silence, she raised her head and said, "I think she has the same problem I had. The sound has no room—although it *is* powerful. I believe an incredible beauty is hidden under Hilde's raw power."

Garcia nodded and turned to Hilde. "Hildegard, stand aside for a moment, and let's hear Juliette sing the same arpeggio." Hilde stepped nervously to one side, and Juliette took her place. Professor Garcia played the same arpeggio. Juliette sang a beautifully coloured 'high C,' then warmed the notes further as she descended the octave in three increments.

Professor Garcia looked at Peter and asked, "Even a tenor can hear the difference… am I right?"

Peter nodded. There wasn't a chance in hell he was going to say anything.

The Professor pointed at Juliette, then Hilde. "You each need something of what the other has got, and I am going to see that you get it."

Juliette immediately understood, looked at Professor Garcia, who nodded, then turned to Hilde and said, "Why don't you sing 'Smoke gets in your Eyes' for Professor Garcia."

"Go ahead," said the professor and asked Hilde, "Original key?"

Hilde, puzzled, looked at the professor, then Juliette. She nodded and said, "If you insist, but that isn't my opera voice. I sing popular music without the same support I use in opera."

The sound filled the room, and when Hilde finished the first section, Professor Garcia stopped and said, "Can you do that on a high C?" He played the arpeggio top down, and Hilde shook her head. "No, I can't do it."

"Of course you can," said Juliette. "I can hear it in your voice."

"Why don't we try this," said Professor Garcia. "I want you to relax and let the sound come out exactly as you would sing the smoke song."

"But, I will crack the note."

"Yes, that's right, but I want you to relax, aim for the centre of the pitch, and crack it, but without what you think of as supporting the sound." Professor Garcia grinned. "I guarantee nothing will break, and no one in this room will laugh."

He played the note; Hilde looked at Juliette and made a stab at it. Peter snorted when her voice splattered the note all over the room, and Hilde gave him a look that should have killed him, then laughed, and Juliette and the professor joined in.

The professor used a cutting motion to halt the laughter and played the arpeggio again. "Crack it again, but this time I want you to relax and let your larynx fall as though it had nothing holding it up. Do not support!"

"Don't support? But a singer must support!"

"But you are not lifting weights; you are blowing air through a slot between two little strips of flesh. Give me a light crack, not a heavy one… think of a kitten mewing."

Hilde shrugged and sang the arpeggio, but the crack didn't happen.

"Put a little of your 'Smoke in the Eyes' honey in it and crack it again. Forget that you are an opera singer."

Hilde sang the arpeggio a little louder, smoother, and much more beautifully.

"No, no, find the crack!" Garcia pretended to be angry and played the arpeggio again, and Hilde sang it louder but still brimming with honey.

Professor Garcia's black eyes shone when he said, "That is the most beautiful sound I have ever heard come out of a human throat, but you can do better!"

Hilde sang the arpeggio again, adding power as she descended. She giggled and said, "But it's so easy—I can't believe I did that! I can't believe I can do that again…" and she did it again.

Juliette hugged Hilde, looked into her eyes and said, "My God, Hildegard, what a voice you have!"

"And you, young lady," the professor pointed at Juliette, "are a born teacher! You have a teacher's ear for sound!"

Felix wasn't there an hour and a half later when they left the studio, as high as a kite, and the assumption was that he had gone to the *Sängerhaus.*

Music theory, history, language studies and repertoire classes didn't start until the next day, so Juliette, Hildegard and Peter decided to prowl around the 'Old City' for a while.

Juliette steered everyone to the Deutsches Theater to check on the movies. A *"Keine Jüden"* sign plastered over the window at the entrance blasphemed a "Morocco" poster beside it showing a reclining Marlene Dietrich with Gary Cooper leaning seductively over her. The evening performance was at seven.

"Look at that piece of…." Hilde pointed at the *"Keine Juden"* sign and let Juliette and Peter fill in the rest.

Juliette blew a kiss at the poster. "Gary Cooper is so romantic!"

Hilde laughed and stared at the poster. "No, Dietrich is the romantic one! She's so sexy!" She turned to Juliette. "You know, I heard she kisses a girl in the film. The Americans were horrified at the première, but Americans are horrified if they see a girl's knee or hear someone say 'fuck.'"

Juliette looked at Peter. "Would you like to see Marlene Dietrich kiss a girl?"

Peter's face turned red, and while he was trying to think of an answer, Hilde cut him off.

"What would you say if I kissed your girlfriend?" She grabbed Juliette, planted a kiss on her mouth and said, "There! What have you got to say about that?"

Peter looked around to see if anyone was watching, grabbed Juliette's shoulders and kissed her. It immediately turned into something more.

"Okay, okay, I know when I'm beaten."

Juliette wasn't entirely convinced when Hilde so obviously feigned disappointment.

Juliette grabbed Hildegard's arm. "Do you want to see it tonight? The box office is open."

"Juliette, dearest, I have no money, and I saw it two years ago in Hamburg."

"I have bags of money, and I want to see Dietrich kiss a girl."

"I won't help you spend your money."

"I'm buying three tickets in the front row of the first *Rang,* and I will go alone if you and Peter don't come with me. Peter has to come, or Marcel will kill him, but I want you to come because you are my friend."

"Well, I would like to see it again. It's the sexiest film I've ever seen, and I could use a little sex in my life right now."

Juliette said, "Stay here... I'll be right back," and headed for the box office.

By the time they reached the *Sängerhaus,* Peter and Juliette knew most of the plot, and Hilde had sung Dietrich's cabaret song. They went to their rooms, and Peter found Felix sprawled on his bed reading *Der Stürmer.* Peter sat on the edge of his bed facing Felix and said, "We're going to the Deutsches Theater to see 'Morroco' tonight. It starts at seven, so we will leave here at about six-thirty. I'm sure there will be lots of empty seats if you want to go."

"I wouldn't go to that piece of shit if someone paid for my ticket!" said Felix. "Dietrich does a Lesbian thing… God, I find a girl kissing another girl so damned disgusting, don't you? Hitler killed that fag Röhm because he was a homo!"

Peter decided not to answer the question. He said, "Well, Juliette is going, and I have to go with her so she will be safe. Hilde is coming too."

"You know they don't allow Jews in the theatre, don't you?"

Peter felt his face burning but said nothing.

"Juliette can get away with it here in the residence because her father knows someone, but the theatre won't be so blind this time."

"Do you think Juliette is Jewish?" asked Peter incredulously. "And what do you know about what happened at the theatre?"

Felix laughed. "Are you blinded by love… of course, she's a Jew!"

Peter stood up. "She is not a Jew, and I've got to go to the bathroom." He turned and left the room, slamming the door. On his way down the hall, Peter told himself he was offended because Juliette would be in danger, but as he closed the bathroom door and unbuttoned his fly, he wasn't as sure of his reason.

The afternoon flew by as singers in the residence who had no classes performed an impromptu concert. The sopranos sang seductive cabaret songs, and Hilde put everyone to shame.

Felix went to his room and returned with sheet music to a new song, so excited he dropped it twice while trying to put it in front of Juliette, the delegated pianist. It was a march, and Juliette was impressed by the mesmerizing melody as she read it. The title was simply *Panzerlied*, and *Oberleutnant* Kurt Wiehle, a member of the *Wehrmacht's 'Panzer Corps,'* had composed it.

Felix had the piece memorized and had sung the first verse in a voice best described as 'loud noise' when Juliette stopped playing. He sang the first line of the second verse unaccompanied, stopped and asked Juliette, "What's wrong? Is my voice that bad?" Everyone laughed.

Juliette wanted to say, "Yes, it's that bad… how did you get into this school?" but held her tongue. The other two male singers in the audience said, Let's sing it together!"

Juliette stood up from the piano and said, "This is Hitler music, inciting people to go to war, and I won't have anything to do with it!"

Peter followed Juliette to her chair in the bay window and sat beside her. He said, "He thinks you are a Jew."

"Yes, well, I *know* he's a National Socialist!"

Hilde took over the piano, and three baritones took over the stirring march.

"Hilde has no problem with that song. You have to be more tolerant, Juliette."

Juliette stood up, stamped her foot and said, "I do not have to be more tolerant when it comes to what is happening in your country! I am not so naive that I think Hitler's ambitions stop at the German border! He talks about Austria as though they should welcome him as a conquering hero, and Czechoslovakia and Poland as though they are holding Germans against their will! He says he will take back the Alsace Loraine Germany lost in the Versailles Treaty, but do you think France will say, 'Please, Mister Hitler, help yourself?' And what country lies between Germany and France? What country was torn apart the last time the Germans went crazy?"

Juliette began to cry, and Peter tried to comfort her. She twisted away and ran up the stairs without caring that everyone had stopped singing and the whole room was staring at her.

Abendessen was on the table when Juliette came down the stairs, and the looks on the faces of the other girls were pathetic. Her competition, a sweet young thing from Duisberg, was already sitting beside Peter when he pulled back a chair he had been saving for Juliette. She deliberately sat on the other side of the table beside Hilde. It took a few minutes for the embarrassment to evaporate, but the ten students who had stayed to eat *Schnitzel und Pommes Frites* soon got over it, and the chatter was back at full throttle when black forest cake and coffee were served.

"How do you know so many popular songs?" asked Juliette, further cutting the tension.

Hildegard responded, happy to discuss something besides Hitler and the Panzerlied. "That's where Professor Garcia found me. I was singing cabaret songs in Hamburg, but he heard Brünnhilde."

"That answer demands the question, 'What was our esteemed professor doing in an… 'illegal cabaret?'"

"You are on the right track, but you will get nothing more from me. The second time Miguel came to hear me, he asked if I liked opera."

"What did you say?"

"I said I had never heard one."

"And then…"

"He took me to hear *Die Walküre* at the Hamburg State Opera. I was hooked when they played the 'Ride of the Valkyries,' and he pointed at Brünnhilde and whispered, 'That's you!'"

Hilde and Juliette walked to the Deutsches Theater side by side, leaving Peter to trail behind. They talked and laughed all the way there while Peter strained to hear. What he heard wasn't encouraging.

They sat in the centre of the first row of the first balcony in a half-empty theatre, and Juliette was shocked when Marlene Dietrich actually kissed a young woman full on the mouth and, despite knowing it was coming, the audience gasped. Sitting at a restaurant table with her boyfriend or husband, the woman on the screen giggled and played the kiss as embarrassing. Juliette noted that the director didn't have the character show even a modicum of disgust. She observed the actor's reaction closely, and was sure the woman was happy about the kiss!

They left the theatre surrounded by a crowd of people whose conversation was exclusively about Gary Cooper and Marlene Dietrich. Juliette hadn't heard a word about the kiss as the crowd dispersed when they reached the sidewalk.

A hundred metres from the theatre, Juliette and Hildegard walked ahead of Peter, ignoring him as they had on the way to the theatre. They were deep in conversation about the film when an open car stopped beside them. Two brown-shirted *Sturmabteilung* soldiers got out of the back seat and stepped in front of them. People on the sidewalk crossed the street or hurried away.

"Ausweis!" said the smaller man while the other stood with his hand on the butt of his pistol. He had unbuttoned the holster.

Juliette opened her purse, found her passport and passed it to the officer. Hilde already had hers in her hand under the officer's nose, but he waited for Juliette to give him hers. Peter stood to one side with his *Ausweis* in his hand, but neither officer showed the slightest interest in him.

The man opened Juliette's passport, fumbled through the pages, looked at her and said, *"Eine Judin darf nicht ins Theater!"*

Juliette said angrily, "I am painfully aware that Jews are not allowed in the theatre, but if you are insinuating that I am a Jew, you are mistaken."

Peter stepped between Juliette and the officer, pushing the man backwards. "Leave her alone! She is not a Jew; she's Belgian."

The soldier beside Peter drew his pistol, pressed the barrel on the side of Peter's head and said, *"Lass dass, Junge."*

Hilde stepped up to the man holding Juliette's passport, pulled her hand out of her purse and put the barrel of a small pistol against his forehead. "Your friend has until I count to three to put his gun on the ground. One…two…" The soldier with the Luger carefully put it on the ground as a gray Mercedes with the SS symbol on the doors stopped behind the SA car. Two SS uniforms got out with machine pistols in their hands. One of them approached Hilde.

Hilde said calmly, "You are just in time. I was about to shoot this scum!"

The SS officer smiled as he said, "You must not do that… That's our job." He pointed at the Beretta. "Make that disappear—your friend is in no danger now."

Hilde slipped the gun into her purse.

The SA officer stooped to pick up his Luger, but the SS officer shook his finger, and he straightened up.

He turned to Peter. *"Herr Schweitzer, bitte holen Sie mir die Pistole."*

Peter picked up the Luger and passed it to the officer, not at all surprised that the man knew his name.

The officer snapped his fingers at the SA officer still holding Juliette's passport. *"Ausweis… Bitte?"* The red-faced officer passed it to Juliette.

"And now, get out of here before I arrest you for harassing these German citizens and their guest. I don't think anyone, even scum like you, is happy in Dachau."

The SS officer followed the SA soldiers to their car and, when they were seated, passed the luger to the officer with the empty holster. He said something to them that Juliette couldn't hear, and the man responded. The SS officer slapped the side of the car, and the driver pulled away.

The officer pulled Peter aside and said, "Do not trust your roommate… he reported Juliette as a Jew spy, and those bastards were going to take her somewhere unpleasant." He turned to Juliette. "Please tell your father what has happened here."

The SS officers got in their car, the officer who had done the talking waved, and it drove away.

As the taillights disappeared around a corner, Hilde said, "Juliette, I am impressed! You must tell me more about yourself."

Juliette took Peter's hand, put it against her lips, kissed it, and said, "Neither Gary Cooper nor Marlene Dietrich has a chance! You will always be my hero!"

Juliette turned to Hilde, took her arm and led her down the sidewalk. She put her hand in front of Hilde.

"Will you show me your gun?"

Chapter Eleven

Irreconcilable Differences

It is natural that Hypocrisy's agenda is always hidden

JULIETTE WORKED ON THE MOON SONG for a month, and twice in that time, Professor Garcia brought Hilde into her lesson to sing it with her. Juliette could hear Hilde's voice becoming more beautiful every time they sang together and wondered if hers could be improving at the same rate.

The song ends with a string of low D-flats, then climbs to a high B-flat that must be sung beautifully, without the slightest hint of tension. Juliette had no problem with the high note... as long as she didn't sing the string of low notes first. Her low notes were anemic if she sang them placed high in her head to prepare her cords for the following high B-flat. If she used a heavy voice as the words and music dictated, tension crept into the high B-flat, and the note became a frightened woman's scream.

Hilde had the opposite problem. She could sing low notes all day, and they always rumbled like a train going over a trestle. For her, the high note was another beast entirely. She could blast the paint off the walls with a high-C, a clear and powerful sound, dead in the centre of her voice's most potent resonance. However, when she sang a B-flat softly—and she could do that—it sounded like a drowning cat.

"Juliette, sing these notes," said Professor Garcia as he plunked a middle C, then a high-C two octaves above it.

Juliette sang the two-octave jump, controlling the impulse to smile when she nailed the perfectly placed top note.

Hilde gave Juliette a suspicious look, but Juliette didn't turn her head away from the professor.

"Hilde, listen again, then sing the same notes."

Professor Garcia played the 'C' again, and Juliette nailed the notes perfectly, holding the top note as he directed her. He indicated she should swell the note, and she followed his direction until she had nothing more to give.

Professor Garcia turned to Hilde and said, "Before you try it, yawn."

Hilde yawned, let her larynx fall to her esophagus as he had trained her, and lifted the soft tissue at the back of her throat, opening her echo chamber as far as possible. She relaxed, and he said, "Again, but stop pulling your lips back." She started, felt her face move and started again.

"Juliette, face Hilde and sing it again." He plunked the same notes.

Juliette concentrated on relaxing her face, opened everything as much as she could and sang the notes. The sound resonated more than it had since she had begun singing.

Hilde laughed. "My God, Juliette, I didn't know you had that sound in there!" She turned to Professor Garcia and opened her mouth to say something, but he played the notes again and said, "Don't talk… Sing! Now!"

Hilde sang the bottom note, then the top. She followed Professor Garcia's hand gestures to soften the sound, then swell it until he cut her off with his hand.

"That's as loud as you need to sing, and that's the most beautiful sound you have."

Hilde beamed and looked to Juliette for reassurance. Juliette said, "That sound is as loud as anything I have heard you sing, and trust me, it is incredibly beautiful!"

Juliette looked at Professor Garcia—he smiled and shook his head.

They worked on the aria for an hour, stopping to put every phrase into their technique. Juliette felt her voice opening, and for the first time since coming to Professor Garcia, she felt she could add power without sacrificing beauty.

Soon, Hilde blew the roof off at *Übungsabends,* and the beauty in Juliette and Peter's singing made other students want to give up and go home.

Peter's voice grew to match Juliette's and, as his musicianship reached the professional threshold that Professor Garcia demanded, his interpretation of the repertoire changed. As the notes fell into place, a high 'C' became routine—the 'breaks' in his voice became the ringing sound every tenor uses to thrill his audience.

Following the incident at the Deutsches Theater, Felix didn't return to Peter's room or the school, and Peter didn't get a new roommate. Every night, Juliette fought the urge to go to his room, but soft spring breezes and the First Act duet from La Bohème took Juliette past the point of no return.

She waited until she thought Hilde was asleep, then sneaked into Peter's room and awakened him by sitting on the edge of his bed. When he stirred, she whispered, "I can't sleep."

Juliette told herself she didn't intend to do anything more than talk to Peter, but when he rolled over and put his arm around her, his hand brushed her breast, and she lost all hope of controlling herself.

He asked, "You want to talk?"

Peter wasn't sure what to do, so he let go of her and sat up.

"I don't know what I want." Juliette looked at Peter, and a tidal wave of heat began at her hairline and worked its way down.

She put her hand on Peter's hip. "I lied… I know what I want, but my mother and the priest keep telling me I shouldn't."

Peter's desire was dangerously close to Juliette's hand, threatening to grow out through the slit in his pyjamas. She slid her hand closer to the lump.

Peter said, his voice husky, "Oh God, Juliette, I don't know what to do."

"I do!" She grabbed his hand, put it between her legs, and kissed him.

Peter groaned, pushed his hand against her, and she thrust her tongue between his lips.

"No, we can't!" Peter grabbed her wrist and made a half-hearted effort to pull her hand away.

"Oh, yes, we can!" Juliette twisted onto her back, pulled her pyjama bottoms off, then whipped the top over her head. "Take off your pyjamas."

A few minutes later, Peter had taken care of her screaming desire, but she wanted much more. Only her Catholic upbringing and her mother's dire warnings of the consequences kept Juliette from taking what she desperately wanted.

She slept in Peter's arms until daylight brightened the window and then got out of his bed, put on her pyjamas, and quietly went to her room without seeing anyone.

As Juliette lay down, the clock beside her bed said ten minutes after six, but sleep was out of the question.

"Was that your first time?" asked Hilde, startling Juliette.

"We didn't go all the way."

"Why not?"

"My mother stopped me."

"Your mother doesn't have to know. You are a big girl now."

"She would know, and what if…?"

Hilde chuckled. "I lied, but my mother knew." She turned on her side and rested her head on her hands. "She gave me a book."

"Did you stop doing it?"

"No, it was a book on how to avoid getting pregnant."

"What about the boy? I assume you didn't marry him."

Hilde was silent for more than a minute.

"We wanted to get married. I was twenty at the time and…" She paused, then said, "His parents didn't like my socialist views. They found out I was a member of the Communist Party, and I haven't seen him since."

"I'm sorry," said Juliette, "but you will find another."

"Well, there's no need to feel sorry; I got an excellent book out of the deal." Hilde laughed without mirth. "Maybe you should read it before you get into the trouble your mother is worried about."

"No, we found out how to have fun without that."

"I wouldn't trust you two for a minute! Read the damned book!"

Juliette read the book in a day but decided she couldn't trust the rhythm method or any of the book's other suggestions, the most asinine of which was withdrawal before ejaculation. Once Peter was inside her, there wasn't a chance in hell she was letting him out!

Juliette tried to limit her visits to Peter's bed to once a week. That didn't work out, so they agreed on twice. Two days later, she crawled into his bed early in the morning, throwing away the idea of a schedule.

Finally, they agreed to a simple solution…Peter's penis would stay away from Juliette's danger zone.

The morning after their third encounter, Professor Garcia laughed when they entered the studio holding hands and said, "I see it's time to take out the Don Pasquale duet again."

As they sang, Juliette couldn't tear her eyes away from Peter. He stroked her hair, she touched his cheek, and their breath mingled—they couldn't keep their hands off one another.

When the duet ended, and the professor played the last few bars, they kissed, and Professor Garcia said, "Now, that was a love duet! Every woman in the house is panting, and the men have their legs crossed."

When Juliette and Peter came up for air, he said, "I will book it for the *Übungsabend* on Tuesday."

He smiled at them. "Is there any chance this will cool before next Tuesday…?"

Juliette shook her head, and Peter looked at his feet.

"…And what about before the Bohème duet is ready?"

Juliette shook her head again.

"…Before you audition this fall?"

Juliette and Peter said, "This fall? Audition?" in unison.

"You will need four arias, this duet, both Bohème duets, and the Roses in Tyrol. Can you do it?"

Juliette looked at Peter, he nodded, and they said, "Yes" in unison.

"And If you sing like that, you will have a contract a year from now!"

The *Übungsabend* duet was more successful than either Juliette or Peter dreamed it could be. The piece is deceptively simple, but in its simplicity Donizetti embraced a passionate love story. Faking it won't work, but Juliette and Peter didn't have to fake anything; they needed only to look, touch and breathe. Love dripped onto the stage and floated into the audience, and when it was over, the super-critical students shouted, stamped their feet and stood for four curtain calls, unheard of in the school.

In January 1935, the National Socialist Party took another step against the Jewish community, announcing they would enforce the "Law for the Reconstruction of the Civil Service," passed in April 1933. The law banned Non-Aryans from working in the civil service and included Lawyers, notaries, and tax advisors, all of whom were forbidden to provide legal services in the courts. The law even extended to such mundane jobs as swimming instructor, church musician, and art or antique dealer. However, missing in the law was a clear definition of Non-Aryans, making it nearly impossible to enforce. Its principal effect was to drive more Jews, together with their talent, money and education, out of the country.

Juliette and Peter were cuddling on the sofa after working on their audition music when Juliette decided to bring it up. She had not mentioned Hitler or the National Socialist Party since the SS had rescued them in front of the theatre, and since then, she and Peter had become so close Juliette had convinced herself he would listen to reason.

"What do you think Hindenburg would think of Hitler now that he is enforcing the civil service law against the Jews?" Juliette softened the question. "Of course, he died in August, so his opinion is irrelevant. However, unintentionally his death gave Hitler the power he was missing. Adolph Hitler inherited the presidency—and now he can kill *anyone* without trial... not just Jews and communists!"

"I haven't been reading the papers," said Peter, "and the radio hasn't said anything about a new law."

"It's not a new law...it's the law they passed two years ago but mostly didn't enforce. It was in the *Beobachter* and *Der Stürmer,* so I supposed Hitler's supporters would have seen it."

"Well, I haven't read those newspapers for a while, and I don't know anything about this civil service law."

"You think Hitler is a friend of the Jews, and his minions think I'm a Jew, so you really *should* know what the law says!"

Juliette knew she had already gone too far and wanted to stop. Still, Peter was becoming important to her—she was encouraged that he didn't read National Socialist newspapers and thought this might be an opportunity to enlighten him.

"The law is called the *Berufsbeamtengesetz* and bans non-Aryans from working for the government—becoming teachers, lawyers, even swimming instructors—any job paid for by the government. When Hitler's *Reichstag* passed the law two years ago, in April, Hindenburg was against implementing it, and so to delay it, he inserted a list of exceptions. There was no clear definition of who is Aryan and who is not, so until Hindenburg died, the government only rarely tried to enforce it."

Peter said, "Can't we forget about that? I don't care what you believe… why do you care what I believe?"

"I care because I love you, and I can't love someone who is blind to what is happening in Germany."

"Juliette, since Hitler became chancellor, he has had two policy referendums, and ninety percent of the people supported him. Do you think the whole country is stupid?"

"Not stupid… unwilling or unable to see the truth because they are afraid it would mean Germany might return to the misery of three years ago."

Peter, obviously frustrated, said, "Yes, of course, they are afraid of returning to the time before Hitler. You weren't here when a stamp cost a day's wages, and you live in a world where a job is something you only do if it pleases you. You cannot blame the German people for wanting safe streets, a roof over their heads, and enough to eat!"

Juliette didn't have an answer. If it hadn't been for her father's connections and money, the *Sturmabteilung* or even the police would have done something to her she didn't want to think about—and she could be in a concentration camp like Dachau, or even dead! When the SA tried a second time, the SS had interfered again, and Felix, the rat, was now mysteriously gone.

She said, angry, "But there has to be a better way than Hitler!"

Juliette waited until, finally, Peter said, "Perhaps Hitler is right; it took absolute authority to fix the mess he inherited when he became chancellor."

He stopped talking, but Juliette couldn't think of anything to say, so he continued.

"I agree that if the National Socialists attack non-Aryans, that will be a catastrophe, but most Germans don't think they'll do that. Even if they fire a few from the civil service, perhaps we must sacrifice their well-being for the greater good."

Juliette's voice reflected her frustration. "Oh, Peter, you are so naïve. It's not only Hitler; it's the National Socialist Party machine. Goebbels, Himmler, Göring, Heydrich and probably dozens more are whispering in Hitler's ear. Like children trying to get his attention, each one is trying to come up with something more sensational than the others, all of them sycophants competing for Hitler's praise."

Juliette didn't give Peter enough time to interrupt.

"My father told me that Hitler killed his best friend, Ernst Röhm, duped by Himmler and Göring so they could take control of the *Sicherheitsschutz,* the *Gestapo,* and the *Stürmabteilung.* They killed hundreds of Brownshirts to get command of a three-million-man army of criminals."

Juliette was on a roll that couldn't be stopped. Peter looked at the floor, holding back tears.

"And now, Germany has the *Gestapo,* a federal secret police force with tremendous power. Already, they are accumulating information that they can use to control their competition."

Peter shook his head and came close to sobbing as he said, "Juliette, you are saying things that are not true. Hitler is now *Der Führer,* our supreme leader, and those people you are so afraid of serve under him. He controls them!"

Juliette stood up as two students came into the room. She said softly, "I don't want to talk about this anymore. You can't have both me and your insane loyalty to Hitler. You must choose." She looked around... no one was looking at her.

Peter wanted to tell her about his grandparents—Jews who lived fifteen minutes from the *Sängerhaus*—but he had promised them and himself that he would never tell anyone. And then, there was his Jewish mother....

Five months later, Peter and five other students sat facing the radio on chairs borrowed from the dining room, awaiting Hitler's speech to the Reichstag like excited children anticipating the first day of school. It was the twenty-first of May, a beautiful day, and Juliette sat curled in her chair beside an open window, with Hilde facing her, each with a glass of beer on the little table beside them.

A few weeks earlier, Hitler had rejected the limitations to Germany's armed forces imposed by the Versailles treaty. He had asserted that the Allied signators of the Versailles Treaty had expanded their armed forces while limiting Germany to one-hundred-thousand men, breaking the treaty's terms. He had further announced that Germany would be universally conscripting fighting men to a strength of four hundred and eighty thousand, a total of thirty-six divisions. Britain and France warned Hitler of the consequences, and the German people held their collective breath.

Hitler began his speech by affirming Germany's commitment to the 1925 Locarno Pact of Treaties, limited by and conditional upon France also halting any increase in armaments.

When Hitler stopped for applause, Hilde said to Juliette, "France won't stop building their army, and Hitler is going to occupy the Rhineland."

Hitler then deflected to attack Western democratic political systems, reminding the Reichstag that a referendum on his autocratic government had resulted in thirty-eight million Germans giving their resounding approval.

When the applause died, Hitler began a rant on the futility of war and Germany's commitment to peace. The audience clapped at every opportunity, and at one point, Hilde said, "It looks like Hitler will bring peace to Europe by building another great German army."

Hitler went on to list the arms Germany had demolished—every box of ammunition, every airplane, every ship and every gun—dozens of items.

Hilde laughed. "Yes, Germany has melted outdated junk to build modern weapons. Today will mark the end of the Versailles Treaty."

Juliette wrung her hands. She wanted to leave the room screaming.

Hilde put her hand on Juliette's. "He has gone too far. The Allies won't allow him to build an army stronger than theirs."

Hitler turned to the 'Memel Territory' in Lithuania, traditionally German with 140,000 German-speaking inhabitants, now ruled by a Bolshevik government. Hitler claimed the territory, separated from Germany by all of Poland, saying it should be returned to Germany. The applause thundered for five minutes.

Hilde said, "My God, he is going to invade Poland and say he is liberating Memel!"

Hitler turned to Austria, assuring the Reichstag members that Germany harboured no intent to force Austria into an *Anschluss* against their will.

Hilde whispered, "He is going to annex Austria!"

The last half of the speech was a convoluted diatribe of Hitler's "poor me" version of Germany's persecution by France, Russia, and England, culminating in his contradicting claim that Germany wants only peace and equality. He again asserted that his country's people wanted a peaceful Europe and, to prove their sincerity, would agree to an international ban on gas warfare and bombs used against civilian targets. Germany would agree to limits on the number of submarines, sizes of surface ships, number of bombers, and certain restrictions on tanks and artillery.

Hilde laughed during the applause. "The peaceful Europe he envisions is a National Socialist Europe with no Gypsies, Communists or Jews. An international reduction in arms is a farce."

When Hitler ended his speech, Juliette suddenly felt cold. She closed the window and said, "Is this the end? Will the world let Hitler start another war?"

"He wants what Napoleon wanted… authority to rule over all countries bordering on those he already ruled."

"So, Hitler will take over Austria, then attack Poland?"

"And Czechoslovakia. The French won't let him do that, so Germany will go through Belgium and Holland to attack France, just like in 1914."

Juliette said, "Surely someone will stop this maniac before then. There must be a limit to his ambitions!"

"No, there is no limit. That man has no conscience, feels no guilt no matter what he does, and his hunger for power can't be satisfied. Everything that goes wrong is someone else's fault, and only he can fix it!"

As Peter and his listening companions discussed the speech, Juliette kept her voice low when she asked Hilde, "How do you know these things?"

"I studied Freud and Jung in university—I have a master's degree in psychology. But there isn't much market for that outside academia, so I tried cabaret singing, and it worked." She looked wistfully outside. "Sometimes I wish it hadn't."

Peter dragged his chair over to Juliette and Hilde's and sat where he could talk with them privately. He was still excited.

"Wasn't that a great speech? Hitler certainly made Germany's intentions clear, and I hope the Western Allies are hanging their heads!"

Hildegard said, "He threw out the Treaty of Versailles, made sure everyone understood that he would conscript three-hundred-and-eighty-thousand men, invade Austria and Poland, and replace all Germany's outdated arms with modern offensive weapons. Did I miss something?" She looked at Peter's puzzled face.

"That's not what I heard." Peter said, "Where did he say he would scrap the Versailles treaty?"

"I will show you when we get the *Beobachter* on Saturday. They will print the highlights."

"I didn't hear that!" said Peter.

Hilde said, "Peter, that is precisely what he said; perhaps you hear what you want to hear. You still ignore Hitler's intention to kick every Jew, Communist and Gypsy out of Germany, even though he has told you and passed laws that do exactly that!"

"But he said that he would not annex Austria!"

"And then he said—I wrote it down in case you asked—" Hilde read from notes she had taken.

"Born of a simple feeling of solidarity due to a common national origin, the German Volk and the German Government have, however, the understandable

desire that not only alien peoples but also the German Volk be guaranteed the right of self-determination everywhere. I personally believe that any regime which is not anchored in the people, supported by the people and wanted by the people cannot endure for any length of time."

Hilde looked up. "He will force the Austrian government to hold a referendum, send in his 'SA convincers,' and drive the new German army across the border when the referendum comes out in his favour."

"When?" asked Juliette.

"When he has conscripted four hundred thousand men and built enough planes and tanks. Two years, maybe three."

Peter said, "But he said that Germany would agree to a limit to its forces."

Hilde shook her head. "Only if everyone else will do it. They won't because Hitler's idea of arms equality would be suicide for everyone else."

Peter stood up. "I can't listen to this; you are twisting his words!"

Hilde's voice took on a note of cynicism. "I would show you what the foreign press says if Hitler would let me. Unfortunately, he has censored all the neutral press in Germany and now allows only papers like *Der Stürmer*—pure government propaganda. Foreign papers are no longer allowed into the country…the truth is dead and buried."

Peter's voice rose, and everyone in the room looked at him.

"Hitler has done more for Germany in two years than the Weimar Republic did in ten. In those ten years, democracy ruined Germany. People starved to death in the best, hardest-working country on earth! Hitler fixed that and now will make Germany into the world power it was before the Great War!"

Juliette felt sorry for him as he walked out of the room, hiding his face. She suspected he was crying.

"I'm sorry," said Hilde, "I shouldn't have done that!"

Juliette said, "Peter can't hear what you and I hear. Hitler is Houdini with words; he has carefully hidden the truth in the fabric of his speeches so only an open mind can find it. Peter can't see past his father's job."

Chapter Twelve

A Fork in the Road

A fork in the road has three choices, and sometimes the best choice is the one most people overlook—to return to where you started and begin again

JULIETTE SLEPT IN HER OWN BED until the semester ended. Peter left for the train station in the early morning fog and Marcel, in Munich on her father's business, picked up Juliette and her luggage shortly after. Distraught, Juliette talked about Peter and his Hitler fascination until they changed trains in Köln. Marcel couldn't get a private compartment to Brussels, and two elderly women joined them. They chattered in German, Juliette stared out the window, and Marcel read.

Marcel left Juliette with the baggage and brought the Rolls Royce to the main doors, where a baggage handler helped load her luggage. Marcel paid him, and Juliette climbed into the front seat.

"I want to talk about Peter," she said.

"I hoped you had talked that subject to its death."

"Why can't he see what you, Hilde, and I can see? It isn't reasonable that someone of his intelligence doesn't understand what Hitler is doing!" Juliette had to focus on keeping her voice down. She wanted to scream.

"He isn't alone. Almost all of Germany agrees with him. You and I weren't there when people starved—they fought one another for scraps of food they found in garbage cans. Thousands slept on the streets, in train stations and in lobbies. There were no jobs, nowhere to live, and they had nothing to feed their children!"

Juliette remained silent while Marcel thought of what he wanted to say. She could see his discomfort but wanted his opinion before she asked her father for his. Finally, he began as though giving a lecture.

"The Treaty of Versailles demanded that the German people pay reparations for a war they hadn't started and didn't want—money they didn't have and weren't permitted by the treaty to borrow. It financially ruined the country and drove the people, who had forced their government to negotiate the peace, into despair."

Juliette said, "I remember when people slept on the Brussels streets. We didn't look for a maniac to lead us!"

"Juliette, we are working through a worldwide depression that started seven years ago. Germany's problems began in 1916 and got worse every year. When the world economy collapsed in twenty-nine, Germany's problems went from bad to horrible…they paid a day's wages for a stamp! Mothers couldn't afford milk for their children, and old people froze to death in the streets. You can't imagine the agony they went through…."

"But that doesn't excuse electing a man like Hitler."

"You are looking at him through the lens of hindsight. His Brownshirt bullies drove the communists away, and yes, they were too aggressive, but the people were tired of demonstrators upsetting the work of the government. They wanted bread, milk for their children, and medicine for the sick. The communists' civic rights were a small sacrifice."

"But…"

"Peter's family knows what hard times do to a man's soul. His father, a master machinist, swept floors and cleaned toilets. Like most workers, Heinz had lost hope until Hitler resurrected M.A.N., the company he now works for. You cannot persuade Peter's family that Hitler is bad for their country because they know what he has done for them, and Peter's family represents Germany."

"But…" Juliette expected Marcel to go on, but he let her finish her sentence… "he has made a law essentially taking citizenship from Jews, Romani, and anyone who doesn't have Aryan blood! He is taking away their jobs and telling people not to shop at their stores!"

"Yes, but the law doesn't define those people, so the law can't be and isn't widely enforced. Basically, the fanatics can't agree on who to persecute."

FOOLS, ANGELS and the DEVIL

The Rolls Royce rolled quietly into the gravel driveway of number 6 Saturn Drive, stopping at the end of a short gravel walkway leading to the house's main door. Juliette got out of the car and met her mother halfway down the walkway with her arms spread. Her mother wrapped her arms around her, and Juliette's worries about Peter and German politics melted in their embrace.

Jacques Durand waited until mother and daughter came up the walk to him, then hugged Juliette, kissed her on both cheeks and said, "It's so good to see you, *ma chérie!*"

The family took the afternoon to catch up, assisted by pastries and coffee. Marcel left to do errands, and the valet, Charles, kept the food and coffee coming. When the chit-chat was over, Juliette turned the conversation to Peter.

"Mama… and Papa… I have a problem with Peter, and I need your advice."

Veronique said, "Then may I assume you and Peter are more than friends. May I also assume you are not doing anything we may regret?"

Juliette knew her mother's ability to read her mind, so she didn't bother lying.

"Mother, we aren't taking any risks of my getting pregnant, but please don't ask me for anything more specific. It's enough for you to know I'm unhappy when I'm not with Peter, but sometimes… Mama, I love everything about him except his utterly stupid worship of Adolph Hitler!" She looked at her father.

Jacques said, "Perhaps worship is a bit too strong, and if you look at Hitler from Peter's point of view, 'stupid' isn't the word that springs to mind. What if you said, 'I'm in love with Peter, but I disagree with his political opinions?'"

"Papa, it's much more than that. We watched the *Sturmabteilung* shoot people in the street!" Jacques nodded, and she added, "Four SA soldiers beat up a Jew and his wife right in front of us because they had sold a hat to someone the SA had used to trap them!"

"And what did Peter do? Did he support the murderers in the street or the men beating the Jews?"

Juliette shook her head and looked at her hands. "He was appalled and risked getting a beating himself when he tried to stop the Brown-shirts from beating the Jews."

"And didn't he defend you when they arrested you for being a Jew in the theatre?"

"Yes, he did everything he could. He risked his life…."

"…for Jews. That doesn't sound like a National Socialist to me."

"But, Papa, Peter doesn't understand what Hitler's statements, and even his laws, imply!"

"Juliette, the German people had a democracy from the end of the Great War until Hitler became Chancellor, and that democracy brought only misery. After four years of war, the German people rioted in the streets; food was rationed; trainloads of young men's bodies arrived home to be buried. They forced the Kaiser to sign a truce, and then, four months later, those democracies double-crossed the Germans when they based the Versailles Treaty on vengeance for French grievances, not President Wilson's 'Fourteen-Point Plan' as promised."

Juliette said, "Marcel explained that to me, and I get the point."

"I don't think you do, or you would understand Peter." He stood up and began pacing.

"Germany had trusted Wilson and the Allies, but the Western Al-lies betrayed that trust when they forced Germany to sign a document placing all responsibility for the war on them. The Allies ignored the Wilson document, crushing Germany under a mountain of debt and shame it could never repay."

"Papa, Hitler is a murderer, a thief, and has no conscience!"

"But if you are a German, he has lowered unemployment from thirty to ten percent. He even executed his friend and probably hundreds more to make the streets safe. You've had some experience with that."

"Yes, someone told the SA I am a Jew, but I think the SS knows I'm not."

Jacques smiled. "I assure you the SS knows who you are."

He sat down and leaned back in his chair.

"Peter is not a fanatic. He has clear motivations to like Hitler, and his reasoning is sound. Don't underestimate Peter's intelligence."

Juliette hung her head, twisting her coffee cup back and forth in her hands. "I can see what Hitler is doing…why can't Peter?"

"Adolph Hitler is a clever manipulator."

Juliette said, "Hitler says he cares about the German people, but at the same time is conscripting three hundred thousand men this year, more than doubling the size of the *Reichswehr*." She looked at her father. "Won't that cost a lot of money? Where will he get it… from the Jews?"

"He is financing his 'miracle' with a bearer bond, a promissory *Mefu Bill*, short for *Metallurgische Gesellschaft*. The rich industrialist families buy those *Mefu Bills* to get government contracts, and the National Socialists agree to repay them in cash in five years. When the bonds come due, the cash will come from plunder taken from non-Aryans before they leave Germany and countries the Germans will invade. Hitler openly talks about *Lebensraum* in the east where a larger proportion of the population is Jewish and Romani because they are a gold mine for the Reich!"

"Hilde said he would march into the Rhineland now that the French pulled out, then Austria, Czechoslovakia and Poland, using ethnic Germans in those countries as his excuse. While we listened to his speech to the Reichstag, she pointed out…"

"Yes, I heard that speech, and your friend is astute—much wiser than the average German."

Juliette decided to say what she had been thinking since the *Reichstag* speech.

"Papa, despite what you say, I can't stay with Peter. I am losing the battle—I can't compete with an evil force that powerful."

"I don't know what to tell you, *ma chérie;* I believe Peter is a good man, and I don't think he will ever be a National Socialist."

Monique Desjardins visited Juliette the following day; she knocked on the door before Juliette was awake. Veronique led her to the breakfast table, Charles put a cup of coffee in front of her, and Veronique went upstairs to wake Juliette.

"It's nine o'clock, and Monique is downstairs. Did you know she was coming?"

Monique had telephoned a week before Juliette had left Munich, telling her she had an exciting proposition. Through the fog of a fading dream, Juliette suddenly remembered they had agreed to meet this morning at nine. She jumped out of bed and ran to the bathroom.

When Juliette arrived in the dining room, Monique was sipping coffee and talking to Juliette's mother. Juliette kissed her former teacher's cheek and said, "I'm so pleased to see you, Monique. I apologize and must admit I forgot our meeting until *Mama* woke me."

She sat down; Charles poured her a cup of coffee and, a minute later, set a plate of croissants in the middle of the table.

Veronique emptied her coffee cup and said, "I will leave you two to get reacquainted. Whatever you discuss won't concern me...." She looked at Monique... "Will it?"

Monique shook her head, and Veronique reluctantly left the room with Charles.

"Your mother told me things aren't going well between you and Peter. She said you can't live with his political views, and I can't say I'm surprised. I also despise what is happening in Germany, as any reasonable person must. But what baffles me is how a modern country full of intelligent people can fall for that man's drivel!"

Juliette shrugged her shoulders. "I don't understand what is happening, but I can't be part of it. I've decided not to return to Munich."

"But your letters... and at Christmas, I heard the improvement in your voice! Are you going to let this thing with Peter...?"

"It's not just Peter; it's soldiers dragging Jews into the streets and beating them because they sell something to a non-Jew; it's the signs on theatre doors saying '*Keine Juden!*' It's the feeling I am being watched by someone who will hurt me if I do something wrong. They even call *me* a Jew because I can't prove I'm not!"

Monique shook her head. "Then I agree; you can't go back to Munich. It isn't worth the risk even if Professor Garcia is the best teacher in the world and Peter is Don Juan reincarnated!"

She smiled sheepishly. "But I'm afraid I have a selfish motive for wanting you here. I have started an artist's agency and would love to have you as my client. The Bach Kammer Orchestra wants you to sing the Coffee

Cantata at the Café every week and one of the soprano solos in the B-minor Mass in late August. I think I can still get you into the summer festival in Amiens if you want to do a concert there, and Lyons is…."

"…Wait, wait… I must think for a moment. I've never sung the B minor Mass, so first I must look at it. I don't think I want to sing a solo concert and…."

"I already have a tenor for the concert. He was the narrator in the Coffee Cantata you sang, and he will sing in the B minor Mass. He's also not married, and he likes women."

Juliette laughed. "Mademoiselle Desjardins, you are incorrigible! You must give me a few days to think."

Monique picked up her oversized purse, pulled out a piano score, and passed it to Juliette. "That's the Mass, and could you do the Coffee Cantata on Saturday? Please? I'm afraid I told them you would… otherwise, I would do it, but I would rather concentrate on my new business."

"Monique, you do move fast," said Juliette, trying to remember the tenor's face. She remembered he wasn't as tall as Peter, but…."

"I've arranged a tentative time for your audition at the Monnaie Theater. Will two weeks be enough time to get ready? They're doing La Bohème in the fall, and their soprano is pregnant."

Strictly to buy time to think, Juliette picked up a fresh croissant and poured hot coffee into her cup.

"I need to think. You are moving so fast I need to catch my breath." She opened the Bach score, found the first soprano aria and skimmed it to get a feel for the tessitura.

"I don't see anything unusual, but I've never heard it. I see two sets of soloists… which soprano would I sing?"

"You can choose; they don't have a second soprano yet. Perhaps you should learn both, just in case."

Juliette laughed. She thought Monique's audacity was her best quality, but sometimes the woman stirred up a lot of dust.

"The conductor might want to have something to say about that!"

Monique sipped her coffee dry, stood up and shook Juliette's hand.

"Okay, I'll be in touch. Rehearsal for the Coffee Cantata Friday morning at nine in the Café. Same people… shouldn't need more than a run-through."

"I don't remember agreeing to…."

Monique laughed as she went to the door. "See you at nine Friday morning."

Juliette felt the Monnaie Theater would hire her, but she wasn't sure she wanted her first contract to be with a theatre her father supported financially. They might give her the contract even though she wasn't ready to handle 'Mimi' yet, and if she embarrassed herself on stage—if she made a mess of it in front of everyone she knew….

Juliette decided to talk to her father.

Chapter Thirteen

Roads that Bend

The most interesting roads weave around mountains and across bridges over rivers and valleys

JACQUES HAD JUST HAD A VISIT from his wife, warning him that Juliette would be knocking on his door to ask his advice about what she should do about her singing career, and he wasn't looking forward to it. His daughter had an annoying habit of listening to his advice, then doing the opposite.

Nevertheless, when she tapped the door, he said, "Come in," as a loving father would.

Jacques had a good relationship with his daughter. She talked to her mother about things too intimate or trivial to discuss with her father, but when it came to life decisions, she sometimes told her father more than he wanted to know, and he feared this would be one of those times.

Juliette threw herself in the padded leather chair she and her mother used when they came into his office for an extended conversation and began talking by going directly to what was on her mind.

"Papa, I don't know what to do. I love Peter, and my teacher is wonderful, but I hate Hitler and Germany!" She pouted, looked at the Turkish rug and waited.

"Please excuse your *Père stupide*… he doesn't see a problem."

"Peter loves Hitler…we discussed that."

"For the moment, yes, Peter has a high regard for Hitler, as do about fifty million other Germans. I thought we were done with that.

"Of course, I agree that Hitler is evil, but would you disown me if I told you I thought Hitler had performed an economic miracle in Germany? And if I said I respect him for rallying his people around the glory of work and the need to work together? Would you hate me?"

"Well, of course not, but it's not the same thing."

"If you love Peter, it is the same thing, *ma chérie*. And if he is the man you want to spend the rest of your life with, it is even more important that you understand your love and his limitations."

"But, Papa… "

Jacques put his hand up as a stop signal.

"Some people drive others crazy with their unfounded opinions, incessant yapping about insignificant subjects or events, and empty-headed commentaries on things they know nothing about. I could not live with someone like that, nor could you."

He got up from his comfortable office chair and went around the desk to face his daughter.

"I could also not live with someone who had no opinion about anything. I appreciate intelligent people who think seriously about who or what they support or do not support. They give you their well-thought-out reasons and listen to your counterarguments. This doesn't make them fanatical—quite the opposite." He let it sink in while Juliette waited, then said, "You must ask yourself whether your ego will allow you to live with someone who disagrees with you politically. It's that simple."

Juliette sulked for a minute while Jacques waited.

She said quietly, "I could live with someone who thought we should spend more or less on the poor than I did; I could live with someone who believed in a different God; I could even live with an atheist. But Hitler is a devil who has a powerful country in his spell, and I'm terrified he will do what he says he will do with that power." She stood up. "Papa, this is different. Peter is addicted to Hitler's magnetism and can't break the spell. I couldn't live with a drunk, and I won't live with a fool!"

Jacques nodded. "I understand, but Marcel is of a different opinion. Although he has never met Peter, he knows enough about him to advise you not to do anything rash. Give it the summer—perhaps Peter will come to you."

Jacques watched his daughter, knowing the signs. There was something else.

"Monique Desjardins has become a talent agent and is offering to get me singing jobs. She says she can arrange an audition at the Monnaie in two weeks—they need a Mimi in the fall. Monique has already found me a regular job singing on Saturday nights at the Café, and I'm singing the Bach B minor Mass in August. I've decided not to return to Munich and instead to begin my career in Belgium."

"That would leave Peter out in the cold—you told me that either Professor Garcia teaches both of you or neither. Are you so sure you could do that to Peter?"

"Yes, Papa, I must because I can't live in that awful country!"

"Then you must immediately write to Peter and Professor Garcia so they can make other arrangements."

"Papa, I need one more thing… I want you to talk to the manager of the Monnaie Theater for me."

"I won't use my influence to get that job for you. You're on your own."

"That's not what I'm asking. You automatically influence the Monnaie Theater because you are its patron. When I audition for them, they will know I am your daughter, and if I sing like a frog, they will still hire me because they don't want to offend you. I don't want to sing Mimi if I am going to embarrass myself and my family. Please speak to them before I audition and tell them that if they let me sing Mimi when they know I am not ready, you will do something they will regret!"

Jacques smiled. "I will speak with *Monsieur Guignard,* but I will not threaten him."

Juliette put writing a letter to Peter before writing to Professor Garcia. She began with the date, *3 July 1935,* at the top, then *Liebe Peter* under it. Should she have written *"Liebe?"* Juliette could admit to herself she still loved Peter, but did she want him to know that? How could she tell her lover that she couldn't stand to be around him because he admired the things she hated most in the world? She wrote:

I'm writing this letter because I couldn't say what I must if I saw you face-to-face. I need to think about every word without input from you or anyone else.

Juliette read what she had written, thought she should tear it up, then decided not to. She desperately needed him to understand why she couldn't live with his Hitler fascination.

I can't expect you to give up your ideas when I can't give up mine. I know you don't hate anyone or anything, not even those who would hurt you. I have seen that you are also brave, sometimes to the point of foolishness, especially when you defend me. But you have made Adolph Hitler a part of you, and I will not and cannot tolerate anyone who is part of that devil!

She read the paragraph and decided she had said enough. She now knew Peter would never give up his idol, and she could never tolerate the mention of the devil's name. It was time for the *Coup de Grâce.*

Peter, I love you and know I will die inside without you, but I also know I will get over it. Life will go on for both of us, and perhaps someday, when this madness is over, we will meet and laugh about this letter.

Juliette got up, went to the kitchen, poured a glass of milk and stole a croissant. As she ate, she thought about the letter. Should she tell Peter she would write to Professor Garcia, wrecking his chance of studying with him when he was doing so well? Perhaps Garcia would keep him as a student…tenors are scarce; good tenors are almost impossible to find.

She returned to the writing desk.

I am writing to Professor Garcia to tell him I am not returning to Germany because I don't feel safe there. I don't think he would ever drop a tenor as talented as you are, and, as a member of that rare species, I know you will get a good contract in a theatre.

Juliette read it, reread it, and knew it didn't matter how she said it; her rejection of Peter would break his heart. She cried as she wrote,

I will love you until I die. Remember your Mimi forever.

She folded the letter, sealed it in an envelope, addressed it and pasted a stamp on the corner.

The letter to Professor Garcia wasn't as hard to write but just as regretful. Juliette knew she would never have the voice she would have if she studied with him another year, and without Professor Garcia's blessing she couldn't stay at the opera school. She wouldn't be missed— sopranos are like flies in the opera world.

She dried her eyes, washed her face and found Marcel in her father's office. She looked at her father as she handed the letters to Marcel.

"What's this?" Marcel read Peter's address on one of the letters and Professor Garcia's on the other. "Is this what I think it is?"

Jacques said, "I'm afraid so. Juliette has decided to leave Germany and start her singing career in Belgium."

"And Peter? I thought you loved him."

"I do, but I can't be with him and Hitler."

Marcel tapped the letters against his hand.

"I guess you know what is best. But just for the record, I think you are making a mistake."

Juliette could feel her face burning and wanted to say something hurtful about the chauffeur keeping his opinions to himself, but she bit her tongue.

"I've made up my mind, and nothing will change it. Mail the letters."

She slammed the door as she left the office, and her eyes filled with tears as she ran upstairs to her room.

Elizabeth Schweitzer loved her son and husband without limits or conditions. They freely admitted her intelligence level was far above theirs and knew that if they had a problem, no matter how impossible it seemed, Elizabeth could solve it. And that was the reason for Peter's visit to his mother's kitchen a week after he arrived home. She stood at the stove, her back turned, stirring gravy in a cast iron roaster with a wooden spoon while shaking flour from a bottle to thicken it. Heinz had drilled holes in the top.

Peter said, "Mother, I love Juliette so much it hurts, but she doesn't love me. Tell me what to do."

Elizabeth smiled but didn't turn around.

"How do you know she doesn't love you? Have you told her how you feel?"

"Yes, I told her, but...well...I know she doesn't love me anymore, and if... Mother, I can't stand it!"

The bubbling gravy was the correct consistency when Elizabeth turned around and said, "You're just in time. The roasting pot is too heavy for me—would you fill the gravy boat?"

Peter put on oven mitts, lifted the heavy pot and filled Elizabeth's china gravy boat. As he poured, his mother began her search for the facts.

"Something is missing from your story. I know from your letters that you and Juliette…perhaps you wanted to go too fast. Did you…"

"No, Mother, I would never do that until we get married, even if she wanted to!"

"That isn't what I was going to ask, but it's good to have it out of the way."

Elizabeth wiped her hands, took a long wooden-handled fork and carving knife out of a drawer and said as she looked at the pork roast on the counter, "Your father is in the shop. Perhaps you…."

Peter took the tools, and his mother reached for a pot full of peeled potatoes still on the stove, turning off the gas in the same motion.

"When did she stop loving you?"

"Uh…the twenty-first of May."

"So precise? Perhaps you should become an engineer." She dumped the last bit of water into the sink and the potatoes into a large bowl. "Put those on the table while I make a salad. You can tell me about the twenty-first of May."

"Uh…" Peter searched for a way out of the trap and said, "Hitler spoke to the *Reichstag.*" He put the bowl in the centre of the table and turned around.

"Juliette and I got in a fight about what Hitler said. She hates the National Socialists, and so does Hilde, her roommate. They ganged up on me."

"Son, she and Hilde are not alone. Sometimes I find it hard to love you too… because of Hitler."

Peter sat down at the table and began fiddling with a fork. His mother pulled a chair to the opposite side of the table and said, "Tell me about Juliette. Why do you love her?"

Peter said, "The food will get cold. Maybe I should get Dad."

"The food doesn't matter. Tell me what you love about Juliette."

"Mother, Juliette is the most beautiful woman in the world and has the most beautiful voice. When we sing together, I feel we are one person... is that possible?"

Elizabeth reached across the table and put her hands on her son's. "Peter, I still feel like that with your father. It's called love, and you mustn't lose it."

"But she can't stand that I agree with most of what Hitler has done for Germany. He has made mistakes, but he is correcting them and...."

"Stop! Stop! I can see why you will lose Juliette; she sees the real Hitler, and you, my son, can't recognize the devil right in front of you!"

"But Hitler has...."

"Peter! Stop! You will say something stupid and expect me to think it's logical. Even a mother can't put up with that, and if Juliette has any sense, she will run away from you as fast as she can. I would worry about her sanity if she stayed!"

"But Mother, don't I have a right to...."

"To rant like a lunatic? To force people to accept your views? Your attitude is your problem—Adolph Hitler is in your head!"

Peter was silent as his mother stood up and poured a glass of milk for each of them. He drank some of it while waiting for his mother's advice.

She put down her glass, wiped off the white moustache with the back of her hand and said, "Think for a moment how you would describe your father, then tell me about him."

Peter shrugged. "I love Dad, and we get along better than most fathers and their sons. He and Rolf and Dieter don't get along as well as Dad and me."

"You haven't described your father. Tell me what he does that makes you respect him."

"I respect how he can machine a polished shaft from a rough casting to within a hundredth of a millimetre. I respect how he works with other men... he shows them how to do something without insulting them. He can teach the most stubborn man in the shop how to do things perfectly!"

"I understand what you are saying. Heinz is patient, kind, and very good at his job. He helps everyone else to be better, and he does it while making them feel good about themselves." She took another drink while Peter thought about it. She wiped her mouth and asked, "Is that what you are trying to say?"

Peter nodded. "Yes, exactly—that's it."

"Tell me, Peter, who do you respect more, your father or Hitler? Which one would you trust with your life? Would you trust Adolph Hitler with *my* life?"

Peter thought for a moment, then said, "I would trust my father with your life. Dad would die to protect you—but I wouldn't trust Hitler with anyone's life!"

"And yet, you worship that man, not your father. You go on about Adolph Hitler as though he were God, but I have never heard you praise your father, the better man by far. Hasn't it occurred to you that your Hitler fascination might be unreasonable? Perhaps even foolish?"

Peter sat motionless, looking at his mother, feeling like something heavy had run over him.

"But Mother, Hitler saved the country and rescued M.A.N. My father has a good job because of the National Socialists, and I can't believe you don't see that!"

Elizabeth squeezed her son's hand. "Peter, you are a victim of National Socialist propaganda. Juliette sees that and is frightened that you will destroy yourself and take her with you. If you love that girl, you will write to her and tell her about this conversation. You will never again speak of Herr Hitler to her or say his name anywhere she can hear you!"

She squeezed her son's hand so hard he wanted to pull it back, but he didn't.

"Peter, for everyone's good, you must break the spell that man has over you, and you can only do that if you don't listen to him on the radio or read those trash propaganda newspapers. Sing with Juliette; concentrate on her and the path you have both chosen. Take politics out of your life."

Elizabeth stood up. "Go and get your father while I finish making the salad."

Before Peter reached the door, she said, "As soon as we finish *Abendessen,* I will help you write a letter to Juliette."

Peter went to the shop behind the house, his mind churning. He paused at the door, listening to the sound of his father grinding a piece of steel. When he opened it, a stream of sparks landed at his feet.

Peter ate without saying anything more profound than "Pass the potatoes." Heinz returned to his shop when they had finished dessert, and Peter picked up a dish towel.

Without looking up from a plate she was washing, Peter's mother said, "I will dry the dishes...you write that letter."

Peter went to his mother's writing desk without a plan. He had spent many hours with his elbows on that desk, thinking about a project he wanted to build and sometimes a school assignment, but never a letter to a girl.

He sat in the straight-back oak chair that his mother insisted was essential for keeping her spine straight, pulled a sheet of paper out of the top drawer, and was reaching for Elizabeth's second-best pen when she said from the kitchen, "Not that paper...that's for the government. Look in the bottom drawer."

Closing the top and opening the bottom drawer, Peter pulled out a sheet of slightly blue paper and laid it on the desk as his mother shouted, "Use the good pen and the black ink."

Peter changed pens, took the stopper from the black ink bottle, dipped the point and wrote the date on the top corner: *6 July 1935.* As he touched the ink with the tip, then the nib on the rim of the ink bottle to remove the excess ink, he tried to shake the feeling that Juliette had already written him off.

Peter had postponed talking to his mother for more than a week. But he was confused, nervous and depressed and hadn't slept through the night since the argument with Juliette and Hilde. He couldn't give up Juliette unless she said it was over.

He wrote: *Liebe Juliette,* poised his pen for the first sentence and waited for inspiration. His mother had given him a sheet of expensive paper and told him to use black ink. He had to get it right the first time.

"Apologize first, then tell her how you feel about her."

Elizabeth stood behind her son, holding a newspaper. When he turned around, she said, "Come to the table. I have a copy of that speech." An hour later, Peter had tears in his eyes.

Elizabeth put her hand on her son's shoulder. "If she loves you, she will forgive you."

He returned to the writing desk, and his mother followed, standing behind him while he dipped the pen.

"Don't worry about the paper; I have enough."

Peter sighed and turned his head to look at his mother. She returned to the kitchen.

He wrote: *I haven't been able to sleep since I got home—Every night I have nightmares about you leaving me. I'm a stubborn fool, and I'm terrified it's too late to fix things. I was wrong to argue, and you were right about everything. I couldn't understand what you and Hilde were trying to tell me, but my mother and I read Hitler's speech in the Beobachter together, and now I understand. Hitler intends to take over Austria, Poland, and everywhere else Germans live.*

I promise I will never attend another Hitler rally, and I will not read the newspapers. Mother told me to concentrate on you and our music, and that is what I will do. Please forgive me for being such a fool.

Peter sighed and leaned back. His mother said from the kitchen, "Do you want me to read it?"

He had 'no' on his lips but thought better of it and said, "Yes, please."

Elizabeth came into the room, drying her hands on a towel. She looked over Peter's shoulder, rubbed the back of his neck with her hand and said, "You listened. She will like that." She leaned over and kissed his cheek. "Now, tell her how much you love her, and I promise I won't ask to read it."

Peter spent the rest of the page telling Juliette how much he loved her, how he loved to sing with her, and how he wanted to spend the rest of his life singing love duets with her. When he finished, he reread the words and was embarrassed at the childishness. He picked up the sheet, thought about crumpling it, and his mother shouted from the kitchen, "Don't worry if it sounds silly; love shouldn't sound like engineering."

He thought, "Maybe not," and put it down.

His mother shouted again from the kitchen, "Read it one sentence at a time. Love seems silly when you write it down, but ask yourself whether what you wrote is how you really feel, then read the next sentence."

Peter read aloud, *"I loved you the first time I saw you on the singer's bench, and from that moment on I knew I couldn't live without you."*

He said, *"Scheisse*, I sound like an idiot," and slapped the desk.

Elizabeth came into the dining room. She leaned on the table and said, "Read the sentence to me." Peter read it, and she waited a few minutes before she said, "I fell in love with your father the first time I saw him. He was cleaning our yard, and he smiled at me. That was enough."

"But what about the sentence?"

"It's wonderful. Juliette would be a fool not to love you, and that girl is not a fool."

"But what about…?"

"Mail the letter. Juliette will cry when she reads it."

Chapter Fourteen

Everything Works Out in the End

If everything hasn't worked out, it isn't the end
Tracy McMillan

THE COFFEE CANTATA REHEARSAL became a bit more than a run-through. The baritone who sang the father was a cold fish, had never sung the piece and couldn't remember his entries. He complained that the eight-piece chamber orchestra was not playing loud enough, and Bach had meant it to be played slower. The conductor then pointed out that the orchestra was already covering his voice, he was mumbling the words, and the tempo was correct. There followed an argument about what in the score was Bach's writing and what was the editor's.

The tenor took the disruption as an opportunity to approach Juliette and began his pitch, proposing she sleep with him when the rehearsal was over. Juliette fenced with him for a few minutes before she cut him off at the knees.

"I have a boyfriend who I intend to marry, and he is the best tenor I have ever heard. If you can't work professionally, leave, or I will."

"But I heard...."

Juliette turned away and went to the conductor, who was still arguing with the baritone. The baritone was mid-sentence when Juliette interrupted.

"How long before you get the rehearsal under control? I don't find this useful in the least." She turned to the baritone. "Perhaps if you used the score for the rehearsal, you wouldn't need to sing with only half your voice. And you had better have this memorized tomorrow."

The conductor blushed, looked at the baritone and said, "Shall we sing? I will find a tempo that works for you if you will sing over the orchestra. And I don't mind if you carry your score if that will help."

The baritone carried his score, sang in full voice, and the rest of the rehearsal went well.

As Juliette and Monique Desjardins walked to her apartment where Marcel would pick Juliette up, she said, "I wrote to Peter and told him it was over, but I don't want the world to know. Jean was under the impression that I was a candidate for his bed."

"I am sorry. I thought since you had broken it off with Peter, and Jean is a tenor, so…."

Juliette wanted to be serious, but she couldn't help laughing. "Are all tenors really like that?"

"All the tenors I know are either homosexuals or sleeping with anything with a skirt."

Juliette chuckled. She knew that Peter was interested in girls, especially a certain Duisberg soprano, and she felt a sudden twinge of pain when she thought of him singing love duets with her.

The Coffee Cantata went off with a few baritone memory lapses, which Juliette cleverly covered up, and everyone was a friend when it was over. The soloists went to an Italian restaurant for a late-night snack, and the topic of the B Minor Mass came up. Monique informed everyone that Juliette would sing the first solo soprano, Jean would sing the first solo tenor, and the baritone would sing the second solo bass. Everyone toasted everyone else, their sex partners, the B minor mass, Bach, and the excellent wine. When Juliette and Monique wobbled out of the restaurant, Marcel was waiting for them in the Rolls.

"Your father has good taste in cars," said Monique as the car soundlessly rolled through the streets, "I don't see why anyone would buy anything else."

She laughed, Juliette laughed, and in ten seconds, they were out of control.

Marcel said, "If you pee on those seats, I will get fired. Either quiet down, or I will stop and kick you out."

"Party-pooper Marcel!" said Monique.

They stopped laughing, and Juliette asked, "Heh, stick-in-the-mud, did you mail my letters?"

"You asked me to, didn't you?"

Juliette said, under her breath, "So just once, why couldn't you make a mistake?"

"What was that?" asked Marcel.

"Oh, nothing," said Juliette. "You are just so damned reliable you're boring!"

Juliette got home in time to throw up in the toilet, and the following day she woke with a headache. Not an average hangover headache, but a debilitating, stay-in-bed-and-let-your-mother-feed-you ache. Her mother caught her crying when she entered the room with a tray of croissants and coffee. Juliette pushed herself to a sitting position, and Veronique put the tray on her legs. She poured a cup of coffee for each of them, pulled a chair over to the bed and sat down.

Juliette didn't touch her cup or the croissant. She said, "The tenor made a pass at me. He invited me to sleep with him."

"Well, did you?"

"Mother! No, I would never do that with *him!* He's a *philanderer!*"

"Hmmm... philanderers can be fun, I guess! They certainly have lots of experience."

"I wanted to slap his face."

"What about Peter? Would you slap his face?"

"No, I would never slap Peter. But he would never be so...so... *vulgaire.*"

"You regret writing that letter, don't you?"

Juliette started to cry. Her mother leaned over the croissant and hugged her.

"Perhaps you should write another letter."

"No, he wouldn't read it; I was awful. I broke Peter's heart, and he will never forgive me! Furthermore, he would be insufferable about Hitler!"

"Eat your croissant, drink your coffee and come downstairs. Your father wants to talk to you about the Monnaie Theater.

It took Juliette an hour to eat, drink a cup of coffee and bathe. She covered the lingering smell of up-chuck with perfume, but her breath still smelled of alcohol when she sat beside her father's soft leather chair. He had a glass of cognac on the small table between them.

"I don't think I've ever seen you drink too much."

"And you never will again!" said Juliette.

"A small glass of cognac would help. Shall I pour one for you?"

Juliette waved her hand. "No, Papa. I think that would kill me right now."

"I had lunch with Monsieur Guignard yesterday, and your name came up."

Juliette smiled. "An amazing coincidence?"

Jacques almost smiled. "He telephoned me this morning after Mass. Apparently, he had dinner in your Café last evening. He heard you sing."

"And…"

"And he wants you to audition. He needs a Mimi this fall—early October première, I think—and he said if you've got the notes, you can have the role. He will tell you if he thinks you shouldn't sing it, no matter how badly he wants to hire you."

"When is the audition? It's not quite ready yet."

"Whenever you like, but the sooner, the better. Monsieur Guignard will try to have the tenor there for the duets if you have them ready."

"I can have the entire role ready on the fifteenth."

"That's only a little over a week. Are you sure?"

"Papa, Peter and I have been working on the role at the school. We're going to audition this fall."

Jacques smiled. "I thought you weren't going back. Didn't you write to Professor Garcia and tell him that?"

Juliette felt a jolt. She felt sick and started to get up.

Jacques said, *"Ma chérie,* you don't look well—perhaps you should rest."

Juliette made it to the bathroom and sent her croissant and coffee on their way to the river.

Juliette's mother brought Peter's letter to her room. She was still sick and sleeping, so Veronique put it on the table beside her bed. An hour later, Juliette's mother woke her and said, "You got a letter from Peter. I have to know what he said."

Juliette looked at the letter, now in her mother's hand.

"*Mon Dieu, Mama,* I don't want to know!"

"You must read it sometime. I think it could be something good."

"Good, Mama? It could be a suicide letter!"

Veronique pushed the envelope toward Juliette's face. "Please read it. I have one of my feelings, and I don't get one like this when something is bad."

Juliette took the letter, and her mother gave her a silver opener. She slit the end and pulled out a single sheet of perfectly folded light blue paper. She looked at her mother and held out the still-folded piece of paper.

"Read it, Mama, but don't let me hear it if it's bad."

Veronique pushed her daughter's hand back. "No, *chérie,* you must read it first."

Juliette unfolded the paper without looking at it, then lowered her eyes.

As she read, tears began to form and flow down her cheeks, gradually increasing until rivers of them streamed down her face onto her nightgown.

When she finally looked up, she was crying like a child. She passed the letter to her mother.

As Veronique read, she became more excited every second until, holding it in front of Juliette, she said, "I knew it was something good! Jacques has never written such a wonderful letter to me! Peter loves you enough to give up everything he believes in, and you are the luckiest woman in the world!"

Juliette wailed. "You don't understand, Mama... when he wrote that letter, he didn't have my letter yet! He will hate me when he gets it! I have ruined my life, and probably his too! What if he kills himself?"

Juliette cried inconsolably. Veronique held her until her cries became sobs, then left to go downstairs. She found Jacques in his office.

"How long should it take a letter to get to Augsburg?"

"A day, two at most; why?"

"Juliette just got a letter from Peter posted on Monday."

"Yes, that's two days. That sounds right."

"Peter hadn't gotten Juliette's letter when he wrote this one. If he gets her letter now, there will be a *désastre.*"

"Oh, he will already have her letter. It was mailed on… Wednesday last week. The letter was at his home on Friday, Saturday for sure."

"Maybe we should call his parents; perhaps they can find the letter before he does. Maybe his mother read it and didn't give it to him. Maybe…."

"I'll get Marcel—he's the only one who can clear this up. He took the letters to the post office."

Five minutes later, Juliette entered her father's office wearing her night dress and nothing on her feet.

"Where's Papa?" she asked. "Maybe we can stop the letters."

Veronique said, "No, your father said there is nothing to do, but he went to get Marcel to check when he put them in the mail. Peter should have had your letter when he wrote to you."

Juliette sat in the soft chair she always sat in when she talked to her father. She chewed her fingernails until, a few minutes later, Jacques and Marcel entered the office.

Jacques motioned to Marcel. "Give them to her."

Juliette jumped to her feet as Marcel put the letters she had written in her hand. She said, incredulous, "You didn't mail them?"

"I thought you shouldn't have written them, so I decided to wait a few days. I didn't think waiting until you cooled off would hurt. As a matter of fact, I was going to check with you today."

Juliette started crying again. She tore the letters into small pieces and threw her arms around Marcel's neck. She kissed him on both cheeks and said, "If I didn't have Peter, you would be in big trouble!"

Veronique looked at Jacques, but he didn't seem to notice.

Juliette's letter arrived four days after Peter had sent his offer of unconditional surrender. His mother put it on the table in front of his chair, and Peter took it to his room when he and his father arrived home from work.

Ten minutes later, he sat at the table, a broad smile stretched across his face. Elizabeth whispered in his ear as she passed his chair with a bowl of peeled and boiled yellow potatoes.

"I assume she forgave you?"

Peter nodded.

Heinz was never the quickest cat in the herd, but whispering was a sure sign his family was hiding something. He growled pretentiously, smiled at his wife and said, "Something I shouldn't know about?"

Elizabeth put the potatoes in the middle of the table, kissed her husband's neck and whispered, "Mother-son thing, and don't embarrass your son."

Heinz looked at Peter and winked. "If it's a girl problem, listen to your mother."

Peter blushed. He decided to tell his father.

"I wrote to Juliette to say I wouldn't talk about Hitler. She's like Mother; she thinks Hitler will destroy Germany and hates to hear anyone say something good about him."

"Good move, son. I never mention that name in front of your mother either." Heinz added, "But I'm not a *Dummkopf*—I know that's not what you were whispering about."

Elizabeth said, "I don't think you want to know about your son's love life—or am I wrong?"

Both men blushed, then Heinz and Peter said, *"Nein!"* together.

"I didn't think so. Now, who wants a *Jäger Schnitzel?"*

Peter and his father exchanged looks and, laughing, said, *"Ich!"* together.

They had just thanked God for their food and family, and Peter had picked up his fork when his father said, "Does this mean that you can't go to the rally with me?"

Peter looked at his mother, and she said, "As long as you say nothing to Juliette. No matter what she says, not a word about Hitler or the rally."

"What if she directly asks me whether I went to the rally?"

"Tell her the truth… that you went to the rally but not a word more, even if she beats you!"

Heinz spoke with his mouth full.

"Like me! I won't tell your mother *anything!*"

Elizabeth waved her spoon at Heinz and said with a hint of threat in her voice, "Now I want to know what you won't tell me!"

"Ich sage kein Wort! You can beat me, but I will never talk!"

Elizabeth waved her spoon again.

"There are ways a wife can get her husband to talk without beating him!"

And everyone laughed.

Chapter Fifteen

Everything Worthwhile is Difficult

The greater the degree of difficulty, the more satisfying the victory

THE WEATHER WAS PERFECT on the day of Juliette's audition for the Monnaie Theater, so she and Monique decided to walk there. Juliette told her about Peter, his touching peace offer, and the delayed letters. Monique was openly disappointed, and Juliette reassured her she wasn't losing a client or a friend.

Juliette said, "If I get the role, you will get your agent fee. It won't matter that I'm still in the *Münchner Hochschule.*"

"Yes, Juliette, I know, but it's more complicated than that. I've decided to move to Paris this fall, and I was hoping you would make Paris your headquarters."

Juliette was taken by surprise. "Paris? Why Paris? There must be a hundred agents and thousands of sopranos in Paris."

"I am originally from there, and I know most of the church musicians between here, Amiens, Paris and Lyons. I have four singers and a professional Bach choir on my list now; two singers live near Paris, and the others, in Belgium, want to get away. You would be my most important client."

Juliette said, "I'm sorry, but I want to sing opera. There are about sixty full-time opera houses in Germany and Austria and only three in France, and they aren't full-time repertory houses."

"Juliette, I understand, and your father says he will help me if I help him with some things that I can't talk about, even to you. Don't worry about me; I can take care of myself."

Mimi was a role that had always suited Juliette's voice; everything about Juliette was Mimi. Most singers and conductors agree that

Puccini's writing was inspired by the drama in the human voice, with the orchestra subservient to it. Juliette's voice was the one Puccini heard when he wrote *Mimi's* role.

Juliette began the first-act aria, and twenty seconds into it, Monsieur Guignard said, "Skip to before the high note."

Juliette felt insulted, but the pianist nodded and played a two-bar lead-in to the last phrase. Juliette sang it perfectly, then was interrupted again.

"Enough... I want to hear the duet from *'O Suave Fanciulla'* to the end. I promise not to interrupt."

Juliette was about to ask whether she was expected to sing the duet alone when a man, only slightly taller than she was, entered stage left. He walked like a woman, weighed only a few kilograms more than Juliette, and when he shook hands, his fingers wrapped gently around hers. He lifted her hand, and Juliette let him kiss her fingers.

"I am called Jules Ouellette. I will be your Rudolpho."

Juliette smiled broadly when she said, "I am Juliette Durand, and I would be delighted to be your Mimi."

Jules said, without a hint of the boaster, "I have sung the role many times, and I am told this is your first Mimi. Monsieur Guignard wants me to help you through the First Act duet. Don't worry; I won't kiss you, but I believe the scene requires intimacy... perhaps more than you would like."

Juliette kissed his hand coquettishly, knowing there was no risk. This man would respect her. She said, "You can kiss me if the director wants a kiss."

The tenor stood facing her, half a meter from her, nodded to the pianist, and began singing precisely on cue. She joined him at the appropriate moment and kept her eyes on his as he moved so close their breath mingled."

Jules' voice wasn't close to the size of Peter's, but it shone with resonance, and she let her voice blend, needing most of the power Professor Garcia had found. Juliette sang *'T'amo'* with all the passion she sang it with Peter, then let him lead her to the edge of the stage. Juliette put her lips inches from his as they sang *"Amor"* repeatedly, rising to a blended and relaxed 'C' and holding it until the chords in the score demanded they let it go.

Juliette kept her eyes on Jules long after the last note. Finally, they relaxed, and Jules turned to the theatre manager. Laughing pleasantly, he said, "If you don't hire this Mimi, you will also have to look for a Rudolpho!"

Monsieur Guignard ignored the comment and asked Juliette, "Tell me why your father was worried you might embarrass yourself. I have never heard a better Mimi, and your natural sense of the role is quite extraordinary. Don't you agree, Jules?"

"I have rehearsed for hours with five other Mimis and have never before felt that kind of connection. This woman can sing *and* act. If she told me she loved me, I would believe her. If she told me she hated me, I would kill myself. And that is what opera is all about, *n'est-ce pas?*"

On the way home, Juliette fought an excitement she had never felt before. She wanted to tell Professor Garcia that she understood now—she had learned his secret.

Juliette could have called Marcel to pick them up with the Rolls, but the cloud she found herself on was too high; she had to cool off. She wanted to talk to someone who knew something about what she had tried to do on stage. Juliette wanted to curl up in the bay window with Peter.

Monique broke the silence.

"You know Jules isn't interested in women, don't you?"

"Yes, it is a bit obvious. Jules is charming, intelligent, and so musical he breaks my heart. I wish Peter could work a phrase like that man!"

"It doesn't bother you that he likes men, not women?"

Juliette laughed. "So do I."

"You know what I mean."

"I know I like Jules very much, and I feel safe and comfortable around him. I look forward to singing Mimi with him, and Monique; my father taught me not to look for a problem where none exists."

Monique was quiet for a minute, then said, "That's a good point. I must start thinking like that."

They walked for a while, Juliette's emotions returned to normal, and she said, "What did you think? Is my Mimi good enough? Tell me truthfully what you think about my acting and singing."

Monique didn't hesitate. "Your singing was exquisite; you're the best Mimi I have heard. Your acting was so convincing I was sure you had missed Jules's sexual preferences. My chin is on the floor when I think about what you did without rehearsal or coaching! Marlene Dietrich… move over!"

Reichsparteitag der Freiheit is what the Nazi Party called its 1935 Nürnberg rally, so named to celebrate conscription, the last act necessary to free Germany from the terms of the Treaty of Versailles.

Heinz and Peter took the early train to Nürnberg, leaving before daylight and arriving at the zenith of a glorious sunrise. They walked to Zeppelin Field, sure of having their choice of seats. Indeed, few seats were occupied, and they chose theirs high in the grandstand above the podium Hitler would use to make his speech to the men of the *Wehrmacht*.

The *Münchner Beobachter* promised a parade of the armed forces through the Nürnberg streets that included men and equipment from three branches of the armed forces, over a hundred vehicles, a hundred thousand men, and the *Luftwaffe* crisscrossing the city overhead.

Adolph Hitler had openly thrown out the terms of the Versailles Treaty, and Germany's new Panzer, no longer classified as a 'farm tractor,' could officially carry guns and use the more appropriate name *Panzerkampfwagen I*. It would make its maiden public appearance as a tank during a mock battle fought by seventy thousand men, including a cavalry platoon. The war would be fought on eleven hectares in front of seventy thousand spectators, and a hundred and thirty Panzer I tanks would display their power. Heinz Schweitzer and his son had helped develop the tank, and half the *Panzers* on display were built in the M.A.N. factory in Nürnberg. They didn't mind a four-hour wait.

When Heinz put his lunch bag on the seat between them, Peter asked, "Are we saving a seat for Georg and his wife?"

"Just Georg. His wife hates these rallies as much as Elizabeth does."

Fools, Angels and the Devil

Georg Baltzar worked in the M.A.N. (Munich. Augsburg. Nürnberg) factory as a *Fliessband Ingenieur*. He had designed assembly lines to build *Lastwagen*, engines, and now the *Panzer I* tank and was responsible for the technical functionality of every production line in the factory. As the company's lead research and development machinist, working from the research facility in Augsburg, Heinz worked hand-in-glove with Georg. Working with his father, Peter spent many hours with the *Fliessband Ingenieur*, increasing the production of *Lastwagen* and now *Panzer I* tanks.

Peter had been in Munich beginning his singing studies when the first German tank prototype built since the 'Great War' was tested. Following evaluation, Peter had worked with his father on design modifications during his first summer at M.A.N., but neither had ever seen the little tank in action. Krupp was the lead company in the tank's development, but M.A.N. had designed specific parts of the suspension, tracks, and drive train. Heinz had been directly responsible for machining the final drive gears and shafts.

Georg joined them a few minutes before Hitler's speech, and they listened impatiently. For the first time, Peter found Hitler's speech confusing. He spoke of *Wehrbefreiheit*, the blatant act of breaking the rules of the Versailles Treaty and the League of Nations, something Juliette had predicted, as though the Allies were threatening Germany. He talked of "Modern Weapons," which Peter knew could hardly be called "Defensive." He spoke only of men joining the armed forces to learn "obedience, subordination and an utmost sense of duty," certainly referring to conscription, precisely as Juliette had predicted. Every paragraph was a version of the same sacrifice, obedience, and, consequently, the superiority of the German soldier.

At that point, Peter's mind went to Juliette and the guilt he felt for deceiving her. As Hitler continued to broaden the context of men joining the *Reichwehr*, twisting two years of servitude and slavery into a privilege, Peter wanted to talk to Juliette but knew he must keep his presence at the rally a secret.

The mock battle kept everyone on their feet for an hour. Panzer I tanks drove back and forth, spewing smoke from their guns, driving through smoke clouds created in strategic locations. Lovers of machines like Peter, his father, and Georg watched the mechanical ballet, accompanied by a hundred and thirty noisy air-cooled engines, with elevated heart rates.

Having spent the past two years designing and building these mechanical marvels, they clapped and cheered every time the carefully choreographed action changed direction. Peter looked at the women around him, all of them seated and trying to talk to one another over the racket, choking on the cloud of dust drifting into the stands. He imagined Juliette covering her ears and pulling her coat over her head.

The battle continued with the tanks overwhelming a mock defensive position, followed by the infantry shooting and bayonetting the survivors, reminding Peter that, as Juliette had pointed out, every army is, by its existence, offensive.

Planes flew over the field, some only a few meters above the clattering tanks, attacking positions with bombs and machine guns, perfectly timed explosions behind them simulating the destruction they had wrought.

Peter stopped clapping. He put his hands in his pockets and watched the demonstration, his excitement waning. Watching soldiers bayonet dummies and shoot wooden man-shaped targets, Peter swallowed the bile rising from his stomach. The idea of fighting amongst that chaos didn't frighten him as he thought it would... it made him sick.

Conscription was on Peter's mind as they left Zeppelin field and followed the crowd lining the streets. The discipline, subordination, servitude and sacrifice that Hitler had spoken of echoed in his mind, and he wanted to talk to Juliette... he had to tell her she was right.

Peter watched rows of soldiers march twelve abreast, columns of *Lastwagen* and rattling tanks, and, listening to the roar of the rabid crowd, was suddenly frightened. The feeling remained as he and his father walked to the train station when the parade was over. Georg and Heinz talked of how they could improve the manufacturing process for the Panzer I, excited and motivated to work on the next tank, a much heavier model with a cannon and even faster and more maneuverable. M.A.N. hoped to get the undercarriage and drivetrain contracts from Krupp, guaranteeing their employees another two years of work.

Chapter Sixteen

The Devil Tightens his Grip

Democracy rarely disappears overnight; it is slowly, almost imperceptibly squeezed out of society like water from a soaked sponge

THE FOLLOWING MORNING PETER'S TRAIN WAS ON TIME, It stopped at track two at the Munich *Hauptbahnhof* when the round white-faced clock at the end of the platform showed precisely two minutes after nine. It was Tuesday, 17 September 1935. Classes wouldn't begin until Wednesday, but Juliette would arrive today, and Peter wanted to be there when she did. Flush with money from his summer's work, he took a taxi to the *Sängerhaus*.

Juliette had written to tell him that Marcel would drive her to Munich in her father's new Rolls Royce, so after emptying his suitcase, Peter went to the bay window to watch for her. It was a twelve-hour drive, but Marcel had left Brussels yesterday, planning to stop along the way to take care of Jacques' business. He and Juliette had stayed in Karlsruhe overnight, and the drive to Munich would take about five hours.

Peter guessed that Marcel would try to get Juliette on the road early but that eight would be the best he could do. That meant he had two hours to wait, so he decided to work on his voice.

At first, Peter had intended to exercise his voice every day, but as the job with his father became more demanding, he had to work twelve hours six days a week. They had begun the summer working on a twelve-cylinder diesel marine engine using a new Bosch direct injection fuel pump. And then, when General Heinz Guderian made up his mind on the specifications, the war department decided to allow M.A.N. to bid on a new tank, creatively named the *Panzer III*.

They won, and the contracts collided, meaning overtime and nothing but work.

The new *Panzerkampfwagen III* suspension system necessitated a two-hour longer workday for the department and a full day of work on Saturday. The M.A.N. suspension design utilized a system of torsion bars, lowering the tank's profile while allowing more vertical travel in the tracks. The tank weighed twenty-three tons, but Guderian insisted that it must ride like his new Mercedes.

Peter began with a few soft arpeggios, then scales, but his voice was not cooperating. When he tried a B-flat, nothing but air came out of his mouth. He added a bit of effort, but the harsh sound told him what his throat muscles had already warned; he was tense, and the sound reflected that.

Angry with himself and worried that he was damaging his cords, Peter stopped singing and sat in his chair to watch for Juliette while his vocal cords recovered. He put a few 'falsetto' sounds in the front of his head, gently beginning above his break at B-flat and descending to the B-flat an octave below.

He watched a flock of sparrows chase a crow up the street as he switched to the 'you' sound on the same descending 'glissando.' The breaks smoothed out until he couldn't feel his voice transition from falsetto to full voice.

He went to the piano, screwed up his courage, and sang a relaxed B-flat, aiming for and counting on a squawk, but the sound was pure and rang against the plastered walls. He swooped down through an octave, expecting his voice to break, but nothing but a beautiful ringing sound filled the room. He picked a high-C out of the air, then a D. He sang the last phrases in Rudolpho's first aria, holding the 'C,' increasing the volume until he felt the line where he had to trade beauty for power.

"I can't believe it!" Peter danced to the window, wanting to see Juliette at the door, then hurried back to the piano. He plunked a B-flat, then sang the first B-flat phrase in the Bohème third act duet. Holding what he knew was a thrilling B-flat, Peter walked to the window and wanted to shout as Juliette climbed out of the back seat of her father's new Rolls and looked up at him. He held the note as he stared at her, and then lost it as they both began laughing and waving.

Juliette disappeared into the house—Peter heard her running up the stairs, and when she entered the room, she threw her arms around him. They kissed and she said, "Oh, Peter, sing it again!"

He plunked a 'C' on the piano, nailed it, increased the volume, then softened the note until it almost disappeared.

Juliette jumped into his arms. "Peter, it's so beautiful! I love you!"

Peter put his arms around her, the note forgotten as he pulled her against him.

"Marcel is late for a meeting and is leaving the luggage on the sidewalk." She smiled sweetly. "Would you help me carry it to my room?"

Peter heard the car drive away as he went down the stairs.

It took Peter fifteen minutes and three trips to carry everything to Juliette's room, and Hildegard showed up before he finished, ruining Juliette and Peter's plans. Hilde's summer had been full of adventure, and Juliette listened while Peter went to the living room.

The room had begun filling with chattering students, most of them talking excitedly about their voices and the concerts they had sung, but some were clearly suffering from the angst of leaving home.

Two hours later, Juliette found Peter waiting for her in his chair, shooing away anyone who tried to claim hers. The call to dinner came before Juliette could ask Peter about his summer.

After dinner, Juliette suggested she go to Peter's room, ostensibly to 'catch up' on their summer. When they got there, Peter didn't have a roommate, at least not yet, and he sat on the bed he had slept on for the past two years. There were two hardwood and two upholstered chairs in the room, and Peter didn't try to hide his disappointment when Juliette made a beeline for the one she knew to be the most comfortable.

She said, "Peter, your voice has improved so much I can't believe it!"

Peter said, "It isn't because I practiced," and then changed the subject.

"I've got some blackberry tea in the cupboard. Would you like some?"

"That sounds like a good idea," said Juliette, as nervous as a cat in a dog pound.

Peter put two cups of water in a kettle and turned on the hot-plate. As the element gradually turned orange, he checked to see if the cups were still in the cupboard over the sink—and they were precisely where he had left them.

Juliette said, "Despite what you said, you must have worked hard on your voice. It's much bigger than I remember—I could hear you as soon as I opened the car door."

"Truthfully? I worked with my father all summer, twelve hours a day, six days a week. M.A.N. received a contract from the war department, and everybody had to put in an extra two hours a day."

"Another Hitler make-work project? What were you building... tanks?"

Peter's face turned red, and he looked out the window.

Juliette said, "That violates the League of Nations rules."

Peter recovered quickly, but not quickly enough. Juliette knew she had pressed the right button.

"I can't say anything about what we worked on, but when I got home every night at seven-thirty and had my *Abendessen,* I had no energy left for my voice. But I warmed my cords on Sundays, and I think I can sing Rudolpho from memory."

Juliette didn't want to tell Peter about her upcoming contract at the Monnaie Theater—somehow, it felt like a betrayal—but she would have to inform Professor Garcia tomorrow, so she couldn't keep it from Peter.

"I did a lot of singing this summer. I sang the Coffee Cantata every Saturday for a month and the Bach B minor Mass a couple of weeks ago."

"Yes, you told me about that in your letters." Peter took the whistling kettle off the hotplate and poured the water into the cups. The loose tea was contained in tiny, perforated steel balls he and his father had made in the M.A.N. shop.

"But I didn't tell you I auditioned for the Monnaie Theater."

"No, you didn't." Peter pulled the small table between the chairs and set the teacups on it. He was suddenly afraid of what she would say next.

"They hired me to sing four performances of La Bohéme—two in October and two in March. The soprano who was supposed to sing Mimi is pregnant."

Peter was relieved Juliette hadn't signed a house contract. He said enthusiastically, "Just Mimi? That's great! I can help you—we can work on the role together!".

"That's what I told Monsieur Guignard. I will have to be there for blocking and orchestra rehearsals... they begin on October ninth, and the performances are on the nineteenth and twenty-second. I will be back here the following weekend."

Peter couldn't decide how he felt. He wanted to sing his first performance with Juliette and assumed that was the way it would be. But, of course, although he feared it, her career would have a different trajectory than his. They would audition separately; the odds were against any opera house simultaneously needing a lyric soprano and a tenor.

Peter sat down opposite Juliette. "You will turn their heads, Juliette. Someone will hear you and want you *Fest Angestellt.* By Christmas, you will have a long-term contract in a good opera house."

Juliette sipped her tea. "Professor Garcia told us we would audition together. I'm hoping we can sing in the same opera house, but I suppose that's too much to expect."

"Yes, I suppose it is. Maybe your Rudolpho will break a leg, and I can take his place. What's he like? Have you heard him sing?"

"He sang the audition with me. His voice is sweet but smaller than yours. He has good high notes."

"But, what's he like?" Peter felt a gnawing anger that he recognized as jealousy.

"He is sweet, like his voice. He's only a few centimetres taller than I am and not much bigger."

Juliette was pleased to see Peter's jealousy. "You are jealous, aren't you?"

Peter felt his face burning.

"I guess that's obvious, isn't it?"

Juliette put down her teacup and went to Peter. She sat on the arm of his chair, kissed his cheek, then whispered in his ear, "Jules only likes men."

Peter smiled, relieved. "Do you mind working with him?"

"I would rather work with him than the tenor I sang with in the Coffee Cantata—he expected me to sleep with him!"

Juliette went back to her chair. As she sat down, she said seductively, "I'm only going to sleep with you."

Peter's spirits rose, along with something else and he asked, "When?"

"Juliette put her cup on the table and stood up.

"How about right now?"

Peter stood, suddenly lightheaded.

And at that most uncomfortable moment, someone knocked on the door and marched in, suitcase dangling from his right arm.

Peter was taller than average, but this man was fifteen centimetres taller than Peter. His shoulders barely fit through the door frame, and his arms were as muscular as Peter's thighs. Even discounting the slight stomach bulge, he was the largest man Juliette had ever seen, and when he spoke, he sounded like God telling the Israelites they were special.

"I was given a key to this room, but if I'm interrupting, I can go away."

Peter's mind told him one thing, his urges told him another, and Juliette spoke before he got it sorted out.

"I was just leaving; I'm Juliette Durand." She took three steps toward him and offered her hand—it disappeared in his, her fingertips short of reaching past the edge of his palm.

Peter stepped to Juliette's side, making it awkward for the big man to keep her hand. Peter offered his in place of hers.

"I'm Peter Schweitzer, and it appears we will be roommates."

"Yes, that is what I was told. My name is Maximilian Holzmann, and of course, everyone calls me Max."

Peter was uncomfortable as he shook hands with Max. He wasn't accustomed to looking up at people, and he sensed that the man's hand was powerful enough to crush his bones.

"I wasn't told I would have a roommate."

Max took two folded pieces of paper out of his shirt pocket. As he passed them to Peter, he said, "My instructions are there, and the second sheet has the new rules."

Peter looked at his bedside table. He had seen the paper on it but hadn't gotten around to reading it yet. He read the preamble on Max's sheet about protecting the reputation and integrity of the school and respecting other students' privacy. Peter then read the first rule, making it clear no girls were allowed in boys' rooms, and no boys could be in girls' rooms for any reason, day or night. No second chances for an offence—just immediate expulsion from the school.

The big man smiled. "Yes, that one got my attention too. It's a bad sign that they put it at the top, and it's the only offence that will get you expelled. I'm almost thirty years old and didn't come here to become a monk!"

Peter read number two—no practicing in the room, but it gave permission to sing in the 'common' room between eight in the morning and ten at night. And, as expected, there must be no noise during *Mittagspause,* from one until three in the afternoon.

Number three forbade radios except in the 'recreational' room, and the penalty for changing the frequency, prohibited by German law, was immediate arrest by the Gestapo.

The fourth rule didn't bother Peter: Homosexual activity, or even suspicion of such behaviour, must be reported to the Gestapo immediately.

Number five forbade criticism of the Nazi government, the *Führer,* or Nazi policies. The consequences were left to the readers' imagination.

There followed a list of mundane items like meal schedules and bathroom courtesies, and the final rule was a notice that the house door would be bolted at 22:00 and opened at 06:00 in the morning. Between those hours, the inhabitants would be virtual prisoners.

Peter passed the papers to Juliette, and Peter and Max waited while she carefully read each one. When she returned the document, she said, "There was one of these on my table, but I hadn't read it yet."

Juliette wanted to say more, but Max was an unknown quantity. She decided on the spot to find an apartment, a *Wohnung* close to the *Hochschule.* She wouldn't need luxury; it would only be for a few months.

Peter was about to vent his frustration when Max spoke.

"Yes, that's an impressive list, isn't it? I got mine over a month ago, and I've been looking for a place to live ever since, but no one wants to rent to a student."

Juliette kept her tone neutral as she asked Max, "And which rules couldn't you live with?"

"The first rule is enough, but it isn't clear who determines criticism of the government, the Führer, or, most importantly, who reports it. I would also be interested to know who can inform the Gestapo of homosexual or suspected homosexual activity."

Max paused, then said, "I don't know you, and it's dangerous to talk openly in Germany right now. I can't even listen to *Radio Östereich* without breaking the law! When I look at that list, I'm nervous someone will catch me brushing my teeth in the wrong direction!"

Juliette was relieved; Felix had made her gun-shy of the other students, but her instincts told her this man was different.

She said, nodding, "I feel the same way about the rules, but Professor Garcia says Peter and I will audition in late October or early November, and he wants us to live in the *Sängerhaus*. He has a reputation for getting jobs for his students, so I'm not going to create any confusion. There are ways to work around this."

"I hope that's true because he will be my teacher, and he promised to let me audition as soon as I am musically ready. I sang for him in Vienna, and he said my technique would only need a few tweaks, but I needed to work hard on my musicality. I guess that means music theory?"

Peter and Juliette looked at one another. Peter said, "That's what I thought when I started, but now I know I started from scratch two years ago, and I'm still working on my technique and musicality. Juliette is way ahead of me."

Juliette put her arm around Peter and said, "Musicality is more than theory—it's ear training, phrasing, shaping the sound, and a generous dose of natural instinct. Generally, your musicality is measured by how well you express music with whatever instrument and type of music you play. Still, even with excellent musicality, your possibilities will be limited if you don't have a good technique."

"I haven't sung much classical music; I sing mostly *Volksmusik;* I can even yodel, but most people laugh when I do."

Juliette said, "Then you must yodel and let us judge."

He chuckled and yodelled a short phrase. Juliette laughed, and Peter shook his head, thinking that a yodelling bass sounded remarkably like a braying donkey.

The dinner table chatter came from two camps, one stridently in favour of the rules, the other objecting to them but choosing their words carefully. The discussion continued as students filed into the living room, eventually turning to the new race laws that Hitler had recently unveiled, with about the same division between the same people.

News of Juliette's contract to sing Mimi had somehow reached the students, and when they became tired of talking about what the race laws would mean, they turned to her, pestering Juliette and Peter until they agreed to sing La Bohème's third-act duet.

Hilde played the piano, the only baritone in the house sang Marcello, and a new mezzo-soprano sight-read the insults Musetta flung at him.

They began the scene with Rudolpho's arrival, something Peter hadn't sung in four months. It was the first time he had sung it with enough confidence to forget about his technique, and he now understood what Professor Garcia had meant when he said, "Stop looking at your vocal cords!"

Listening to Rudolpho's broken heart, Juliette found herself close to tears. She became Mimi, ill with tuberculosis, knowing that the draughty garret Rudolpho lived in would drastically shorten her life. Left unsaid was that Mimi must live with someone who could offer her the warmth, food and medicine she needed. The heart-rending duet ended with an agreement to part, but not until spring.

The tragic couple's long phrases soared, floating romantically through the room as Marcello and Musetta fought in the background. Their high notes rang from the plastered walls—Juliette felt her resonance meshing with Peter's until the sound overlapped.

The end came too soon for everyone, and no one heard the final loud chord from the orchestra, despite the punishment Hilde inflicted on the innocent piano.

Peter didn't want to let go of Juliette, and she wasn't ready to help him. They held their embrace until it came close to embarrassing, then reluctantly parted.

The other students congratulated Juliette and Peter, wishing them well, some with tears in their eyes. And then the madrigal books came off the shelf. They sang until curfew at ten, and every break brought the conversation back to Juliette's contract. She was the envy of every soprano in the room—a handsome, humble tenor and an opera contract: for a soprano, heaven's ultimate reward.

Max joined Juliette and Peter at the singer's bench opposite Professor Garcia's studio a half-hour before their lesson. Max still had an hour and a half to warm up his voice. When he sat down, Juliette stood up and said, "If you like, I will show you how to prepare for a lesson." He immediately followed her into a practice room.

Juliette taught Max a few simple arpeggios, marvelled at his natural voice's deep, profound power, and found she enjoyed teaching his cords to find sounds almost as much as singing herself. As she guided his weak falsetto down the scale through the break, Juliette was sure she heard why Professor Garcia had chosen him over the dozens who had likely auditioned. She was fascinated when Max's voice immediately responded and was annoyed when Peter tapped on the door and said, "It's time, Juliette."

Juliette reluctantly left Max to join Peter in Professor Garcia's studio.

The professor shook hands with Peter and Juliette, pointed at Juliette and said, "You have been a bad girl. You took a contract without consulting me."

Juliette blushed. "I wrote to you."

"After you signed the contract."

Professor Garcia had a smile that belied the scolding he was giving. Finally, he said, "If you had called me, I would have told you to sign it. You are ready to sing Mimi."

An enormous weight disappeared, and when Juliette asked him about the rehearsal and performance schedule she had sent, Professor Garcia said, "The rehearsal plan works well. I scheduled your audition with the Nürnberg Theater for late November, and I booked the Odeon concert for the first week in November, so everything works out perfectly."

"Odeon concert?" said Peter.

Garcia nodded. "Providing your voice has appreciated the rest your mother told me it had."

"My mother?"

"Yes, well, I called her to see how you were doing. Juliette's father suggested it."

Juliette looked at her professor, then Peter, and decided things were becoming too complicated. She said nothing, and Peter came to the same conclusion. But the Professor wasn't done.

"I am going to assume your affair is back on the road, and I'm sure you are both disappointed with the first rule."

Juliette's face burned, and Peter looked at his feet.

"Yes, I thought so." Garcia added, "There are hotels in the city that won't ask whether you're married, but with the Gestapo spies now in town, there is some slight risk. They pay our highly principled citizens well for such important *Nachrichten*. The Gestapo won't care, but the school will expel you. You must be careful."

"*Scheisse…*" whispered both Juliette and Peter under their breath.

"Indeed!" said Professor Garcia. "And now, let us sing something cheerful. We shall warm up with the Tyrolean roses."

Peter started to say he hadn't brought the score, but the look he got from Professor Garcia reminded him that it was a duet he should know.

"*Schenkt man sich…*" was as far as Peter got before Professor Garcia stopped him.

The professor put his hands on his lap and asked, "What happened to your voice?"

"Didn't my mother tell you I could only practice on Sundays? M.A.N. got an important contract and…."

"You misunderstand—your voice has found itself—you sang that as though you knew what you were doing!"

Peter shrugged. "I just woke up one morning, and everything worked. I thought I would lose it like I always have, but it's so easy now that I...."

"Yes, yes, but I didn't expect it so soon...you are so young!" He smiled, thoughtfully played a scale and said, "Maybe this singing together is a better idea than I thought." He raised his eyes and moved them from Peter to Juliette. "And perhaps it's because... Juliette, did the same thing happen to you?"

"Nothing that dramatic, and it happened gradually over the summer. When I heard Peter singing as I arrived at the *Sängerhaus,* I could tell he had made a huge breakthrough. Last night, we sang the third act of Bohéme for the other students, and it was exquisite. The other students said things...."

"Sing the last phrase." Professor Garcia played the bars leading into the last romantic phrase in Act III, and Peter and Juliette sang it. They held the B-flat, playing with the sound, looking into one another's eyes until the professor waved his conductor's hand, then dropped to the final passionate notes.

Professor Garcia looked from one to the other, then said, "I took a chance. I spoke with Herr Johannes Maurach, the Intendant of the *Nürnberg Stadttheater,* and I thought I might have gone a little too far—until now."

He said, "Neither of you has to worry about La Bohéme. If you sing like that, you will make me look like a genius, and I'm confident he will hire you."

Peter and Juliette's "Both of us?" overlapped.

"Yes, both of you. I told the director he couldn't have one without the other. Fortunately, he has no reasonable prospects for a Rudolpho with a solid 'C,' and his lyric soprano is off to Hamburg next year.

It suddenly occurred to Juliette that this might be an arrangement Garcia had been planning for a while.

She said, "I don't suppose they are doing *Der Vogelhändler* next year?"

Professor Garcia chuckled and nodded. "Yes, and he wants to do *La Traviata* in thirty-seven, so you will need to sing that devilish aria at the audition."

"The one with the high 'E,'" confirmed Juliette, nodding. "I worked on it this summer, and I can sing it on a good day."

"It's my job to teach you to sing it on a bad day." The professor's fingers ran up and down the keyboard, then began the introduction to the "Roses in Tyrol."

Peter finished singing the first verse; Juliette repeated his lines and was surprised at how much she enjoyed singing the romantic duet with him. Peter's voice had the ringing quality that made old ladies swoon, and Juliette got the full benefit when they sang close together. They sang the romantic ending, their voices blending like sugar and water, their cheeks half a centimetre from touching.

Garcia said, "Well, we can put that aside and work on *La Traviata*."

Peter sang Alfredo's lines before and during Violette's awkward and extremely difficult mood-swinging First Act aria at an *Übungsabend* a week before their audition. Juliette received the universal acclaim of thirty students, and Peter, bowing alone, got polite applause. Juliette's 'E' was no longer at the top of her range, and the 'F' in the dreaded *Königen der Nacht* aria from Mozart's *Zauberflüte* was still not the limit of Juliette's range, and she sang with confidence born of skill. The *Regisseur* in the opera school had worked out a staging for Juliette's *Violette*, and she lost herself in it.

The audition in the Nürnberg *Stadttheater* was not something Peter ever wanted to do again, but Juliette had sung dozens of them and helped him through it. Juliette began with Violette, and twice Herr Maurach's *Musik Director* cut her off. The second time, he told Juliette to skip to the end, and when she took the optional 'E,' holding it a bit too long, he smiled for the first time and said,

"*Herr Schweitzer… Bitte singen Sie die Aria von Rudolpho.*"

The pianist played the short introduction, and Juliette took her place beside Peter on their hands and knees on the floor, searching for her key in the dark. Their hands touched. Startled, she made a slight sound, and Peter sang, *Che gelida manina...* "Your tiny hand is cold...."

The opera school had staged all of their duets for them as part of their acting classes, and Juliette had smoothed Peter's stiffness to the point where he was better than passable when he sang with her. He immediately became Rudolpho, forgot about voice technique, and sang to Mimi.

He wanted to scream at the music director when he stopped him two lines into the aria and said to the pianist, "Go to *'Poiche...* you know the place...."

Peter sang it perfectly, beginning the first *"La..."* with the lightest colour he could, keeping the three approach notes the same heady mixture of top and chest voices, then nailed a bright, ringing high 'C' from the top. Peter turned his head as he increased the support, sweeping the sound across the theatre, manipulating a relaxed, focused vowel to a ringing insistence, adding pressure as he dropped to the last syllable.

Peter was surprised when the director let him take Juliette's hand and sing the following phrase, asking her to tell him her story.

The *Musik Direktor* talked to the *Intendant* for a few seconds, Herr Maurach left, and the director said, "We have decided that we want you both in our ensemble, and Herr Maurach is preparing the contracts. But for my information, I want to hear what you can do with *Schenkt man sich Rosen...* and the Bohème Third Act duet. I'm afraid I don't have enough time to hear it all, so I will choose as we go."

As they sang the third act of *Bohème*, Juliette couldn't help comparing Peter's Rudolpho with Jules Ouelette's. The Monnaie Theater was built for smaller, sweeter voices, and the Large Nürnberg Theatre for powerful, exciting voices. When she sang La Bohème with Jules, Juliette had tempered her voice so she wouldn't cover Jules' sweet sound, but Peter matched whatever she did seemingly without effort. His passionate interpretation blended perfectly with hers, dramatically contrasting Marcello and Musetta's background fight.

Contract negotiations with Herr Maurach were short—as *Anfänger,* the singers had no negotiation position—but the three-page list of conditions and rules was onerous, and Juliette balked when she had to state her racial origins and religious affiliations as Aryan or non-Aryan, Protestant or Catholic. She explained that she was many-generations Belgian Catholic, which prompted Maurach to instruct his secretary to write 'Aryan'... and 'Roman Catholic.' He didn't have to ask Peter...the secretary had a copy of his information gleaned from the *Bürgeramt*. She took the original, retyped it in triplicate and returned it for signatures.

Juliette reread every word, and Maurach ranted about government interference in art as he waited. When Juliette finally signed the last page, everyone shook hands and Intendant Maurach said, "I wish I could negotiate a longer contract term, but the end of thirty-eight is as far out as I can go with an *Anfänger Vertrag,* and even if I could go further, you would be fools to sign it.

Chapter Seventeen

Some Rules are Intended to be Broken

If you obey all the rules, you miss all the fun
Katherine Hepburn

Professor Garcia broadened his experimental duo-teaching to include Maximillian and Hildegard, compelling them to spend more time working together. If there had been a question of where Max's voice would fit in the opera repertoire, it was answered when he sang Wolfram's "Song to the Evening Star" from Wagner's *Tannhäuser* at an *Übungsabend*. No one who was there would ever forget that voice or the man. Any flicker of doubt that remained was extinguished when he and Hilde sang the last scene from *Die Walküre* in January. Maximilian's *Wotan* and Hildegard's *Brünnhilde* left the audience stunned.

Hilde returned from their triumph in a mood Juliette had never seen, and she waited for an opportunity to ask the obvious as her distraught friend paced, ranting about the 'first rule.' Finally, when Hilde sat on the bed, hung her head in silence, and looked at the floor, Juliette asked, "Is it Max?"

Hilde looked up and said quietly, "Of course, it's Max. I love that man!"

"Does he know?"

"If he doesn't, he's too stupid to live."

Juliette sat beside her friend and tried to put her arm around Hilde's shoulder to comfort her but gave up when she couldn't reach that far. She looked straight ahead, put her hands on her lap and said, "Well… I'm going to rent a hotel room. They won't want to turn business away, so all we must do is give them an excuse to turn their heads."

Hilde nodded. "Yes, that's all there is to it, but a false *Ausweis* that shows us as married is out of the question. I'm not sure that a night in bed with Max is worth the punishment, but it might be. The problem is, if someone is on the ball, it's easy to prove."

Juliette and Hilde looked at the wall. Juliette said, "So… we can't pretend we're married, but…."

"Give me a couple of nights in a bed with Max, and I guarantee he will beg me to marry him."

"Peter would marry me tomorrow, but I don't want Hitler in my house."

Hilde said, "I didn't think it was possible, but Max hates that piece of dog crap worse than I do."

Juliette said, "Tell him to beat some sense into Peter." She stood up and looked out the window. "There has to be a way!"

Hilde stood beside Juliette, rested her hand on Juliette's shoulder and asked, "What if we rented two rooms?"

Juliette thought about the idea for a moment before the light came on. "Peter and Max rent a room, and we rent one an hour or two later?"

"Yup—Max sneaks into our room and you go to theirs. My God, is it that easy?"

"What could go wrong?" Juliette's excitement threatened to overwhelm caution.

"All we need is a hotel that won't think too hard about it."

Juliette laughed. "If it works, how often can you afford it? If you need it, I have bags of money, so…."

"Cabaret singing pays very well—a lot better than opera. Even if I paid for his room, I could do it every day for a year!" She clapped her big hands together. "I can live with that!"

"Same here," said Juliette, "but the boys don't have that kind of money, and they won't take ours, so…."

"Okay, so maybe I can live with once a week…how about you?"

"We could take a taxi to a hotel outside the city!" Juliette smiled sheepishly at Hilde. "Uh… those hotels are cheaper, and maybe we could make it twice a week."

They looked at the wall for a few minutes, then Juliette said, "We should take turns… someone should be in this room every night." They exchanged glances, shook their heads, and said, "No, we'll go out together."

The following day, Juliette and Hilde went hotel hunting. One by one, they crossed off the cheap hotels where the worst shenanigans were encouraged and were walking past the Bayerische Hof when Juliette stopped and looked at the entrance with the hotel's name in gold letters over the door. As she and Hilde watched, two taxis dropped off couples with no bags… the woman in both cases was at least twenty years younger than her companion and carried nothing but a large handbag.

Juliette said, "The National Socialist spies probably watch the hotel for Jews, but if they arrested every couple that came here for recreational purposes…" and Hilde finished the sentence… "They would lose half their clientele!"

The pitch of Hilde's excited voice rose, "We could come straight here after classes, have dinner, and eat breakfast together the next morning. The more we spend, the less likely the Gestapo, or whoever guards the Munich *Mädchen's* virginity, would bother us!"

"If the men sat together without us, and we sat together, someone would think we were queer, wouldn't they?"

"Yes, they would. Hitler has made it clear what he thinks of homosexuality… look at Ernst Röhm; Hitler probably killed him more because he was a homosexual than on the flimsy evidence that Röhm had betrayed him." Hilde put her cold hands in her pockets. "You won't find two men having breakfast together in a Bayerische Hof restaurant!"

"My Rudolpho in Brussels is homosexual, and he doesn't hide it. I enjoy his company more than anyone except Peter's, but that lovely man will never sing in Germany!"

Hilde said, "Trust me; no one will ask questions if we are heterosexual couples in an expensive hotel like that! You wouldn't believe what goes on in those rooms, and if the Gestapo starts asking questions… well, they wouldn't dare start that ball rolling down that particular hill!"

Juliette smiled. "And there won't be any singing students in that expensive hotel to rat on us."

Hilde looked down at her and said, "You've got it bad, haven't you?"

Juliette nodded and bit her lip. "It's been over six months since…."
She looked at her feet and dragged her toe over the ground.

Peter and Max were sitting in the living room drinking a beer, waiting for the evening meal to arrive at the dining room table, when Juliette and Hilde entered the room. Juliette sat on the sofa beside Peter; Hilde stood behind Max's chair and put her arms around his neck.

Juliette said, loud enough for a few other students in the room to hear, "We've decided we want to go to the Deutsches Theater tonight, and before that, we want to eat at the *Spatenhaus*."

"Okay, thanks to the summer job Hitler gave me, I can afford to go out." He mocked Juliette with his irresistible grin, easing the sting of the forbidden name.

He expected a sarcastic comment, but the look on her face wasn't one that would indicate retaliation; in fact, it switched on a stab of joy in Peter.

Hilde turned Max's head, leaned over and kissed him.

"We'll meet you here. Why don't you put on some nice clothes?"

Max looked at Peter; he shrugged, and they followed Juliette and Hilde up the stairs.

The *Spatenhaus* had a table for them, and Juliette ordered a bottle of expensive wine.

"What time does the film start?" asked Peter while they ate a sweet blackberry pudding.

"Soon," said Juliette. She looked at her watch. "In fact, we're too late."

Max looked at his watch. "It's ten after... if we hurried, couldn't we...?"

"No," said Hilde, "we couldn't."

No one spoke for almost a minute. Hilde finally broke the silence.

"We've got a surprise for you. But you have to do what we tell you."

"Uhh...." said Peter. "Nothing illegal, I hope...."

"Well, technically, I suppose...."

Juliette giggled. "Trust us. It won't hurt, and you won't get arrested."

"Where are we going?" asked Peter as the girls led them toward the Bayerische Hof. "The Deutsches Theater is that way." He pointed down the other side of *Promenadeplatz*.

"Yes, it is," said Hilde, "but we're not going there."

"Oh? Where are we going?"

Juliette pointed at the hotel. "We are going there."

Max stopped walking and stared. "Why?"

Hilde said, "Because I want you to sleep with me." She raised her large handbag in front of his face. "I've got my nightie and everything we need right here."

Max looked at his feet. "I don't know if we should."

"Do you have a wife or a girlfriend you haven't told me about?"

"No, not anymore. A week after I left home, my girlfriend found someone else." He looked at Hilde, grinned and said, "As planned."

"Do you want to sleep with me or not? You know, you've sent a few signals, and it's impolite to ask for something you don't want."

"Yes, more than you know, but, to tell the truth, I'm not very good at it, and I'm afraid...."

"You weren't a good Wotan either until Professor Garcia taught you how to sing! Trust me; I know how to do this."

Max looked at Hilde, probably one of half a dozen men in the city who had to lower his head to look into her eyes.

Hilde said, "Max, I'm already old for a singer, and I want a family with you. I also want to sing in America, but not tonight."

Juliette told Peter, "I now know what it feels like to be a nun, and I understand why my catholic school teachers screamed and threw things."

She straightened his twisted collar. "I want to do this, and you will let me pay for everything. I asked Papa to send lots of money, and it's in the bank."

Peter opened his mouth but then closed it to think. Finally, he said, "If I sleep with you, will you marry me?"

"Did you go to the National Socialist Party *Tag der Freiheit* rally?"

Peter felt his face burning.

"I see you did go to the rally. You know you promised you wouldn't!"

Peter opened his mouth, but Juliette put up her hand.

"Stop, Peter; nothing you can say is better than saying nothing. I want to forget about Hitler for a few minutes...well...hours, but I won't marry you yet. If I married you, I would marry Hitler, and then

223

I would get pregnant, and then… It just won't work, but perhaps later…" Juliette pushed Peter toward the hotel. "Let's go practice our love duets."

Juliette gave Peter a wad of Reichsmarks, and he and Max headed for the bar.

Juliette and Hilde checked into a room on the third floor, carrying oversized handbags. When the clerk rang for the bellboy, they gave each of them ten marks. The clerk smiled and nodded as though it happened all the time.

Hilde appeared at the bar and slipped a key into Max's hand as she said, "Room three hundred and twenty-two. Come as soon as you can."

Half an hour later, Max showed up in the girls' room. Hilde was on the bed dressed in a nightgown with a book in her hand when he asked, "Are you sure?" She licked her lips and pointed at a door. "The bathtub is in there."

Juliette held out her hand. Max handed her a key and said, "He's waiting for you in room three-sixteen."

Juliette had her hand on the door handle when Hilde said, "Tomorrow is Sunday—not before eight!"

Juliette chuckled. "You don't have to worry about that!"

Juliette looked forward to Saturday night every week until the end of the semester. The foursome added the theatre to see a movie, the *Staatsoper* if it was something in their repertoires, and sometimes the *Shauspielhaus* to see a play if it wasn't blatant propaganda.

A month before the school year ended, Professor Garcia arranged a private audition for Hilde and Max at the Hamburg Staatsoper. The Intendant pushed a contract in front of them, hiring them to sing Tannhäuser. A week later, *The Bayreuther Festspiele* hired them as the *Zweitebesetzung*, alternates for the *Wotan* and *Brünnhilde* in the 1937 summer festival Ring Cycle.

Hilde decided Max could ask her to marry him and set the wedding date as the last day in August.

Professor Garcia reserved the Odeon Theater for June nineteenth, when Juliette and Peter would sing their *Reifeprüfung* concert, the final part of their graduation exams. The public was invited, and Peter's parents and grandparents were there. Juliette's parents were, unfortunately, in England searching for art objects.

They divided the concert into two parts... the first, opera arias, German *Lieder,* and French *Chanson;* the second, a half-hour of opera duets. The applause didn't stop until Juliette had sung her encore, Rusalka's "Song to the Moon," and Peter had sung a short aria from "Fedora," titled *Amor ti vieta...* "Love forbids you not to love."

The school had arranged a reception for those who wanted to meet the budding artists, and the first people Juliette and Peter looked for were his parents and grandparents.

Peter held Juliette's hand as he introduced his mother.

"I have heard great things about you," said Elizabeth. "I know it is presumptuous of me, but I hope you will someday be part of our family."

Juliette wanted to put her arms around Elizabeth and was considering whether she should do it when Peter's mother wrapped her in a warm hug. She whispered in Juliette's ear, "We are winning on the Hitler thing. Please, Juliette, don't give up on my Peter."

They still held one another's hands when the embrace ended and Juliette said, "I assure you, I never give up!"

Elizabeth stepped sideways and pulled a grinning, self-conscious and uncomfortable man forward.

"This is Peter's father, Heinz." Heinz looked as though he would like to run, but Elizabeth pulled him close to her and said, smiling, "And this is Juliette, the woman Peter loves."

Heinz awkwardly stretched out his hand, and Juliette impulsively bypassed it to hug him. She whispered, "I love your wonderful son."

When she let his embarrassed father go, Peter turned Juliette around and said, "And these are my grandparents... Moshe and Hannah Metzger."

Juliette couldn't move. After an awkward moment, she saw that her shock had stunned Moshe and Hannah and knew they had misinterpreted the cause.

Elizabeth said gently, "I see Peter didn't tell you my parents are Jewish."

Juliette was suddenly furious with Peter. She turned to him during the embarrassing silence but could only helplessly search for words that wouldn't come. Hannah finally whispered to her back, "Peter doesn't understand… he thinks we're the same as he is."

Juliette didn't turn around. She stared at Peter, found words she knew she would regret, and said them loud enough to be heard by others in the room.

"How can you be so stupid and insensitive about Adolph Hitler and National Socialism? My God, Peter, he wants to destroy your family!" She turned to Hannah. "He still believes Hitler doesn't want to hurt Jews!"

Moshe said calmly, "We live in Munich, but we're safe now that Röhm is gone." He whispered, "Perhaps this isn't the place to discuss this."

Something snapped in Juliette's mind, and she looked around at the people waiting to speak to them. They were giving the family space, but she suddenly realized that some of them must have heard the conversation. She turned to Hannah.

"I'm so sorry I made assumptions I had no right to make. Please forgive me."

Hannah put her arms around Juliette. "My dear, there is nothing to forgive. We are not ashamed of our heritage—she looked at Heinz—and we are not ashamed of our Aryan son-in-law."

Heinz grinned, but when he realized everyone was looking at him, he broke eye contact by looking down.

The people who had stayed for the reception, if they had heard the exchange, didn't acknowledge it. A few left, but most stayed to talk to Peter and Juliette, basking in the glow of their success.

When they finally broke free of the crowd, Hannah and Moshe took the family to a small Jewish restaurant owned by friends and introduced Juliette to *Shabbat,* a traditional once-a-week meal. It began with asparagus soup and balls made from shaved and pressed potato, moved on to roasted *Shabbat* chicken, two loaves of *challah,* and finally, dessert—*Babka,* stuffed with cranberry.

Juliette forgave Peter before dessert, and they decided to walk home, although Heinz had offered to drive them in his car, parked behind the restaurant. Hannah and Moshe lived only a block away, so everyone gathered on the sidewalk to say goodbye.

Hannah said, "I cried when you sang the second duet from La Bohème. You two have something special; you were born to be together."

Juliette felt a kinship with Hannah and Elizabeth that calmed her fears of Peter ever becoming a National Socialist. Heinz was the picture of Hitler's Aryan without the ideology, and his son proved the fallacy of the National Socialist belief in racial purity. An Aryan father and a Jewish mother had produced a son equal to his parents, even superior to them, in meaningful ways. As Juliette locked arms with Peter, she told Hannah, "Peter has a wonderful family, and I intend to be part of it someday."

Hannah touched Juliette's arm.

"Then, when you come to my house, I will teach you to make Peter's favourite *perogies."*

Juliette tried to rein in her disappointment with Peter for not telling her about his grandparents. They lived close to where she and Peter had been living for three years, he hadn't mentioned them, and there was only one explanation. As they walked, Juliette picked a moment to confront him without causing an explosion.

"Why didn't you tell me your mother and her parents were Jewish? Why haven't I met them until now?"

"My mother is officially Protestant. She left the Jewish church when she married my father."

"My dear naïve Peter, People are born Jewish, they don't and can't choose. Your mother will always be a Jew, and she is in danger every day she remains in Germany."

"The *Bürgeramt* says she is a Protestant married to a Protestant."

"Peter, you shouldn't be ashamed of your mother or your grandparents, and you must recognize the danger they are in."

227

Peter stopped, took his arm away and said, a little too loudly, "I am not ashamed of my mother or her parents!"

"You didn't tell me about them when we argued about Hitler—why didn't you say something?"

Even in the darkness, Juliette could see tears reflecting the streetlight. She said softly, "You didn't tell *anyone*, and it's because you are afraid for them. Peter, you don't trust Hitler any more than I do!"

Juliette took Peter's hand and squeezed it.

"Peter, it's time to admit that the National Socialist 'miracle' has a price, one your mother and her parents will pay if they don't leave Germany. Hitler probably won't do anything until after the Olympics, perhaps not until a year has passed, but don't you see that the only possible reason for the Nürnberg race laws is to set the legal groundwork for enforcing laws against Jews and Romani?"

Juliette looked deep into Peter's eyes as she said, "Peter, I have a terrible feeling about this, and I am not alone. I am terrified now that I know about your mother and her parents. They should leave Germany as soon as possible! My father can help them, and perhaps he can find...."

Peter shook his head. "My grandparents won't leave Germany— München is their home—and my mother will stay with my father no matter what anyone says or does. They built the house I grew up in, all their friends live in Augsburg, and my father would never leave his work."

Juliette squeezed his hand hard.

"Peter, Hitler doesn't care about any of that, and you must believe him when he says he will 'eliminate' Jews, communists, and Romani. In January last year, he passed a law that Jews couldn't work in the civil service, and he has built work camps in Dachau and Oranienburg, mainly to house his political opponents. Jews who sell to Aryans are also sent to Dachau, while Aryans go unpunished for breaking the same law by buying from a Jew. The sign over the entrance to Dachau says, *"Arbeit Macht Frei,"* but the work there doesn't equal freedom; it is slave labour and is intentionally debilitating. Peter, I'm terrified... Perhaps this is only the beginning!"

Peter had sworn he wouldn't fight with Juliette about Hitler, but what she said was not what he saw, so despite the little voice telling him to say nothing, he charged onward.

"*Opa* and *Oma* Metzger said that this is the first time in years they can walk down the street without someone spitting on them or hitting them. No one has called them filthy names since Hitler cleaned the antisemites out of the *Sturmabteilung*. Moshe says Hitler has learned that Germany can't afford to lose the Jews, their businesses and their money."

"Yes, I've heard that argument from my father, but he can't answer this question: what if the Jews aren't allowed to take their money with them?"

Peter said, too quickly, "Most Jews have their money invested in their businesses, homes and real estate. Would the National Socialists take over and run the businesses the Jews left behind? What would they know about running a business that serves only Jews?"

"Hitler's minions can legally take the Jew's business and everything he owns, including his home! Hitler has that power and more in a decree he wrote. I'm not saying he would, but according to that law, Adolph Hitler can legally execute anyone who resists!"

Peter threw up his hands. "You are exaggerating what Hitler can do. The people, including Jews, have been behind him since the 'Night of the Long Knives,' and he knows they would leave him if the violence returned. Many Jews say that the persecution against them is over; the streets are safe for everyone! The firing of Jews in the civil service has stopped, and non-Jews ignore the law forbidding them to buy from Jewish-owned stores as they always have. Violence is rare, and when it occurs, the police interfere on the victim's side."

"Peter, you are wrong, and you are repeating Goebbels' propaganda!"

Juliette thought she felt Peter weakening. "Jews with enough money are taking advantage of the lull, making arrangements to go to England, Palestine, America; they're going to any country that will take them—and they aren't planning to return. Papa says his business of turning Jewish-owned paintings and jewellery into Swiss Francs or American dollars is booming. Thousands of non-Aryans are buying their way into America or

England with cash, paying exorbitant fees for a visa. And, in Germany, the National Socialists force Jews who want to leave the country to 'donate' valuable objects and cash to the 'Party,' then either sell the valuables to someone like my father or find a discreet way to store them.

"My father says the National Socialists put their cash in Swiss banks, not German, because even the well-connected rich don't trust Hitler. Papa thinks the bubble he has created will eventually burst."

Juliette pointed at Peter as she said, "You would do better to sing at a festival than to work with your father; there are a dozen on the bulletin board in the *Sängerhaus*. You might learn something working with like-minded people. The Bayreuth Wagner Festival needs choir singers, and they never turn down a tenor! Weikersheim posts opportunities to sing at their festival, and they specifically need tenors."

Peter shook his head. "I can't let my father down. He needs me to help him, and the work is important for the country."

"What is more important for Germany than your singing career? You are a singer with a rare talent, not a machinist. Peter, you are much more valuable as a singer than anything else you could do!"

Peter put his arms around Juliette, and she pulled herself against him.

She said, "Perhaps, for now, you have doubts, but you have never taken four curtain calls and seen people crying after hearing and seeing you perform. You will find out how valuable you are when you sing Rudolpho."

Juliette pulled back to look into Peter's eyes without putting her head back.

"Saturday will be our last day at the Bayerische Hof, and it's the last performance of *La Bohéme* at the *Staatsoper*. We must make it last until we meet in September."

Peter grinned and began singing, "*Schenk man sich Rosen in Tyrol....*"

The narrow street and houses built against narrow sidewalks reverberated Peter's shining tenor sound like a stone church. Juliette joined him, and they sang the duet in one another's arms.

When they finished, Juliette turned her face up, Peter kissed her, and applause and cheers came from open windows everywhere.

Chapter Eighteen

When the Devil Schemes, Nature Trembles

When the sky is black, lightning flashes, and the wind rises, you must believe a storm is imminent and seek shelter

JULIETTE WAS HARDLY THROUGH THE DOOR when she told her father, "Peter's mother and grandparents are Jews, and he didn't tell me!"

Jacques smiled at his daughter. "I didn't tell you either."

"You knew?" Juliette looked from her father to her mother, who had joined them on the terrace. They both nodded, and Veronique said, "Yes, we knew," and began knitting.

Jacques said, "You didn't think I would look into the background of the man my daughter is in love with?"

"I didn't say I was in love with Peter—I'm still not sure about him."

Veronique laughed and kept knitting as she spoke.

"That's nonsense, my dear; why else would you care whether he likes Hitler, and why would you care about his grandparents?"

"I care because his mother and her parents aren't safe in Germany. They must leave immediately!"

Jacques poured a little brandy into a glass and offered some to Juliette and Veronique, but they shook their heads.

"Hitler has been careful since he debuted the race laws last September, except for occupying the Rhineland in March. He was lucky that move turned out well for him. The Olympics begin in August, and he won't do anything to stir up trouble for a while after that. I don't believe Peter's family is in immediate danger; they're probably safe for at least another year, and everything could change in that time—for example, Hitler could die."

Juliette decided on her points before she spoke, then began with a question.

"Papa, what do you know about the labour camps? There are stories about bad food and beatings at Dachau, and Germans are making jokes about Goebbels' *Arbeit Macht Frei.*"

The edges of Jacques' mouth curled slightly upward, almost becoming a smile.

"I am sure the people in those camps are mistreated. And because that is where you're going with your argument, some are Jews, but most are petty criminals and Hitler's political enemies. There are now two labour camps, and I know another camp will be built this year in Sachsenhausen, north of Berlin, followed by a fourth camp next year. Each *Arbeitslager* can house tens of thousands of people—there aren't enough petty criminals, homosexuals, and political enemies to fill them, so one must ask, why build them? Are they the solution to unemployment? Perhaps they will house slaves—cheap labour for National Socialist Party supporters?"

Juliette said, "Maybe they are a place for Jews who don't or can't leave the country. He did say he would get rid of them. If Hitler goes after the Jews, Peter's mother and her parents would be among the first!"

Jacques lit his pipe. "A primitive retirement home for Jews and Romani? That would put a hole in his budget, and I don't see why he would do it, but you could be right. I will stay with my theory of cheap labour for the business friends of National Socialism."

Jacques repacked his pipe and relit it to give Juliette time to recover, and she patiently waited for him to go on.

"If you believe my theory, Peter's mother and grandparents are safe for now. In a year… perhaps, if Hitler is genuinely insane, he might move on the Jews. But it's too early for Peter's grandparents to think about leaving their life in Germany and starting over somewhere else."

Veronique stopped knitting and asked, "If Hitler begins putting Jews in camps, not because they broke the law but because they are Jews, would the world protect them?"

Jacques shook his head. "No, the world won't attack Germany to protect Jews. Hitler's idea of 'racial purity' came from America—they call it *Eugenics,* a euphemism for pure racism. America has an anti-Semitic movement that rivals Germany, and it's led by famous celebrities!

"England is also not a safe haven for Jews. Unfortunately, most of Europe is, at the moment, not safer for them than Germany, even if they would allow them in. No country is interested in allowing a Jew to immigrate without a lot of money changing hands."

Juliette said, "But, England and France...."

Her father stopped her by shaking his head, and his facial expression was tinged with disappointment. He puffed on his pipe, then took it out of his mouth and blew the smoke away from everyone.

"I'm sure you know that Hitler defied the Versailles treaty and the Locarno agreement when he occupied the Rhineland. The world thought Hitler had finally gone too far, but, in the end, England and France backed down, allowing him to do much more than reverse the Versailles Treaty. The Europeans know Hitler is building a modern army so powerful the rest of Europe won't dare challenge him, allowing Germany to take whatever it wants until and unless someone grows the backbone to stop him. The Olympics will distract the world's media from Hitler's intentions and actions—they are nothing more than a Goebbels public relations ploy designed to buy Germany time to build an army."

Juliette, now depressed, said, "What's wrong with people? Where is the League of Nations? The Great War—we optimistically call it 'the war to end all wars'—killed millions and appears to have accomplished nothing! The Allies took what should have been a lesson on the stupidity of hate and prejudice and used it to humiliate Germany. Because of that, Adolph Hitler happened, and the world is now stumbling headlong into another conflagration—probably a worse one because we are inventing much better war machines every day! Will anyone be safe?"

Jacques thoughtfully sipped his brandy. He had given up on the pipe and let it go out.

"Perhaps we can invent a weapon so destructive it will destroy an entire army or city in seconds."

"But wouldn't someone use it to take over the world?"

"Not if both sides had the weapon. Neither would dare use it because, for the first time since the caveman, everyone, women, children, and politicians, would be as vulnerable as a soldier! But, of course, such a weapon is generations away, and hopefully, by then, man will have learned the futility of violence."

Jacques put his brandy down and leaned ahead in his chair, using his hands to express what he was saying.

"For now, picture this." He looked far away and waved his palm in front of him. "A small concrete room with no windows—the walls, floor and ceiling are smooth. Two men, locked in a fight over some principal, threaten to kill one another and each other's wives and children. We give each of them a rifle loaded with steel bullets, lock them in the concrete room, turn off the light and leave them there until they find a way to agree."

Jacques looked at Juliette. "How long before they work out a compromise?"

She smiled. "Just before they die of thirst."

"When we have a weapon that is so fearsome no one on either side would survive if they used it, peace will be possible—not before."

Veronique stopped her knitting and looked at her husband. "Do you know of such a weapon?"

Jacques shook his head. "Not yet, but a physicist in Berlin has a theory that one could be built. His name is Albert Einstein."

Veronique shook her head. "Then God help us all!"

As the days passed, Juliette's parents became more worried about her. Whenever Juliette and her parents sat together, she talked about nothing but Adolph Hitler. She became more depressed, turning to anger and avoiding reasonable discussion whenever Jacques or Veronique tried to calm her fears.

Her first performance of the Coffee Cantata went badly. She screamed at the baritone and, following the performance, cut the tenor to pieces when he tried to point out that she had acted hostile. Juliette attacked his voice, musicality, and personality, leaving him with his mouth open, shocked, and humiliated.

Jacques heard about the fiasco the following day and asked Juliette into his office for a "chat." She threw herself into the soft chair she and her mother used, and he sat facing her on the hard wooden chair he preferred when talking to them about something that he knew would be difficult. Veronique placed two cups of coffee and two croissants on the low table in front of Juliette, smiled at her daughter, then left, quietly closing the door. Juliette turned sideways in her chair so she wasn't facing her mother's peace offering. Jacques sipped his cup of coffee before he spoke.

"Charles can't make coffee like your mother can. I must say I enjoy her Sunday coffee."

"Papa, stop playing with me. I know why I'm here, so just say I was a bad girl last night and get it over with so I can go to my room and cry."

Jacques looked at the croissants and said, "I don't think I've ever seen you turn away from a croissant. They are fresh, you know."

Juliette turned to face her father and almost knocked over her coffee. "Enough already! Do whatever you feel you must, say whatever you want to say, but get it over with!"

Jacques reached for Juliette's hand, but she pulled it away and turned, sheltering her face with her arm so he wouldn't see her tears. She was silent, waiting for the onslaught she knew would come, but her father leaned back in his chair and waited.

Juliette wiped her face with her sleeve, half sobbed and said, "I don't know what's wrong with me. I know I ruined the performance for everyone last night, and the audience knew it too. I was thankful when they didn't whistle."

Juliette waited, but her father didn't move. Finally, she said, "I need Peter. To hell with Hitler!"

"Your mother and I have been waiting for that, hoping you would realize that Hitler and National Socialism are not your problems."

"But Peter... "

"...is not a National Socialist, and Hitler is not his idol, you are. He loves you as much as you love him, and you are pushing the devil himself between you. Isn't Adolph Hitler causing enough misery without your adding to it? He can't come between you if you don't allow him to... It's up to you, not Peter."

Juliette faced her father. "Papa, I love him so much! But if I become pregnant, I...." She looked at the croissante.

"So, that's the problem you've been dodging since you came home. Hitler is the excuse you've been using for not marrying Peter."

"I want to marry Peter, but if I do, we'll have a child and then... Papa, I want to sing."

"Don't tell the bishop I told you, but there are ways to prevent pregnancy."

"My roommate gave me a book, but I think the Pope wrote it. I wouldn't trust Peter and me with any of that!"

"Your mother and I had the same problem, but after you were born, the doctor said your mother shouldn't have any more children and performed a minor operation. Please don't ask me about it; your mother doesn't discuss such things with me, but that's why you are our only child."

Juliette brightened. "Perhaps the doctor could do that for me!"

Jacques shook his head. "Not a chance! It's permanent, and you will want children someday." He smiled. "*Ma chérie,* now that we've cleared that up, what about Peter's Hitler fetish? Realistically, can't you live with that until he gets over it?"

"Are you sure Peter won't join the National Socialists?" Juliette reached for the coffee with one hand and a croissant with the other.

"Juliette, Peter has a Jewish mother and grandparents and doesn't differentiate between religions or race. Aryan or non-Aryan, he really doesn't care. If he belonged to the National Socialist Party, they would kick him out!" He laughed. "Live with his little incon-sistency... when the time is right, his mother or his grandparents will straighten him out."

Jacques watched his daughter's expression change.

"But I want to live with him. I want to wake up beside him."

"This is where your mother and I don't agree." Jacques took a bite of his croissant. "I think you should live together, if you can avoid becoming pregnant. You can't ask me to discuss how you should do that, but I know you will be taking some risk no matter what you do."

"But... "

"You must never tell your mother I said this, but I consider your relationship with Peter a marital one. You and Peter have signed your marriage contract with love, which is more important than paper and ink. I've been a businessman too long to put faith in contracts—I look at the person holding the pen."

Juliette burst into a torrent of tears, stood up and met her father in an embrace that bruised the back of his neck.

"Oh, Papa, I've been feeling so guilty I almost told the priest at confession! Peter and I have been sleeping together in a hotel every Saturday night for months, and I want to marry him, but I don't want to live with Hitler, and I'm not ready to get pregnant yet."

"Yes, I know about the Bayerische Hof, and I can accept that the world is changing. I understand your wanting to sleep together but be careful, or you *will* get pregnant. Your mother would love to have a grandchild, and so would I, but don't ask her to give her blessing if you force the issue."

He stood up. "I think you know what you should do."

Juliette tried to smile, wiped her face with her sleeve and left the office ahead of her father. Her mother waited in the living room chair closest to the office and stood up when she heard Juliette open the door.

"Are you alright, *chérie?*" She took Juliette's hand and looked into her swollen red eyes. Juliette smiled and nodded, then went up the stairs.

Jacques poured a drink and sat in his comfortable chair. Veronique sat beside him and picked up her knitting.

"Did you discuss the business in the hotel?"

Jacques looked at her. "I said I understood. But we know she's walking a tightrope with grease on her feet."

"Do you think she will get pregnant?" The needles clicked a steady rhythm, slowly becoming a small sweater.

"She is young and in love with a fine young man, and he is in love with her. We cannot let her feel guilty for what they do; we have no choice but to trust them. Right now, she uses Peter's political views as an excuse for fighting nature, but that will only work until Peter surrenders.

Until then, I think we're safe, but we must be prepared to look after the consequences if it comes to that."

Veronique smiled and looked at Jacques thoughtfully as she pushed the pink yarn back on the needles.

"Don't you dare tell her... You didn't, did you?"

As the clicking resumed, Jacques folded the paper at the article he wanted to read. "She thinks you don't approve of her sleeping with Peter, and if a consequence should be born, she thinks her career would be over."

"And you had better see that she continues to think that!"

"Are you sure you wouldn't like to take care of a little consequence for a few years?"

Veronique said, *"Merde!"* as she dropped a stitch.

Juliette threw herself into her music, singing the Coffee Cantata every Saturday and, in early August, a Bach religious Cantata written for trumpet and Soprano, the most challenging piece she had ever sung. Over the summer, she tried to steer her mind away from Hannah, Moshe and Elizabeth, but their situation haunted her.

Juliette and her father watched the Olympics live in the theatre, broadcast for the first time on a new invention—television, and tickets cost a fortune. Everyone in Belgium cheered for Jesse Owens, an American runner, and each time the black man defeated Hitler's 'Master Race' opposition, they stood and cheered as though he could hear them. But when, despite Owens' four gold medals, Germany won the games by a wide margin, Juliette's depression returned.

When Peter's parents installed a telephone, they spent a fortune on their first long-distance call—from Peter to Juliette—a day's wages for Heinz. When Jacques figured out what it was costing Peter's family, he offered to fund their calls twice a week, and Veronique set a timer for fifteen minutes. Juliette's mood changed as quickly as the wind, and her father didn't say a word when she called Peter every night for a week. When, on the first call, they spent five minutes saying goodbye, Veronique pushed the lever down to disconnect them.

"You will never again say you are not in love with Peter!" With her hands on her hips, Veronique faced her daughter, who was kissing the receiver.

"Peter will reject Hitler eventually, but first, you must stop your pathological reaction to him and concentrate on Peter and your music."

Juliette passed the receiver to her mother. "Okay, I admit I love him, but I will never marry him until he sees what a monster Hitler is."

Veronique hung up the phone and took her daughter's hand.

"Juliette, anyone can see that he is the only one for you, and waiting won't help turn him away from Hitler. If Hitler's government does anything more against the Jews, Peter's grandparents will set him straight, and if Hitler doesn't go after them, your fears will be dispelled."

Juliette couldn't accept her mother's logic.

"Mother, you are living in a bubble! Germany is not Belgium, and the German people are quickly becoming fanatics. Before Hitler, they already valued machines more than people and perfection over everything, so they were easy for a man like Hitler to manipulate. They didn't object to Hitler's laws allowing the government to kill mentally ill people or those with certain physical disabilities. So-called 'sexual deviants' are sent to work camps like Dachau without trial. *Mama,* it's now a crime to disagree with National Socialist philosophy, and who knows how long it will be before they enforce it?"

Veronique touched Juliette's cheek.

"*Ma Chérie,* you must stop listening to such rumours. The German people are not different from the Belgians, and we would never tolerate such things. Even Adolph Hitler has a conscience and would never do the things some people say he is planning."

Juliette looked at her mother with tears in her eyes.

"*Mama,* Hitler does not have a conscience and will do whatever increases his power. You are not safe in Belgium—no one in Europe is safe. In fact, I don't think anyone in the world is safe!"

Veronique's sadness seeped into her words.

"Juliette, you cannot take all the world's sorrows on your shoulders. You must trust God to look after Hitler and the National Socialists."

Juliette shook her head. "No, Mama, God isn't in Germany right now, and the devil is winning!"

CHAPTER NINETEEN

Creating Something Beautiful

To succeed in any artistic endeavour, you must first find inspiration; but without hard work and talent, inspiration will dissipate like morning fog in bright sunlight

PETER BEGAN HIS OPERA CAREER in the Nürnberg Stadtsoper at the first *Stellprobe* for *La Bohème,* a blocking rehearsal to set the staging. It started at nine o'clock on the last day of August, coincidentally when Hilde and Max were reciting their wedding vows in front of a few family members in Bremen's city hall, the *Rathaus.* Because they couldn't attend, Juliette and Peter had sent a telegram and a wedding present—two towels and an ashtray with "Bayerische Hof's" coat of arms and name on them. Juliette added a box of her favourite Belgian chocolate.

The only *Stellproben* Peter had previously experienced were haphazard affairs in the Munich opera school that lasted for hours and accomplished little. The school trained stage directors, conductors, orchestra musicians, sound engineers and singers—anyone involved in producing an opera. Every rehearsal was, by necessity, a mishmash of teachers and students, each with an agenda and needs. There was no shortage of ideas and opinions, and everyone with one demanded to be heard. It wasn't surprising that it took a semester to stage an opera. Peter was dumbfounded when Juliette told him the Monnaie Theater had blocked the entire La Bohème opera in two days.

The first surprise for Peter was a slightly sloped stage leaning toward the audience. The sloped plank floor, painted black and scattered with pieces of white tape marked with numbers and letters, was empty except for a table and chairs, a stove, and an easel. The props sat on spots marked with bits of white tape or chalk. A pianist sat on a hard chair in front of the keyboard of an upright piano perched at the corner of the stage, and almost everyone else stood around holding a piano score and a pencil.

As nervous as a caged canary in a house full of cats, Peter stayed close to Juliette until the stage director beckoned him to sit at the table.

"Rudolpho, you're a writer and will have a pen, an ink bottle and a pile of papers in front of you. You are writing your novel when Marcello, frustrated with his painting, begins singing."

He turned to Marcello, standing at the easel, half turned to the audience. "You will paint with your back to the audience until the curtain rises, then turn to Rudolpho to sing your first line, then back to the painting and paint furiously as you 'drown the Pharoah.' Turn back to Rudolpho when you sing, *'Che Fai?'*"

He said to Peter. "Rudolpho, you will then respond with your first line."

He waved at the pianist, who played the short introduction. While he played, the director said, "Curtain rises," and Marcello turned to Rudolpho. He sang *mezzo voce,* half voice, as he expressed his annoyance. He finished venting, turned to Rudolpho and asked, "Che Fai?" What are you doing?

Peter sang his response in full voice while looking at the audience, and Herr Schulmann, the director, stopped the music with a wave of his hand.

"No, Herr Schweitzer, you are not singing a concert, you are singing Rudolpho, a character in an opera, and you are trying to concentrate on your writing while your friend is complaining about his painting. You must focus on Marcello, but you don't know anything about his painting, so you point out the window and tell him about all the warm furnaces in Paris, while yours—you point to the cold, lazy, good-for-nothing stove in your apartment—does nothing but sit there!" He turned to the pianist. "Marcello's entrance, please, and Rudolpho, *Bitte, Markieren.* If you sing full voice, you won't last until the *Pause.*"

Juliette had explained to Peter that he must "Mark..." his way through the rehearsal, using as little voice as possible, but he had forgotten. He felt sick and began his next entrance tentatively and a bar late, but the stage director ignored it.

Herr Schulmann let them sing their back-and-forth about freezing to death until Marcel reached for Rudolpho's chair, then raised his hand.

"Herr Schweitzer, Marcello needs the chair. You must stand up and move toward the stove as you sing, 'We must have a fire...'" Schulmann turned to the pianist. "Marcello's line... 'dying of hunger,' please."

The pianist played the line; Peter came in late again and forgot to stand up. The pianist stopped—Herr Schulmann said, "*Nochmal,*" and the pianist played it again. This time, Peter nailed the entrance and remembered to stand up. He looked at Juliette, hoping for help, but she was busily writing notes in his score.

The first act staging moved too fast for Peter. Confused, he missed entries and forgot lines as his frustration increased, along with the director's. Finally, just before Mimi's entrance, Herr Schulmann called a break, sent everyone but Peter and Juliette away, and took Peter aside, beckoning Juliette to join them. He sent his assistant for a glass of water for each of them.

"Herr Schweitzer, we will work a great deal together... May I call you Peter?" He smiled kindly but didn't wait for an answer and used the familiar 'du' reserved for children and good friends.

"Peter, I am sure you have a wonderful voice, and I believe you are intelligent, but you must relax. All we are doing here today is getting the lay of the land; acting will come later." He turned to Juliette. "I see you are writing notes for him. Can I assume that you work together?"

Juliette grinned awkwardly. "Yes, Peter and I work together."

"Excellent...excellent. Please continue to do that, and if you could work with Peter on his stiffness, I would be grateful."

"Oh, don't you worry; I will take the stiffness out of him, Herr Schulmann!" She laughed like a barmaid, and the stage director joined her. Peter caught on too late.

They drank their water and returned to the stage, where the pianist waited...cross-legged on his chair, taking the final puff on a cigarette.

Herr Schulmann said, "Begin a few bars before *'Non sono in vena,'* please."

He turned to Peter. "You are trying to write—you become frustrated and drop the pen as you sing the line."

Juliette and Peter were comfortable acting the scene as they had in the opera school. They searched in the darkness for the room key that Mimi had dropped, touched hands, and Peter sang his aria, *"Che gelida manina..."*

Peter sang in full voice, and just before Mimi told her story, Herr Schulmann stopped them by clapping and shouting, "Bravo...Bravo... Bravo, you were born to sing together! May I assume you have the rest of the duet as well-prepared as this scene?"

Juliette said, "Yes, but of course we can adjust to whatever you want."

"Then there is no need to do the rest of the scene now. We will move on to Act II, but first, everyone to the Mensa while the stage crew moves things around."

A fifteen-minute break turned into a half-hour, and when they returned, the Act II props—tables and chairs in Café Momus—were in place.

Rudolpho's participation in Act II was limited to interactions with Mimi, so Peter relaxed. Herr Schulmann's direction contained a great deal of latitude—no one cared about or paid attention to notes, phrasing or voice quality—it only mattered that the character was in the right place at the right time—and acting was optional, if not downright discouraged.

The first musical rehearsal began at three, after *Mittagspause,* under the baton of Maestro Chiera, who would conduct La Bohème. When Juliette and Peter entered the spacious rehearsal room, a pianist played scales on a three-metre Steinway and, with the cover raised on the long stick, the sound rang off the papered walls, oak floor and rough, plastered ceiling.

Juliette and Peter listened, waiting to introduce themselves to the pianist, but Maestro Chiera entered the room before they had the opportunity.

The conductor, a short man barely as tall as Juliette, wore a wide moustache and a triumphant smile as though he were pleased with something he had just done. He moved quickly and smoothly to Juliette's outstretched hand, then surprised her by putting it to his lips and kissing her fingers.

"I am called Giuseppe by my friends, and I assume you to be Juliette Durand, alias Mimi." Giuseppe turned to Peter, glancing back at Juliette as he said, "I have heard good things about both of you and look forward to working with you... *È vero.*" He shook Peter's hand, pointed to the piano and said, "That's Kristina—my right hand." The pianist waved from her bench.

"I would like you both on the raised platform; I will conduct from the podium. No marking; I need your normal singing voice." He looked straight at Peter. "You have never sung with a conductor... *È vero?*"

Peter said, "Yes, that's true."

Juliette jumped in. "He's a fast learner."

The maestro smiled at Juliette, then turned to Peter. "I will teach you to look at me without looking at me." His smile widened.

Juliette and Peter went up on the raised narrow stage, stood behind their music stands and put their scores on them.

The conductor moved to his podium and said, as he opened his score, "We will work first on the scene at the beginning of your *'Che gelida...'* aria, starting just before *'Non sono in vena.'*"

Kristina played the flutes' bird sounds, then the heavier chords leading down the scale to Peter's entry. Peter watched the maestro and entered precisely on the upbeat, as written. Kristina stopped playing, and Maestro Chiera lowered his baton.

"Peter... you're late; you're listening to the piano. You must watch my baton and ignore the piano until you find the beat."

Peter was puzzled. He was sure he had nailed it.

"I see you don't understand." He looked at Juliette. "Can you sing Peter's part for me?"

She nodded.

Maestro Chiera began at the same spot, talking as he waved his baton.

"Listen to the piano; Kristina is following my baton, not behind it or anticipating it."

Peter heard the piano's fraction of a second delay. Juliette sang Rudolpho's line, *"Non sono in vena,"* with the same tiny lag behind the baton that the piano had, putting them exactly together. Peter listened closely and realized the delay was the musician's reaction time to the conductor's baton.

Juliette knocked on her music stand to simulate Mimi's knock on Rudolpho's door; Maestro Chiera waited, then moved his hand downward, and Juliette reacted by singing, *"Chi è La?"* She was slightly behind the conductor's baton and precisely with the piano.

Giuseppe asked, "Do you hear it?" and Peter nodded. "You must follow my baton, even when that's not what you want to do. You will sing *when* my baton reaches its turning point, not *as* it reaches it... *Capisce?"*

Peter said, *"Capisce!"*

Maestro Chiera raised his baton and said, *"Di nuova. Una barra per niente."* He gave the piano and Peter an empty bar; Peter watched and listened until his entrance, then sang, *"Non sono in vena."* It felt right... Juliette tapped the music stand, again simulating knocking on Rudolpho's door... Peter waited, followed the Maestro's downbeat, and sang, *"Chi è la?"*

"Precisely! *Bene... bene!"* He kept his baton going; Mimi said, *"Scusi,"* Rudolpho said, *"Una Donna!"* They sang the dialogue to the touching of her cold hand and the beginning of Rudolpho's aria.

Peter had sung the aria so many times it was part of him, which was his first problem. Maestro Chiera let him sing the first two phrases, then stopped him.

"You are accustomed to the piano taking your tempo, *é vero?"*

Peter felt his face warming. "I wasn't with the piano, was I?"

Maestro Chiera held up his baton. "You weren't with this. You will sometimes have difficulty hearing the orchestra when you are on the stage, and it will feel strange, so you must trust me and my baton. If you get ahead or behind, I can help you, but only if you look at my little stick. The orchestra will follow me to hell and back, but remember, they can't hear you. Everything on the stage can go to pieces, and they won't know it; they only know this!" He held up his baton.

He said, "Sing the aria *a cappella* without the piano as you follow my stick."

He began beating. "Whenever you want to come in...."

Peter picked the first beat of the bar and began. The maestro quickened the pace for the second phrase. He held the first note much longer than Puccini had intended, and Peter held it with him. He finished *a tempo.*

"*Excellente!* Now, I want you to look at Juliette, and Kristina will be our orchestra."

Juliette faced away with a demure smile, puffed a sexy "Ah..." at precisely the right moment, and Peter sang, *"Che gelida manina...."* Juliette whispered, "Peek at the maestro out of the corner of your eye."

Everything went fine until Peter lost himself in the music. Suddenly realizing he was a half-beat behind the orchestra, he stopped, but the orchestra and the baton kept going. Maestro Chiera said, "Find a place to get on... I can't stop the train!"

Peter immediately found a spot, watched the baton and entered at the beginning of a phrase.

"Look at Mimi, Peter. Sing to her!"

It took an hour and a half to feel comfortable, but Peter finally figured it out. They had worked their way through the first act, and no matter what the baton did, Peter followed, precisely with the orchestra.

When the rehearsal ended, Maestro Chiera shook hands with Juliette and Peter.

"Peter, you learn very quickly, and Juliette, you are the most musical singer I have ever worked with." He turned back to Peter. "We will have two orchestra rehearsals in this room and one in the theatre. You will find the change in acoustics difficult, but Juliette and I will help you. He slapped Peter's back. "Just don't get sick—there is no second Rudolpho!"

Chapter Twenty

It's Worth Doing Because it's Hard

It doesn't take a miracle to successfully stage an opera, but the occasional act of God does increase the odds of success

THE 1936 NAZI PARTY RALLY, *Tag der Ehre*, 'Day of Honour,' promised to be one of the largest exhibitions of military power Europe had ever seen. A celebration of the return of the Rhineland, Hitler, in effect, announced the death of the humiliating Versailles Treaty.

In March, motivated by the French ratification of the Franco-Soviet Treaty of Mutual Assistance in February, Hitler trashed the last vestiges of the Versailles Treaty and the 1925 Locarne agreements. He violated both agreements by sending twenty thousand *Wehrmacht* soldiers to occupy the cities and towns along the Rhine. German citizens, fed up with bowing and scraping, lined the streets as German forces symbolically retook the area along Germany's beloved river.

Against his military advisors' advice, Hitler dared France and England to do something about it. Although the Allies threatened and blustered, all they accomplished was reducing the number of occupying soldiers from a hundred thousand to twenty thousand.

Every day of the rally, Juliette expected Peter to say he was going and was delighted when he ignored Hitler's arrogant demonstration of raw military power. Peter lied when he told his father he didn't have time to watch endless rows of soldiers pretending to fight a non-existent enemy, and Heinz didn't fool Peter by saying he was tired of watching soldiers march anyway.

Peter and Juliette had been fortunate that the previous soprano and tenor's departure had meshed with their arrival, conveniently allowing them to take over their apartments. Juliette's *Wohnung* on the third floor had a bay window not unlike the *Sängerhaus in München,* where she spent hours sitting in a soft chair studying her music and enjoying the birds that fed at her bird feeder. From her chair, she could see the door into Peter's building, a hundred metres up the street and two floors below.

They walked home from rehearsals every day. Juliette said *"Gute Nacht"* every evening, climbed three flights of stairs, went to the window, and wistfully watched Peter walk a hundred metres farther and open the door that separated them. She tried to imagine living with a man who supported Hitler, risking her future if she became pregnant. Despite her *Papa's* advice, Juliette wrestled with the same dilemma every night.

On Monday, the last day of the National Socialist Party's Nürnberg rally, she watched row after row, twelve men abreast—thousands of soldiers—pass under her window. Half the windows on the street were open, people leaned out, waving and cheering, and blood-red flags with black swastikas fluttered from most of the buildings. Juliette understood that the people were cheering for the leader who had led them out of a crippled, devastated economy into a bustling, prosperous beehive of activity where everyone who wanted one had a job. Juliette couldn't hate those people who cheered Hitler; he had given them back their pride, confidence and self-respect. *So,* she asked herself, *why can't I accept Peter's admiration of Hitler?*

Juliette and Peter rehearsed their solo parts separately, each with their own *répétiteur,* and Peter had not gotten out of the opera house before the parade began. He watched the spectacle from the sidewalk, and it was dark when he arrived home. Juliette watched him unlock the door, a plan already hatched.

Both apartments had telephones, and Juliette impatiently waited for what she thought would be a decent interval before calling him.

The tone that signalled Peter's telephone was ringing sounded in Juliette's receiver three times before Peter lifted his.

No one but his mother had ever called him. He said, *"Peter Schweizer,"* expecting his mother to put his father on the line.

"It's Juliette. I've got a Jägerschnitzel for you—it will be ready in five minutes."

Surprised—it was the first time Juliette had invited him to her apartment—he said, "I'll be there in three."

"Bring your pyjamas."

Juliette heard Peter suck in his breath, take a few seconds to process the implications, and finally say, *"Jawohl!"* with more than a little enthusiasm.

When Peter rang the doorbell, Juliette was already flying down the stairs to open the door. She fumbled with the lock, smoothed her dress, and breathed from her toes twice before opening the door.

Juliette said, as elegantly as she could, "Come in, Peter; the schnitzel is almost ready."

She suppressed a giggle and forced herself to turn around and walk up the stairs. Peter was close behind, his pyjamas in a paper bag on his arm, hoping it looked like a gift for the house.

When they had finished the main course and shared a bottle of wine, Juliette put a bowl of fresh blueberries and a quarter litre of thick cream on the table. Something that Juliette interpreted as disappointment flashed in Peter's eyes. She chuckled and said, "Perhaps we should have these later?" inserting a suggestive note.

Peter's crooked grin was pathetic. "Uh…Yes…uh… I ate too much; perhaps later would be better."

Juliette put everything in the ice box, then turned around suddenly and said, "Why don't you have a bath while I clean up the kitchen?"

The blueberries had to wait until morning when Juliette made porridge and coffee to accompany them.

They barely made it to their ten o'clock orchestra rehearsal on time, and a buzz spread through the room when they walked in, holding hands and beaming like searchlights.

Maestro Chiera took a few minutes to let the room settle down, tapped his baton on his music stand and turned to the forty-four musicians in his rehearsal orchestra. When the last sound had died, he waved his arm in Juliette and Peter's direction.

"I will now introduce our Mimi and Rudolpho. First, Juliette Durand will sing Mimi...." Juliette curtsied. "She comes to us from Brussels, where she sang the role with the Monnaie Theater. She is a renowned Oratorio singer who graduated from the Munich Opera School." He clapped, and the orchestra members followed his lead as they were trained to do. When he stopped clapping, everyone lowered their hands and waited for him to speak.

"Our Rudolpho, Peter Schweitzer, is, like Juliette, a graduate of the *Münchner Musikhochschule.* Rudolpho is his first opera role since opera school, and he will need our help."

Peter bowed, and the orchestra musicians clapped until Maestro Chiera signalled them to stop.

"Peter, please take your place beside Marcello. We will try to get through the first act before *Mittagspause.*" He turned to Juliette. "Why don't you sit at the back of the room until we reach your first scene?"

Juliette sat behind the orchestra, where she could see Peter.

When the orchestra played the opening passage, the sound bouncing off the rehearsal room walls was nothing like what Peter expected. He forced himself to concentrate only on the conductor, focusing on the Maestro's baton, picking out the first beat of each bar as Juliette had told him. But the tip of the little stick didn't stop anywhere—the first beat wasn't as straightforward as it had been for the piano. Maestro Chiera waved his left hand at Marcello, who began singing his frustration over his painting, perfectly synchronized with the smooth pattern the baton carved in the air. Marcello turned to Rudolpho and asked, *"Che fai?"*

Maestro Chiera waved his left hand to give Peter his entrance, and he sang his little *arietta,* comparing the industrious chimneys of Paris with the useless stove in their garret, and found himself slightly behind the orchestra. His effort to catch up momentarily put him ahead, and he couldn't seem to correct it.

Marcello entered again; Peter focused on Maestro Chiera's baton. Luigi, the Italian baritone singing Marcello, put his hand on Peter's shoulder, squeezed and said, "Look at me." Peter looked away from the podium, and Luigi eased the pressure. He checked with the baton;

he was behind the beat…the orchestra was pulling ahead. Luigi hissed, "Look at me!"

Peter found the baton in his periphery and slipped into the sweet spot with the orchestra. Whenever he turned away from Marcello to look directly at the conductor, Luigi touched his shoulder and turned him back.

The orchestra rolled on like a train—relentless and unstoppable. Peter had no control; there were too many variables. He tried to imagine how he could do this while running around the stage!

Rudolpho burned the second act of his drama…the action moved so fast that there was no time to look at the baton!

Colline entered the fray, complaining that he couldn't pawn his books, and Peter found the sweet spot again. He imagined the staging, picked places where he could look away from the conductor during the action, looked at the baton when the music ebbed and flowed, and more and more often found a place where he and the relentless orchestra were precisely synchronized. Eventually, he rarely lost that perfect oneness with the music that every soloist must have.

The fast pace persisted until Benoit, the landlord, knocked on his music stand at the far side of the small stage. He promised to say only one word; Schaunard opened the door, and Benoit said, *"Afitto!"* "Rent!"

The banter between the landlord and four starving artists with no money finally ended with the artists manipulating Benoit into admitting he had cheated on his wife, and they kicked the shameless landlord out of their virtuous abode.

Peter fumbled his words twice in the exchange but didn't lose the thread. He felt he had found a balance between playing a role and following the baton.

Maestro Chiera chose that spot to halt the music for a fifteen-minute break, released Marcello, Colline and Schaunard for the day, and everyone headed for the *Mensa*.

Peter and Juliette waited for the mob to clear before they made their way to the crowded cafeteria, and when they finally succeeded in getting through the line, there were no empty tables. Maestro Chiera stood up and waved, two orchestra members conveniently left his table, and Peter and Juliette sat down. Peter sat opposite the Maestro, Juliette beside him.

Peter was barely seated when he said, "I apologize for missing those entries…" and Juliette interrupted… "I will work on those banter scenes with Peter tonight."

Chiera chuckled but kept his eyes down. "I've heard you work at more than music together." He paused, choosing his words carefully. He looked at Juliette, then Peter and said, "I must caution you. There are people in this city who are, to put it kindly, troublemakers. The Gestapo listens to tattletales who have nothing better to do than poke their noses into other people's private affairs, and they question the alleged perpetrators rather energetically. Many self-righteous people believe the "Morality Law" outlaws sex outside of marriage, although, if that were true, half the adult population of Germany would be in jail. However, if someone reports such crimes, the Gestapo can make it easier to confess than to endure questioning. Guilt, innocence or law have little to do with the outcome."

Peter stirred sugar and milk into his coffee, trying to prolong lifting his head.

Juliette, who had no such inhibition, said, "Are you saying my personal *Wohnung* is not private?"

"I am saying that an innocent *tête-à-tête* can be intentionally misinterpreted and reported to the Gestapo, with catastrophic consequences."

"Without evidence of anything more than that?" Juliette looked at Peter, who had frustration etched all over her face.

"I'm afraid so."

Peter finally stopped stirring and sipped his coffee, remembering his pyjamas were still in Juliette's bedroom.

Maestro Chiera cut a piece of *strudel* and turned to Peter.

"I am confident that you will have no problems with your entries when the *répétiteur* and orchestra rehearsals are finished with you, but perhaps Juliette could help you as well. The fast-moving scenes are relentless, and Herr Schulmann's stage direction will add more confusion, but you mustn't become discouraged. Today was shaky, but you are learning quickly. I know it is selfish of me to put my needs at the top of the list, but in those scenes you have two anchors; my baton and the *souffleur*.

Startled, Peter asked, "What's a *souffleur?*"

Juliette and the maestro exchanged glances. Juliette explained.

"There's a bump in the stage floor, close to the front. It's open to the back of the stage, and someone, usually a retired singer, sits on a stool under the bump with their face just above the stage floor. Whether you need it or not, the souffleur gives you every entry an instant before you sing it."

"But if I can hear this souffleur, can't the audience?"

Maestro Chiera shook his head. "No, the audience can't hear her, although sometimes you won't believe it. Our prompter is a retired soprano with perfect pitch and a singer's sense of timing, so you can trust her."

But isn't it confusing when she sings along?"

Juliette laughed. "Of course, it would be, but she stops singing as soon as you get the entry. She works both parts in a duet and can keep up with stage antics. Believe me, you would never have missed an entry if she had been there."

Maestro Chiera said, "You will learn to love her, and it's good policy to buy her a coffee and something sweet if you see her in the *Mensa*. A souffleur rarely pays for her lunch."

They arrived in the rehearsal room to a cacophony of orchestra musicians tuning, chattering, and working on difficult passages.

Juliette and Peter climbed three steps to the small, elevated platform and opened their scores, already on a music stand with sharpened pencils beside them. Peter hadn't made a mark, but Juliette had filled the margins in her score with notes, most of them for him.

Maestro Chiera stepped to the podium, tapped his baton on his music stand, and the raucous room became suddenly silent.

"We will begin at the tenor entry, bar three-twenty-five. '*Non sono in vena.*' I will give two bars for nothing." He waited until the sound of rearranging pages stopped and the first violin's bow hovered near the strings, raised his baton, then swept down with a flourish, beginning the scene.

When the birdsong introduction reached his entry, Rudolpho vented his frustration on the pen, beginning the dialogue with Mimi. The scene moved flawlessly through the search for a lost key. Rudolpho stretched out his arm to touch Mimi's cold hand, Juliette reached across the space between them, their fingers touched, and Peter began Rudolpho's aria, the most famous in opera.

For the next two hours, Maestro Chiera stopped the orchestra to correct slight instrumental problems, pointed out improvements to Peter's musicality, and often used different tempi and musical interpretations than Peter had drilled into his head. When Juliette and Peter sang their final high 'C' at the end of the act, it was with a sense of relief. The orchestra musicians tapped their bows, stamped their feet and cheered, but Peter and Juliette were too exhausted to do more than wave and walk off the stage.

Juliette's abode was a five-minute walk from the opera house, and she talked Peter into going there for *Wurst und Sauerkraut*.

As they walked, Peter asked Juliette, "Is Maestro Chiera a good conductor?"

"I've only sung with a few conductors—not more than a dozen, and I think a couple were quite good but not as good as Maestro Chiera. I like singing for him. His sense of phrasing suits me… I can feel what he wants to do before he does it because his interpretation seems to anticipate mine."

Peter had no idea what Juliette was talking about, but he nodded, and she continued.

"A singer has to watch a bad conductor like a cat watching its prey because he will be unpredictable. It's enough to glance at Maestro Chiera in critical places, and I think it will sometimes be possible to turn away and sing with the orchestra once we get the feel of what he's doing."

Juliette put her arms around Peter's right arm and pulled it against her body. "Don't worry; you will understand before the first performance."

"When we begin rehearsing the staging, you will appreciate Maestro Chiera's conducting. Herr Schulmann will scream at you for looking at the conductor, and Maestro Chiera will want you to keep your eyes on his baton! It's helpful if the conductor doesn't throw in a surprise *ritardando* where you don't expect one."

It took only a few minutes to sear the wurst, open a bottle of sauerkraut, and pour the apple juice. They sat down at the table and hadn't taken a bite when Juliette told Peter why he was there.

"I wanted to come home because we need to discuss what Maestro Chiera said about our relationship."

"You believe that the Gestapo will arrest us? Who do you think would tell on us?"

"Peter, I know you don't want to believe that your friend Adolph Hitler would set up a secret police to spy on Germany's people, but the Gestapo apparently does precisely that! Don't forget—Hitler condemned Ernst Röhm to death without trial, and on the 'Night of the Long Knives' he had two homosexuals shot on the spot because they were caught in bed together!"

"That's a rumour! And Röhm was shot because he plotted against Hitler!"

"Perhaps it is a rumour, but they are dead. The only evidence that Hitler's friend and head of the *Sturmabteilung* was plotting against him was that provided by Himmler, now coincidentally head of the *Gestapo and* the *Sturmabteilung*. It is not a police force tasked with investigating, arresting and turning criminals over to the courts. The Gestapo is Himmler's monstrous dream, an extension of his evil arm into private lives. They are his private police, judge and executioner. Himmler's power now equals, or even exceeds Hitler's."

Peter found himself in a corner and decided not to fight it.

"Should I take my pyjamas home?"

"You can't carry them back and forth, so...."

Peter suddenly felt sick. He stood and turned toward the bedroom, but Juliette caught his arm.

"You could buy a second pair and, once a week, we could take a chance. If you don't carry anything, how would anyone know?"

Peter thought about someone, perhaps a nosy neighbour or a rival soprano, seeing him enter her building in the evening and come out the following morning, but he didn't say anything.

Chapter Twenty-One

The Worst Thing That Can Happen

We worry too much... unless we're a singer with a cold... In that case, panic is appropriate

WHEN JULIETTE AND PETER ARRIVED in the orchestra rehearsal room, it buzzed with activity. A children's choir stood quietly to one side while the adult choir, busy exchanging recipes and discussing politics, drowned out almost everything else. A beautiful tall soprano introduced herself as Lynda, the production's *Musetta,* and Bruno, the character tenor who would play *Parpignol,* the toy seller, made the rounds, shaking hands with everyone. The young soloist from the choir who would sing the rich old *Alcindor* sat in a corner studying his lines.

A choir soprano handed Juliette a blue bonnet with an intricately embroidered pink border. She said, "Try it on—I made it for Mimi. You won't want to wear the one they'll give you."

Juliette pulled it on, tied the ribbons under her chin and said, "It's perfect! Thank you so much; I won't forget to return it."

"No, please keep it... you will sing *Mimi* many times, and it will be enough if you think of me when you wear it."

Maestro Chiera stepped up on the podium, tapped his baton, and everyone scurried to their place. When they were ready, he dropped his stick, starting the fun.

The time is Christmas Eve, the place Café Momus, an artist's hangout in Paris. The soloists, orchestra, and a choir of fifty townspeople and street vendors jump into a fast-paced, chaotic scene. Shaunard barters for a horn, claiming the 'D' is out of tune; Colline buys a used coat, then complains that it was worn.

Mimi and Rudolpho arrive and go straight to a milliner's shop to buy a bonnet for Mimi; Colline finds a rare book; Marcello offers his heart to anyone for a sou.

Mimi admires a coral necklace in a jeweller's window—Rudolpho mentions a rich uncle with one foot in the grave. Rudolpho tells Mimi that, when the inevitable happens, he will buy a much better necklace for her!

Peter nailed every entry.

Rudolpho and Mimi join Marcello, Colline and Schaunard at a table in front of *Café Momus,* and every one of the penniless artists orders an expensive dinner.

Parpignol, the toy vendor, hawks his wares, and excited children gather around him, begging for toys. Their mothers catch up to them, and the children shout out the toys they want for Christmas.

The artists order more food and wine.

Mimi and Rudolpho talk of love; Marcello equates it to poison. The artists raise their glasses to love, and Marcello says bitterly, "Let me drink poison."

Musetta's shrill laugh halts the chaos, focusing everything on her. Dressed like a Queen, Musetta leads *Alcindoro de Mitonneaux,* a pompous but wealthy admirer, to the table next to the artists, driving Marcello crazy. She treats the rich Alcindoro like her pet dog.

Although he had little to sing, Peter found the fast action confusing; entries came and went; an arrietta here, a remark there, a short duet, then a shouted comment; and then, there was the loud and imposing choir....

The scene was a music rehearsal, but Juliette used it to prepare Peter to play his part and to react to her within the limited space. She tried to teach him to anticipate and plan his next move while he sang.

While Marcello and Musetta bantered back and forth, Peter and Juliette touched, kissed, and flirted their way through the tumult. When Musetta finally ended the chaos with a burst of song, Juliette had done everything she could to throw Peter off, but without success.

Musetta finished her aria and went to Marcello, and Rudolpho used that as an excuse to kiss Mimi.

Fools, Angels and the Devil

Maestro Chiera stopped the music frequently to correct something in the orchestra or berate the choir for dragging. Once, during Musetta's aria, when she tried to set the pace, he stopped, stared at her for a moment, then restarted at the tempo he wanted. She gave Maestro Chiera a look that said everything, but adjusted her tempo to fit his interpretation.

The second act took until six o'clock without a break, and the tension sapped Peter's strength. He missed entries, looked at Juliette when he sang to Marcello and was guilty of several wrong notes.

Exhausted, Peter walked home with Juliette, who seemed as fresh as she had been when the day started.

Juliette said, "I've got some ravioli I can warm up for supper," and then, seeing the exhausted look on Peter's face, added, "We'll go shopping for your new pyjamas in the morning. You can leave your old pair in my bedroom."

Peter's expression changed, and miraculously, his energy returned.

They were starved, the ravioli was good, and they ate in silence until Peter said, "I'm still nervous about the second act. I was sure I could get my entries, but I only know them if I'm in the studio. I need to work on all the back-and-forth scenes we did today. The beginning of the fourth act has another of those scenes, even a mock sword fight, and I know I won't get it right. Maybe I should go home and work on my music as soon as I'm done eating."

Juliette smiled. "I will help you with your role after *Abendessen*. That's what Maestro Chiero suggested, isn't it?"

Juliette had planned to offer Peter a piece of Belgian pastry she had made but decided to wait until after they worked. She put her plate in the sink and headed for the piano.

"Let's start where you introduce me to your friends. Maestro Chiera didn't stop you, but he pulled and pushed the tempo there, and I'm afraid you didn't follow him. Puccini uses those little ariettas to contrast the steady background rhythm; in that spot, Puccini gives you a syrupy love song that contrasts with the action... And I'm afraid you sing it like a German engineer."

Juliette went to the piano, opened her score and began playing. Peter sang, *Chi guardi?* Juliette sang, *Sei geloso!* and embraced Rudolpho. They sang the romantic interlude to an imaginary audience. Juliette then conducted Rudolpho's short solo, telling Peter to look away but keep her in his periphery. She pulled and pushed the tempo, and he followed her perfectly.

The solo ended, and Juliette approached Peter, mischievously smiling as she pressed against him. He made a token effort to push her away as he said weakly, "No, Juliette, don't... I have to go...." She pressed her lips against his, thrust her tongue into his mouth, and pushed Peter backward toward the sofa. "No, Juliette, we can't...."

She pulled down her panties, kicked them away, pushed him down when he tried to get up, and unbuttoned his pants.

"Juliette, the Gestapo...."

"I can't handle more than one man at a time, and if they were coming, they would have been here by now. This won't take long."

Peter swung his feet onto the floor. "What if someday I can't stop?" He hung his head, knowing how close he had come.

Juliette shivered. "Don't you mean, what if I won't let you stop? If we go too far, I will be pregnant in a week and goodbye career! I won't let that happen!"

Peter said softly, without lifting his head, "Don't you want to have children?"

Juliette sat up with her back to Peter. "I want to be free to choose. I'm only nineteen; I want to sing for a while before I have a family." She looked into his eyes. "We both need time and as long as we can satisfy one another... Tell me why that isn't enough."

"Are you satisfied?"

Juliette laughed. "Of course not; I'm satisfied for the moment, but I am dying to let you make me a woman!"

Peter grinned. "No more than I want to." He kissed Juliette's hand. "I won't do it, even if you try to make me."

Peter whispered in her ear.

"I gave up Hitler for you; are you telling me that's not enough?"

Juliette stood up. "You have done nothing of the sort, but I will admit you are trying."

"What about meeting me halfway. Come to the rally next year and hear Hitler speak."

"I'll think about it!"

Peter stood up. "I need to go home, and I'm not going to help with the dishes. You're still dangerous!"

Juliette stood up and leaned against Peter, rubbing against his leg. "Spoilsport!"

Peter headed for the door.

Rehearsals became routine for Peter, as did his visits to Juliette's apartment. Juliette taught him how to keep both of them happy. They began to finish one another's sentences, said the same word simultaneously, and did what one another wanted before they asked.

Peter's voice blossomed, and he felt confident on the day of the first stage rehearsal with the full orchestra. Happy, believing that nothing in his perfect life could go wrong, Peter's confidence rose into the stratosphere.

But when the conductor's baton fell, Peter sensed something was wrong... The beginning chords were marked *Forte*, and he could hardly hear the orchestra! Peter looked at Maestro Chiera; he looked back, smiled and nodded. The souffleur gave Marcello his entrance, and Peter was shocked when the baritone's voice nearly covered the orchestra. Seated at a table facing Maestro Chiera, Rudolpho could look directly at him without stepping out of character. The maestro looked straight at Peter, smiled, nodded and said, exaggerating his mouthing of *"Sehr gut!"* and nipping a complete breakdown in the bud.

Marcello sang his frustration with his painting, then turned to Rudolpho and asked, *Che fai?* The souffleur gave Rudolpho his cue, and he began singing.

Peter had no idea whether he should give more or less sound. The first note he sang pushed the orchestra away into the distance, covered by the resonance in his head. The theatre soaked up Peter's voice like a sponge—the sound seemed to drop out of his mouth and fall on the floor. Juliette had warned Peter this would happen, but he thought she was exaggerating.

Panic wrapped its fingers around Peter's throat, shrinking the sound. He increased his support and immediately felt his throat constrict.

Terrified, Peter heard Juliette in his head saying, "Relax, Peter, don't manipulate the sound—trust it and let it go! Feel the sound resonate; don't try to hear it!"

He sang Rudolpho's short arietta about Paris chimneys and his useless stove, sure no one had heard it. Ready to run off the stage, Peter looked at Maestro Chiera, who nodded, smiled and said silently, *"Bene! Eccellente,"* saving the day once again.

Juliette had lectured Peter about panic being part of a singer's repertoire, and he repeated in his head the remedy she had given him.

"Faith—have faith that the audience can hear. Accept what you have; don't adjust anything! The little devil on your shoulder saying your voice is too small is full of *Scheisse!*

Peter put everything out of his mind except Rudolpho, determined to do precisely what Herr Schulmann and Maestro Chiera had rehearsed and to remember Juliette's words.

"The conductor is your anchor. Look at him, don't worry about the role—do the big things, the little things will follow naturally!"

The action developed at breakneck speed; Peter focused on singing Rudolpho's lines at the correct place and time. He used the conductor directly when he could and was always conscious of his baton somewhere on the edge of his vision—he let the souffleur help him nail his entries.

Marcello sang—Rudolpho turned to face him, Maestro Chiera still in the corner of his eye. Everything clicked.

The landlord knocked, Marcello asked who was there, and the answer, "Benoit," came back. Rudolpho scrambled for a place to hide, and Peter relaxed. The action, entwined with the music, pushed panic back to its lair. Rudolpho came to life, joined the fun with Benoit, and Peter was entirely in Rudolpho's skin when the artists tricked him into admitting he had cheated on his wife and kicked the wicked landlord out.

When Rudolpho sat down to write an article for "Beaver" magazine, Peter was comfortable. When Mimi knocked, Rudolpho opened the door and fell in love.

Juliette played Mimi so convincingly, and Peter was so far into the role that he reacted to her as though meeting for the first time. Mimi showed him her dead candle, and he was back sitting beside Juliette on the bench in front of Professor Garcia's studio.

His candle went out; they searched for her key in the dark and touched hands, all as natural as breathing. The coquettish scene flowed as though instant love were as ordinary as sunshine.

Peter unconsciously kept the conductor somewhere in his vision. The lilting music carried the flirting dialogue—Rudolpho kissed her cold hand, then sang, *Che gelida manina...* beginning the most-loved tenor aria in Italian opera.

The phrases flowed like water until, from nowhere, Peter felt a scratchy overtone creeping into the sound. He looked at Juliette, terror on his face... Juliette knew Peter was in trouble!

Close to panic, Peter looked at Juliette, then straight at Maestro Chiera as he sang, *Poiché... Poiché v'ha preso stanza,* preparing his voice for the high C. He lightened his tone and began, *La speranza,* the Italian word for hope. He sang the arpeggio, and launched opera's most famous tenor note.

As he ascended, Peter prepared everything as Professor Garcia had taught him—his cords and larynx performed as they had been trained, but the intoxicating resonance wasn't in the sound.

Juliette froze; she wanted to grab Peter before he fell off the cliff. Still hoping for a miracle, she heard his vocal cords stretch and tighten to reach the pitches in Peter's head, but then resigned herself that they could not thin themselves enough to create the overtones that must carry the ultimate note. Juliette's heart tore as she looked into Peter's eyes, saw the terror in them as his cords tried to save themselves by fluttering, shattering Peter's note into a thousand pieces, scattering fragments everywhere.

The sound was what most people imagine as the scream of a tortured cat, and the shock took Peter's breath away. Terrified, he stopped singing, looked at Juliette and was considering running away when she said, "Don't stop!"

Peter, terrified, stopped singing, looked at Juliette and was considering running away when she said, "Don't stop!"

Now completely out of the role, Peter mechanically sang Rudolpho's next line, asking Mimi to tell him about herself, giving her the cue to sing her aria.

Peter had a few terrified minutes to think of the duet. He had no idea whether he could sing it, and halfway through Mimi's aria, if it hadn't been for the *souffleur,* Peter would have missed singing his *Si,* responding to Mimi's asking Rudolpho if he were still awake.

Mimi finished her aria, and Rudolpho's friends shouted at him from the sidewalk, telling him to hurry and join them at Café Momus. Peter responded, feeling a slight tickle in his throat, but the sound was clear.

Juliette said softly, "Relax; don't try to fix it!"

Like a condemned man when the hangman drops the noose over his head, Peter decided to accept his fate. He sang the romantic duet looking into Juliette's eyes, close to tears, dreading the moment they would sing the 'C' together. In the pause before the first *Amor,* Juliette said softly but loud enough that Peter heard, "No 'C,' take the 'F!'"

Peter found the note and held it while Juliette sang her 'C,' blending their sound as they walked off the stage holding hands.

When the orchestra stopped playing, Peter was shocked to hear everyone clap until he and Mimi came onstage and bent at the waist to recognize the praise. He asked Juliette as he waved to Maestro Chiera, "Don't they care that I missed my most important note? That was the worst moment of my life!"

Juliette blew a kiss to the maestro. "They are musicians and actors... they feel your pain. You kept going, and they are applauding your courage."

Maestro Chiera met them in the hallway on their way to their dressing rooms, obviously upset.

"My God, Peter... do I hear a cold in your voice?"

Peter shrugged. "I don't feel like I have a cold, but my voice isn't right; I'll try to fix it before the second act."

Juliette nodded her head. "Sir, you are right, he's got a cold, but no, he can't fix it."

"Okay, I'm going to phone the specialist we have on call." The maestro turned to Peter. "The doctor will be here when the rehearsal's over, and we will see what he says. Do you think you can sing the third and fourth acts?"

Juliette said, "I know a lot about colds... how to sing with one and when to shut up. Peter must be careful not to sing it into his vocal cords, but he can do it."

"Can you help him? I need him to sing Rudolpho for the rest of the rehearsal, but I can't risk ruining his voice for the première."

"There are ways a singer can protect himself while singing with a cold, and I'm an expert at that! Today's performance will suffer, but I'll show Peter how to do it without damaging his cords."

Maestro Chiera looked skeptical. He said, "I don't have any other options. I checked with the agents yesterday, just in case, and no Rudolphos are available on our performance dates."

Juliette took Peter's arm. "Come to my dressing room, and I'll show you a few tricks to get you to the end of the rehearsal."

Maestro Chiera went toward his office, wringing his hands and mumbling to himself.

Juliette opened the door to her dressing room and let Peter go ahead of her. When she closed it, she was shaking her head.

"Peter, I'm not sure about this—you are coming down with what could be a bad cold, and I don't know whether I can prevent it. The doctor will see inflamed and swollen cords and recommend no singing until they heal, but unfortunately, without you, there will be no performance." She crossed the room to a piano, sat on the piano bench, raised the cover and played an octave arpeggio beginning and ending with a 'G.'

"Colour the bottom note as light as possible and let the notes naturally darken as you go up. Don't manipulate... let the top note find its place. When a singer has a cold, it is tempting to add pressure, but don't do it—that could cost you six months of work with Professor Garcia."

Peter sang the first note with the resonance high in his head, then went up the arpeggio and held the top 'G.' It felt too light and easy to use on the stage, but Juliette said, "That's it… don't put any more support under it than you have now."

When she waved him off, Peter said, "It doesn't sound loud enough, and the ringing sound isn't there."

Juliette looked at the keys and said, "Don't look for the ring… you are right; it isn't there. Your cords are swollen, rounding off the delicate edges that produce the 'ring.' If everything goes well until Saturday, you will know whether you can give a little and when you must accept what your cords can deliver." She pointed at Peter. "If you feel the faintest tickle, stop singing; your cords are touching, and a few seconds could destroy your voice for weeks!

Juliette worked Peter carefully up to the high C in falsetto…not an exciting note, but it was on the pitch.

"You must sing the rest of the rehearsal like that. Your voice will work, but you won't impress anyone."

Peter thought about it for a moment. La Bohème would be his opera debut. No one would blame him if he didn't sing with a cold, but if he sang badly….

Peter decided to put his voice in Juliette's hands and asked, "What if the high notes crack?"

"Let go of it but don't panic. You must keep going any way you can, but above all, don't cough!" Juliette stood up and took Peter's hand. "If you fear a note, sing it in falsetto or leave it out. A good falsetto is better than pushing your voice or cracking; no note is better than no Rudolpho on Saturday. A century ago, tenors sang everything above a 'G' in falsetto!"

Peter made it through the rehearsal without falsetto, and his B-flat notes in the third act duet floated easier than he had ever sung them. But when he sang the last sobbing "Mimi" in the final scene, he felt a tickle and immediately knew what he had done. Despite Juliette's warning, Peter let his emotions take over when Mimi died in his arms.

He fought the urge to cough and ran off-stage, the tickle on his cords bringing tears to his eyes. When he saw a stagehand holding a beer bottle, he grabbed it and drank it dry, despite the man's objections.

Juliette waited until the last chord stopped resonating, then rose from Mimi's deathbed and ran to Peter. When she caught him, his face was red, and he was fighting the urge to cough. A choir member gave him a glass of water while another opened a bottle of honey.

Juliette held up a hand. "Don't talk! Gargle before you swallow!"

Peter gargled, the tickle disappeared, and he wiped the tears with his sleeve. He opened his mouth and got a spoonful of honey, then another.

"No talking!" Juliette put her hand over his mouth.

Maestro Chiera met them at the stage door, his face a mask of fear. "Please follow me. The doctor is here."

He opened the door to his office, and a middle-aged man wearing a pleasant smile stood up, stretched out his arm, and Peter shook his hand.

Maestro Chiera said, "This is Doctor Kemp. It is our policy to do whatever he says."

The doctor said, "Please sit facing the back of this chair; I'm going to look at your vocal cords."

Peter straddled the hardwood seat.

"Put your head back and open your mouth."

Using a wooden stick to push Peter's tongue out of the way, he shone a small flashlight down Peter's throat. It took Doctor Kemp only a few seconds before he turned to Maestro Chiera.

"His cords are badly swollen. I suspected as much when I heard those last two notes. I'm afraid he won't be able to sing for at least a week, more likely two."

Maestro Chiera's expression became more apprehensive, crossing the line to desperation. He said, "We have our *Generalprobe* in three days and the *Premiere* two days after that. Someone is trying to find a replacement, but there is little hope they will succeed. Can't you give him something?"

The doctor shook his head. "No, it will take a miracle for him to sing this weekend. I can only recommend rest, aspirin, and drinking fluids. The cold symptoms are just beginning, and it's for certain he won't sing the dress rehearsal. Perhaps, if he rests his voice, he will survive the Première, but the risk to his voice will be high." He turned to Peter. "Giuseppe told me you are from Augsburg. Perhaps it would be best to go home for a week or two."

Peter looked desperately at Juliette, and Maestro Chiera quickly said, "No, no, he needs you to see him every day and…"

Juliette cut him off… "Peter can move in with me. I will see that he sings on Saturday, and I can get him through the *Generalprobe.*"

Juliette kissed Peter's cheek, and the doctor said, a knowing smile crossing his face, "Yes, of course, that would be much better for Peter. If he stays with you, I will come to see him every day."

Peter grinned, and Juliette took his hand.

Doctor Kemp turned to Maestro Chiera with a look that did everything but shake a finger in his face. "But I will not let him sing if his cords are inflamed!"

Doctor Kemp faced Juliette. "You got Peter through the rehearsal and, looking at his cords, I would say there is no damage. It's a lot to ask… Are you sure you want to do this?"

Juliette squeezed Peter's hand as she looked up at him, then returned to the doctor.

"Peter has no experience singing a role like this nor singing with a throat infection. I have sung professionally since I was a child, and I can't remember when I've cancelled. I've learned to sing with an imperfect voice, and I can show Peter a few tricks."

Doctor Kemp chuckled.

Juliette gave him a stern look and said, "My experience is that singers tend to be over-cautious. They go to bed when they should exercise and get some fresh air." Juliette looked at Peter and said, "I will see that Peter gets lots of exercise."

Peter lowered his head until he was staring at his feet.

Doctor Kemp said, "I understand the benefits of exercise. Peter has a bad cold, so in addition to aspirin, I prescribe all the exercise you can give him, but you must keep him quiet. If he uses his vocal cords, he could be in trouble for a long time. I know from experience that he could ruin an amazing instrument!"

"I promise I will take good care of his instrument."

Juliette took a grinning Peter's hand and led him out of the room.

The doctor said, "I will see Peter tomorrow afternoon." Juliette heard Maestro Chiera laugh as she closed the door.

CHAPTER TWENTY-TWO

All is Not Yet Lost

Sometimes the cure makes the disease worthwhile

JULIETTE TOOK PETER HOME, gave him a pot of chamomile tea, a pillow, a blanket, and a book, *Bomben auf Monte Carlo,* then went to the *Apotheke* to fill Doctor Kemp's list. The first item was an order for *Spirsäre,* commonly known as aspirin, Bayer's wonder drug for arthritis, rheumatism and fevers. Then came the naturopathic items: elderberry tea, lemon tea, and *Erkältungsöl* pressed from eucalyptus leaves and a smelly mixture of Olive and garlic.

Juliette had added lemons, oranges, garlic cloves, hot mustard powder and a bottle of rum to his list.

Juliette left the *Stadtmitte* with her two-wheeled cart full and spent the time walking home working out her *Erkältungsstrategie.* She was ready for the battle against Peter's cold when she pulled it into her *Wohnung.*

Peter was asleep on the sofa with the book on his chest when Juliette checked on him. She let him sleep while she boiled water in the kettle, added a teaspoon of salt and poured some of it into a glass. She warmed a hundred millilitres of foul-smelling *Erkältungsöl* in a measuring cup, then put it aside.

When she roused Peter, he opened his mouth to say something, but Juliette said, "No talking," and he closed it.

Juliette put the book on the small table in front of the sofa while Peter turned to a sitting position.

He looked at the floor, desperately wanting to speak.

Juliette said, "You can ask a question if you speak softly, but no whispering."

"Can't I sleep in the bed? That sofa is as hard as the sidewalk, and I promise...."

Juliette cut him off... "Yes, you can sleep in the bed, and I will sleep on the sofa."

"That's not what I meant. I...."

She cut him off again... "I know what you meant, but you need all your strength to fight this miserable cold." Juliette tried not to laugh at the expression on Peter's face.

"I've made you some tea, but first, I want you to go to the bathroom and gargle with this warm salt water." She held up the glass.

Juliette followed Peter to the bathroom.

"Are you going to watch me?" Peter had no intention of letting Juliette criticize how he gargled.

Juliette read his mind. "It's not as easy as you think. Have you ever gargled?"

Peter said, "Yes, I gargled in the theatre, and you watched me do it!"

"You can do it better." She gave him a look that said the discussion was over.

"Take a mouthful of water, sing 'aaahh,' and tip your head back. Hold the note as long as possible, then spit the water in the sink."

Juliette handed Peter the glass, he filled his mouth with what he guessed was enough water, and again, Juliette read his mind.

"That's enough water. Now, start singing before you tip your head back!"

Peter sang, "aaahh," tipped his head back and felt the warm water gurgling on his larynx. Gradually an ache in his throat that was beginning to worry him disappeared.

"Tip your head forward and spit out the water before you stop singing. Don't inhale until the water's gone, and keep your head tipped until I tell you to stop."

Peter tipped his head forward, spit the water in the sink and stopped singing. He turned his head sideways without lifting it and grinned at Juliette.

"Alright, I'm a nag, but nags always win. But it's for your own good... if water touches your vocal cords, you will cough for five minutes, and I guarantee you won't sing the Première!"

Juliette went to the kitchen, Peter gargled until the glass was empty, and she returned with the warmed oil.

"If this tastes as bad as it smells, you will do well not to gag, but despite that, you must gargle with it; I think three times a day should do it."

Peter took the cup, smelled it and screwed up his face.

"I can't do it."

"I won't get in bed with you unless you do."

"I thought you said...."

"That was before I smelled that oil; that changes everything, but don't breathe on me!"

Peter used all the noxious mixture in two gargles, then reached for Juliette, but she pushed him away.

"First we eat, then I have some pills for you, and elderberry tea...."

"And then we go to bed?"

"No; you must have a hot bath, drink a hundred millilitres of rum, inhale eucalyptus steam...." she smiled..." And then we go to bed!"

Juliette's doorbell rang the following afternoon, and she opened the door for Doctor Kemp. She brought him up to date as they walked up the stairs, and they had to wake Peter for the examination.

The doctor examined his patient, then sat on the sofa to write his notes. Juliette gave Peter an aspirin washed down with *Schlaftee,* code for tea made with a sleeping potion—probably an opiate derivative—and led him back to bed.

Juliette put a pot of black tea on the small table in front of Doctor Kemp, filled two cups and sat on an upholstered chair that matched the hard, dreary, gray sofa.

Juliette said, "I hear an improvement in Peter's gargling voice, and the rasp in his speaking voice is gone. I make him gargle four times a day with salt water and *Erkältungsöl.* I feed him warm honey twice at night and Shlaftee for breakfast and at bedtime—so he sleeps a lot." She sipped her tea, waiting. "What do you think? Do his cords look better? Should I do more, or less?"

Doctor Kemp smiled. "There is minimal swelling and only a slight redness. It's the first time I've seen a cold stopped in its tracks!"

Juliette said, "My goal is to have him sing the *Generalprobe* gently, using falsetto on the high notes. I think he can do enough for the dress rehearsal without damaging his voice for the Première."

The doctor nodded his head. "I wouldn't have said that yesterday, but today… You could be right. Is he getting lots of fruit?"

Juliette nodded. "I feed him oranges until he threatens me, and I make him drink five glasses of warm lemon water daily."

Doctor Kemp smiled. "What do you threaten him with?"

Juliette said innocently, "I assure you, it's nothing bad. Actually, it's more like a reward for good behaviour."

Doctor Kemp laughed. "Too much 'reward' affects the vocal cords… or so my singer patients tell me."

Juliette wanted to contradict the popular idea but felt it would be better to let sleeping tigers rest.

Doctor Kemp finished his tea, and Juliette escorted him down the stairs, noting that the landlady's door was open a crack.

The doctor said, "I will see you and Peter tomorrow at the same time?"

"Yes, Peter and I will expect you."

When Juliette passed Frau Berchtoltzhofen's door on her way up-stairs, she noted that a floorboard in the Wohnung squeaked.

The following day, Doctor Kemp was again satisfied with Peter's prog-ress—the redness was all but gone, and Peter's voice was without any roughness at all. Doctor Kemp stayed for tea and, in the conversation, established that his Wallonian mother may have a connection to Juliette's mother's family. He stayed for a pleasant hour and, as they walked down the stairs, Juliette laughed at his imitation of a tenor pretending to have a cold. The tenor tried to get a *Krankenzettel*, confirming a non-existent throat infection because his high notes weren't there.

Frau Berchtoltzhofen's door was open a crack when they passed. Juli-ette had only spoken to the woman once but, on that occasion, couldn't get away until she heard the woman's tragic life story. She had learned Frau Berchtoltzhofen had lost her husband five years ago to a prolonged illness—the lingering effects of gas during the Great War.

Fools, Angels and the Devil

Juliette said, *"Auf Wiedersehen"* to Doctor Kemp and closed the door, intending to check on her landlady, but her door was closed when she passed, so she climbed the stairs to check on Peter.

A day later, when Juliette opened the door for Doctor Kemp, Maestro Chiera was with him. Again, Juliette spotted the landlady's open door but pretended she didn't notice.

Peter was awake, sitting on the sofa dressed in pants and shirt and eating an orange when Juliette led Doctor Kemp and Maestro Chiera into the *Wohnung*.

Doctor Kemp took a few minutes to examine Peter, listened to his lungs, shone a light on his vocal cords, then listened to Peter vocalize effortlessly to a high 'C.'

Everyone looked expectantly at Doctor Kemp as he sat at the table, set for four, with a platter covered with *Kuchen* in the middle and a choice of tea or coffee. He chose coffee and talked as he poured.

"I'm reluctant to say Peter is healed enough to sing a role like Rudolpho, but Juliette has conquered the symptoms, at least for now."

Maestro Chiera looked at Peter. "How do you feel about it? Can you sing the dress rehearsal tomorrow?"

Peter shrugged. "I feel great, and you heard my voice… I didn't feel any tickle or raspiness, and the *Generalprobe* is a good place to find out if it works, isn't it?"

Juliette put her hand on Peter's. "Peter, you must resist the temptation to sing full voice at the dress rehearsal. I suggest you save your voice as much as possible and take the high notes in falsetto."

She looked around the table. "Maestro Chiera… do you agree?"

"Juliette, I don't care what he does in the *Generalprobe* as long as he stays on the stage. But I need him to sing the Première. Do whatever you must do at the dress rehearsal, but if he doesn't sing the Première.…"

Juliette filled in the blank. "It's Peter's first opera performance, and he has no idea what to expect." She turned to Peter. "You've never sung a full performance, and rehearsals don't count because your nerves aren't involved. The cold symptoms are mostly gone, but your cords are still very sensitive."

The door to the apartment shook as someone pounded on it. A loud voice shouted, *"Gestapo… Mach' die Tür sofort auf!"*

Juliette got to the door at the same time whoever was on the other side smashed his fist against it again. She opened it quickly, hoping to avoid a broken door, and a gloved fist hit nothing but air.

The Gestapo officer, dressed in a black suit, shirt and tie, looked ridiculous holding a pistol in his left hand.

Juliette stepped to one side, and the man entered. He looked at Peter, Doctor Kemp and Maestro Chiera, now standing in front of their chairs. The embarrassed man holstered his Walthers pistol with a confused look and stepped into the room. Frau Berchtoltzhofen stood in the hall behind him, and Juliette beckoned to her as she said, "You might as well come in too; I have enough *Kuchen* for all of us."

The Gestapo officer said, "I am *Kriminalkommissar* Heinrik Krause." He looked from one person to another, at the *Kuchen* and coffee, and then at Frau Berchtoltzhofen. Embarrassed, he asked, "What is going on here?"

"We are all members of the Nürnberg Stadtsoper, and perhaps I should introduce you," said Juliette. "First, the General Musik Direktor, Maestro Chiera… The maestro left the table and shook hands with the Gestapo officer. "Doctor Kemp, the opera house's doctor." The Gestapo officer shook his hand. Juliette pointed to Peter. "Peter Schweitzer is our lead tenor, and my name is Juliette Durand. I'm from Brussels and also sing in the theatre." She turned to Frau Berchtoltzhofen. "And this is Frau Berchtoltzhofen—my landlady who lives downstairs."

Frau Berchtoltzhofen's face reddened, and *Kriminalkommissar* Krause gave her a look that told a pathetic story.

"I have enough Kuchen for everyone," said Juliette, "Why don't we sit down and talk about this?"

Too embarrassed to refuse, the kommissar and landlady sat across from one another. Juliette brought them cutlery, plates and cups and asked whether they wanted coffee or tea.

The Gestapo Kommissar took a piece of strudel from the plate of kuchen and poured his coffee as Juliette asked him, "I understand that someone told you we were breaking the law, but could you tell me what you expected to find when you came into my home?"

"Uh... I suppose it wouldn't hurt, so... I thought, from the description I was given, that I would find an illegal prostitution ring, or at least a prostitute working outside the legal market."

Juliette looked at her landlady. "I can understand how that conclusion would be the logical one... but why not ask me? My door is open to you at any time."

Frau Berchtoltzhofen lowered her head. "I thought you might hurt me. I heard that the Gestapo police would investigate illegal prostitution and homosexuality, so I called them."

"Yes," said the *Kriminalkommissar*, "we handle those crimes, but it isn't something we like to do. Our job is to find those who are plotting or actively working against the state."

"You get rid of Hitler's competition," said Juliette, and everyone at the table cringed.

The kommissar looked at her and said nothing for a long moment.

"I wouldn't put it that way if I were you, but you are right. The law states that Hitler's enemies are the State's enemies, and vice versa. So, Hitler's enemies are criminals according to the law. And it is our job to find and arrest those criminals."

Maestro Chiera, who seemed to enjoy the banter between Juliette and the Gestapo officer, asked, "And when they are tried, what is the charge, and what is the penalty?"

"If Juliette were arrested for illegal prostitution, the penalty would be a small fine, and she would have to register as a legal prostitute. However, she would have to move to an area of the city where prostitution is allowed."

Maestro Chiera nodded. "And what if the crime were homosexuality?" He saw the expression of disgust on the officer's face and quickly added, "I only ask because I am curious... I have a wife and a child, and I assure you I am not homosexual."

The kommissar almost grinned. "I don't doubt your sexuality, but to answer your question, it depends on whether we are discussing male or female homosexuality. Female homosexuality isn't illegal, but male homosexuality is. However, technically, male homosexuals must be caught in the act. But if convicted, they are often given long or indefinite terms in a prison camp like Dachau." He looked at Doctor Kemp. "It is the opinion of the law that homosexuality is not a disease, but a crime and so can't be cured or controlled."

Doctor Kemp nodded. "It is, as you say, not a disease, but whether such activities are immoral or criminal is a matter of opinion."

Frau Berchtoltzhofen asked, "And what is your opinion, Doctor?

"I try to stay out of emotional debates. I don't consider anything which doesn't damage others to be immoral or criminal." He looked straight at the landlady. "Many people who harbour resentment or jealousy view normal sexual behaviour as something immoral. It is an easy target because the accuser is not open to the same scrutiny as the accused."

Peter said, "I don't understand what the Gestapo or the police have to do with people's private behaviour. Why would the secret police be interested in such things?"

"I wish I could answer that question," said the Gestapo officer. "We are the most professional police force in Germany, and we spend half our time chasing reports that amount to neighbours getting even with neighbours by making up a story. It is natural for neighbours to quarrel occasionally, but they get over it because they must live together. We have given people who want to hurt others a powerful weapon with our morality laws, and they are too eager to grasp it."

Peter said, "That's why you must catch them in the act. Hitler knew that would happen."

The Gestapo officer shook his head. "No, those morality laws are older than Hitler. They were in place during the last century, but intelligent law enforcement didn't look for trouble. Unfortunately, we now have strict instructions to enforce those laws."

Juliette asked, "By 'we,' you mean the Gestapo enforces those laws?"

"Yes, and we enforce them over all of Germany."

Peter started to speak, but Juliette was there first.

"If a man... Say, my friend Peter..." she pointed to him in a general way... "were to come to my house for dinner, and just for discussion purposes, let's assume he stayed overnight, would that violate the morality laws?"

"Is money for sex involved?"

Juliette laughed. "Of course not! I would never take money for sex! I'm not *that* good at it."

The Gestapo officer laughed. "Then I would never arrest you. If we arrested every person who had sex outside of marriage, I would have been arrested when I was sixteen and spent the rest of my life in jail!"

There was a short silence, and *Kriminalkommissar* Krause added, "Of course, if one of you were Jewish, that would make it a crime. But, of course, neither of you is Jewish, so the race laws don't apply."

Maestro Chiera asked, "Herr Krause, are you an opera aficionado?"

"I go when my wife makes an offer I can't refuse."

"The Première is Saturday. I will leave two tickets for you at the box office. I promise you will like this opera."

Juliette looked at Frau Berchtoltzhofen. "I can't offer you tickets, but I can let you come to my dressing room. I will leave a note with the man who guards the stage door, and he will show you where to go. Perhaps you can help me with my makeup and hair." She checked the maestro with a look. He nodded, so she took another step.

"Perhaps I can find a chair so you can watch from the wings." Maestro Chiera nodded again.

The *Generalprobe,* a full dress rehearsal with a sold-out audience, went off without a fault, always a bad omen for the Première. Peter's voice worked as well as ever, but he obeyed Juliette's strict instructions and sang the top notes lightly, mostly in falsetto. Peter anticipated a reward when he went home with her, but she kissed him goodnight at the door.

"No fun tonight, but come for breakfast with some fresh *Semmel* rolls, and we'll spend the day looking after your voice."

Peter moaned but knew there was no point in arguing. At nine the following day, he turned up in her Wohnung with *Semmel* fresh from the bakery.

Peter had a runny nose when he arrived at the opera house for the première, but when Doctor Kemp examined his vocal cords, he pronounced them healthy.

Juliette was not as convinced and said, "I will listen to Peter warm up; he will sing, but he isn't ready to give everything he has."

Doctor Kemp said, "Juliette, you've performed a miracle to get him this far, so I yield to your judgment." He laughed. "And I don't want to argue with a woman who wraps Gestapo officers around her finger!"

Juliette chuckled. "Gestapo officers are nothing—what about Frau Berchtoltzhofen?"

"I assure you, I haven't forgotten Frau Berchtoltzhofen."

Juliette heard the fragility in Peter's voice, and when he sang above an 'A' even for a second, she could hear his cold. When the warmup was over, she told him to sit down, pulled a chair beside him and sat on it.

"Despite what Doctor Kemp said, your voice is not yet healthy. Do you hear the raspiness when you get near your upper *passagio,* between 'G' and 'A?'"

"No, it feels…uh… normal to me."

Juliette heard the fragility in Peter's voice when he sang above an 'A,' and decided she could hear his cold. She said, "Despite what Doctor Kemp said, your voice is not yet healthy. Surely you hear and feel the raspiness."

"No, it feels…uh… normal to me."

Juliette shook her head. "Peter, you must be careful. If you sing the 'C,' I'm afraid it could break. In fact, it probably will because you will be nervous. You can't count on those top notes."

"Juliette, you are making me nervous. Just leave me alone, and I will be fine."

She wasn't sure of anything as she left Peter and found a chair and a place in the wings for Frau Berchtoltzhofen. When Maestro Chiera passed by, he nodded his approval, then asked about Peter. Juliette smiled, gave him a *"Schon gut"* and a wave.

Peter was frightened when the curtain rose and Marcel began complaining about his painting, but it dissipated when he sang his little arietta about industrious Paris chimneys.

The repartee between Rudolpho and his garret friends felt natural, and Peter ran around the stage as comfortably as he walked around his *Wohnung,* inserting impromptu gestures at opportune times. The others caught the bug, and the scene with the landlord brought howls of laughter from the audience.

Juliette knocked on Rudolpho's door and, when Peter sang his lines, she could hear his cold. As the famous 'cold hands' aria approached, she debated whether to tell him to take the 'C' in falsetto, but concluded she had done enough and he must sink or swim on his own.

Peter felt confident as he touched Mimi's hand, and grinned when she uttered a small, but audible, "Ah!"

He sang the aria, forgetting himself in the beautiful lines as he held Juliette's hand and looked into her eyes. Rudolpho sang to Mimi while Peter's heart went to Juliette, losing himself in the music and the character.

Juliette saw the love in Peter's eyes, heard his voice soaring as though it were bulletproof, and knew it meant trouble. She considered 'accidentally' kicking him or perhaps pinching his arm, but the uncertainty of his reaction to her breaking the spell tipped the scales against it.

Peter sang the phrase leading to the most loved yet feared note in the tenor repertoire with an aggressive, flowing tone… perfect if his voice had been healthy, but nitroglycerin in his present situation. Once again, Peter stood on the cliff's edge as he sang the notes leading to the 'C.'

Juliette already heard the cold on the 'F,' the first note of the *arpeggio,* and desperately wanted to stop Peter—to hell with the audience, to hell with their careers—if Peter crashed and burned, she would never forgive herself!

Peter knew he had nailed the 'C' when his cords first gripped it. Attacking the note *Sotto Voce* from above, his confidence growing, he increased his support and grip. He added more support as he dropped to the B-flat, then the E-flat, increasing the volume on the last two notes in the phrase. Peter turned his head, swept the sound across the theatre, then back.

Tears of joy welled in Juliette's eyes, and she had to suppress an urge to fling her arms around Peter.

The sound of the last note hadn't died when the crowd stood as one person, shouted "Bravo," and slammed their hands together. Peter froze, his eyes on Juliette, his heart pounding. He wanted to laugh and dance across the stage, shouting, "I did it!" but held his position. The only thing he didn't control was the broad smile on his face and the light in his eyes.

Finally, the audience, tired of clapping and shouting, sat down, still excitedly murmuring to one another.

Juliette squeezed Peter's hand so hard he winced, then sang her aria surrounded by a world of happiness.

The duet to the end of Act I was the best Peter and Juliette had ever sung it, and Peter's 'C' at the end was clear and resonant, even though they sang it offstage. The third-act duet brought the house down, and the heart-breaking fourth-act conclusion started a river of tears in the audience.

Seven curtain calls followed with no letup in the applause. Juliette and Peter waited in the wings beside Frau Berchtoltzhofen, who stood beside her chair, crying, laughing, and pounding her hands to a pulp. Maestro Chiera put his arm around her, turned to Juliette and Peter and said, "One more for the road?"

They ran onstage, Herr Schumann came from the other side with the other soloists, and the choir ran noisily onto the stage behind them. Everyone bowed, kissed, waved to the audience, and someone began rhythmic clapping that went on and on. The theatre, filled with joy, tears, and the anticipation of Christmas, finally realized they had done enough, and as they rested their tired hands, the ensemble retired to the wings for the last time.

Juliette and Peter waited, and when the audience was quiet, Juliette wrapped her arms around Peter, pulling his head down so she could kiss him, and the theatre exploded! They kissed in a long and passionate embrace, then turned to face their new fans. The darlings of Nürnberg waved and threw kisses as they walked off the stage, blissfully ignorant of the chain of events their love had set in motion.

Keep your Friends Close—your Enemies Closer

(Sun Tsu, Chinese general)

Christmas passed without a break; La Bohème on Christmas Eve, and two days later, *Der Vogelhändler* rehearsals. The work with the *répétiteur* left no time to go home—Juliette and Peter only had a month before orchestra rehearsals, and the première was scheduled for February twentieth.

Peter and Juliette adopted a routine that brought him to Juliette's nest almost every day to work on their music, interspersed with romantic interludes.

On Saturday, January thirtieth, Juliette was alone—Peter had gone home for the weekend to help his father at work. She played the phonograph for an hour, then became bored and switched on the radio just as the announcer introduced Adolph Hitler. He was at the *Reichstag,* celebrating four years since becoming Chancellor.

She reached for the knob to turn the radio off, but something made her change her mind.

Juliette was surprised when Hitler began his speech, not with self-congratulations but with humility, leaving his list of accomplishments for the media to expound on and criticize.

Juliette sat on the sofa, fascinated with the sound of Hitler's voice. She had thought of him as a brute, a screaming fanatic, but this man's voice projected neither. Juliette decided the voice belonged to a smooth manipulator—not unlike her father in that respect.

She listened to the most powerful man in Europe bow to his people, blaming the communist Bolsheviks for everything that ailed the world and crediting the German people for their rise out of servitude. He only once mentioned the Jews and then only briefly. The speech ended with prolific thanks to political leaders—officers in the *Wehrmacht,* workers, and especially, Germany's women, with special thanks to Germany's mothers.

Juliette switched off the radio, went to her chair at the window and looked down at the door to Peter's building.

She said aloud, "Peter, I understand your idol is a genius; he has, after all, molded puppets from Germany's people. No one can control him because he is always in front, like *Der Rattenfänger von Hameln*. The Pied Piper of Hamlin has driven the rats out of Germany, dismantled the Versailles Treaty, and given the German people back their pride... But at what cost?"

And then, looking down the street, remembering thousands of soldiers marching with torches while people hung out of their windows and cheered, she said to herself, *The price the Pied Piper exacted was Hamlin's children... Will Hitler settle for less? Is he a Wagnerian hero for the German people, or the most devious and evil villain the world has ever known?*

She thought as she looked again at Peter's door... *Perhaps I should go with you to hear Adolph Hitler speak,* but didn't say it out loud. The *Devil* could be listening!

THE END

Message from the author

I HOPE YOU ENJOYED THE BOOK, and I invite you to read the first book in *The Songs of War* series, titled *A Song of Sorrow*. But before you do, I have a favour to ask.

Most people pick books by looking at the cover, reading a short description, and checking the reviews. I can control the first two, but the third is up to you, and your honest review will help others decide whether the book is for them. Most importantly, a good review, honestly written, is a justification for my writing. If you don't tell me whether you liked it or, (shudders and shivers), hated it, I might assume the latter, and that would be depressing.

If you are on Amazon, you can leave a review there. Tell everyone what you liked or didn't like about the story or my writing.

Alternatively, if you aren't on Amazon or your review is rejected, use the links or the QR code to reach me, join my newsletter, and tell me whether you liked the book. Please give a rating, 1 to 5, and leave any comments you want to share. Unless you tell me not to, I will submit an Editorial Review in your name.

Web site: *thesongsofwar.com.*
Facebook: *Robert Faulk, Author*
Email: *robertfaulk@thesongsofwar.com*

Join my newsletter on the website, by email, or on my Facebook page, and I promise to keep you updated on what I am doing. I will send you tidbits I cut from the books, historical context, and previews of new books I am writing.

A Song of Sorrow

JULIETTE SPENT THE SIX-WEEK SUMMER BREAK with her parents, and agreed to attend the Nürnberg National Socialist rally with Peter. The rally's theme, Germany's working men and women, would be celebrated by a cast of Thirty-five thousand performers, and a hundred-and-fifty-two searchlights pointed at the heavens to form Albert Speer's *Cathedral of Light*. A one-hundred-piece orchestra would accompany a chorus of thousands singing Germany's praises. And Juliette couldn't deny her interest in hearing Adolph Hitler speak without the marvel of the radio between them.

Peter met Juliette at the train station the day before the rally, and the following morning, they left her apartment with their arms locked, stepping in unison, German hiking fashion. Deliriously happy, they talked of their summer, laughing at the slightest provocation. The morning air was brisk and dew still dripped from the leaves when they reached Zeppelin field and joined the happy throng.

In the first book of *The Songs of War*, Juliette's world is turned upside down when she experiences the terrifying power of Hitler's charisma. Nothing in Juliette's life has prepared her for the horror to come. Her innocence taken, Juliette joins the Belgian Résistance, staking her life on her ability to deceive the Nazis and outwit the Gestapo officer who has sworn to catch her. Thrust into a whirlwind of war and espionage, Juliette must outmaneuver the oppressive system that threatens the world. If you enjoyed Fools, Angels and the Devil, you will be captivated by Juliette's journey in this thrilling tale of courage and strength.

The four books of *The Songs of War* will take you through that horrible time, seen through the eyes of the people who lived it. You will laugh and cry; your heart will break as you travel through time with the people who endured the systematic violence of the Third Reich. In the end, you will understand more than you do now.

About the Author

Robert Faulk, a Canadian, born on a farm and educated in a small rural school, grew up in a world of hard workers—men and women who farmed the land and harvested the forests and the sea. He studied engineering in university and worked in construction before taking his family to Germany to pursue a career as an opera singer.

Over the next ten years in Europe, Robert met many Europeans willing to share still-fresh memories of the Second World War. Their stories, often traumatic and always deeply personal, expose the most devastating cost of any war—the human cost. Robert captures the spirit of these people and their stories in a series of four books of historical fiction that he calls *The Songs of War*.

www.ingramcontent.com/pod-product-compliance
Lightning Source LLC
Chambersburg PA
CBHW030805210726
48290CB00002B/430

* 9 7 8 1 7 7 8 0 7 8 1 8 7 *